On a rush of air, Ian pulled away from Taylor. He stared at her, the sad eyes, the tormented soul, the weariness. The rain slowed, trickling to just a mist as the only streetlight blinked on. Drips hit him between the eyes and snaked down his nose, but the tremble didn't come from the cold or the tickle.

It arose from the memory. The vision. The thoughts that had passed through his mind while they kissed.

Not real. Just weirdness from being outside.

"Ian?" Taylor asked.

"Yeah?" His voice escaped breathy and unsure.

"Did you . . . I mean . . ." She exhaled against him. "Never mind." Taylor leaned up, laid a touch to the side of his lips. At her shiver, he wrapped his arms around her, drawing her tighter against him, and rubbed up and down her back. "I think I'm going crazy. I have to be."

Praise for Hide & Seek, Book 1 in the Games of Zeus

"To say this is well written would be a major understatement … It's one of those one in a million finds, an exceptional book."
— The To Be Read Pile

"Hide and Seek is a brilliantly written and sexy book. [with] so much heat, passion and danger you'll be left breathless for more!"
— Best Books

"I really enjoyed this book. I loved it so much! It was exciting, the characters were amazing, it kept you guessing, and it was so different than the books I am used to reading."
— Synchronized Reading

"Hide and Seek takes established Greek mythology, sprinkles it with a dash of paranormal, and then shakes it all up with a healthy dose of passionate romance."
— Bex Book Nook

"I have to say this is one of the best mythology books I have ever read. It completely blew me away, and I could not stop reading."
— K-Books

"… just know love must, can, will, and does conquer all."
— J.A. Belfield, author Darkness & Light

Silent Echoes

aimee laine

J. Taylor Publishing

SILENT ECHOES

Published by J. Taylor Publishing
www.jtaylorpublishing.com

ISBN 978-1-937744-21-2

First Printing: March 2013

To love,

Here's to taking only one lifetime to finding a soul mate.

That moment.
When I suck in air as if I haven't breathed in hours,
Sweat trickles down my neck,
My entire body shudders, muscles tensing, straining, poised
For something I cannot grasp.
When sight and sound,
Touch, taste,
Smell
Merge
Somewhere between life and death,
Awake and sleep,
Today and tomorrow.
When I know I've died,
Yet around me,
Life begins.

1

The sledge hammer circled through the air, whipping around Taylor Marsh's head. Wood splintered. Fragmented pieces shot off like shrapnel.

With another heave, she drew the tool over her shoulder, and with one step, swung with every bit of force she could muster.

Decades-old siding crumpled under her attack of the shed.

A deep breath and a growl preceded the stretch of her arms and the twist of her body as she propelled herself forward again.

The weighted head hit first, yanking the tool from her sweaty palms and throwing Taylor sideways. On an 'oomph', her chest, arms and cheek kissed the red clay of southern North Carolina soil.

Taylor pushed up to her elbows, twisted toward the old building she'd vowed to tear down, and sighed. She sat, ran a hand through her failing hair, where blonde streaks had turned brown, and resecured the tail at the nape of her neck as sweat dripped from her brow.

Despite its age, several of the shed's planks remained standing—a testament to construction of years gone by.

"One barn to go, and it wants to stay upright longer than the Titanic."

Beyond the mess, her home stood—a white, clapboard bungalow she'd renovated herself.

"Okay. One more time." With the sun high in the sky and bearing down upon her with the force of the coming summer, she stood. "It's no bigger than a kid's play house. This shouldn't be so hard."

Taylor positioned her feet at the front corner, spreading them to give herself a wide base. "Right. One hit to the figurative solar plexus." She nodded as if the pile would respond. The crunch of a car's wheels on gravel made her turn. She faced the Jaguar as it rolled to a stop.

Two very recognizable men stepped from within the vehicle. Their long strides spoke of power and confidence, the smiles suggested warmth, and the punch one gave the other—playfulness.

Taylor brushed off grime from her jeans, tapped her boots against the ground and wiped a hand across her brow. "Like that's going to help." Giving up on her attire, she headed toward them, leaving her pile of work for later. "Hey, Tripp." She took his extended hand, gazing again at the tattoo on his neck she'd found so intriguing the first time they met. "Ian." Taylor switched her hand-held welcome toward the man who did more to her libido than anyone she'd ever met.

He held up his hands, palms out, bejeweled right ring finger glinting in the sun.

"Afraid of a little dirt?" She let her true southern come out, even added a bit to the tone as she spun the only ring she owned around her fourth finger—nothing like the ostentatious, gaudy, show-offy thing Ian wore.

"No. But you're a . . . more . . . I got a flight to New York in an hour," Ian said.

Tripp chuckled. "Why don't you have a crew come knock that thing down?"

Taylor glanced back at her project. "What fun would that be?"

"Fun?" Ian asked. "Fun's hiring a company and sitting back with a beer." The muscles in his chest jumped under a thin, blue shirt that hugged light mocha skin—a color and smoothness she wanted to run a hand up against. Green eyes contrasted with the chocolate tones and penetrated her psyche, drawing her in and throwing her out at the same time.

Since their first introduction, he'd brought up a mix of interest and an outright fear Taylor didn't understand.

A grin took hold of her lips. "What brings you two to no-man's-land, then?" She raised a hand over her eyes, blocking the blinding sun, and kept her gaze fixed on Ian's defined form, his clothes better suited to Sunday lunch after church—as her mother would say.

Tripp shifted from one foot to the other. "Lexi says she has a client who's looking at the original Weaton Farm estate house. She hoped you might get over there, do some preliminary renovation estimates and give her that insider info you're so good at so she can do an upsell."

"So … Lexi sent you to ask me about the house?" Taylor wiped at a droplet making its way down her temple.

"I told ya, man." Ian gave Tripp a backhanded slap to the bicep. "She's busy. And, I gotta go … anyway … need to get back to some real civilization for a while."

"What's that, Ian?" Taylor turned on her thickest drawl. "You don't like it down here in North Carolina? You want that rush of adrenaline you get with them city folk?"

"Damn right." Ian tucked his hands in his pockets. "Too damn slow down here. I need real lights, not lunar ones, or Tripp's white ass mooning his wife."

Taylor's lips retained their curve upward. "That's just how I like it." *Oops.* "I meant the moon part, not—" *Well, not his, but yours.* "Well, you know." *Shush it, Tay.* She tapped a finger against her cheek, turned to Tripp and tried to ignore the pull from Ian. "Tell Lexi I'll be in touch after I get this thing down."

"Really, why not hire a crew?" Tripp crossed his arms over his chest, his wedding band glistening in the sun.

"I need to work off a little steam." *And a whole lotta lust.* Taylor snuck a peek at Ian's retreating form, leaving her gaze stuck to his backside for an extra moment. *Yup. That under the moonlight. I could make use of it. Dammit thoughts, shut up.* "Since there isn't anything else to do 'round here—as Ian so eloquently put it—I might as well do my own demolition." She hefted the sledgehammer. "Unless you want to help, that is."

"Oh, look at the time. We really gotta skedaddle," Ian said from the car, his tone full of mockery.

"It's a private flight." Tripp earned a glare from Ian and a chuckle from Taylor. "Fine." He spun back toward Taylor. "Just remember to call Lexi, or she'll ride my ass and say we didn't stop by."

Taylor saluted with her free hand. "No problem, chief."

Tripp stood at the driver's side door and held up a finger. "Oh, and Lexi says to tell you 'yes'—whatever that means."

A larger smile pulled at Taylor's lips. "Got it."

"What's that mean?" Ian said from the passenger side.

"I have no idea."

Taylor's laugh rang out as the two boys slipped into their car. As soon as their vehicle disappeared down the road, she turned back to the shed. "All righty, you bastard, it's time to come down." She lifted her arms just above her head and let the tool fall backward behind her shoulders.

"Three."

The sledgehammer's handle pressed into her shoulder.

"Two."

She twisted backward to prep for her swing.

"One."

The ten pound rock clamored against metal and wood, sending vibrations up her arm. Birds took to the sky. The caw of a crow passed through the air, and a long, low creak of wood sliding against itself began. It increased, creating a stream of chalkboard-like screeches until the entire housing collapsed upon itself.

"Yes!" She kicked out her legs, prepared to bask in her success. "We don't need no heavy equipment." A chuckle burst from her.

Taylor meandered to her pile and grabbed one of the freed

planks. It slid from the clutches of the others without much effort. A second one did the same as if it had never been nailed in.

The third took a bit of maneuvering, and the fourth came away with three attachments.

She yanked, pulled, shoved, pushed and twisted pieces and parts away, making new piles. One for wood that could be recycled and another to burn.

Wiping her hands against each other sent dust into the air. A cough cleared her lungs and gave her a breath of fresh, untainted air. "Women can do anything men can do . . . and better. So there."

As the sun started its dip at the horizon, she tugged at the floorboard planks, bringing up the whole lot.

In the center of a patch of charred earth, a skull faced the sky.

Taylor's lungs constricted.

The sledgehammer fell at her side.

She dropped to her knees, clawing at the dirt.

On an intake of air, the red clay remained in her view.

With the exhale, the blue of the sky showed through closed lids.

Dirt.

Sky.

Red.

Blue.

Nothing.

She kicks at the granules falling from the surface of the earth. Rock, sand, dirt, grit. An entire shovel-full covers her face, coating her nostrils until she can no longer see the man above her. A snort forces some of the bitter granules out as he throws another toward her.

"Stop! Somebody help!" Her shoulders move side to side. Her head turns, following the same motion. "Someone, please!"

A torrent of dust, dark with clay and soil, lands on her stomach. He leans forward, scooping and throwing another upon her.

"Please!" Her screams echo off the walls of her building grave.

"Someone!" Her tone takes on a hollow effect.

Her location six feet beneath the surface of the earth, with her hands bound behind, prevents escape. He'd planned well, taking away her ability to save herself.

She sheds no tears. Those she has long since given up. She'd begged and pleaded, promised love. Falsehoods, she knew, but she'd tried.

"Please. John!" Another deluge of earth hits her midsection. "Stop! I'll do whatever you say!"

The man covering her claimed she spoke untruths.

"Somebody!" Her scream fades as her face is again covered by falling debris. She spits it from her mouth, coughing and gagging. "Help!" Her words garble.

More dirt fills the hole.

She lifts her chin, but only the tip reaches outside. A breath draws in more earth, and nothing is expelled. Unable to take in air, unable to keep life, unable to save herself, to survive, pain radiates through her.

To struggle would only increase her own torment.

She stills.

Weight lands on her toes. Her torso. Her head.

To the world, she no longer exists, merged with the earth she loved so.

His laugh breaks through the growing weight of dirt. "Next time, I will not fail."

She gasps for a final breath, and life no longer exists.

Ian Sands paced the floor of his New York flat. Thoughts of the blue-eyed blonde back in North Carolina had filled his mind on the flight up, the ride from the airport, in the elevator, and even as he keyed himself into his apartment. He'd been unable to sit still in the few hours since.

Damn woman.

"Dude ..." Dressed in jeans and an NYU T-shirt, Michael

Sands looked every bit the undergrad, despite the fact his next diploma—in another four years—would include the letters M.D. "You gotta relax, bro. I've been here a whole three hours, and you haven't sat once."

Despite his brother's insistence, Ian paced to the window, where his reflection mirrored back at him. Beyond the glass, the city moved by at its normal pace—fast. "I don't know what's happening to me."

The woman.

Her.

Something, he didn't know what, clawed at him. Had for months—since the first time they'd talked on the phone.

"You're sounding southern, too." Channels changed one after the other on the flat screen. "That means way too much time in slowville." Michael switched the station yet again. "Maybe your body's trying to regulate itself—like jetlag . . . only we'll call this . . . mindlag." He grabbed a handful of chips, waving them in the air. "We need a night on the town. Few beers. Some women."

Ian traipsed back to the couch and plopped down. "Distraction." *Drunkenness will take away all thoughts.* "That's exactly what I need." He grabbed the snack bag and pulled it toward him. "Don't know about the women, though. They do nothing but complicate life."

"Not mine." Michael crossed his ankles, dropping his bare feet on Ian's coffee table, but continued his direct-from-the-bag snacking. "Not Tripp's."

Ian eyed his brother. "Celibacy does not make you an expert on relationships. And, Tripp fell right into Lexi's hands the night they met. She's been a total pain in his ass since."

A crispy tortilla pinged Ian in the cheek.

He brushed it off and glared at his brother.

Michael chuckled. "And yet, he married her. Maybe you're a little jealous. You know, like he got himself a woman, and you've been oddly womanless for a while."

Ian headed toward the kitchen. "I don't need a woman."

"Hypocrite." Michael coughed through the word.

"What?" An eyebrow winged up on Ian's face. "*You* might need one. I don't need one. I need beer, tortilla chips and some salsa."

A smirk crossed Michael's face. "Uh-huh. Tripp took my advice once. Maybe you should, too." Crumbs landed on his shirt as he leaned back again.

Ian dropped down and rolled his eyes. "You haven't given me any brotherly *advice*."

Michael shrugged. "Last girl you had an interest in."

"What's that got to do with any of this?" Ian grabbed a handful of snacks for himself.

"Just answer me."

"You didn't ask a *question*."

Michael's evil eye speared Ian.

"Taylor Marsh." His voice cracked on her name. *Son of a bitch!*

"That was four months ago!" Michael's resounding laugh burst out. "I knew it! One girl in four months?" A 'whooeee' whistled from him. "Hot, blonde chick was at the wedding and giving you the vibes, bro. Why didn't you tap her?"

"She was not," Ian shot back. He dug through the bag. "And, that's just plain rude, Michael. I may have had my fair share of lovely ladies, but I would never just *tap* one."

"Dude ... she was playing for you."

"You don't—"

Michael sat up straight. "How else would I remember her after so long? She twisted her hair. She leaned toward you as you talked. Her hip swayed out. Her head fell back when she laugh—"

"Those are all just normal people things." *That I saw every bit of.*

Michael shook his head. "No, they aren't. Well, yes, they are, but—" He circled a hand in the air.

Ian pressed two fingers to his eyes.

"It was a come hither move." Michael jutted his hips up. "I am a student of the people."

"Sick people, Michael." Ian pinched his arm. "See? Still alive, healthy and . . ." He rubbed at the spot. "Not in need of your head shrinking or body healing services."

"You had the same body language, you know. I was just waiting for you to touch each other as close as you were. God, the vibes were rolling off you two." With a deep head shake, Michael faced Ian. "What stopped you from taking her?"

"I—" What had stopped him? Beautiful—no—gorgeous woman. She'd met every criterion he had, yet after their conversation at the wedding, the drinks and chatting, they'd parted ways and not looked back.

Michael shifted to the edge of the couch, turning toward Ian, and motioned stabbing into his heart. "You're my role model. How can I go out into this world and expect to get some—"

Ian's fist made contact with Michael's shoulder, though he pulled the punch.

"Ow." Michael rubbed at it. "You're the worst big brother ever."

"And you're full of—"

Michael's snort of laughter preceded the, "Yeah. I am. But you are 'the man' when it comes to women. Blondie got you by the short hairs? You do something—"

"Hell, no." With a capital H. He'd wanted to. Every urge within him said 'take', yet he hadn't. He'd walked away.

"Is it 'cause she's white?"

"No."

Michael huffed air. "That's wrong on so many levels since Mom and Dad have been married for forty years."

"I said no." Ian gave Michael a measured glare. "Of course it's not that." Ian draped a hand over his forehead. Race had no bearing on the women he'd sought. Never had. Never would.

"Then what? 'Cause bro, if a drink and a pretty smile didn't send you to the priesthood, what did it?"

A deep, long, extended sigh left Ian's lips. "Her roots are in

North Carolina. Mine are here. That's not going to work."

"Excuses, excuses." Sarcasm dripped from Michael. "Your roots are wherever Tripp is, and he's in North Cakalacky. Give me the real answer."

"It's not that simple." Ian stood again and meandered to the window. *It's just not that simple.* His green eyes reflected back at him under the darkening sky. *I just don't know. She's different. I want her like nobody's business.* Ian held up his hands. "Enough sappy shit. What bar you want to hit?"

"Rocky's down on fifth has unlimited nachos on Thursdays."

"Give me a sec to change." *It's time to get Taylor Marsh out of my head for good.*

2

Yellow caution tape ran from Taylor's garden to barn, to rear fence post, and back around to her house. Blue lights spun in a dizzying array as she sat on her front porch under the watchful eye of Sergeant Dale, a Rune police officer. The fire trucks and ambulance had come and gone, replaced by a couple extra official-looking vehicles.

"Ms. Marsh—"

She tilted up, raising an eyebrow. "Riley Dale, do not talk to me like you don't know me."

Riley, in his grey and blue uniform, with his smooth cheeks and deep, dark blue eyes, chuckled. "C'mon, Tay. I'm a Sergeant. I can't be informal on a crime scene investigation." He tapped her toe with his, pointing out toward a set of spotlights that hummed and warmed up as the light of day faded.

"We're practically siblings, Riley. Been neighbors since we were twelve."

Riley shifted his weight and returned to his earpiece. His half-smile fell into a full frown, his shoulders drooping while he alternated between touching his earpiece and glancing in her direction.

"Spill it, Dale."

His lips curved but stopped at smirk level. "Can't just yet."

"Why are all these people here? What do they think the bones are?"

More gravel crunched while, at the same time, a unit of

jumper-clad people stepped from another SBI van, which had taken the last non-yard spot. If anyone else showed up, he'd have to park on her near-pristine lawn. At a quick glance, seven cars filled her drive and yard while a dozen-and-a-half suited worker bees milled about in various stages of doing 'stuff'.

Riley's lips firmed. "They're human, Tay."

She leaned back on the porch. "I know that part. That's why I called you." *After I woke up with my face in the dirt.* "But, why is the SBI here?"

"The State Bureau of Investigation comes when they are called." His gaze strayed toward the mess of people. "Now hush. I really can't talk to you about this."

"Rile—"

"Shh."

A man in a suit and tie pointed toward the site of Taylor's find before he made his way toward where she sat.

"Rile—"

Riley held up a hand. "Say nothing, Taylor. Nothing, got that?" He turned as the suit joined them.

Taylor stood, crossing her arms over her chest and spreading her feet wide enough to keep her balance. She intended to create a bit of perceived stubborn confidence, despite the nerves tingling throughout her body.

"Ms. Marsh?" the suit asked.

"Yes?" She kept her tone firm but kind.

"I'm Jeremy Faine … with the SBI Crime lab." He held out his hand.

Taylor shook once and let go. "I'd say nice to meet you, but I think that would be inappropriate given the circumstances."

Jeremy gave her a short nod. "Right." He faced Riley. Nodded. He turned to the site. Nodded.

How robotic is this guy? The head gestures added to her curiosity, but at the same time, they brought the hairs on her arms to a stand.

"Anything I can—" Taylor's words earned a glare from Riley.

Jeremy swiveled back to her, his hand slipping into his jacket. He pulled out a paper, opened it and held it up, but Taylor couldn't read it in the darkening night. Jeremy gave yet another nod to Riley.

Riley's eyes hardened. "Taylor—"

Cuffs appeared from within Jeremy's suit coat. Riley bumped him out of the way.

A shiver ran the length of her body. "What's going on?" She spun out of Riley's way as he reached for her.

His lips went to a thin line as the cuffs came closer. "Don't freak out. You're not under arrest." Through gritted teeth, he added, "And keep your damn mouth shut."

Wide-eyed, Taylor stopped moving as Riley took her arms and drew them behind her back. The action brought with it a familiar muscle constriction to her entire upper torso. Her throat seized. Her eyes watered. "Can't—"

"Just stay calm. Breathe through it." The click of handcuffs registered before the pressure on her wrists took hold. "I'm right here with you. Right here."

Her mouth opened and closed, but air failed to go in or out. Taylor's eyes burned. She stared hard at Jeremy, willing him to hear her unsaid plea. *I need air! Why does this happen to me?*

"Breathe, Taylor," Riley said from behind her. "It's just a formality."

Tortured, her lungs screamed for air, and her legs wobbled.

Jeremy grabbed her as she pitched forward. "Ms. Marsh?"

She opened and closed her mouth again.

Riley jumped around to Taylor's front, taking Jeremy's place. He laid his palms against her cheeks. "Look at me, Taylor. Here. Look at me."

Her eyes failed her. *Arms ... need ... untie.* A watery view of Riley's face came into focus right before Taylor's body slumped against him. *Bound. Again.*

Her eyes rolled back until even her thoughts went silent.

Rocky's couldn't have been louder and still met the noise ordinance for New York's night crowd. Michael and Ian had walked in, headed straight for the bar and both ordered beers. Around them, the place reeked of sweat, secondhand smoke from those bringing it in with them from outside and spilled alcohol.

A DJ pumped music through the room while at least two dozen televisions displayed a variety of stations, none of which interested Ian.

He downed the contents of his beer and tapped the bar for a second.

"Might want to pace yourself there, bro," Michael said.

Ian shook his head. "Better to just get drunk. Then all the thoughts go away."

Michael snorted. "Temporarily. Until you puke all night."

"I don't get sick. I know my limit."

A waitress with her blonde hair tied in a ponytail sidled up to them, her tray, pad and pencil in hand. "You boys care for some hors d'oeuvres? Or a meal?" She leaned over the counter, dropping a small piece of paper onto a stack, which a second bartender picked up. Her breasts piled up as she pressed into the walnut countertop, her blue eyes daring Ian to take in his fill.

"I'll take a burger," Michael said as Ian said, "You're not my type."

The slap to Ian's shoulder accompanied the waitress's pout.

"What the hell?" Ian asked.

"When has blonde and blue eyed not been your type?" Michael asked.

Never. "Tonight." He drank deep from the beer and signaled for a third.

"We came here to get your mind off her. To get you back in the saddle." Michael jutted his hips out as if that would entice

Ian to jump on a horse he didn't want to ride.

"I know. I'm just not . . ."

"You need the right motivation." With beer in hand, Michael pointed toward a group of women who eyed Ian over their shoulders every few minutes. One, with straight black hair, licked her painted red lips. Another, with red hair to her butt, crooked her finger at him. "They're motivated."

"Then, by all means, go get them."

Michael nudged Ian's shoulder. "No, you go. You have to get out of this funk."

"They're too young for me."

"Dude, they're over twenty-one, and that's close enough to half plus seven."

Ian snorted a laugh. "Who told you that was the rule?"

"Grandma."

They both laughed again.

"Go, man. Let tonight be the get-back-on-the-horse night." He clinked his beer against Ian's. "Or, you be the horse and let her ride." With another bump to Ian's shoulder, Michael stood. "I'm going after the group in the back right."

By the largest of the TVs, a group of barely-over-twenties stood together.

Michael gave Ian a nod and sauntered away.

Two of the women in the group eyeing Ian stretched and curled fingers his way. With a deep sigh and a third beer to begin the dulling of the senses phase of the night, Ian began his walk toward them.

A hum filled Taylor's mind, ran up through her legs and into her arms. She blinked tired eyes, working to focus on her surroundings of black and metal, flashing red and blue, and the humidity of southern springtime.

"Taylor . . ." Riley's voice penetrated the fog.

A cop car. Riley's cop car.

The engine hummed, sending vibrations through the vehicle. As her mind whirred, she jerked her arms and found them attached one to the other.

Riley leaned over the open door and reached in, offering her shoulder a light squeeze. "I'm sorry, Tay. I didn't think the panic attack would come on so strong. I really didn't."

He'd cuffed her. He'd pulled her arms behind her and made her into a common criminal. Hurt and disappointment filled her. Not at Riley, but herself. Her cheeks flamed with embarrassment. She hadn't reacted so strongly to her phobia in ages—ten years, in fact.

"Tay?"

She focused on her breathing, anxiety ebbing like the ocean's tide. "I'm okay."

"I should have told you before I did that. It was Faine—" Riley shook his head. "No, totally my fault. No excuses. I knew and didn't—"

"It's okay. I'm …" *Wigging out.* "Okay."

"You were right. I'm really, *really* sorry. I should have been your friend. Not a Sergeant. I won't let that happen again."

While she couldn't believe how strong her reaction had been—blindsiding her with paralyzing fear—she believed his apology and that he meant it. Beyond the car, people continued to work, lights buzzing as they illuminated her yard, and in the center, her pile of wood sat just where she'd found the bones.

"You're not under arrest. They just wanted you secured for questioning because of the … nature of the situation. God, I'd swear that Faine has something against you, and he doesn't even know you. Showed up outta nowhere like he owns the crime scene."

Crime scene?

"But, I told them I'm staying with you right here until they do whatever or take official action."

"I'll be okay, Riley. Really. I will. What happens next?"

"Ms. Marsh?"

So focused on the activity beyond the car, Taylor hadn't noticed anyone else join them.

"I'm Lieutenant King." His deep voice rumbled over the hum of engines and lights.

"Dale." Faine's voice chased after them, pulling Riley from the car.

"Would you be willing to answer a few questions tonight?" King asked.

She tracked Riley and Faine's path away from the car as she answered, "Sure."

"When did you purchase your house?"

"Ten years ago." *The day I returned from Alabama.*

"And you're a native of this area?" He scratched something on his pad.

She didn't need to think for that one. "Yes."

"You own Marsh Construction?" King barely looked up when he asked or wrote anything.

"Yes." She squished up her nose, shooting a glance at Riley, whose arms flailed while Faine wagged a finger in Riley's direction.

"Why did you call the police today, Ms. Marsh?"

She wanted to roll her eyes. They knew very well. "Because, in the demolition of a shed on my property, a set of bones turned up underneath." The image of the face, its jaw wide as if in a scream, forced Taylor to close her eyes. She inhaled, focusing on happy thoughts of her house unencumbered by yellow caution tape, and calmed.

"Can you tell us what happened in Alabama ten years ago?" the lieutenant asked.

"No."

"Ma'am?" The lieutenant's tone turned irritated. "You cannot give us any clarity?"

She raised her lids and stared straight at the officer. "What happened in Alabama isn't relevant to today in any way, shape or form, and I wish to leave the past … in the past." That they knew about her time there surprised her. Their bringing it up made her blood boil.

Faine stepped into Taylor's view again. "Is there a problem here?"

"No," King said, eyes narrowed.

"Have you—" Riley received a glare from both the other men—superiors if Taylor understood their gestures.

They all faced her again.

"It would be in your best interests—" King started.

"If ya'll want to ask me about stuff that happened ten years ago, that wasn't my fault, that was all a setup, you go on ahead, but do so during part of the day where I'm not exhausted and wondering if my roses are going to be trampled on."

"Our investigation—"

She stared hard at King and moved to Faine as he threw up his hands. "Your investigation is about a set of bones on my land. Now, what would you like to know about that?"

"We'd like to know who you murdered and why," Faine said in as monotone a manner as possible.

Taylor jerked back. She hadn't expected anyone to say murder. She expected to hear she'd unearthed a cemetery plot, and they'd have to bring in an excavation team, archaeologists or historians.

When her gaze landed on Riley, he hung his head.

Uh-oh. "You know what? I think, if you're going to ask me any other questions, I might just want to have my attorney present."

Faine puffed up his chest. "Something to hide already?"

Taylor wanted to clock the attitude right off the man.

"No, sir. But I like to cover my ass, and I do believe it's best to do so right up front."

"If that's the way you'd like to play this game—" Faine started as King withdrew a paper, his own expression sour. "Taylor Marsh, you're under arrest."

Not again.

3

Pitiful whines, muffled sniffles and cries of 'I didn't do it!' pierced Taylor's ears as the Corrections Officer, Breck—by her name tag—led Taylor down a grey-walled hallway toward booking.

The warrant King held had, in fact, been an arrest warrant, executed by the newest judge on the bench and delivered under orders per one Jeremy Faine. 'No point fightin' it', Riley had said. 'It'll only make it worse. Just get through it, and I'll come by in the morning'.

He could only escort her as far as the outer walls of the female wing, but he'd convinced Breck to keep the cuffs in front and sent her off with his signature smile and a promise to call her attorney for her.

Taylor kept her head up, banking the sigh wanting to escape. She wouldn't fight it, didn't even have the first-timer nerves about her, since she already knew the drill. Once had been enough of a lesson.

'Least this time, I have help from the get-go.

"Have a seat." Breck pointed to the row of orange, plastic chairs and held on to Taylor's arm as she dropped into one. "Someone will come get you in a second." The officer disappeared around a corner.

Taylor fell back as exhaustion weighed heavy on her. Her mind spun to Riley, her home and the bones. With deliberation, she closed her eyes and remembered what had stared back at her. The blank eyes. The smoothness of the features that had barely been covered in any dirt.

The familiarity bugged the living daylights out of her, but she couldn't figure out what gave her the impression she'd seen the bones before.

"Taylor Marsh?"

Her body jolted back to reality, and Taylor held up a hand to the new woman who'd called her.

"Come on, honey. It's after two on this fine—" The woman spun her watch around. "—Well, I'll be damned, it's Earth Day. It's no wonder I'm ready for summer and my dinner break." A sweet smile graced her face. "I'm Officer Hough."

At the wave of Hough's hand, Taylor stood and walked toward her and another jail hallway.

Hough directed Taylor through photographing, took her fingerprints, and swabbed the inside of her cheek. She led her to a room with a flat, steel desk, a locked, metal cabinet, a chair, a table and a female officer with a shotgun in her hands.

Taylor's calm dissolved as her wrists flexed within the cuffs digging into her skin. A cramp knotted her foot as heat flushed through her body.

"Now. It's just us girls in here, and if you cooperate, we'll have this over in a jiffy." As Hough talked, she set her clipboard on the desk, slid on a pair of rubber gloves and took Taylor's wrist with the gentleness of a kitten. "I'm going to secure one hand to the bar, and the other you can use to undress. Murder charges get the full work-up, but I'm inclined to make this fast. Got a Lean Cuisine waiting for me."

A small laugh bubbled up inside Taylor along with resignation to her fate.

"Shoes first, please."

Taylor toed her work boots off since they hadn't been fully laced after leaving the hospital. She nudged them toward Hough.

"Thank ya, ma'am." Hough jotted stuff down on the paper,

the gaze of the other officer never leaving Taylor. "You'll get all these articles back. I'm just cataloging them."

Taylor offered a slight nod. *I remember.*

"Britches next, please. Eye color?"

"Blue." She pushed herself up against the wall to undo the buttons and let her jeans fall to the ground. She wanted to scream at the injustice, to yell and ask why she'd be put through a full body strip search experience a second time. Who had it out for her so bad that she couldn't live in peace?

"Height?"

"Five-seven."

"Weight?" The pants went into a bag.

"One-forty." Her underwear and socks disappeared.

"Any diseases, drug use or alcohol use?"

"No." Removing Taylor's shirt would require Hough's assistance due to the cuffs. Same for her bra. She banked the embarrassment.

"Let me help you with those." Throughout it all, Hough hummed a calming lullaby that contradicted the situation, especially the fact Taylor stood, naked, attached by a metal ring to a wall. Hough grasped her hand, slid a key into the lock and led her to the table where she dropped a plastic bag she'd pulled from the cabinet. The cuffs were reconnected to yet another metal bar.

Hough plopped onto her chair. "Go on ahead and suit up. I'll need that ring, too."

The plastic ripped without effort, and a jumpsuit fell to the ground. Taylor slid her grandfather's ring from her finger. She rubbed around the knuckle, feeling more naked for having removed it than any of her clothes.

"Got a man in your life?" Hough kept on writing as she asked.

Ian's face jumped to the front of her thoughts, bringing both a tremor and desire to Taylor. "No." She slid her legs into the awful jail attire, trying to force him out of her mind. She turned to Riley, his lifelong friendship and smile, but Ian's image replaced it.

"Pretty girl like you?" Hough chuckled.

"Why are you being so nice?"

"Honey, they ain't no reason not to be nice to people. Just 'cause you screwed up—" she held up her hands "—or didn't screw up, don't mean you aren't a human and deserving respect. You give it to me; I give it to you."

Taylor blew a breath. "You should give that advice to the folks in Alabama."

Hough narrowed her eyes. "Am I wrong about you, hun?"

"What do you mean?"

"Well, I got a track record says I know when someone is guilty, and you ain't."

A light chuckle escaped along with a quirk of Taylor's lips. "How do you know—"

"It's the 'mean' in someone's eye. Look for it, and you'll know if they're telling the truth. Works ever' time. What happened in Alabama?"

Taylor stared into Hough's sweet, chocolate irises, wishing she could spill her entire history. "Let's just say, it wasn't quite so pleasant in their jail, and the woman there didn't believe in 'innocent until proven guilty'. And . . . she let me know it every step of the way."

Hough stuck a hand on her hip and jutted out the other one. "Naw, girl. You ain't nothing but someone stuck in the wrong place, maybe even wrong time. Probably even been with the wrong man one too many times, too." She motioned with the clipboard toward the other officer who hadn't said a word through the entire experience. "Ask Nell over there. Tell her, Nell. Ain't I right about people?"

Nell's answer came in the form of a nod.

"You've got gorgeous eyes," the redhead said as Ian stood just outside their circle.

The group of four all turned toward him.

"What nationality are you?" The second lovely to speak had thin legs up to her breasts and breasts up to her shoulders. "I mean, what with the green eyes and the milk chocolate skin. The simple cheekbone structure says European, but the tones say African."

"I'm American, born and bred, like, I presume, all of you beautiful women are."

They giggled, clearly having had too much to drink already—or just too young to care if they acted silly. "So, are you here with anyone special?" Raven-haired girl asked.

Ian shook his head, not wanting to mention Michael.

"We're here for Kimmie's twenty-first birthday." Two of them pointed to the blonde with blue eyes—a girl who looked nothing like Taylor yet rivaled the others in the room.

Knowing they were Kimmie's friends meant none of them would meet Michael's age calculation.

Fuck it. This is about getting my groove back. "Twenty-one, huh? How about I buy you ladies a round of drinks?"

They whooped and brought Ian into their fold, surrounding him with their bodies, touching and rubbing as they asked questions and he answered, about where he lived, who he'd come with and finally reached the ultimate. "So, what do you do? For work, I mean," Red asked.

Ian had decided not to learn their names—except for Kimmie. He figured the less he knew, the better. "I'm a treasure hunter."

"Ooh, is that like a bounty hunter?" Raven asked.

Holding back the eye roll, Ian said, "Yes." *And yet nothing like it at all.* He'd get nowhere if he acted his age.

The women giggled and downed a Tequila shot—their drink of choice, according to Red.

The more Blondie stared into Ian's eyes, the more Taylor's face appeared in his mind. He shook his head, trying to get the image to go away. "How about another round?" *Or ten.*

The women whooped again and spun, picking a whiskey shot and beer chaser for their next venture. As they waited to be served, Ian chatted up each one of them.

All in one sorority.

All having just turned twenty-one that year.

All looking for someone to help them after they ensured Kimmie reached her fully drunk state.

Red sauntered up, ran a finger down Ian's cheek and to his chest, where his button down had somehow been unfastened further. "There's something else our friend wants to do for her twenty-first."

Ian wound an arm about Red's waist. "Oh yeah? What's that?" He downed another shot, holding back the cringe as the heat trailed his throat.

"She wants a ménage. With a guy like you." Her lips remained right at his ear, and a split second later, the wetness associated with a lick sent a chill through Ian.

He grasped Red's wrists and pulled her in, crushing his lips against hers. When he withdrew, she stared up at him. "Is that what *you* want?" he asked.

She quirked an eyebrow. "All four of us. We've heard the myth about your kind."

"My kind?" *Older men?*

She tilted her head left, right and left again. "Yeah, you know, if you go black, you never go back."

"Ah, that one." Ian picked up another shot glass, thankful he'd ordered a set, and swigged it, knowing if he agreed to their little fling, he'd have to be thoroughly drunk not to have Taylor's face peer back at him from all four of them. "Some say it's true, but the true test is not in the size of one's dick, but of just how it's used."

The four of them wound their arms around Ian. "We're staying at the Ritz. Just one night. Room fourteen sixty."

"Will you come?" Raven asked.

"For me?" Kimmie asked.

“And me?” Red asked.

The fourth in their party remained silent, standing still, her newest drink still in her hand. When she licked her lips and fluffed her mousy brown hair, Ian knew they’d all agreed and chosen the best man for the job—whether or not he’d ever been part of a ménage before.

Which he hadn’t.

First time for everything.

“Okay, ladies. Let’s go.”

They packed up their bags, swiping credit cards with their server, and Ian gave Michael a nod and a wave. He received the same and a giant smile in return.

Teetering on the highest of high heels, the foursome struggled their way out the door and onto the finest sidewalks in New York.

Ian waved to a cab as it slowed its way down the street. Red held out her hotel key, jiggling it as the car pulled up. Rather than pile in with the four of them, Ian said, “I’ll meet you there.”

They squeezed into the back and front seats, jabbering on and on the whole time, squealing that they’d found just the right man and that they couldn’t wait to get his clothes off.

“Drunk as skunks. I can’t believe I’m doing this.”

He whistled for a second cab, and once one pulled to the curb, hopped in. “Follow that one. It’s time to forget.”

Psychologists claimed pink calmed, but the wails of the women in the cells surrounding Taylor’s suggested the experts knew nothing about human nature. Confinement, small spaces and lack of freedom put everyone in a sour mood.

Hough had walked Taylor to her cell, given her a single blanket and pillow and one bit of advice: “Just like a bad dream, honey. They, too, go away, and the sun shines again. Hang in there.”

Taylor shifted to her side, blinked through exhaustion, though her body refused her sleep. Across from her, a woman sniffled light sobs. Beneath her, one snored louder than a lawn mower rolling at top speed. Despite the hour and the darkness, silence failed to engulf the women's side of the correction facility.

She flipped onto her back, the ceiling coming within three feet of her face. A shiver ran through her body. She switched to her side again, despite the protest of her muscles suggesting she should stay the other way. The proximity to the wall could induce an attack like the ones she'd had at home—of claustrophobia instead of just being hog-tied.

Why she had so many issues remained a mystery, but Taylor had learned to cope.

As long as she could breathe and keep her hands to her front, she could deal, alone, with her place among the criminally challenged.

4

Groggy from lack of sleep and dreams about a certain gorgeous blonde, deep down in the southern part of the US of A, Ian clutched his massive, morning erection and groaned. He rolled over, the hangover pounding his head, and crawled his way toward the bathroom.

The scent of burnt toast and syrup wafted through, smack to the center of Ian's stomach, making him want to both hurl and curl up in a ball.

He managed to reach the bathroom, rise for some Ibuprofen and down a few by drinking from the sink's tap.

"Never, ever, ever drink so much in one night," he said to the mirror. The face staring back at him reflected the night's binge, but not the guilt he'd expected when the night started. Hand on the marble countertop, Ian balanced himself upright, letting the swimming room come to a stop. A gritty dryness coated the inside of his mouth, and he needed something stronger than water. "Time to face the judge," he said and staggered from the bathroom in his boxers.

"You look like hell," Michael said the moment Ian stepped into the kitchen.

Ian blinked at the brightness in the space and found Michael sitting at the round table in a kitchen designed for a chef, but rarely used to its capacity. "And you're a horrible chef."

"ThaswhyI'mgonbeadoctor."

Ian withdrew a glass from the cupboard and poured the remaining inch of orange juice from the container, attempting to process what Michael had said. *That's why I'm gonna be a doctor.* Thinking while still hung over did not bode well for the rest of the day. "You talk with your mouth full around Mom and Dad?"

Michael wiped at his lips. "Never. She'd beat me black and blue if I did."

With a roll of his eyes, Ian sipped at the lukewarm juice. As smart as Michael had been, top of his class, he acted pre-pubescent half the time. *Which is exactly why I went to the bar with him last night.*

"So ... why were you home before me?" Michael asked. "I mean, I saw you leave with four lovelies. Figured you'd be out all night."

Ian set the glass on the granite counter. He knew the subject would come up but had hoped it wouldn't. "Tired. I had a long—"

The shake of Michael's head went farther than any words could have. "Liar. Liar. Liar. Liar." He scraped off some of the charred remains on the bread and slathered jelly on top. "You left with them. *With them*, my man. If you weren't going to actually make use of them, you could have passed them off to me."

"You're old enough to get your own women." Rather than try to drink any more of the juice, Ian dumped it, rinsed his glass and set it in the dishwasher. His cleaning lady would take care of it later that afternoon.

"But four! You had four of the most gorgeous girls." Michael leaned forward, hands pleading. "Tell me one of them—"

"Nothing to tell. They were drunk. Too drunk. And by the time they reached the hotel, two of them threw up on the sidewalk." Ian ran a hand over his head. "So, I did the gentlemanly thing and kept going."

"So wrong." Michael hung and shook his head. "But yet again, this is why you are you, and I am me. The one chick I met last night?" He faced Ian as if Ian should answer the non-question.

"Her boyfriend showed up as we were walking out. How crazy is that?"

Ian waved a hand through the air. "Sorry. But don't you have anything better to do than sit here eating burned toast?" *And asking me about an adventure that didn't happen? And making my stomach curl with your inability to cook?*

A nod accompanied Michael's, "Nope. No classes today. Just need to study." He didn't even seem hung over.

This is why men my age don't get wasted. Ian headed for his couch where he intended to lie down and do nothing all day.

At the musical chime singing from his bedroom, he continued on and grabbed his cell off his dresser. "It's eight o'clock in the morning, why are you calling me so early?"

"Hot date last night?" Tripp asked.

"Well ... if you must know ... yes." *No.* Rather than sit on the bed and twiddle his thumbs while he talked, Ian opened his balcony doors, breathed in the pre-polluted morning air of New York City and basked in the glory of just being home. The thirty-fifth floor offered him a full view of the city below, the cars on the road and the ever-present horns and sirens.

"Time to come back," Tripp said.

"What the hell? No way. I got ... stuff to do. Women ... and—" *Fuck, this sucks.* Wind bit at his cheeks, a reflection of the varying springtime temperatures and of the morning.

"Are you drunk?"

How the hell could he tell that? "Of course not." *Anymore.*

"Good. Then get on the pla—"

"Did you find us a new gig?" Ian's lips curved. They'd done nearly no work in the six months since Tripp married Lexi. Or, no 'real' work as Ian liked to call it. "What is it? No, wait, better yet, *where* is it? Bahamas? Europe? Somewhere completely exotic with an everlasting supply of tequila—" His stomach lurched. *Or not.*

Tripp chuckled. "Exotic, yes. No idea on the tequila."

"Where, then?"

"Trust me, Ian. You want to be in on this one. The plane will be ready in an hour. Get your ass on it, and I'll pick you up."

"Wait . . . if you're picking me up, that means I'm coming back to Slowville. Back to Noville. Back to—" Ian had never refused Tripp's business offers before, and the excuses only escaped out of pure frustration over a woman. One woman. *One damn woman.* He thumped his forehead against the glass of his balcony door, inciting a headache the size of Mount Rushmore. "You're not telling me everything."

"I'll fill you in when you get here."

"Oh, no. If I have to come back—" The line died. Ian held the phone away from his head. "Bastard." He slipped back through the doors and grabbed his bag—one he hadn't even unpacked—ripping through it for clean clothes.

Michael appeared in the frame of the door, yet another piece of toast in hand. "South for the winter?"

"It's spring, but apparently so."

"Coming back?"

"Of course I am. Why would you even ask?"

The clang of nightsticks against steel bars forced Taylor's eyes open. She hadn't even realized they'd closed. She'd been roused at six for square meal number one and replaced in her cell immediately afterward. As nine rolled around, her cell mates had been taken away, and three new ones returned, each with a brighter smile on her face than the previous. By ten, she'd grown restless and almost considered asking to make another phone call.

Though she'd talked with Tripp Fox about becoming her attorney, she hadn't called her parents and wouldn't dare interrupt their annual vacation. Riley, though, he'd help if he could.

She just wouldn't ask. Doing so would put him in an unfair position.

When the clangs continued, Taylor's heart raced with memories of her time in Alabama.

"Something freak you out up there, honey?" Her lower bunkmate's drawl carried over the sounds.

Taylor hadn't realized she'd moved enough to bring any attention to herself. Unsure whether she should play tough, demure, or be herself, she rolled to her side and said, "It just never gets quiet."

"Nope, never does." The voice came from the lower bunk on the other side of the cell. "I been in—" The woman tapped one bright red fingernail against the other. "—fourth time this month." She lowered extended-length lashes, revealing bright browns a second later. "Prolly gonna stay inside this time. Might as well get used to the noise."

"Why?" Taylor held back the cringe at an extra-long stay. She hoped for a summons to the magistrate that morning. Expected it even, if Tripp could get her on the docket.

"Done did it this time. Actually killed the bastard. Thought I did it last time, but he prit-near killed me instead. I got him, though, this time. Damn cops didn't help one damn bit before. Had to take control. Use my own hands. Shoulda done it three tries ago, but I kept thinking I'd change him."

The other two women hummed agreement.

"I'm Tanya, by the way." She held out a hand.

"Taylor."

"You got a boy name?"

Taylor gave a small snicker. "How else would I get by owning a construction company?"

"Girl, you got it goin' on. What'd you do? Stiff a client? Shoot someone with a nail gun?"

"Plaster their head into a wall?" one of the others asked.

"Put up the wrong tile? You know them southern women. You mess with their shit, and they'll sue." The third whooped.

"Actually, I didn't do anything," Taylor said.

Loud guffaws accompanied hoots of laughter. "That's what they all say."

It seemed the game called 'Taylor Marsh's innocence' had already created two sides.

The flight back to North Carolina proved uneventful. Tripp picking Ian up at the airport's curb in his black Jaguar suggested nothing out of the ordinary. Though, when they bypassed the turn-off from the freeway that would take them to Tripp's house, Ian narrowed his eyes. "*Where* are we going?"

Tripp gave a slight bobble of his head. "We have a client to see."

"Is this *the* client you wouldn't tell me a rat's ass thing about? Or something else? Because if it's something else, drop me off at your house first."

Tripp's eyes stayed fixed straight ahead. "It's *the* client."

"Why the hell are you being so secretive?" Ian twisted so he could face Tripp. The Jag blew past the few cars on the road with them. Ian glanced at the speedometer, found Tripp going over ninety. "I hope you got your can't-catch-me-o-meter on."

A light chuckle breezed from the driver's side. "You know I can't use my *talents* without Lexi right next to me."

"Get a radar detector then."

Tripp shrugged.

"Your funeral, if you get a ticket and Lexi finds out." Ian smiled at the thought of the argument the two would have. Lexi would tear into Tripp without a doubt. "So, you wouldn't tell me when I was in New York, and you're not telling me now. What gives, Fox?" Ian's body tensed. "Wait . . . you're not telling me because something happened. What happened? Is Lexi—"

"Lex is fine. This is about the woman you so affectionately refer to as 'blondie'."

"Wait . . . you brought me back here for her? *Her!* What the—"

"She was arrested last night, Ian."

"Blondie? You're shitting me." Ian's mind whirled with curiosity and uncertainty. "What for? She saw someone up with one of those power tools? Drill into them with one of those thingamabobs? Ooh … a wood chipper—"

"There were bones found on her property."

"She buried someone? That's not very creative for someone in construction."

"And, that's a pretty big leap for you to assume," Tripp said. "Why'd you jump to her burying someone?"

Ian realized he had no idea why. "Logical guess." He rubbed a hand across his face. "So, tell me why you're involved."

"She hired me as her attorney."

"For what? I mean, why would you even take a criminal case? Which again, since you haven't said, I'm guessing is the truth. That's not your kind of deal."

Tripp glanced toward Ian. Trees lining the edge of the freeway rushed by as Tripp picked up more speed. "Because, sometimes, it's necessary."

"Necessary?"

Tripp eyed Ian as they came to a stoplight. "Yes. Necessary. We can't have the girl of your dreams rotting in jail, Ian." Tripp oozed sarcasm.

"She's not—" Ian couldn't finish the comment without lying. She'd been exactly that for months *and* throughout the previous night. Any time he closed his eyes, she took over. He thought himself good with women, attentive and never shy, but the fantasies that played in his mind put her in the lead with him following. In everything. "Why would you tell me we got a gig then?" Ian's earlier curiosity moved into downright suspicion.

"I didn't, remember? You assumed. Would you have come down here if I told you *blondie* asked for a lawyer because of some bones in her yard and cops in her face?

"Of course …" *not.* A knuckle to the temple relieved some of the pressure building behind Ian's eyes.

Tripp shook his head. "Ian, Ian, Ian. I took it because I know she's innocent."

Ian's eyes widened. "You convinced Lexi to use your moojoo-joojoo on a person?" According to Tripp, and Lexi herself, she refused—as in flat-out, punch in the face, don't-go-there—to use her Zeus-given gift to search for people.

"Sorta."

Ian huffed. "So, now that the fun is gone from the game, who dunnit?"

"No idea."

"What the hell?" Ian thumped the dash with his fist. "How do you—what do—what good is your voodoo-mental-mojo if you can't even find that answer?"

Tripp chuckled. "I didn't say we looked for a killer, Ian."

"You know that's the logical thing to do, right?"

"Who says it's a murder?"

"Well, if she's in jail . . ."

Tripp eyed Ian.

"Okay, so yeah, there are innocent people in jail." Ian waved a hand through the air and air quoted. "I'll believe that when I see it. What did you look for, what did you find, and if she's 'innocent', why is she in jail?"

"I don't kno—"

"Fuck that, Fox. This whole marriage thing went and made you soft. If you wanted an answer before, you'd have gone and gotten it." Frustration ebbed from Ian. "You know what? I'm calling a cab when we get to wherever-the-hell we're going and getting on the next flight home. This is not a job I signed up for. We don't do stuff without information. We made a deal twenty-five years ago, and until now, you've stuck to it. But I'm not—"

"You didn't let me finish, Ian." Tripp brought them into the jail's parking lot. "And, you're not going anywhere."

"Watch me." Ian kept his voice serious, with a hint of 'don't fuck with me'.

The jail, in all its bland glory, loomed ahead of them—a ten story building in sandstone brown. As soon as Tripp pulled into a spot, Ian unbuckled, jumped out and slammed a fist on the roof.

His emotions went every which way when Taylor became a part of the conversation. He had to get her out of his system—to purge her from his mind.

Tripp walked around the car and laid a hand on Ian's shoulder. "Have I ever, in those twenty-plus years you referred to, done anything to steer you the wrong way? Ever?"

Ian clenched his teeth. Tripp hadn't. "There's always a first."

From within the car, Tripp withdrew a briefcase and a stack of folders. "And, it's not now." He handed Ian the pile. "You get to be my assistant in here. Take copious notes, keep your mouth shut, don't ask any questions, don't say a word, and no matter what you do, don't touch her." He strode off. "Oh, and I am going to need *you* to bail her out."

"What the—Fox! Have you gone fucking mad, man?" Ian stood, gawking, waiting for Tripp to return. When he didn't, but drew closer to the building's entrance, Ian took off after his so-called friend. "You want *me* to give up *my* money for a woman I know nothing about. Son of a bitch got balls." Ian nearly bumped into Tripp as he reached the doors. A grab of Tripp's bicep had him spinning toward Ian. "Say something . . . *anything* . . . that'll make me want to walk through those doors."

Tripp closed one eye, scrunched his nose and shut the other. "I'll give you five million dollars if you don't ask her to marry you by—" He turned his watch toward himself. "—the end of May." The sliding glass opened on a whoosh, and Tripp slipped inside, leaving Ian standing alone.

On a deep sigh, and with multiple head shakes, Ian followed.

5

The buzz of the lock release sounded a moment before Taylor's cell door opened. "Taylor Marsh?" a guard asked.

"That's me." She held up her hand as if in kindergarten, waiting to be picked by the cool kids.

"This way."

Being escorted by two armed guards to a small, empty, white-walled room had an upside. The claustrophobia Taylor had begun to experience faded.

The small conference room held one table, three seats and nothing else. Taylor sat when told to sit. Walked when told to walk. Waited when told to wait. If she had a clock, she'd have guessed five minutes passed before the door opened.

Tripp, in tieless suit, and Ian, in cream slacks and a seafoam green button-down, strode in.

Taylor's breath stuck even as her eyes riveted themselves to the second man. Her heart hammered in her chest. She hadn't expected Ian. *Hadn't he gone to New York?* She drew her fingers through her mess of hair as if that would do any bit of good and tucked them below the table, between her knees.

"How are you, Taylor?" Tripp asked.

She eyed him before answering, "Peachy."

Ian snorted a laugh but hid it between pursed lips a moment later.

"You look like a woman caught in the middle of a tragic comedy," Tripp said after a few seconds.

Her head tilted. "What exactly does that look like?"

The two men pulled chairs from across the table and sat. Ian dropped a stack of folders and paper on the solid surface and, with pen in-hand, began to write. From upside down Taylor could read her name. A moment later, Ian rested his elbows on the flat surface, fingers intertwined.

"So … tell me what you found yesterday," Tripp said.

Taylor's entire body tensed. *They were just bones. Someone's skeleton. A cemetery for sure. That's all.* She relayed what she'd been doing before they showed up—as if they didn't know. "The bones though—I don't know. It was … really weird. I mean … the face was pointing to the sky with the jaw open. That's all I saw." *With my eyes.* "I don't know where it came from or why it was there. I have no idea who they were. Are." She shook her head at herself. "I bought the house with the shed. I tore it down so I could put in a garden. I don't understand any of this, or why they think I'm connected to this in any way." Taylor clasped and undid her hands underneath the table.

"Can you tell me about the previous owners of the house?"

"Not really. Other than it came through the original estate, but the place had been a rental for years. I snatched it up on a foreclosure. Did the entire renovation myself—just like on your place." She closed her eyes, bringing to mind Tripp's farmhouse. "I picked my house because I fell in love with the land and the possibilities … and because it's the last of the Weaton farm bungalows." The image of cars, people, equipment, tools and anything else running itself over her roses and the new lawn she'd sodded no more than a few weeks before had her grimacing. "I'd just bought it when I came back from Alabama and was just starting my company. I wanted a showpiece, but not like this."

Ian separated his hands and fiddled with the gaudy, gold monstrosity of a ring around his finger.

Tripp clasped his hands in front of himself. "The press, obviously, has gotten wind of this, and there's talk about something happening before you came back here. I can get the files, but I'd rather hear what happened from you."

"In Alabama, you mean?" She knew, at some point, that experience would come back to bite her.

"Yes," Tripp said.

Anger boiled. "I should have killed him." *Good gracious, what are you thinking, saying that out loud?* She closed her eyes, drew in a breath and exhaled. "Strike that. Pretend I didn't say that."

"Okay. Who?"

"An ex." Memories of that day flooded her mind.

"Tell me."

Ian picked up the pen again.

"He staged his own death—a murder of all things—and set me up. I'd come home to blood all over my apartment, a shotgun on the table and a lack of a body. Of course, despite the number of cop shows on television, I went straight for that damn gun and grabbed it, coating my hands in blood. Cops showed up ten minutes after I got home, as if they'd been called. I never even dialed 9-1-1." She heaved air. "Took 'em two days to test the blood, found out it was his, figured I stashed the body. They spent over a week interrogating me, and the newspapers were all over it. 'College student murders boyfriend in jealous rage'. That's what the headlines said. I was guilty before I ever got a chance to get my story told." Her hands clenched even with the cuffs around her wrists. "I lived in the county jail, in podunk Alabama for two weeks, going back and forth with their investigators until someone at a bar saw the bastard—alive and well—and reported him." Taylor's cheeks flushed with heat as anger filled her. "He ended up in jail, himself, but not before I had the *full* experience." She faced Tripp. "I never imagined I'd see the inside of another one of these places, especially for yet *another* trumped-up charge."

"Didn't they test the blood to find it wasn't all his? If there was that much of it, it can't have been, right?" Tripp asked.

Taylor remembered that question being her own at the time.

"He'd planned ahead. He drew his own blood and stored it in a garage fridge. Then, when he needed it, he made one hell of a mess and scattered to the wind." Her nails dug into her palms.

"What was his name?"

"Tanner Meadows."

A visible shiver ran through Ian as one made its way down Taylor's body. She forced herself to calm.

"Why were you in Alabama in the first place?" Tripp asked.

"School. I wanted to start over. Yes, even just at twenty, I wanted change. Get away from Mom and Dad. Used my middle name while I was there . . . or for part of the time. Never expected to get involved with a psycho."

"I believe you," Tripp said.

"What?" Her lips refused to curve. "Not that I—I mean, I'm grateful you do. But—no. Never mind." She waved her combined hands in the air.

"Stop." The forcefulness of Tripp's tone had her freezing, hands mid-air. Even Ian's blank expression had moved to wide eyes.

"Did I say something wrong?" Taylor's gaze flitted between Ian and Tripp.

"Let me see your hand. Lay it on the table," Tripp said.

Taylor lowered them—a bit at a time—until they both lay flat against the tabletop.

Tripp and Ian both leaned forward.

"May thirty-first," Tripp said.

Ian couldn't believe it. He knew exactly why Tripp had stopped Taylor, had her put her hands down, but not why he repeated the date—six weeks from then.

"What's going on?" Taylor asked.

"Your finger." Tripp pointed to her hand. "Where'd you get that tattoo?"

Taylor rubbed at the blue lines snaking around the top bone

of her right ring finger. Her hands shook while she continued to twist and turn as if the ink were a ring—and she could pull it off. "It's not a tattoo. It's been there all my life."

Yup. Knew it.

Tripp turned to Ian. Ian to Tripp. Both adjusted back to her.

"Tell me about it," Tripp said.

Yes, please do.

"Why? How is this related?"

Yeah, I'm with her. How is this related?

"It's not. Just humor me."

Taylor took a deep breath. "Okay. When I was little, this looked like a vein wrapped around my finger funny. My parents took me to doctors and everything, trying to find out what it was. They just all said to leave it be unless it changed."

"And did it?" Tripp asked.

Nope.

"A few times. Usually, when it gets itchy, it's doing something. It's a little darker right now than usual, but it's not abnormal . . . to me, at least. I think I've gotten used to *that* weirdness in my life."

Hers changed? Why? How? Ian leaned and shifted until he met Taylor's gaze again, but he said nothing, per Tripp's orders.

"You normally wear a ring around that finger, don't you?" Tripp asked.

How did he remember that? Ian slipped his own hands beneath the table, twisting the class ring he kept on his own right ring finger.

"Yeah, my grandpa's. He gave it to me before he passed away. I hate that they took it last night."

"Understandable," Tripp said. "Why do you cover it up?"

Taylor inclined her head and closed her eyes. "Because when you're sixteen, and your best friend tells you that having a tattoo on your finger is going to send you to hell, it kinda gets old. So, I covered it and have gotten used to it being there. Plus, I like Grandpa's ring, and that's the only finger it fits on." She gave a small shrug. "He gave me my first hammer. Taught me how to drive a nail. How to work with people and how to listen to them." Taylor pressed at her eyelids. "I miss him."

Her pain washed into Ian, making his heart flip flop and bringing up an urge to reach out to her.

Tripp turned to Ian. "Put it up here."

Ian jerked back, lips pursed.

"Now."

On a deep sigh, he raised his hands and set them on the table, like Taylor.

"And take off the ring."

With a huff and a grab of his own ring, he slid it off.

Taylor gasped. She rose from her chair. "What the—"

Ian wiggled his fingers. *I'm never going to get this woman out of my head.*

Taylor couldn't believe what reflected back at her from Ian's skin. Her tattoo. Her mark.

Her symbol etched into his finger.

Under the gold and platinum, the same blue lines decorated his finger. "Please tell me . . . that's . . . a real tattoo."

Tripp waved a hand toward Ian.

Ian said nothing.

Taylor caught each of their gazes.

"Go ahead, Ian," Tripp said.

Ian still said nothing.

Tripp ran a hand over his head. "You are hereby authorized to speak, Ian."

Ian wrote 'Are you sure?' on the paper, adding, 'because you told me not to talk and, apparently, I do everything you ask.'

The glare Tripp gave Ian had a smile brewing on Taylor's lips. The two couldn't have looked different, yet they acted like brothers.

Tripp wrote back, 'Yes, you idiot.'

"What . . . is it?" Taylor asked. "What is this, Ian?" She pitched her voice low, pointing to her finger. "Why do you have one?"

After a long while, Ian said, "I've had this on my finger forever, too. Since birth. It wasn't an add-on." He swiped a hand over his head.

Not a tattoo. Taylor's breath caught.

"It's called the branches of life."

Taylor lowered to her seat again, her body shaking with the fact that the man she'd thought of so much in the previous months sat in front of her with an insignia like her own.

"It comes from the tree of life, an interconnection between all life on the planet."

She'd heard of that. "I thought that was depicted as a real tree, though."

Ian nodded. "That's why I said sorta." He reached for Taylor's hand, but Tripp stopped him. With a frustrated sigh, Ian held out his own finger and pointed to the markings. "There are four circles going around my finger. Four distinct patterns."

Taylor brought hers closer to her face. As Ian pointed to the outer part and traced it inside, around and back, she did the same on hers. "It's a closed loop, but it breaks and jumps over to another one."

He continued on, following the second line. It, too, completed a circle, ending on a line that moved it to a third. The third did the same. At the fourth, it stopped midway around.

"Mine does the same." Taylor traced her own. Her entire body, her entire being resisted what stared at her. The breaks matched without a millimeter of error. *They stop at the same point.* "Why doesn't it reconnect?"

Ian's gaze didn't shift from Taylor's. "According to the guy who translated this for me, it's a cycle of four. Lives, that is. Each of the three previous has ended before something happened that would allow it to reconnect with the other side."

"What did?"

"He couldn't tell me. Rather, he said it was unique to every individual. Like snowflakes. All of them. But . . . according to him, and he said he was an expert on this stuff, this is the last chance to rectify whatever happened the other three times."

"Why do we both have this?" Taylor asked.

Ian shrugged.

"There's no way this is coincidence," Taylor said.

"And, there's no way this is related to you being in jail, so, why don't the two of you finish your conversation, I'll play secretary, and we can all go home," Ian said.

A pang hit Taylor. She couldn't go home right then, and of all times, she wanted to, just so she could do some research. "When can I get out of here?"

"They've got you on the docket in twenty-four hours," Tripp said.

"Another day?" She couldn't keep the incredulity out of her voice. A pull back of her feet and her leg restraints caused a clank against the floor.

"Seems there was a full moon last night, and with that came a whole host of crimes and a plate so full, the justice system is backed up further than normal."

"Lovely." Sarcasm riddled her tone.

Tripp tapped on the table, sending an empty, metallic echo through the room. "The police are continuing their investigation."

"How can they keep me while they do that? Don't they have to have proof?" She spat out the words as anger replaced frustration.

"They had a warrant, which I'm waiting for a copy of. My guess is they've got their claws in some piece of information and are hanging on to it by a thread."

Taylor jumped forward. "Riley."

"Riley?" Tripp asked as Ian leaned back in his chair, a scowl growing on his face.

"He's . . . a friend. On the police force. Just got a promotion. He'll help if I ask. Can I? I mean—"

"No." Tripp shook his head. "Just leave this to me."

An inner war began within Taylor. Riley would help her with anything. "So, what happens next?"

"We get in front of the judge tomorrow. We plead not guilty, get bail, get you out and figure it out from there. Or, I find a way to convince them you had nothing to do with this and get you off completely."

"How the hell can we have matching symbols on our fingers?" Ian asked as he slipped into Tripp's Jaguar.

"I told ya," Tripp started, "when you first looked up those lines. I told you it was going to lead to a woman."

"But you didn't say a criminal."

"She's not." Tripp drove them from jail and onto the freeway toward home.

"Yet, we were the ones to walk out of that jail and oh! Oh! She *stayed.* So that puts her on the wrong side of the law." Ian leaned his head against the window.

"So pessimistic." Tripp chuckled. "Lexi will be so disappointed you think that way when she tells you what she found."

6

Ian slouched against the back of Tripp's favorite chair, sat up, leaned elbows on knees and relaxed again. He couldn't get comfortable. They'd spent over three hours with Taylor but had no real plan, no next steps as far as he could tell. Ian had itched to touch her, to make a physical connection with her, until the moment he'd seen the lines—the bands—the symbol.

On top of that, criminals, whether proven or not, did not fit into his future.

Tripp plopped next to his wife on the couch, sneaking an arm around her shoulders. Lexi's black hair fell over his arm as she snuggled into the crook.

A desire for the same hit Ian. A picture formed in his mind of him and Taylor sitting much the same way. He shook it off. "Okay, Lex, tell me what you know about Taylor Marsh."

Emma, Lexi's twin, though her complete opposite in every way, with her ultra-bright, blonde hair and crystal blue eyes, snagged a beanbag. "Ooh. What do you know about Taylor? I would love some good gossip."

"She's in jail, Em," Lexi said. "No gossiping allowed."

Emma stuck out her tongue. "You're no fun."

Tripp coughed over a laugh. "So . . . I didn't tell Taylor this . . . but we already got some intel from a source."

"You mean, Riley?" Emma asked.

Ian raised an eyebrow. "What happened to *my* question?"

"What?" Emma shrugged. "They've been friends for years.

He's on the force. I can put two and two together really fast." She tapped her temple.

Lexi pulled her hair into a tail and stood. "You guys keep going. I'll be right back."

I'm never going to get an answer.

"So . . ." Tripp tilted his head toward Emma. "My . . . source . . . says the bones are beneath the surface, by a couple feet, and at a semi-angular tilt—head up. Whatever the hell that means. They have to dig around the entire area where that shed was. Seems they need to cull through an eight by four by three foot section to get to everything and won't let anyone touch anything until they have it all mapped out. They got a judge to agree to the arrest, and according to my source, it's legit. Again, *how*, I haven't a clue. Worse, it's probably going to take a week to find, catalogue and validate that they have all the bones and do their search of her home . . . everything."

"Bones are bones, right?" Ian asked. "Have them date 'em, for fuck's sake. How hard can that be?" Ian rolled his eyes, closing them for a second. "Or, has innocent until proven guilty been forgotten?"

Emma's gaze strayed his way with a discernible tilt to her head and furrowed brows. Ian mirrored her look. Tripp gave him a similar one.

"What?" Ian asked.

Tripp leaned forward, elbows on knees. "An hour ago you were complaining that she was a criminal, now you're advocating for justice?"

Lexi returned with a small pint of ice cream in her hand. She stopped, turned to Tripp, to Ian, Emma and back to Tripp. "I'm sensing some emotional upheaval."

With a smirk, Tripp said, "Ian's in love and doesn't like it."

"I am not!" Ian stood and stormed to the sliding glass door, facing out where a spring thunderstorm brewed.

"Ian's in love?" Emma asked. "With who?"

"Taylor Marsh," Lexi said.

Ian spun. "Son of a bitch! What is up with you three?"

They all smiled.

"Well, that explains three things," Emma said. "The moodiness. The half-pissed off, half-smart-ass, half-rockin' attitude."

"That's two point five, Em." Lexi sat with Tripp again. "Or four, depending on how you count." She turned toward her husband. "You didn't tell him, did you?"

"And ruin all this fun?" Tripp chuckled. "Not on your life."

"Will someone please—" Ian began.

Lexi patted the seat next to her. "Come on, Ian. I'll tell you."

He flopped back into his original spot.

"When Taylor called me—" Tripp started.

Emma sat bolt upright. "You *already* looked!" She slapped her palm on her knee. "What about your 'I don't use my superpowers on people' deal?"

Lexi licked her spoon clean and waved it at her sister. "This is my story, Em, so zip it. But, yes."

Ian leaned forward, propping his elbows on his knees, as interested as Emma seemed excited.

"So, as I was saying . . ." Tripp pointed at both Emma and Ian. "Stay quiet for a minute, and we'll explain."

"Fine," Emma and Ian both said.

"When Taylor called me and told me she'd been arrested on suspicion of murder, I asked Lexi if she'd be willing to check out the stor—"

"And I said 'no way in hell'." Lexi's body trembled—Ian assumed from the question and not brain freeze from the giant mouthful of ice cream she spoke around.

"That's my girl." Emma giggled. "Stick to those principles you and no one else in the world still uphold."

Lexi rolled her eyes. "I don't use my gift on people for a reason, Em. You know that. And, we don't know that this person was murdered. All it is is a pile of bones. For all we know, that was a cemetery plot." Lexi drew in a deep breath. "But, because said person is dead and gone and thus can't ask anything of me … I decided to bend my rules a little and simply search for who they *were*. That's all. Just 'who', and if that would give Tripp an answer, he could figure out the rest."

Emma's lips curved down. "I thought your gift let you find tangible stuff, like rings and purses, paintings, and people who're alive and kickin'. Not … ones who don't exist."

"I thought that, too, Em, and, well … I didn't exactly get an answer." Lexi's shoulders fell. "Instead, I got a picture … that is, a photograph came to mind."

"A photograph? Of what?" Emma asked as Tripp grinned.

"Of *who* is the better question." Lexi scooped up a big spoonful of ice cream. "What's weirder is that the photo was very clearly hanging on the wall of this house before we bought it. You know, the ones that were up there." Lexi pointed to the fireplace across from where she sat—one that had once been decorated in a pea green, flowered, peeling wallpaper half a year before Taylor had renovated it, had had her hands in the work, had touched the walls and wood, floors and ceiling, doors and every inch of the place.

"So, this picture. *Who* was it?" Emma broke Ian's reaching thoughts.

"It was old. Faded. Black and white. And … I'd have sworn, I mean hand on the Bible kind of swearing, that it was Ian and—"

"Me?" He shot a glance toward the mantel as if the picture would magically appear.

"And Taylor," Lexi said.

Dumbstruck, Ian said nothing.

"It had to be a hundred years old by the look of the clothes and the horse-pulled buggy thing, though, so it couldn't have been either of you. But Taylor has roots here, so, like I said, that leads me to believe those bones are probably an ancestor of hers."

"So, a cemetery, then." Ian eyed Tripp. "So, you said you believed Taylor because Lex imagined some bones, which neither of you have seen, and they pointed you to a picture that doesn't exist anymore?" He knuckled his temple. "How does that make *any* sense?"

"I'm never wrong when it comes to finding this stuff." Lexi paused and took a breath, laying a hand on her stomach. "So, what this proves is that Taylor couldn't have killed that person because she wouldn't have even been born when they lived."

"We're talking a hundred years old, at least," Tripp said.

"All we have to do, then, is prove those bones are one of her ancestor's?" Emma's head cocked to the side.

"Yeah." Tripp turned toward Lexi, one of his eyebrows up higher than the other. "Want a little adventure tonight?"

She ran her hand up his chest as a yawn broke. "With you? Always."

She's tired at two p.m.? "So, you two have the bone acquisition part of our adventure taken care of."

"I want this off the books, too," Tripp said. "We'll find out what we want to find out and then figure out how to legitimize it. I want you to look into Tanner Meadows, Ian."

For the second time, Ian thought the name held a familiarity not unlike the photos on the wall that Lexi had found in her mental missing persons search. Not only for Taylor, but to satisfy his own ridiculous curiosity, Ian said, "I can do that." Research had always been his forte; he only hoped he could find out more about the tattoo on his finger.

"Could you have a certain brother do some forensic science magic?" Emma asked.

Ian blinked. "You do know Michael's going into med school, right? Not morgue work?"

"He'll have friends who need to *pay* for med school, right?" Tripp asked.

"Yeah, but—"

"Ooh!" Emma's eyes brightened. "I just remembered." Emma

pointed toward the wall. "Sherrill has the photos. I'll give her a call."

Sherrill. The woman who's grandparents had lived in Lexi and Tripp's home before them. The woman who held the key to the beginning of Lexi and Tripp's relationship—to the unwinnable game that Tripp managed to outwit.

Why does this feel like a lead I don't want to know about?

Tripp may have wanted Ian to research Tanner Meadows, but Ian needed to know why, how and what force had tattooed him with a mark that matched the woman who plagued his dreams, his life, his very soul.

At the very least, he needed to detach her since he'd spent countless sums of money trying to get the design off, with no success. He'd tried salt water to fade it. Over the counter removal creams. Even went to a professional laser center, and five thousand dollars later, the lines hadn't faded a bit. In fact, to Ian's eye, they'd darkened.

Every search Ian ran pulled up the same information on the markings. No matter the browser, the same sights appeared and reappeared, telling him exactly what he already knew.

Four chances.

He and Taylor seemed to be on the fourth.

The fourth what, though?

Some of the information pointed to success or love. Another article, written by a self-proclaimed psychic, suggested whatever had been the greatest conflict in the life—during the first time phase—would return repeatedly.

Through all of Ian's life, nothing had happened more than once.

"As they say, lightning doesn't strike twice in one spot."

Ian continued his search, having only half-believed the man he'd talked to before, but that niggle in the back of his mind made him want to know if any truth could be hidden *between* the crazy-assed psychic mumbo-jumbo and reality. Somewhere in there, he'd find the details. He just needed to reach the right person.

After two hours, he'd come up with nothing new, and a mounting frustration.

Flat against her mattress again, Taylor stared at the ceiling. She reached out, touched the concrete slab above her and let the pads of her fingertips run across the bumpy texture. As the panic set in, she bit it back, digging her teeth into her lip. Her body tensed. Her stomach curdled. With the exception of the first morning, she had managed to keep the closed-in feeling that came from four people in a room the size of a tin can at bay.

Just a touch of claustrophobia, her pediatrician, family doctor and therapist had all said. *There is no rationale to many of the mind's inner workings*, they'd added. Taylor's list of issues had grown enough that she hadn't been the girl her mother always dreamed of having. Instead, she'd fought off her problems by diving into a career that kept her busy from sunrise to sunset, seven days a week.

She flipped to her side and heaved a breath. *I can get through this. I will get through this.*

"You doin' okay up there?" Tanya's voice carried in the near silence. With the exception of Tanya, Taylor's bunk mates had been replaced again.

Murderers, whether suspected or not, seemed to get priority in one area only—not being moved.

"I'm okay. Thanks." At the edge of the bed, Taylor twisted a loose screw until she tightened it enough that her fingers wouldn't make it go further. If she didn't get something useful and productive to do soon, her head would self-combust from pure boredom.

"You know." Tanya broke the unending silence. "That lawyer of yours is hot."

Taylor chuckled. She and Tanya had built up a trust in each other, to the point Taylor knew Tanya's choice to kill her boyfriend, while wrong, seemed justified. That she'd pled guilty kept her in the local facility—though for how long she'd stay, neither Taylor nor Tanya knew. Overcrowding meant moving to other facilities, but Tanya's sentence had yet to be given.

"My lawyer's married."

"She hot like him?"

Another small laugh bubbled up in Taylor. "She's beautiful." Taylor worked to secure the screw again.

"When they gettin' you outta here?" Squeaking came from the bunk below.

Taylor's arraignment hadn't even happened yet, she had no idea. Delayed, they'd said. Three days. Three times. "I wish I knew."

7

"A million dollars? Who do they think she killed?" Ian stood with Lexi in the hole-in-the-wall barber shop that also took care of bail bonds, check cashing, and sold cigarettes at outlet prices. "I'm gonna lose twenty percent doing it this way. Why can't I just put up the money on my own?" The whine of his own voice forced Ian to take a breath and stop.

"Tripp told you it's safer to go through a bondsman than paying it direct anyway." Lexi, in her heels and professional suit, leaned a hip into the front counter. "And, it's not like you don't have it, Ian. Geez. You and Tripp have been at this partnership long enough that he wouldn't ask you if it were more than a drop in the bucket."

She had a point. Didn't mean he had to like it. The man behind the counter continued filling out a legal-sized document by hand as if he hadn't heard a word. Ian thumped the front panel with a closed fist. "Tripp ought to be ponying up his own cash. *Your* cash, I must add." Ian raised an eyebrow, hoping to throw Lexi off course. "Or don't you trust him?"

Lexi gave Ian 'the eye' back. "I'd have been fine with it. But doing so would be unethical for him since he's her attorney. Besides . . . an overnight of research, to me, suggests you have your own interest in his client." She pinched his bicep.

"I never said that. In fact—" The stink-eye glare Ian gave her in return didn't even make her flinch. *Damn woman.* Even as he thought it, he huffed a breath. "You're setting me up, aren't you?"

"Why would I do that?" A twitch seized the side of Lexi's mouth.

"Son of a bitch, you are! What else did you find in your little lookie-see of those bones and pictures?"

Lexi didn't budge.

"All of ya'll—oh, God." Ian slapped his forehead. "Michael was right. I really have been down here too long."

The clerk whistled. "You forgot occupation on this form."

Ian spun to him. "You believe this shit? I'm all happy in New York, hanging out with my bro—" He wrote 'Treasure Hunter' on the form and turned it back. "—and this one's—" Ian pointed to Lexi. "—husband calls me back with a lie that we had a gig, and it turns out . . . it's a woman in jail—" *Mental note to shut the fuck up, Ian.* "—because they want to set me up with a criminal." *And every time I bring this up, I sound like I'm trying to convince myself.*

Clerk Bob shook his head back and forth in slow motion, shaking a finger in Lexi's direction.

"Worse, he cons me into the racket and makes me post her bail. That's just not right." *You didn't shut up.*

The man held up his fist.

Ian bumped it. "See, Lexi? Dammit? It's not just me who thinks this is weird."

"Actually," the clerk started, "sounds to me like you're justifying it to yourself."

Fuck. I knew that was going to bite me in the ass. "You're a therapist now, too?"

The guy pointed to a sign on the wall. It said: *All services have a price. Advice is free. If you take it, and it fails, it's not our fault. -Management.*

Ian snorted a laugh.

"What he didn't tell you . . ." Lexi angled her head toward the clerk. ". . . was that he met this girl almost six months ago while she was renovating my house, and then sorta kinda hooked up with her at my wedding and hasn't dated since that time, yet he's not known for being alone more than, oh, say one or two nights a week."

The man turned to Ian. Went back to Lexi. "Sorry, dude. She wins. That's the kind of girl shit that trumps all the other stuff."

"I don't do love at first sight." Even as Ian said it, his heart pounded in his chest. He patted it. "Sorry, heartburn." The goofy grin on Lexi's face gave Ian pause. "Aw, hell, no." Ian wagged a finger at Lexi. "It's not happenin'. I came . . . to help . . . *a friend.*" *Who isn't even that.* "An acquaintance. Of your husband. Not mine. Acquaintance, that is. Not husband."

Lexi chuckled.

Ian would have run a hand through his hair if he had any. Or pulled it out. One of the two.

"Well," their bondsman said. "Give me that deposit, that deed on the New York apartment, and you'll be that much closer to on your way."

Ian handed both over, just as Tripp suggested he do.

"In the meantime," Lexi said, "I think I know a way you can stop this emotional roller coaster you're on." Her hand landed on Ian's shoulder.

"How?" He really did want to know.

"Oh, Ian." Lexi shook her head. "Just let nature take its course this time."

Sure. Right. Okay. How?

"Taylor Marsh!" one of the guards called out.

She slid from the bed and stood as her cell mates did the same, each taking her place in the box so the prison guards would be able to see them, in case any tried to bolt or attack or whatever they expected.

Keys jangled as the guard stuck one into the hole and turned. "Marsh. Come with me."

Taylor tensed.

Tanya clapped Taylor on the shoulder. "I hope this is it, and I never see you again. And if I don't, and you get to exact your revenge, do it Tanya style." Her eyes sparkled even as her hands stayed still—another rule as they stood with the door open. "Go out with a bang."

"Thanks, T." She held out her fist.

The guard stiffened, and a rifle aimed her way.

Tanya bumped it and gave her a nod. "Good luck, girly-girl."

Taylor tugged at her coveralls. *One foot then the other, Tay.* "Sorry, ma'am."

"Hands out," one guard said while the rifle-holding guard repositioned her weapon.

Cuffs clicked around each of Taylor's wrists.

"To the first door." The guard motioned her forward.

She found Hough waiting for her in a small, white-walled room. "Miss Marsh! So good to see you, girl!" Taylor couldn't hold back the grin. "This is your day. Yours, yours, yours." Hough wagged a finger at Taylor. "Didn't I tell you?"

"What's going on?"

"In your case, nothing." She pulled her keys from her belt and clicked them into the cuffs as Taylor's heart fell to her stomach.

She rubbed at her wrists. "Am I being moved?"

"No, shug. We're settin' you free of our fine establishment here. I'm to discharge you into your bondsman's capable hands."

Taylor's welcoming committee stood at the release desk while the first of two interior, electronically-operated doors buzzed.

Open. Wait. Close.

Open. Wait. Close.

The open space of the lobby sent relaxing waves through her body. The freeze came when she made eye contact with Ian. *Why did Tripp have to bring him?*

Ian. When they'd talked throughout the renovation of Tripp's house, his voice brought warmth to her soul. When she finally met him at the wedding, she'd thought she might have a heart attack. When he'd shown up at her home, her body had reacted. Every time—different sensations—yet they'd barely talked, let alone spent any time getting to know each other. She didn't understand her own reaction to him.

With a firm resolve, she stepped forward, touching the top of her hair as if a pat-down would help.

Taylor shuffled her way closer to the trio. "Thank you for coming." Tripp gave her a nod, Lexi a pat on the shoulder. Ian said nothing, a clear scowl etching lines in his smooth skin. "No one told me why I didn't have to go to court." She tugged at the hem of her shirt, straightened her jeans. "Am I off—"

"Out, not off," Tripp said. "You'd already been in past the maximum forty-eight hours, the judge asked for a plea, I said 'not guilty', he set a bond, and there you have it."

Taylor flitted her gaze between Tripp and Ian. "Bond?" she asked.

The two men turned to each other and back to her. "It's taken care of," Tripp said.

Oh, God, please don't have called my parents. If they had, they'd be standing here. No, not them . . . Riley. A brief smile nudged her lips. Riley always took care of her.

"So . . ." Tripp broke the silence. "You're a suspected murderer, Taylor, and, of course, the press knows. So, be prepared for a barrage when we step out."

She nodded.

"There will be no comments; no speaking at all."

She gave him one, final definitive head nod.

"Ian, Lexi and I are here to surround you and keep people from getting in your face. Nothing's been officially released to the news, so of course, they know everything. And quite a few have been parked outside your house now for days. So, we go through, get to the car and leave."

Taylor scanned the faces of the people with her. "Where are we going?"

Ian stuffed his hands in his pockets. Tripp's gaze leapt to the opposite side of the room. Lexi bit at her lip. *Oh, God, please don't make me call my mother. Stop thinking like that. Just call Riley.*

"Home is off limits until they finish their investigation." Tripp pulled keys from his pocket. "So, for now, unless you have a better place, you can stay with us."

"Thank you for the kindness." She may not have agreed with her mother often, but Taylor believed in true southern hospitality.

"All right then, let's go." Tripp aimed an arm toward the courthouse doors.

The midday sunshine brought life to Taylor's senses as the microphones and camera flashes, the questions and people in front of them prevented a quick escape. "Taylor Marsh, is it true you were convicted of murder in Alabama?" "Did you kill your former boyfriend?" The voices rushed over one another with dozens of questions she couldn't decipher, and sent a throb to Taylor's temple. "How can a two-time felon be let out even on a one million dollar bond? Do you think the justice system has done its job?"

One million dollars? Riley doesn't have that kind of money.

The questions continued as Tripp and Ian pushed Taylor through the crowd toward a simple, black sedan. A series of large vans dotted the road behind it—their antennae spearing into the sky. Construction jackhammers broke into her thoughts and over the reporters crowding around them again. Their group moved slower than her pet turtle from fifth grade as they waded through the surge of people around them.

Ian pressed against Taylor's shoulder, pushing her toward the car, a cocoon of bodies around her.

What seemed like hours took only minutes, the crowd thinning as the foursome stuffed themselves in the car, shut the doors, and Tripp pulled away from the curb, jostling Taylor into Ian's shoulder for the second time.

He spun to her, his lips a mere centimeter away. Their gazes locked.

Heat spread to her cheeks, not in the form of embarrassment, but in a desperate need to touch him. She forced her hands into her lap, twisted away and reminded herself that the brush of a shoulder did not translate to an invitation for a sexual experience despite the tingling that shot straight to her core.

God, Taylor, you're desperate for a man you barely know and who obviously wants nothing to do with you and don't even have clean underwear on.

With a deliberate nudge, she pulled herself away and leaned into the cool, leather door on the other side of the car.

Ian had touched Taylor only one other time—at Tripp and Lexi's wedding when Taylor had reached out during their conversation and brushed her hand along Ian's arm. Since then, he'd wanted her like no one else in the world. Yet, something had held him back.

The brief brush of her shoulder again brought all the feelings back—the desire, need to keep her safe, the need for no one else. All of it.

Ian pinched the bridge of his nose, letting his fingers move up to his forehead and press against his skin. His thoughts roamed to the how, the why, the what-the-fuck of the entire situation, and why on earth he had an instantaneous desire to kiss her nearly made him to do just that.

She's a damn convict, not a conquest.

Ian turned away, staring at the passing scenery. All the while, his crotch twitched, his hands itched to touch her, and his brain went on high fantasy alert as he imagined taking her lips with his and how soft her tongue would be.

The more the ideas played out, the greater his need grew.

"Pull over, Tripp," Ian said.

"Huh?" Tripp met Ian's gaze through the rearview mirror.

"Just pull over. Now."

Tripp did, into the parking lot of a walk-up burger joint. "What's wron—"

Ian jumped out to the scents of grilled beef and greasy fries, in the midst of dozens of mingling college students. Shouts rang out from the kids as someone threw a football across the small, asphalt area. Ian strode along the sidewalk, cars outpacing him on his way forward and back.

"What the fuck," he repeatedly said.

When no 'aha!' moments hit him, he turned toward the car.

Taylor perched against the back, hair blowing in the wind, wrinkled clothes on a tight frame. A small grin built, the softness of it spreading beauty to her face.

Ian wanted to run a hand along her cheek, to touch, feel and savor the electricity that had coursed through. More than that even, he burned with a desire to lay his hands along the nape of her neck, rub the pad of his finger against the scar at the base of her skull and pull her in for a kiss.

Why would I think she has a scar there?

He blew out the urge to run and sauntered his way toward Taylor until he reached her toes. "No time like the present." He only had to tilt a few degrees to stare right down into her eyes. Despite the grit and torment sleeping in a jail must have caused, her face reflected a beauty that had been burned into his retinas long ago. Taylor's scent—a combination of earthiness, flowers and pure female—drugged him into a stupor worse than his binge at Rocky's.

He followed the motion of her lashes as she closed her lids, finding the small freckle he expected to show up at the edge, and again as she opened them. The simple act, involuntary, but so—her. A dip to her lips gave him a clear picture of what he wanted to savor—had desired for months—yet feared for reasons unknown.

One hand slid to her waist. He pulled her body against his.

Now or never.

Her palms met his chest but didn't push away.

Their breaths stopped.

Lips touched.

The world ceased to exist.

Ian tilted. Taylor shifted.

His tongue darted, teasing and coaxing her to open.

She did.

A symphony of emotion intertwined around the two of them as if their life together started and stopped yet continued across the boundaries of time. He pushed the kiss deeper, reveling in a moment of ecstasy.

Clapping and whistling broke their private reverie. Ian righted himself only to find gawkers in the group of college students. Some snapped photos, others smiled and clapped as if they'd just witnessed two lovers reunited sixty years after their separation.

A hero and his soul mate.

The prince and rescued princess.

"Ian?" Taylor asked.

Tangled emotions forced themselves to the surface. "Yeah?" he asked.

She didn't tear her gaze away as he expected, but held tight, thoughts seeming to formulate in her eyes.

By no means a patient man, Ian broke their temporary muteness. "When you touched my arm at Tripp's wedding, did you . . . feel something?"

He had to know. The question had weighed on him since that moment.

Taylor's big blue eyes blinked once, though her expression remained calm and serene—except for the bags etching deep lines beneath them. After what seemed an interminable amount of time, she said, "Yes."

A simple statement—one tiny answer—grounded him. "What was it?"

"I don't know." Her hair bounced with an indiscernible head movement.

"A hot or cold sensation?"

"Wha—"

"Shock?"

A head shake. "Why—"

"Pinch?"

A chuckle came with her, "No. Why are you asking this?"

Ian blew out a breath. "Familiarity? Did it feel like a touch you'd always known? Something deep inside you'd recognize if you were married to someone for fifty years? Like knowing where someone's freckles are or what the skin feels like where there is an old scratch."

"Mayb—"

Ian shook his head. "Why do I feel this connection? It's getting stronger, too, the more I'm around you. Why, if you don't—"

"When the five o'clock shadow hits your face, and I run the back of my hand over it, there's a little notch in the lower right part of your jaw that dips more when you're a little scruffy." Taylor lifted her chin as if to challenge him to disagree.

His eyes widened. "Son of a bitch, you do feel it." He squeezed where his hands wrapped around her arms, wishing he could pound a punching bag, but at the same time wanting to bring her even closer. "I've spent the last six bass-ackward months trying to figure out why the hell I lost my—" *my entire interest in going after every pretty girl.* "Night and day, I'm hounded by nothing but social impotence. And, I can't believe I just used that word."

"It's unreal, Ian."

"That's putting it lightly." *And I'm going to find out why.*

8

Tripp and Lexi's old farmhouse wrapped Taylor in figurative comfort as she walked in. Four straight weeks of renovation—four months before—and the place gleamed as if it were a new build. Pride swelled in her heart at what she'd helped recreate.

Lexi grabbed towels from a closet, laid them on a bed and added a set of clean clothes. "We got word it'll probably be a week before they release your house." Lexi's calm tone didn't let Taylor's irritation or anger bubble. "I have other stuff you can wear if these don't work, and you're welcome to stay here as long as you want. Or at Emma's. We share and share alike. Or wherever."

"Thanks." Taylor clung to the footboard rail. "Thanks for everything, Lexi. I'm not sure what I'd have done without you guys. I promise not to overstay, though. I'll get with Riley—"

"Not without Tripp's permission, right?" Lexi gave Taylor a light squeeze. "He told me about the whole conflict of interest thing." With another pat to Taylor's arm, Lexi said, "Make yourself at home," and backed out of the room, closing the door behind her.

"Okay, mom." Even as she said it in a whisper, Taylor's lips curved. Emma had once said, during the renovation, that if anyone were on the straight and narrow path, it would be Lexi. Taylor could see that, but the package came with an innate kindness, too, and for that, she'd be grateful—for the friendship, and especially for not having to call her parents.

Taylor stripped off her three-day-old clothes and pulled on the soft underwear, T-shirt and sweat pants Lexi provided. A waft of Ian's scent passed over her. She closed her eyes, drawing it in, not wanting to let it go. It reminded her of being outside, on a farm, where horses and cattle roamed free, and she'd stand at a fence and watch as farmers plowed their fields, their oxen and horses dragging equipment up and down rows of green and dirt.

At a knock, she broke from her mental musings and slipped toward the mirror. "Who is it?" She retied her ponytail.

"It's Ian. I need to talk to you for a minute."

Taylor froze for a second. She steeled herself, and with a deep breath said, "Come in."

Never had a woman brought up so much tangled emotion in Ian, and he'd dealt with all kinds in his thirty-five years. Hand on the door knob, he gripped and turned. He had to know more. Couldn't wait for her to primp or nap or do whatever she wanted while he paced like an angry dog waiting for his next meal.

Once opened, all anger vanished.

Taylor stood by the closet, backlit by the large window, the sun highlighting her in a way that made him want to grab her and hold her tight and prevent all evil from touching her.

She motioned for him to join her. "You can come in-in if you want."

He stepped inside and closed the door with a thunk of old latch hardware.

Taylor lifted a hand, finger extended. "I'll need to update that before—" She stopped. "No, no. Never mind."

"The old stuff gives this place character," Ian finished.

"It does. Yes. That's what I was going to say." She ran her hand along the closet's woodwork. "Do you believe in fate, Ian?"

"Yes and no. Why?"

Taylor gave him a small shrug. "Just seemed like the right question to ask."

"I think fate exists, but it's what we do with it that leads us to our ultimate destiny." Ian repeated the line his grandmother had used throughout his childhood. "That kiss we shared . . ."

"Comfortable," she said.

"Familiar," Ian said, realizing she understood where he'd planned to go with his question.

Taylor nodded. "Real."

Ian quirked a finger in her direction.

She approached until she stood right in front of him. "You asked me if I felt something. And I did . . . Have. Do."

His gaze stayed fixed on hers. Her head tilted as she touched the tips of his shoes with hers. Fingers tracing up his shirt ignited miniature flames along his pectorals.

His thoughts froze as her lips slipped to his. "Don't start this train if you intend to stop it." Ian's hands found the small of her back. "Because the momentum will keep it going."

Hers draped around his shoulders.

Together they drew each other closer.

"I'm a man of my word, but—you play with power tools."

Taylor's laugh burst out, illuminating her face with happiness. "What's so special about that?"

"It's hot. That makes you hot. That makes me hot. And an on-off switch, I don't have."

Her lips caressed his as their hands played across each other, their clothes the only separation. She led; he followed. He pushed; she accepted. Back and forth they moved, a dance as old as time itself.

Taylor tugged him toward the bed.

Ian hesitated.

"What?" Her fingers ran up his chest again.

"This isn't how it's supposed to be."

Taylor gripped the front of his shirt and tugged. "Yes, it is." She crushed her lips against his.

His touch made Taylor melt into him. She closed her eyes, reveling in the sensations of his lips against her—lips she'd desired for ages without a true understanding of why—other than his own excuse. *He's hot.*

Taylor lifted her lids, blinking at the not quite Ian view in front of her.

"I love you," he said.

She flinched, blinking again until Ian came into focus. "What?"

He drew back. "What, what?"

"I asked you first."

Ian raised an eyebrow. "You asked me first what?"

She dropped her arms from his shoulders and tilted her head. "Did you say something?"

"Yes."

"What?"

"I said 'what, what?' And 'you asked me first, what?'."

She squigged up her nose. "That's it?"

His eyes tracked around the room. "I'm pretty sure, seeing as until you said 'what?' I had my lips against you."

"Sorry. Must have heard something else, then."

With his arms still around Taylor, she slid hers back up his chest. "Can I . . . can I try again?"

"Like I said, no on-off switch, no matter what you think the male anatomy looks like."

With her lips curved, she touched them to his again. The sweet aroma—one she'd identified as Ian before he'd walked in—greeted her senses. Eyes shut, they pushed their kiss, deepening it. The sounds of a rooster's caw hit her, along with the brightening of the sun through the open window, the breeze picking up and sending humid air through.

Only as Ian broke their contact did Taylor open her eyes again.

"Hang on," Ian said, pulling back, every muscle in his body telling him to stop yet not to all the same. "This isn't right. You just got out of jail. You're vulnerable. I'm taking ad—"

"Damn you to high heaven if you say you're taking advantage of me." A nudge to his hips suggested Taylor meant what she said.

"Months of waiting and wondering, ignoring and pushing off my baser instinct, and you pick *now* to come on to me?" Ian couldn't contain the grin.

"I've been wanting to do this to you since the moment I laid eyes on you." She pulled him the rest of the way to the bed. "What if this is my only day out of jail? You think I want to miss out on a second of pure ecstasy?"

Her body remained pliable under his touch, a mold that fit against him like dough. Their shapes merged, blended and adjusted as he laid her on the quilt. Ian draped himself over her. Her legs spread open to accept him, offering an intimacy he craved, yet the timing tore at him. How he'd stopped himself, why he'd stopped them—the logic fit—but in any other circumstance, he'd have pursued.

Ian halted before he just took everything he wanted.

"Now what?" Her eyes sparkled with a mischief Ian recognized.

"Nothing." *I'm going to hell for doing this now.* He brought his lips down upon hers.

Moving to her neck, he laid a line of kisses along the ridge of muscle, the tension of tendons, as another brush with familiarity coursed through him.

His hands slid to her waistband.

Hers yanked at the material tucked into his.

She arched, giving him access. "You haunt me, Ian, like no one else ever has."

"Same to ya, and I gotta know why. Just not right now." He pressed his lips to hers, stopping any further commentary. His hand snaked back up her shirt to the smooth skin of her abdomen. Hers tangled with his zipper as frantic met desire, and the two raced toward a finish.

The door handle jiggled a moment before it opened.

Ian flipped himself from Taylor, missed the edge of the bed, and fell to the floor with a crash.

Emma stood in the doorway, one eyebrow raised, as Taylor laughed on the bed.

"Why the hell don't you knock, Emma?" Ian asked.

A snide smirk graced her features. "Payback. Besides, it's not like I haven't seen it before." She wiggled her eyebrows. "Sorry, Taylor. I actually thought you were sleeping since it was so silent. Was going to wake you in case you were hungry." Emma shrugged.

Ian's gaze tracked to Taylor's. "No. No." His hands waved. "Not her. No." He paddled them between himself and Emma. "She's a thorn in my side. Sister material. Lexi's sister, not mine, but close enough."

Emma pushed out her bottom lip. "I'm crushed, Ian. After all the time we spent together—weeks, no months, just you and I … You'd think we'd have come farther. But, hey." She turned as if to leave, but spun back. "Oh, Taylor? Since you were going there … he likes to sleep in the nude. Watch out." Emma shot him a figurative bullet and disappeared.

Heat seeped into Ian's face.

"Snacks are on in five!" Her voice carried back to the room.

Taylor leaned over the side, her face a picture of mirth. "Rain check?"

Maybe he did have a switch after all.

9

Taylor munched on chips and cheese, popping a small one or two into her mouth after dipping it in the creamy sauce. Ian sat as far across from her as possible as if, for some reason, he didn't want anyone else to know about their exploit in the bedroom. She'd take the moment of privacy, but itched to be outside, to soak up the sun's rays and get her hands in the dirt.

Leaving her appetizer aside, she moved to the window, imaging herself gazing upon her own lawn. The rose bushes she'd planted would need fertilizer. The mulch needed compacting. Weeds should have been pruned.

She arced her way from the kitchen doorway back into the living room, from the couch to window and around again.

A glance to her left and Lexi walked in, her hand on her stomach. "Sorry, I think I ate too much."

Taylor dropped back onto the couch and stared out at the bright sun.

"Did you get any more details from the DA?" Emma grabbed some vegetables and dip from the coffee table.

Tripp had joined them, too, and taken a plate of finger food. "Unfortunately not. I highly doubt we'll get anywhere with them for a few more days."

"'Scuse me a sec, gotta pee. Keep going. I'll catch up." Lexi stood and disappeared through the back of the house.

"They didn't really question me much," Taylor said. "That kind of surprised me."

"You lawyered up," Ian said.

"Yeah, but I was there for three days. Wouldn't they have at least tried?"

Munching on a carrot, Tripp said, "That's another thing I'm looking into."

"You have a vibe?" Ian asked.

Tripp nodded, a celery stalk in hand. "I do. Unconfirmed, though. Give me a bit to figure it out before I try to explain."

"Okay," Lexi said at her return. "I have a confession … of sorts."

Ian shifted forward as Taylor did the same, her gaze falling on Lexi.

Lexi closed one eye as if whatever she would say might hurt. "I think you two are meant to be together."

"Say what?" Ian and Taylor burst out. Ian continued, "You said you found a picture that looked like us, but where does that come from?"

Tripp chuckled. Emma belted out a laugh.

Confusion muddled Taylor's thoughts. "Not that I mind the presumption, but why would you think that, Lexi?"

A session of glances went between Lexi, Tripp and Emma. "Let's just say," Lexi said, turning back to Taylor, "I have a gift to … uh … find things."

"Like a psychic?" Taylor asked.

Lexi's head bobbled right and left. "Close enough. See … I found a photo of two people who are the spitting image of you and Ian. And while, at first, I thought they were ancestors, I … think a little diff … er … ently now. I think you were lovers in another life, and I think you're supposed to be together now."

Ian sat up straight, narrowing his eyes. Lexi's tone, the way she spoke and Tripp's vibe made him believe they knew more than they shared.

"How would a-a picture tell you that?" Taylor wanted to see for herself. "Can I see this picture?"

Lexi, Tripp and Emma all did the head swivel activity again.

"Oh, cut it out," Ian snapped. "If you aren't going to tell her what you can do, then stop telling her stuff that isn't going to make sense unless she knows *what* you can do." He held up a hand. "And ... tell me because I still don't get how the two connect and where you've come to your conclusion."

The knock at the door kept anyone from learning more.

Lexi waved as she went through the living area toward the kitchen.

"Who is it?" Emma jumped up as the outer screen door opened. "Oh!"

"I'm Riley Dale."

Taylor raced into the kitchen as soon as he spoke.

He stood in the frame of the door, dressed in jeans and a V-neck T-shirt. "I heard you all had a guest. I was hoping I could get a word with her." He inclined his head.

Lexi leaned forward, motioning him into the kitchen with its wide, copper pots and pans and the old-style, yet brand new, appliances Taylor had installed.

She reached Riley in a few steps, wrapped her arms around him and snuggled into his warmth.

His hands fell to her lower back. "You okay?"

She nodded into his shoulder, the shuffle of feet suggesting everyone disappeared, but Taylor didn't turn around to look.

Riley held her at arm's length. "I'm sorry, Tay. I should have fought them more." He took her cheeks in his hands and kissed her forehead. "I should have stopped it and gotten more information." He leaned his forehead against her. "I should have done all those things for you. I didn't—"

"You had to do your job." She hoped her tone would convey her seriousness.

"But I love you, Tay. I'm supposed to take care of you."

Taylor shook her head against his. "You had a job, Riley."

"I'm not doing that again. You're too important to me. I'm going to take a leave of—"

"No!" Her nails dug into his shoulder. "You can't." Never in her life would she take Riley away from what he loved or his sole income, especially given he'd posted so much money for her. "You've done so much for me, Riley. I'm going to pay you back every little cent. Everythi—"

"What?" He pulled her away again. "What are you talking about?"

She cocked her head as a cell phone rang in the other room. Floorboards creaked as Ian said, "Hello". Taylor recognized the noise from the fifth and sixth steps—a squeak Tripp specifically asked her to keep—as Ian must have moved upstairs.

"Did you—did you talk to Mama or Daddy about this?"

He shook his head. "You know I wouldn't do that. You haven't called them, have you?"

Taylor lifted a hand and rubbed her thumb and finger against her eyelids as confusion reigned. "I didn't want to bother them or you more. You need your job."

"I have a little savings. A leave is temporary."

She patted his chest. "No. Please. I can handle this. Just . . . if this goes south, someone has to talk to Mama and Daddy and convince them what they read in the papers about me isn't true. You're the only one who'll be able to do that. They trust you."

He closed his eyes as if he needed to think about it. "I want to help in other ways, Tay."

"Please, Riley."

"It's unethical for me to play both sides. I gotta take leave to—"

Taylor spun away, wishing for a punching bag to go a few rounds with. She'd dealt with the strip search and the humiliation of the mental attacks, of being stuck in yet another situation that didn't make sense. To have the closest family-like member around be forced to choose pulled at her heartstrings.

"Tell me what you want, Taylor." Riley's arms hung loose at his sides.

She braced herself with her elbows on the butcher block counter and dropped her head into her hands. Footsteps on the ceramic tile floor had her zipping up.

Ian stood in the doorway. "Sorry to intrude." He walked farther in until he stood at Taylor's side. "Ian Sands." He held out his hand.

"Sergeant Riley Dale." Their palms met in a quick, up-down shake.

Why'd he emphasize his title?

"I'm guessing this is one of those ethical line things." Ian pointed between the two of them. "And, though her attorney can't say this out loud, while it's not my place, I can." Ian stuffed his phone back in his pocket. "I think you should go back to work—"

Riley clenched his fingers into fists.

"—because there might be some information waiting for the investigating officers in a few days."

Riley's eyes opened wide. "And they'll need to look into it?"

"If they haven't already figured it out themselves." Ian's voice stayed flat as if he recited details he'd been told.

"And will this have any weight to her case?" A smile played across Riley's lips.

"It might," Ian said.

Taylor stepped between the two men. "This cryptic mess has got to go. Just say it already and be done with it."

"I can't." Ian ran a hand down Taylor's arm. "Not to an active member of law enforcement."

"But he's . . ." *Riley.* Taylor fixed her gaze on him. He'd come to offer his support. She'd told him to keep his job, and yet she needed him in both ways.

"We'll take care of her," Ian said.

Riley tipped an invisible baseball cap in her direction and, without another word, let himself out.

The door slammed shut.

"Riley! Wait!" Taylor turned to race after him. The grip on her arm brought her back around to face Ian. "Let me go."

"No."

Her eyes widened for a brief moment before they narrowed into slits. "I can't just let him walk away. He's my friend. He paid my bond. He's all I ha—"

"If he's your friend, you'll let him keep his conscience clear. He knows that. Gets that. Otherwise, he wouldn't have left."

She yanked away from Ian, but he held on to her wrist. "Let. Me. Go. Ian."

"You want to hear what he's going to learn soon? Or want him to lose his job?"

"Go to hell." She stormed up the stairs, taking them two at a time. In the bedroom she'd been offered, she threw the door toward its frame, but grabbed it to prevent it from slamming.

"Ugh!" Taylor dropped to the mattress and screamed into the pillow.

"Damn women. I can't figure you out." Ian plopped himself into Tripp's favorite chair again.

"Gonna go after her?" Emma asked.

"No."

"Why not?" Lexi asked as Emma said, "But, you just promised Riley you'd take care of her." The scornful looks they both gave him should have made him cringe, but he'd learned to ignore them as often as possible. Their status as 'almost sisters' let him do so.

"I'm not going to let anything happen." He gazed straight at Emma. "You of all people should know I'm a man of my word."

Emma and Lexi huffed breaths, stood and walked up the stairs all at the same time.

"Ennnh," Tripp mimicked a buzzer. "Wrong answer." He didn't

rise to follow them, though.

"What the hell? You, who doesn't do anything the politically correct way, want to tell me—"

"I'm not the one with a relationship hanging in the balance." Tripp's head moved back and forth.

"One—or two—kisses doesn't—no, forget I said anything. I don't even know why she's mad."

"Dude, even I know that one." Tripp's voice took on his complete I-told-you-so tone.

Ian hung his head. "Do I want to know?"

"Yes, but with a beer."

Ian pushed from his seat. "I'll get them."

Two bottles and a bag of tortilla chips later, he returned to the living room. Tripp had overtaken his chair, so Ian took the couch.

"Gonna share what info you got from that phone call?" Tripp drank from the ice cold container as Ian grabbed a handful of fried corn goodness.

"I was going to before ... she went off all half-cocked when her boyfriend decided to do his job instead of your job."

Tripp gave Ian a head bob. "Okay, so what if Michael was in this pickle, and someone said I couldn't handle his case due to ethics? What would you have done?"

"This isn't about me."

"Didn't say it was. Just answer the damn question."

"I'da probably told 'em to fuck off. You're his attorney, and his friend and—"

Tripp crunched on a chip. "Exactly. So, you kinda did the opposite there. You heard her, didn't you? Everything about her says she loves him, trusts him ... you managed to push him away without a second thought."

"Wasn't that the point? To keep him on our side but on the inside?"

Tripp extended a finger toward the ceiling. "Yep."

"Then what the hell did I do wrong?" Ian pulled from his beer, closed his eyes and leaned back.

"Not a thing."

"So, that's your big revelation? I did nothing wrong, only stuff to help this woman, and now she's pissed at me?"

"Yup." Tripp took a long swig from his bottle.

"So, what was your advice going to be?"

"To drink a lot. 'Cause after May thirty-first, it's not going to get any better."

Ian set his bottle on the coffee table. "You keep mentioning that date. What's so significant about it?"

Tripp chuckled. "Not a thing. I just like to up the ante on my bets . . . as you know."

"You're gonna lose." Ian snagged a chip. "Let me ask you something." He waved the corn circle in the air.

"Anything."

"What was your first reaction to meeting Lexi?" The sigh caused Ian to meet his friend's gaze.

"Since we were outside, on the beach at two a.m., it was like a big-ass wave came up out of the ocean and sucked me right in. Damn woman."

Ian huffed a laugh. "That's what I thought. It's the most ridiculous shit I've ever dealt with."

"So, you're chicken, then?" The creases at the corner of Tripp's mouth brought a smile to Ian's.

"I'm not—"

"Boc-boc-boc-boc."

"You did not just do a stupid poultry sound."

"Boc-boc."

"I'm not playing second fiddle. There's a thing with Riley. You even said it." Ian jutted out his chin. "He loves her. I can see it." With a gulp to swash down whatever stuck in his throat, Ian said, "Never mind, screw it. Michael wants a DNA sample from Taylor. Wants it over-nighted."

"That what he called for?"

Ian shook his head, took another swig of the hops. “Nope, not just that. If she hadn’t run off like some girl, I’d have told her the good news.”

Tripp leaned forward, his beer clutched between his hands. “And that would be?”

“Michael says there is no way she had anything to do with those bones. Said it wasn’t obvious at first because they were really well preserved, but he ran some thingamajig to date them, and they’re at least a hundred years old.”

A slap to Tripp’s knee startled Ian enough to make him blink. “Hot damn!”

“He’s stumped, though, on one point.”

Tripp leaned back in his chair. “Uh-oh.”

“Yeah. He has no idea why the bones were so well preserved, but the dating is inarguable. The team he’s gathered is going to run some more stuff. Says we’ll have Taylor in the clear in a few days, week tops.”

“So, all we gotta do is keep her out of harm’s way until then.” Tripp held up his beer. “To teamwork.”

Ian clinked it. “Yeah. And to a clean five mil.”

10

Free but not free. Independent yet reined in. Enclosed but not at home.

All the stresses built up until Taylor could barely contain the judders of her body or the desire to throw a hammer through a window just so she could fix it.

Soft voices arrived outside the door and continued for what seemed like ten or more minutes. They rose. They faded. They whispered. Emphasis took hold of one, punctuated the other and ended with a 'shhh'.

Taylor's lips curved as she listened to Lexi and Emma argue over whether or not they should intrude or leave Taylor on her own—a rivalry that befit any two sisters. For a moment, she wished she weren't an only child.

"This is ridiculous. I'm going in." Lexi's firm decision came just before a tentative knock and the creak of the door as it opened. "Taylor? It's Lexi and Emma."

Taylor's giggle refused to stay inside after having listened to them argue and strategize for so long. "Come in."

Emma bumped Lexi out of the way as she took the bedside Taylor left unused. "How you doin'?"

With a slight nod, Taylor said, "About as well as a deer caught in the crosshairs."

"Doesn't sound so good." Lexi's slide onto the end of the mattress dipped it just a little.

"It sounds downright pitiful," Emma said. The glare Lexi gave

Emma could be none other than a sister would give. "What?" Emma shrugged as if she didn't know. "She's sad. That's a good analogy. I'd be more pissed than sad, if I were her, and Ian hadn't come running up here like an actual man."

"Ignore her, Taylor." Lexi offered her sister another deep glare before giving Taylor her full attention. "Ian got some information he wants to share with you. Tripp's going to make this all go away. Riley . . ." Her head inclined to the side. "Well, if he loves you enough, stepping awa—"

"That's not it." Taylor's head hit the wall as she leaned back.

"That sounded like it hurt." Emma's matter-of-fact voice broke Taylor's lips into a smile.

"Don't listen to the wiseass." Lexi patted Taylor's feet.

"Riley and I aren't a thing." Taylor opened her eyes again. "We never have been."

"It's okay if you are," Emma said and earned another glare.

Taylor drew in a breath. "We really aren't. We've been friends—brother and sister like—since we were—since before we were tweens. And this isn't about Ian, either. It just all caught up with me. Not being able to go home. Not being with my friend. Not having choices. Leaving my fate in someone else's hands." Her hands flitted up and dropped to the bed. "It just crashed on me, and I took it out on the wrong person."

"So, is Ian a hot kisser?" Emma asked.

Taylor's laugh came out full and loud.

"You did not just ask her that, Em!" Laughter bred more as chuckles came from Lexi and Emma.

"Why not? She's obviously past the brood phase of the day. We might as well get somewhere better."

Taylor's mirth continued to toy with her gut. "I can get behind that. And, yes, he is."

Emma offered Taylor a light backslap to the shoulder. "The man has moves. I've seen him in action, though I can't say any of them were used on me." Her hands crossed over her heart. "He can wine and dine with the best of the bachelors."

"Then why is he one?" Taylor angled her head in Emma's direction.

She positioned those hands over her mouth. "Probably said too much."

"Why not let every cat out of the bag then, Em?" Lexi's playful tone returned.

Emma stuck her tongue out at Lexi. "Well, I happen to know Ian's been . . . a bit celibate for the last few months. Since the wedding, actually." She ticked off her fingers. "That's been almost six months now."

Lexi leaned forward. "And, that's a record according to Tripp."

The tension in Taylor's shoulders and neck disappeared as the two around her gabbed.

Girl time. Real girl time. With smart, vivacious women. Taylor had needed that.

On and on they chatted about Tripp and Ian, as much brothers yet nothing by blood. Boys, no matter their age.

Taylor stiffened when Lexi moved a hand to her middle and a small crease grew at her temple. The simple look Taylor received, while Emma continued on, suggested she should stay quiet.

"So . . . Riley . . . Is he available, then? I mean . . . well . . . you know." Emma's eyes glittered with interest.

Lexi and Taylor both burst out laughing.

"Actually," Taylor said. "He says he's not. He's mentioned a girl a few times."

"Damn." Emma snapped her fingers. "All the good ones gettin' away."

"I haven't met her. So, I don't know that I believe him," Taylor said.

More giggles ran through the three of them.

"Maybe we should get downstairs and find out what's going on with *the boys*? And whatever that phone call was?" The mattress shifted as Lexi slid from her spot.

A dark red blotch covered the place beneath where she'd sat.

"Tripp!" Emma's yell came from upstairs with a panic that set Ian's heart to frantic.

Tripp didn't hesitate. He jumped from his seat, took the stairs two at a time, Ian following.

The beating inside Ian's chest didn't stop when he made it to the door behind Tripp.

Taylor gathered blankets into her arms as Tripp whisked Lexi into his. Emma chased them both back down the stairs.

One look to Taylor and Ian read worry and fear.

"Can you help me with this bedding?" She continued to pull, right down to the lower layer. A small patch of red graced the mattress. "I'll just get this cleaned up for her."

Ian moved to the side as Taylor marched through—her familiarity with the house letting her take charge. She stuffed the duvet into the washer first and started it. She grabbed cleaner and a rag and turned. "Oh! Didn't realize you'd followed me." She inched past him back toward the bedroom. "Sometimes, this happens in early pregnancy, Ian."

His heart hammered harder. "What?"

Taylor blinked, the bottle and gloves still in hand. "She didn't tell you."

"I thought maybe … well … something else." He knuckled his temple. "How did you know?"

"Saw her at the doc's. When you and Tripp came by the other day, he said, "Lexi said to tell you, 'yes'."

Ian inclined his head.

Taylor rolled her eyes. "I asked her at the doc's office if I should plan to build out a room as a nursery anytime soon, and she said she'd get back with me. I figured that's what his cryptic message was all about."

"Oh. But, what about—" Ian waved a hand in the direction

of the blood.

"Could be nothing." She went back into the bedroom and sprayed the circle, no larger than a salad plate, but enough to have soaked into the top layer.

Ian leaned into the doorframe. "Why are you so calm about this? About everything?"

"I'm only collected on the outside, Ian. What's inside is running at the pace of a moonshine still with the cops barreling down upon it." She scrubbed until white foam built up on the top. "But there's no sense in letting on if it will do me no good. And, if I wash this little spot now, it'll be gone when she gets back. One less thing for her to worry about and one more favor I can pay back."

"They don't work like that. Lexi and Tripp, that is. Or me."

Taylor's head bobbed as if she agreed, though she didn't say so.

"We have a team working with one of the bones from your house."

Her head snapped up. "How—"

Ian held up his hands. "Don't ask. Anyway ... my brother, Michael, tested it, and it's at least a hundred years old."

Her hands stopped moving.

"We're going to send the results to the police anonymously."

She started scrubbing again.

"He'd like a DNA sample from you so he can run some other tests. More fuel for the defense's fire is good, right?"

The head bob started again.

Ian put his hands on her biceps and squeezed. "Trust them. Trust me. Seriously, trust me."

She stopped. "But what if—"

"Hey." Ian tilted her chin up with a finger. "In my world, we only play the 'what if' game when there is opportunity. Like ... what if there's treasure buried in a cave three hundred feet beneath the ocean's surface? Can we find it?"

Taylor's lids fell. Ian inched closer. Her eyes opened again. "Do you want to go to the hospital? Shouldn't you be there for your friend? I can clean up."

Ian shook his head. "She has Emma. She has Tripp. Anything happens, they'll call me."

Taylor went back to cleaning the spot, though not a blotch of red remained.

Expecting the task kept her mind off Lexi, Ian opted to continue on about their find. "So, one of the questions Michael asked was how old you are. I told him early thirties." He cringed as her head whipped around to him.

The corners of her mouth creased. "Don't you know—"

"Don't play that shit with me. You and I both know you don't care." Though how he knew that, he had no idea.

He just knew.

A small laugh bubbled up from her. "Thirty-one, thank you very much." She dropped the rags and grabbed some light blankets.

Ian coughed into a closed fist. "So, Michael says those bones were preserved so well it had to have been in soil so compact they hadn't been touched in at least seventy, maybe eighty years."

"So, a grave fits then, right"

Ian considered the simplicity, though for some reason, he knew it wouldn't be. "Could be."

"That's what I thought at one point." Taylor tucked blankets around the bed, leaving the wet spot uncovered. "With it being so old, will they put any time into it at all? Wouldn't they just file it away into some dark corner and focus on newer, more pressing cases?"

"No idea." Ian took the other side and tugged the same way she had. "That's not my area of expertise. But I will say, with Tripp on the case, we'll have the inside scoop in no time flat."

Taylor pinched the bridge of her nose. "I really can't thank you enough. I know I shouldn't have called him for this, but it felt … right."

Ian gave her a nonchalant shrug. "S'okay. He takes whatever

cases he wants. It's how he rolls."

She stood straight. "Oh! Does this mean they'll get off my property?"

"Don't get your hopes up. We gotta convince the authorities here that the data is real first."

Her shoulders fell as if the weight of the world crashed back down on her. The open-mouthed yawn suggested sleep would be the most useful tool.

"You can rest if you want. I'll go downstairs—"

"Actually, I'd love a shower." Taylor tugged at a lock of hair. "Or a bath. A massage. Something relaxing that can't even remotely get messed up."

"You installed the claw-foot tub in Lexi's bathroom. I'm sure she wouldn't mind if you used it."

"You think?" Taylor asked.

"Positive. Then, when they get back, we'll both be … refreshed. Ready to help. Or whatever they need. Lexi makes a terrible ward. Been there. Done that. We'll want to take the time now."

"We?"

Ian went to the desk, grabbed his laptop, sidled to the bed and sat on it. He scooted up until he could lean into the headboard. "Oh, yeah. I never get off easy when Tripp's got his claws into something, and when those claws are around his wife? Damn if I get a moment free." He opened the laptop. "Unless you want me to join you in that tub."

Taylor smiled. "I'll take a rain check on that part."

Ian chuckled. "If you change your mind, come get me. I'll be here … doing nothing … but more research."

Taylor's hips swung as she walked to the door. Ian couldn't help but admire them. Head cocked, he tracked her steps to Lexi and Tripp's bathroom, and seconds later, the splash of running water. Once the sounds quieted, telling Ian that Taylor had closed the door, he gave his full attention to the screen in his lap.

Searching public records for a man who had once set up Taylor for his own murder should have been an easy task, but Ian found himself with an ever-mounting frustration level. He found all the new reports from ten years before, with Taylor Claire Marsh's name in them. The victim, one Tanner Meadows, had supposedly been bludgeoned to death.

"It only fits because she can wield a sledgehammer like a rock star," Ian said to himself from his perch on the guest bed.

He read through the articles, the case filings available online, and the information from later when one Mr. Tanner Meadows had been found drunk in a bar.

"It's a tragedy of justice that a young woman was held for so long, without due process, while the alleged victim partied his way across Alabama," the account said.

From what Ian found, Tanner had been drunk off his ass for the entire few weeks, and her set up fueled legislation for victims' rights when the victim had, in fact, been innocent.

"Of course, no one knew that then," Ian said out loud. "How are they gonna know? Gotta go with the facts in evidence." He skimmed a few more articles and found Tanner had been tried for setting Taylor up, though she'd refused to testify against him, citing emotional distress.

Tanner had been found guilty of numerous crimes and sent to prison for twenty years.

"Obviously, he deserved it."

Ian backtracked through various sources, looking for more information on Tanner's background before he hooked up with Taylor. Ian found his target to be well educated, with a Juris Doctor no different than Tripp's, yet at even a younger age.

"Dude, you're five years older than her, a lawyer, and you set her up for murder? I should have known crazy came in all packages, but you'd think someone that smart wouldn't go to such lengths. Just shoot her already and be done with it." As soon as he said it, and though no one had heard, Ian cringed. "Sorry, Taylor. Didn't mean that." His apology, too, wouldn't be heard. "Okay, enough of this. The talking to myself is getting out of hand."

Ian shot off a few emails to friends in various places—the FBI, state law enforcement in Alabama and even a few people he kept up with in the state department. As the day reached five p.m., he sent another series of emails to the prison where Tanner had been incarcerated. Having done enough work for one day, he closed the laptop with a plan to return to it soon. At the very least, Ian wanted to keep tabs on Tanner and ensure he stayed away from Taylor.

11

Water rushes from the falls, tumbling upon itself until it lands with a crash in a natural pool. What should be a soft ripple at the edge bursts with a torrent of spray as her hand breaks the surface and flails in the open air. It submerges again when he refuses to release her or to provide air to her lungs.

His hold of her body against his own tightens.

Her face and head submerge farther with each of his thrusts while her arms and legs seek purchase. She kicks out, missing him. Even when she manages to make contact, the blow barely penetrates.

A smile escapes, though until her movements subside, she will fight.

Her swing extends to his uncovered chest. Nails scrape across his skin, burning deep lines in his flesh.

He twists her hair around his wrist and pushes lower, forcing himself to move backward toward the outer edge of what should be paradise. "Not this time," he says. "You will not betray my love again."

Her feet scrape the tops of his, movements slowing with each passing moment.

Her hands surge in a final attempt to free herself from her captor.

The roar of falling water gives cover to their struggle as does the remoteness of their location.

She'd asked for the islands for their anniversary.

He'd been more than happy to oblige.

Water bubbles around them, each thrash sending cascading lines away from the two of them.

The pace of his heart quickens as the finale to their tumultuous relationship nears.

Her hand dips beneath the surface.

He lessens his grip.

Her body ceases to struggle.

"At last," he says. A step toward the banks drags her with him. He lets go and turns toward the ropes and rocks he'd left gathered there.

His arms weigh heavy with the tools as he brings himself back to her immobile form, face down in the crystal blue, Caribbean water.

He drapes rope over her, pulling it from underneath and wrapping it around a second time. "Just to be sure, darling." His tone is calm and smooth, a perfect accompaniment to the island feel.

A tug secures her within the bonds.

He lifts the wrapped blanket of boulders and attaches them to her restraints.

Her body sinks.

He drags her body toward the center, where the water is near to his shoulders, and adds the final weight. With one solid shove—toward the falls—she disappears.

"Goodbye, my love. May we meet again."

Paradise becomes hell.

Ian blinked open tired eyes. For a moment, confusion plagued him until he realized he'd fallen asleep on the guest bed in Tripp and Lexi's house. His laptop still sat on his lap, cold from having shut off itself.

Two hours had passed.

She hadn't come back.

Leaving his research and the details about Tanner, Ian rose.

The house greeted him with perfect silence. "Taylor?" Ian's footsteps echoed through the empty hallway. "Girl, how long a bath did you take?" He continued toward the stairs, finding nothing. "Hello? Anyone?" No one responded.

Ian peeked into the third bedroom.

Not a soul.

"Maybe I'll take my own bath."

He slipped into Lexi and Tripp's room, noting their bathroom door remained shut. "Taylor?" He rapped his knuckles on the door. "You decent or want some company?" Ian grinned at himself.

With no answer, he figured she'd gone out, but opened the door just to check.

"Taylor!" Ian raced to the tub where Taylor bobbed and pulled her from under the water.

Blue lips and the paleness of death reflected in her face.

He scrambled, sliding her out all the way, falling back to the floor, Taylor's body spilling as fluidly as the liquid itself to the tiled surface.

Ian leaned his ear close to her mouth.

Not a bit of air passed from her to him.

He tilted her head back. His lips met hers, and he offered one deep breath of his own.

With his hands over her chest, he pressed to the beat of 'Stayin' Alive' and moved back to her mouth.

Another breath.

More chest compressions added the crack of ribs under his hands. He wanted to stop, to not hurt her, but knew he had to keep going.

Another breath.

Another crack.

Her body arched, seizing into itself until she flipped to the side and spewed clear liquid.

"Holy shit!" Ian grabbed the towel from the rack and wrapped it around her. One lift up and she fell into his arms. He stormed his way out of the bathroom, through the hall and down the stairs. "You better not die. Not on my watch."

Her head lolled to the side, but the blue tint had been replaced with a light grey.

With her still in his arms, he grabbed cell and keys off the kitchen table and raced outside to the driveway, beeping the car doors unlocked.

Maneuvering her into the front passenger seat of Tripp's Jaguar took two attempts. With each of his own breaths, he checked her face, her color, the movement of her chest. More and more life seeped back into her, but she hadn't yet regained consciousness.

Ian pulled out of Lexi and Tripp's yard, whipping rock and dirt into the air. The car fishtailed as he spun it onto the street and pressed the emergency button. "This is Ian Sands." He didn't even let the operator answer when his call went through. "I have an unconscious woman with me, and we're heading to the ER." He took a deep breath. "She was in—she stopped breathing, and I revived her with CPR." His eyes darted to Taylor as he sped down the road.

"Okay, sir—"

"We'll be at the ER entrance in ten minutes."

"All right. Can you tell me—"

Ian ignored the operator as Taylor groaned, and her head flopped forward. Another gush of liquid burst from her lips. Her hands grasped the door frame. She heaved in air again and blinked. With her body straight upright, her head held high as if nothing had happened, she turned toward Ian and blinked again. Back to the road in front of her, her lids fell, and she slumped against the seat.

"Dammit, woman." Ian pressed hard on the gas, barreling through the roads at double limit. He arrived at the hospital early as blue and red lights spun at the entrance.

Riley stood at the doors along with a nurse and doctor, a gurney and a few gawkers.

Ian jerked the car to a stop at Riley's toes.

The passenger door flew open. Taylor fell into Riley's arms. "What the hell did you do?" Riley asked.

Ian tore out of his side and around as Riley lifted her onto the gurney. The lab-coated people took over, though one approached Ian and took him by the arm, asking a dozen questions a minute to which Ian had only one answer: *I have no idea.*

The doctor pinched the bridge of his nose as he entered the hospital waiting room where Ian sat.

Ian's heart lurched. "Is she going to be okay? Taylor Marsh, that is."

The doctor waved a folder in Ian's direction. "Are you Mr. Sands?"

Ian nodded.

"Great. I was told by the detective to contact you if I couldn't find him. Do you know where Sergeant Dale is? Or any of her other family?"

"Uh . . . yeah." Ian pulled out his cell to text Riley, who'd gone for coffee. "Can you tell me anything about her?"

"And, you are related how?" The doctor tilted his head and half-closed one eye.

"Just a friend."

"Then, unfortunately not. No. I'm sorry. But . . . can you tell me if she's had any incidences like this before? Any reason she might have tried to kill herself?"

She did not try to kill herself. No way. Ian refused to believe it, even as the possibility rang true. "That's something maybe you should talk with Sergeant Dale about." He also didn't know how much to say or not without Tripp's input.

"Was she taking any medication, any—"

"I really don't know." *But, God, I wish I did.*

Riley arrived as the doctor started his next question, and the two walked out into the hallway. Ian dropped into his chair again, his body trembling with a fear he didn't understand for a woman he barely knew.

Had she tried to kill herself? To drown herself? He didn't remember seeing any alcohol or drugs in the room. *How can someone drown themselves in a tub? Wouldn't their body fight it?* Questions ran rampant as Riley re-entered. Ian didn't rise but kept his seat. Riley hitched his gun belt. Ian crossed his arms.

A silent standoff had begun.

"So, once again ... what the hell did you do?" Riley finally asked.

Ian held up his hands. "Don't look at me, man. I was asleep."

The firm set of Riley's lips suggested he didn't believe Ian. "Why didn't you stop her?" Riley's fists clenched. "You were supposed to take care of her."

"Are you kidding?" Ian stood, meeting Riley's gaze straight on. "I drove like a bat out of fucking hell to get her here. I couldn't stop her because I had no reason to believe she'd do anything." Ian punctuated each statement with a finger in the air. "Did *you* expect this? If you did, don't you think you should have said something?"

Riley dropped his chin down. "I didn't. Never. No. She wouldn't. I just—" He ran a hand through his hair.

The paging system called for a Doctor Tackert to Wing D, stat. The urgency made Ian bristle.

"Why are you here, Ian?"

"Because a friend is in need."

"Not because you just put up her bond and want to make sure you get it back?"

Ian balled his fists similar to Riley.

"I know you did it. Don't know why, but she deserves better." Riley gave an upward lift of his chin.

"You son of a—"

"Hear me out." Riley pushed closer to Ian. "Taylor and I have a long history, and she's had it rough a few times. But I *know* she wouldn't do this. So, that means something else happened. And, you were the only one there. If you do so much as break a hair on her head—"

"You'll kill me? What? Are we in middle school?" Ian's snide retort didn't stay under wraps as he'd hoped.

"Yes. And I'm the one with a gun."

"I don't play games with women." *Often. Anymore.* Another call through the speakers for yet another doctor tensed Ian's muscles.

Riley cocked his head toward the sound but turned back to Ian. "It's not a game. She's like a sister to me."

Ian stuffed a hand in his pocket. If ever he stood on one side of a war, with a princess as a prize, Riley stood at the opposite, waiting and at the ready for the attack. Rather than keep up the pretense, Ian held out a hand.

Riley's eyes narrowed.

"Truce. But only for her," Ian said. "For now."

Riley took Ian's hand and shook. "Listen ... if you get asked about parents or others to call, you don't say anything about anyone but me.

"Why?" He thought he'd heard Lexi or Emma mention that her parents lived nearby.

"I told you, she's had it rough. So, let's just leave it at that for now, all right?"

"Fine."

"And I'll ... give them authorization to talk to you."

Ian's brows winged up. "Why? How can you do that?"

"I just can. And, I can't be around the whole time, remember? My job. Our deal from earlier?"

With Ian's nod, Riley offered the same. "Why don't you go get something for yourself—you know, coffee or whatever. Could be a long night."

"Actually ... I have another friend here tonight, and I want to go check on her."

"Go on then. I'll stay here."

"Thanks." Ian stepped through the door and followed the signs for Obstetrics and Gynecology, figuring he might as well offer Tripp support if nothing else.

He traced a path through the hospital, around and down a floor until he found the reception area where he thought Lexi might have been taken. He waited as another series of beeps and calls finished before he moved toward the counter. "I'm looking for Lexi—"

Tripp emerged from a room, his gaze straight on Ian as he left.

"Never mind."

With a quick chin jut, much like Riley had given him, Tripp pushed through to a wide lobby with floor to ceiling windows. Ian hadn't paid a bit of attention to his surroundings on his way in.

"Emma call you?" Tripp asked.

"No. Taylor had an incident."

Tripp's brows furrowed. "She okay?"

"Not really. Still in the ER. She … well … she drowned. In your bathtub." Ian scrubbed at his jaw. "Still trying to figure out how that's possible."

Tripp's eyes went wide. "She try to kill herself?"

"Dude, I just have no idea."

"What do you think?" Tripp asked.

Ian huffed air. "I don't believe that she did, no. Seriously. I don't. But I don't know her. I'm way, *way* out of my comfort zone here and have no idea what to do about it."

"Makes for a great start to a relationship, huh?" Tripp's attempt at humor brought out a small smile.

Rather than keep thinking about Taylor, Ian asked. "What's going on with Lexi?"

Tripp slunk down into one of the vinyl covered chairs. He ran a hand through his hair.

Ian took the spot next to him, his body braced for bad news. "Seriously, man, she okay?"

The slow bounce of Tripp's head should have been encouraging. The face that returned to him came with the glow of parenthood in the making.

"You're looking more like the Cheshire cat every day. Why the hell didn't you tell me she was pregnant?"

"She made me vow to wait until she hit twelve weeks. Something about bad omens or old wives' tales or some such shit." A deep breath left him. "She's only just eight weeks right now."

"And?" Ian's body tensed. Tripp's tone suggested worry. His grin beneath the stress told another story.

"Just one big blob of black on that ultrasound."

The tension in Ian's shoulders dissipated. "Big black blobs are ... good?"

Tripp bobbled his head.

"So, what happened tonight, then? How can—" Ian waved his hands through the air. "—all that stuff happen if she's still pregnant?"

"They aren't sure." He leaned up and back against the wall. "By the time we got here, she'd stopped bleeding. But, they wanted to check it all out, so they did an ultrasound, and there it was." A dad's grin took hold of his features. "I can't read shit on those machines, but they said it was there—a little bigger than they thought it should be, but still there." He hiccuped a laugh. "I'm gonna be a dad."

Ian nudged him with his elbow. "You're gonna be an awesome one, too. You think you'll get a Lexi or an Emma? Or another Tripp?"

"God, I don't know. What if something happens to it, her, him ... to Lexi?" Tripp's tone turned serious. "I mean, what if tonight wasn't a fluke, but is a problem or—"

"You gotta stop thinking like that. Lexi's gonna need you, right? So, no sense filling a shit-full of what-if baskets when she'll be just fine." *Which is exactly what I need to be thinking. Way easier said than done, though.*

That earned Ian a winged eyebrow. "You know nothing."

"I know, but I can make up crap pretty good." He offered his most fake and cheesy smile.

Emma appeared with a white, plastic cup in hand. "She wants

to go home. I think you ought to go in there and tell her she's not going anywhere until her ass is signed off by those people with the big M.D. after their name."

Tripp rose, his feet squeaking on the tile as he did. "Stay close to her, Ian."

"It's what I do best."

Emma leaned back in the chair Tripp had vacated. "What's going on? Where's Taylor?"

Ian went through the story yet again.

"Wow. Well . . . she is an emotional wreck. But, I can't see her trying to kill herself. Find out, Ian." She patted his arm. "It's what you do best, you know. Figure it out."

It's what I normally do best. The doubts crept in—with his failure to find details on key elements of his own physique.

A crackle overhead took some of Ian's attention. "Ian Sands, please report to Emergency. Ian Sands, please report to Emergency."

He bolted down the hall.

For the second time, Ian managed to cross throughout the entire hospital without paying attention to the building or its contents. He entered the Emergency department through its double doors and headed straight for the desk.

"I'm Ian Sands." The stairs and race through the hallways had taken his breath from him—that and the immediate stress of being called upon for who knew what reason.

The nurses nodded toward the far door. Ian spun. Riley sauntered toward him.

"What's going on?"

"My superiors are calling me back to the office."

"Go," Ian said.

Riley nodded. "Don't leave her alone again."

Ian sucked in air, placing his hands on his hips. "I won't."

"Scouts honor?"

"Dude, do I look like a boy scout?" At Riley's smirk, Ian said,

"I won't."

With a nod, Riley disappeared into the night, and Ian took his place back in a waiting room chair.

12

Taylor's body trembled as she forced her eyes open, and put effort into the action when they tried to droop down upon her again. A blurry Ian stood in front of her with some woman she didn't recognize in a white lab coat.

"Need—" A dry throat cracked her words. "—a drink." Running water sprayed to the right within a second of her request.

Ian held out a paper cup. "Here."

Taylor shifted to sit more upright. "Thank … you." Taylor sipped at it, letting it coat the lining of her throat. "What's … what's wrong? Why am I … here?" Each drink gave new life to her voice.

Ian's grip on the rail lightened his knuckles.

"Perhaps we should have this conversation in private?" the doctor asked.

"No." Taylor met Ian's gaze and returned to the doctor.

She held up a pad, pen poised between her fingers. "What do you remember?"

A shiver tore through Taylor. *Being held under water. Being drowned by a face I've seen before. They'll think I'm crazy if I say that.* "I remember going to take a bath. To relax. And then … waking up."

"You were found unconscious in the bath," the doc said. "We found nothing in your tox screen. Did you eat a food you're allergic to?"

Did I? Cheese and crackers. That had been a staple in her house as a kid. "No. I don't think so. Nothing unusual. Is something wrong with me? What time is it?"

"Almost eleven," Ian said.

The doc's lips pursed.

"I want to go home." Taylor reached for the IV in her arm.

The doctor put a hand on her wrist. "I can't let you go just yet."

"Why?"

The doc gazed up at Ian.

"You . . . drowned, Taylor," he said.

"I'm fine." She shivered. "I'll go A.M.A. if I have to."

The doc stopped her again. "Ms. Marsh, we'd like to run more tests, to—"

"No." As her energy returned, so, too, did the memory, the scene, the sensation of being held under water. "I just—I just want to leave." Hospital. Jail. Either or. They both had the same effect.

"Come, on Taylor," Ian started, "I'll call Riley back and he—"

"Riley knows about this?" Anger mixed with embarrassment, heating her cheeks. That Ian still stood in the room only made it worse. "I need to go."

"Ms. Marsh," the doc said.

Ian held up a hand. "Can you give us a second?"

On a low sigh, the doctor nodded and walked out.

"You almost died, Taylor." His comment came out serious and without a hint of humor.

"I know."

"What do you mean, you know?"

Taylor cringed. *How do I tell you that I remember every detail, and I know it wasn't a dream?* "I almost drowned once. Before." *No time like the present.*

He popped back up. "What?"

She wrung her hands. "When I was a kid. I hate most bodies of water—pools, lakes, oceans—because of what almost happened. We were playing Marco Polo—you know, the kids game—when it happened. It was me, Riley, a few friends of his, and a couple kids from school who'd come to join. I don't even remember all the people there. But I can tell you the smell of chlorine is etched into my mind. I can see the surface of the water over my head and the bubbles as they sucked away my air." She heaved a breath as if it would be her last.

"You don't have to tell me this."

"I was hiding under water, coming up for air just long enough to get away. The crystal clear blue kept me from whoever was 'it'. I don't even remember that part anymore. Just the darkness that came over me. I thought it was an air mattress, so I tried to get out from under it." She closed her eyes at the memory. "But then, the whole pool went dark. I couldn't see anyone. I couldn't hear. My head started spinning. I couldn't find the surface. All I could see … oh, God, this is going to sound crazy." She heaved a breath. "I saw a face. And … I saw it again. This time. I remember what happened, Ian. Between getting in the tub and waking up. I didn't want to say anything and make the doc think I'd gone nuts, but … I have to tell you this." She wrung her hands in front of her. "I—I know the face who watched me as a kid, and the one that held me under in the tub."

Ian's gaze stayed on her. After a deep breath, he asked, "Who was it?"

"It was you, Ian. You."

Taylor kept her back to the door as she redressed. The docs had given her discharge papers, but they kept coming back into the room with information and advice, thoughts and ideas as well as what she should look out for in the future. Added to that, they told her, in no uncertain terms, to take at least a week off work due to the fractured ribs from Ian's CPR efforts.

She and Ian hadn't talked any more about her revelation, and Taylor figured that meant either he didn't believe her, thought she'd gone crazy, or he needed to process it. Maybe he just didn't care. She knew it hadn't really happened, just somehow his face had been superimposed in the water, but it had been *his* face. How he'd been there when she'd been a child, she'd never know, but figured faces blurred by the ripples of water could have been anyone.

The swish of the door accompanied a rap and a "knock-knock" in Ian's voice. With Riley back on not-friend-cop-only duty, Ian had offered to be her transportation.

"Come in." She turned as he filled the doorway. "They aren't going to give me any grief, right?" A yawn opened her mouth wide.

"Tired?"

"Yeah. Sore, too." She placed a hand on her rib. "Ian, look—"

He touched a finger to her lips. "It wasn't real. I know what you're going to say, and it wasn't."

"I know, but it felt real. And I remember it. Like, every detail. And while I think it was your face, I know it wasn't."

"See? You've already gone from think to know."

"You don't even seem freaked by this."

"I'm processing."

Taylor couldn't help the smile. "Processing? Is that your word for freaked but not showing it?"

Ian chuckled. "Sure. We'll go with that."

She rolled her shoulders, pulling at the muscles in her chest wall and cringing at the stab of pain on her left side.

Ian waggled a finger in her direction. "I'd suggest a nice, relaxing bath to ease the soreness, but that didn't go so well last time." His grin brought out her own. At least he hadn't lost his sense of humor.

"What time is it again?" she asked.

Ian turned his watch face around. "Ah . . . almost two."

"Still plenty of time to tuck in for a good night's sleep."

"Is that what they say down here?"

Taylor's laugh snuck up on her. "You really are New York, aren't you?"

"Born and bred." He held out a hand. "And two in the morning is prime partying time."

She grabbed her papers. The little touch to his fingers sent heat through her body. "Hey, Ian?" He stopped and turned toward her. "Would you mind driving by my house?"

His gaze stayed on her. "I don't think that's a good idea."

She cocked her head and jutted out a hip. "Would you stay away if it was your place?"

The only description that could fit Taylor's lawn would have been 'war zone'. A single light burned under the pitch black night sky.

"I'm pretty sure they're done gathering, and now it's just a matter of verifying there isn't anything else." Ian cut the engine to the Jag.

Taylor pushed out through the door.

"Hey!" Ian's voice didn't stop her. "You said drive by!"

She traipsed the rest of the way up the drive and marched toward her home.

Tire marks ran along the grass, up to and through her yard. Yellow caution tape, visible under the moonlit sky, caused her heart to flip-flop.

Her rose bushes fell to both sides as if a pole had fallen right through the middle. A foreboding emptiness claimed the entire space.

At the touch of her arm, she whirled. Her hand whipped up. Ian caught it as if she'd simply lobbed a softball and he'd seen it coming.

"Let go of me." The steel tone along with the near punch should have given him a clue as to the seriousness of her request.

"No."

"Dammit, Ian." She jerked, but couldn't free herself. The weakness in her limbs didn't help.

"Why are you here, Taylor?"

"Because I need to take care of my house. I needed to see what was going on. This is mine, Ian. Mine. Nobody has a right—you think they can come in here and destroy—"

He shook his head. "But, right now isn't the time for that." His hold relaxed.

She yanked free and trudged off toward the caution tape corral. The pile that had once been her shed laid out in pieces like a puzzle ready to be put together. The area where she'd found the bones held nothing but dirt and a large hole.

Even with the footsteps behind her, she stared ahead, wishing she could see beyond what the moon illuminated for her. "This is my land, Ian. My home. And under the misguided belief that I killed someone, they jumped to conclusions. Dammit! Everyone around me jumps to conclusions. Here. In Alabama." She stood with hands on her hips. "Why do people do this to me? What is it about me that people want to mess with? What did I do?" Her breath caught, but she refused to let tears form, to succumb to her own plight.

Ian stepped closer, his scent filling her with comfort. "Bad timing, maybe?"

"Well, then. That answers that." Her hands flew into the air and dropped against her thighs.

A hoot called through the silent air. Across the road, lights blinked off, signaling the end of her neighbor's day. Around them both, the earth moved into the night's sleep.

Taylor knelt in the dirt. "I had peace, Ian." She cupped the clay mixture and let it slip through her fingers. "It's mine. It's supposed to be mine."

The hold on both her upper arms caused her body to freeze.

"Please let go." A torturous battle of wills began—her body's versus that of her mind. "I'm sorry. Can you take me back to

Tripp and Lexi's?"

"Sure, but are you okay—I mean physically? Do we need to go to the ER again? You tensed under that touch. I felt it in my entire hand."

Taylor tilted her head low. "I have an issue with my arms being brought behind my back or having anything hold me that way."

"But I didn't—"

"I know." Nerves that had momentarily frozen tickled and teased back into existence. "It's just a thing. I have … a few quirks."

"We all have those."

"So, you see my face trying to drown you, too?" She dropped her head into her hands. "I'm sorry. That was wrong."

Ian stood in front of her and took her cheeks between his palms. "Do you, for a minute, believe I had anything to do with that?"

On a low whisper, she said, "No. I never did. It was just … so real."

A scream froze them for a moment. They spun and separated.

"What the hell was that?" Ian turned toward Taylor and she to him.

The cry came again—a blood curdling sound muffled as if by a pillow.

She ran toward the empty hole but twisted back toward him before he could take a step. "You heard that, didn't you?"

13

For a moment, Ian didn't answer. "I heard something, but by the way you trembled, I'm not sure we heard the same thing." Given the night's events, the fact she'd drowned, come back to life and checked herself out of the hospital, Ian wouldn't discount any rational or irrational explanation. For anything.

Taylor stopped. Each tiny shift toward him came with a low growl. "Why do men do that?"

"Do what?"

"Just answer the damn question when I ask."

"I did."

"Okay then, what … exactly … did you hear?" Irritation coated her tone.

He rubbed at the side of his ear. "Uh … like on the order of a howl? Could it have been a coyote?"

"No. This was …" She ran a hand into her hair and tightened her fists around the tendrils. "It was a scream. A woman's scream. I heard it. Clear as a bell."

"Probably just animals." No way could he say the sound he'd heard had been anything but wildlife given he and Taylor stood alone on her property. Ian opened his eyes wide, searching beyond the edge of her land, to her house, to the only other barn on the property, hoping he would find the animal in question.

He found nothing.

Taylor stood at the yellow tape. "Here."

"Here what? You mean the sound? No, not there. Out there."

Ian pointed toward the line of trees.

A bend and duck put Taylor on the other side of the barrier.

"Wait!" The thought of her imprint on the earth—the scene of the crime—made him cringe. Tripp would roast his balls over coal for letting her touch it. Her shape flitted to the outer edge, and a cold chill caused goosebumps to pop up on Ian's arms. "What're you doing?" His voice carried off with the wind as the only light from above disappeared.

"Looking."

Air swirled around him as darkness took a deeper hold. "For?"

"Her."

"Her who, Taylor? There's no one here." *Except animals. Ones that bite. And hurt.*

"The voice."

Ian itched to jump the yellow line and grab Taylor. "That was a coyote." *Right?*

"Maybe to your ears, but not to mine. It was a woman."

"Please, come back." The hair raised higher on Ian's arms. "To me. To this side of the yellow line. Out of the dirt. Even I'm not stupid enough to put my footprint on it."

"I won't mess this up."

"Dammit, woman, you're standing in the middle of it!" Ian's voice pitched deep and serious. "Come back here." He stepped toward the barrier, but before his foot hit the dirt, he stopped. *I am not putting myself on the line for her. No, don't do it. Not for a crazy woman who thinks I somehow drowned her. Twice.*

"Ian?" Her voice trembled like a bass violin.

His body tensed, feet failing to take him any closer, his gut saying he should remain as far away as possible.

"Ian!" A hitch took her breath.

Another cry echoed through the dark. Taylor still stood in the middle of the spot, her body upright but unmoving.

"Come here already." His own voice shook as the thought of being mauled by wild animals failed to appeal to him. Ian and camping would never cross paths.

"I—I—can't."

Dammit. What is wrong with her?

"Help me, Ian."

"Oh, for the love of all that's human." Ian chucked off his shoes, flung them to the side. He rolled up his pant legs and ducked under the yellow tape.

Three steps took him to the center. A thunderclap shook the earth, and the sky broke. One grab pulled her from her frozen spot and into his arms as he trudged back across the line and into the wet grass.

"Shh." Ian soothed when she didn't let go and trembled against him. "We need to go back to the car." Her head shake and the jerk of her chest against his warred with his desire to get out of the rain. "We're getting soaked," he said.

She stayed quiet, her cheek nestled against him.

Water poured from their heads, drenching them both. Droplets bounced from the dirt up onto his legs. The rush of falling water continued, drowning out anything else.

Ian tipped Taylor's chin up. She blinked as rain soaked her face, dripping down her chin. With a tentative movement, he touched his lips to hers.

Each pulled back but not out of the embrace.

Taylor returned her lips to his, an intoxicating mix of lust, desire and the sweetness of honey. His hands moved upward to take her face between his palms. Their tongues danced against each other. The softness bore down on his heart and caught in his throat.

He'd never hurt her. Ever. Not on purpose.

Taylor poured herself into the kiss, the warmth, the radiance, the beauty of it. While the water dribbled all over her, she ran her hands up Ian's chest and around his neck.

Opening her eyes, she found the face of the man she loved.

"We shouldn't be here," he said.

"I know, but I missed you." She ran her hands down and to the belt around his waist, one fashioned of braided wheat stalks from the farm where he worked.

"Your mama ever finds out about this, she'll skin me," he said.

She smiled up at him, the rain drenching every inch of them, even underneath the oak's broad arms. "Mama need never know."

His lips took hers again as she pulled him toward the tree's trunk, leaned against it and tugged until his body fit hers. He'd always been so welcoming, yet shy.

"You're the man I love. Why must there be these here rules?" Fingertips to face, cheeks, forehead, eyelids and nose. She loved to touch him, to run her hands over his skin, against the hard planes of a working man's muscles, and lower when time allowed.

"Them townsfolk say you've taken up with the belt man."

She pulled back, shock and dismay coursing through her. "And you believe them?"

He shook his head. "Never." His hands gripped her waist, tugging her closer, tighter against the growth in his breeches.

Above them the tree's branches rustled, water falling through and upon them.

"Someday, someday we won't need to hide," she said. "Nor make love only in the dark or in the rain."

His lips curved. "I'd like that, milady. One day, I would like to make love to you under the auspices of the night sky without the fear of death."

"I will make it so, John. I will make it so."

On a rush of air, Ian pulled away from Taylor. He stared at her, the sad eyes, the tormented soul, the weariness. The rain slowed, trickling to just a mist as the only streetlight blinked on. Drips hit him between the eyes and snaked down his nose, but the tremble didn't come from the cold or the tickle.

It arose from the memory. The vision. The thoughts that had passed through his mind while they kissed.

Not real. Just weirdness from being outside.

"Ian?" Taylor asked.

"Yeah?" His voice escaped breathy and unsure.

"Did you … I mean …" She exhaled against him. "Never mind." Taylor leaned up, laid a touch to the side of his lips. At her shiver, he wrapped his arms around her, drawing her tighter against him, and rubbed up and down her back. "I think I'm going crazy. I have to be."

He feared his question, but it had to be asked. "Why?"

Taylor angled up to him. "Because … because I'd have sworn I had an out of body experience just now."

"Like … aliens from space came and snatched you?"

She giggled but bobbled her head side to side against him. Into his shirt, she said, "I called you John."

"You did, yeah."

Taylor jumped back, out of Ian's arms. "You heard that?"

As loud and clear as the coyote that doesn't exist, yup. "Do you want me to have heard it?"

Her lips quirked up. "Can I … can I try something?"

"Sure."

Taylor moved toward him again, slid her hands up his chest and around his neck. She tugged him toward her and merged her lips with his.

Ian accepted the kiss without hesitation, tilting his head left as she went right and reversing their positions a moment or two later.

Taylor slowed their progress, pulling back and meeting his gaze. "Nothing happened," she said.

"What did you expect?"

Her head shook. "I don't know. Something. Something … weird. But you felt it, right?"

"I'm not sure *what* I felt, but you did call me John, and if you want to kiss me in the rain again, I'm happy to oblige." *Always. Forever.*

"We better go." Taylor slipped her hand to Ians, and together they walked back to the car.

Standing at the driver's side door, Ian gazed out at the yard, and in his mind's eye, a large oak loomed in just the spot where Taylor had stood.

When he blinked, it disappeared.

14

Ian woke calm, nude and alone. He'd slept the sleep of the dead, waking at no time during the night. Rested and with as clear a head as he could believe possible, he slipped to the side of the guest bed, grabbed the robe Lexi always left draped over the chair and tied it on tight enough so Emma couldn't yank it off and attempt to embarrass him.

Muffled sounds of chatter reached him from below. A check of the clock showed it to be close to nine, yet no one had bothered to wake him. The stair creaked beneath his foot, and the sounds in the kitchen stopped, but the scent of sweetness spiraled toward him.

Bypassing the empty living room, Ian ended up in the kitchen, where Lexi and Tripp sat on one side of the table with Emma across from them.

"Where's Taylor?"

"Who?" Emma sipped from a mug.

"Want some breakfast, Ian?" Lexi pushed to stand, but Tripp pressed her back down and rose.

"Uh . . . Taylor?"

"Again, who?" Emma tipped the cup up.

Ian pulled out a chair and plopped into it. "What the hell are you up to, Emma? Taylor. I brought her here last night."

"Maybe you were dreaming?" Not a hint of smile broke through.

"Huh?" *Dammit, is that what's happening to me? Am I dreaming these out of body experiences?*

"Dude, do you see Taylor here?" Emma asked.

Ian twisted left and right. "No." *What the hell is going on with me?*

"Exactly."

He dropped his head into his hands. Had it all really been a dream?

Lexi chuckled.

Tripp's slap to the back of the head had Ian popping upright. "Emma's been ready to play that little charade since Taylor woke and told her about your midnight kiss in the rain. She's in the shower, by the way."

Ian raised an eyebrow. "You're one conniving little—"

"Sister." Lexi's interjection couldn't stop his thoughts or the smile.

"Payback's a bitch, Emma. Be prepared." He inclined his head toward her. "How are you, Lex?" Ian twirled a finger in her direction. "I mean . . . you know."

"Well, the docs claimed there was nothing they could do so early in the game, and everything on the inside looked good, and I haven't had any problems since, so . . . I think we're good." The bags under her eyes said her worries hadn't disappeared. She leaned into Tripp's body when his arm draped across the back of her shoulders.

Ian grabbed a banana from the bowl in the center. "What did Taylor say this morning?"

"She said you snore." Emma grabbed a lemon poppy seed muffin from the tray.

"I do not."

"Yes, you do." Taylor's voice came from behind. "Sorry I didn't wake you, but you were sound asleep. I figured you could use it." The kneading of his shoulder muscles sent relaxing warmth through him. "And thank you, as well, for staying with me."

She'd asked him to sleep with her, and sleep they did.

"Welcome." He lifted his mug and put it down, tilting his head in her direction but staring at Emma. "*You* are still on my shit list." He aimed a finger-pointed gun her direction.

"Ah, best watch what you say to me. I'm the one that has your plane booked to take you up to DC today to talk with Sherrill."

"Why?" Ian said as Taylor said, "Who?"

Emma tapped her chest. "Sherrill is the woman who has the photo Lexi told you about. She's going to give you a private viewing. Got a whole box of them, in fact. You get to go through them one by one and see if you can find the actual one Lexi described. Maybe we can match it up with an ancestor."

"Don't I have to stay here?" Taylor asked. "What with the bond and all that?"

"Probably." Tripp's smirk took hold of his lips. "But, what they don't know won't hurt them. And, with you two gone and out of our hair, Lexi can rest and relax, Emma can do whatever she does, and you'll be out working on finding the answer to who those bones were."

Mental note, get the original topology for Taylor's house. Find out if there was an oak.

"And . . ." Emma said, "the plane is set to come back tomorrow night, so when the police have all their little duckies in a row, you'll be fine and dandy to go home, Taylor." Emma uncapped a clear tube and, from it, pulled out a stick-like Q-tip, though much longer. "This is a DNA test kit. We need a sample for Michael. So, if you would just—"

"How do you know how to do one of those?" Ian's surprise came through in his tone.

She stuck her tongue out at him. "I read the directions." She waved the Q-tip in the air. "Open up. This will go off by courier, and if we're lucky, we'll have it back before the end of the week."

Taylor drew closer to Emma. "Anything to clear my name and be done with the crap."

Emma closed in. "That would be nice, wouldn't it?"

"A private airplane?" Taylor took her seat, belted in and tried to calm the butterflies that had taken wing as soon as she stepped from the car.

"Yup." Ian took the spot next to her, leaving the entire rest of the ten-seat space empty.

"How long have you had it?" The engines rumbled as they pushed backward.

Ian's belt clipped. "About five years, though we share it with a few people."

"It's gorgeous." The cream interior, married with a tan and light blue, soothed even as her stomach tightened. Along with the scent, she believed, for a moment, that she sat amidst a giant gingerbread cookie.

"You nervous?" he asked.

She stared hard out the window. The lineman waved them forward with his orange sticks. "A little. It's smaller than everything else I've been in."

"It's not a 747, but it does the trick." His hand slid under hers. "Our Captain is a thirty-year veteran of the fine establishment that is corporate money-sucking airlines."

Taylor linked her fingers with Ian's and held tight as the plane barreled down the runway and lifted from the earth.

"And his First Officer is his son, whom he has trained very well."

The thrust of the engines kept her glued to her seat. "Do they ever come back here?"

"Not unless we need them." He pointed to a handset. "We can call them or knock on the door, but otherwise, they work. We . . . do whatever."

Once in the air, her body relaxed as if one with the empty space that contained them. She leaned her head on Ian's shoulder. "I hear New York in your voice, but not strong, even though you said born and bred once."

"Born and bred is right. My parents are still there as is my brother." Ian's lips touched Taylor's forehead. "But, they come from the south. Grandma and Grandpa Sands were both southerners. My mom's parents, too."

Taylor closed her eyes, keeping herself attached to him. Just the way he talked about his parents and family told her he loved them. "Why'd they move north?"

"Jobs. My dad's a doctor, and he did his residency in Rochester. Ended up in White Plains, and they just stuck."

"And your brother's going to be a doctor, too?" Keeping her eyes closed, Taylor waited to hear his voice again, to listen to it, the soft lilt that came through when he lost the sarcasm. The strength in the depth of his tone.

"Supposedly, yes. He's smart, but he's also a smartass. One of his professors didn't think he was, and I quote, 'physician material' because of his attitude. Michael's out to prove them wrong, but still be himself." Ian's voice wrapped Taylor in warmth. "Someday, I'll own a farmhouse of my own."

She jolted upright, knocking Ian in the chin with her head. As he groaned, she said, "Sorry! Oh—oh, my God. Are you hurt?"

Ian shook his head, covering his mouth and rubbing his chin. "No. Just caught me hard. What happened? Did I bore you with my family history until you fell asleep and had one of those hypnagogic jerks?"

"I—" She'd heard him, in the same tone, same voice, clear as could be, telling her about his family only to switch to a more southern drawl and exclaim over a farmhouse—she knew she had.

Ian held Taylor with both hands. "What's going on? You look like you've seen a ghost."

"I—" She didn't know what to say. Taylor lowered her gaze, dropped her forehead to Ian's shoulder. "I'm going crazy, that's all."

"Tell me."

"I'm sure it's just stress."

He kneaded the muscles around her shoulders. "Sometimes, keeping the crazy in is worse than letting it out."

Taylor let free a small laugh. "That's one way of doing it. Another would be to forget it all happened."

"What happened?" He cocked his head to the side. "Wait—" His head angled to the other side. "Something like the other night?"

Taylor gave him a quick nod.

Ian fell back against the seat. "Tell me."

She drew in a deep breath. "I was listening to you and all of a sudden you said something completely off the wall."

"What was it?"

"Someday, I'll own a farmhouse of my own."

Ian snorted. "Well, that I did *not* say. Who'd want a farmhouse unless they're a farmer? I'm more a New York condo with all the amenities."

As much as Taylor wanted to smile, the fact voices and scenes had begun to play out in her mind without her control really began to worry her. The fact Ian wouldn't want a place she'd love to have added to the problems.

"Right. Yeah. Sure," she said and snuggled back into the crook of his arm.

The plane began its descent as the two fell into silence, and upon wheels touching ground, their pilot opened up the cockpit door. "Welcome to Washington."

A car ride later, Taylor and Ian arrived at Sherrill's house. Together, they traipsed up the limestone path dotted with spring flowers of pink, red and white. A bumble bee buzzed in the center of a lavender sprig.

The front door opened before they reached it, and a woman in her mid-sixties, with flowing, auburn hair, dressed in a pantsuit of raspberry silk, stood in the entry. "Welcome!" Her face lit up as she held her hands wide. "Ian, Taylor. So good to meet a few more of the faces I've been hearing about."

Taylor took the three steps first.

Sherrill clasped her hands around Taylor's. "Emma's told me a little about you, but she didn't mention just how beautiful you are."

"Ah ... thanks." The flush of her cheeks would show, Taylor knew.

Sherrill tugged with Taylor's hand still between hers. "Come, Ian. Come. Come. Come."

Taylor turned her head toward him and tilted her head. A chuckle broke with Ian's smile. They walked through a two-story foyer and into a great room with camel-colored, suede couches and a giant TV paused on a talk show guest's face in full relief.

Sherrill took a spot on the couch, pulling Taylor next to her. Ian lowered to a seat opposite. Between them, a cardboard banker's box sat with its top open. Photos scattered across the coffee table. Some in color. Others in black and white.

"How was your trip up?" Sherrill held a pack of photos still in a plastic sheathing in her hands.

"Uneventful," Ian said.

"Good, good." She patted Taylor's arm. "Emma said you wanted to see my grandparent's old photos, right?"

Ian shifted to the edge of the chair, leaned his elbows on his knees and clasped his hands together. "Lexi thinks she saw a photo of Taylor and me when she did her mumbo jumbo mind-finding thing."

Taylor didn't understand how Lexi could know or see a photograph someone else owned, but figured she must have seen it before, though, even in her mind, that didn't sit well.

"It was a black and white. Would have been about a hundred years old, maybe more," Ian said.

Sherrill reached for the box and pulled a six-inch album from within it. "I've been looking through all these today. They're all the ones that held the photos from the walls. I set aside this box because I thought you might be interested in it most." She laid one book on her lap. A flip of the front cover showed perfectly placed, fully archived photos on the inside. "Where did Lexi see it in their house again?"

"On the wall by the fireplace," Ian said.

Sherrill's head bobbed up and down as she rifled through the pages. "Then, this is the right batch. All those went into a box my mom had when they died. I had them professionally preserved last year." She turned a page over, revealing more photos. "Some were yellowing from the chemicals in the framing materials." Another flip of the page. "Others were crackling from the temperature change over so many years. Some are in perfect condition." A deep breath escaped from Sherrill. "Here." Her finger tapped against an image. She nudged the album closer to Taylor.

The two staring back could be none other than herself and Ian, though the image didn't make sense. He wore overalls—which by the looks of him, he'd never touch, and she donned a bonnet and long dress that covered every bit of her body. Again, an outfit she'd never use in her line of work. They stood three or more feet apart with an old wagon behind them. His subtle look to her and her shy smile away said it all, yet if anyone asked, they might mistake her smile for the small child in the foreground.

"Would you say that looks like you?" Sherrill asked.

Taylor nodded, toying with the ring on her right hand. "Yup. Totally us. I don't know what to say about this. I mean, I guess these are some sort of ancestor to me then, right?"

Sherrill smiled. "Perhaps."

"Why do you have these?" Taylor asked.

Ian leaned over Taylor's shoulder. "Sherrill is the granddaughter of George and Marge Fergs—the people Lexi and Tripp bought the farmhouse from."

That meant little to nothing except that Taylor had remodeled their house.

Sherrill's smile reached across her face. "My grandparents helped Lexi and Tripp solve their, let's call it, relationship issues, so they could have a future together."

"Um … okay." From Taylor's perspective, everyone had relationship issues.

Sherrill flipped the page and patted the album box. "If Lexi saw a photo my grandparents had, and that pointed you here? You're connected to my Grandparents. In some way."

Taylor's head whipped from Sherrill to Ian and back. "What? What does that mean?"

Ian's cell buzzed. He pulled it from his pocket. "This is Tripp. Can we take two minutes?"

"Absolutely," Sherrill said. "Would you care to join me for some lemonade, Taylor?"

As Ian moved to the front door, Taylor stood and followed Sherrill, all the while wondering how her face—her spitting image as her mother liked to say—could be in a picture, in an album, in a house, owned by a woman she'd never met, and no one seemed even remotely wigged out by it.

The afternoon sun brought life to the earth. Fragrance from the various flowering shrubs and plants hit Ian until three sneezes came out in quick succession. "Shit. Sorry." He pinched his nostrils shut to stem the oncoming tickle that pulsed high up in his sinuses. "What's up?"

Tripp chuckled through the phone. "Riley stopped by."

Ian's entire body tensed. "Why?"

"To check on Taylor, of course."

"And?" Ian trusted Tripp not to give away any of their excursion.

"He's a very astute guy."

Ian walked the length of the path as two cars passed on the

road. "What'd he say?"

"It's what he didn't say," Tripp said. "I told him you and Taylor were 'out' de-stressing. His jaw clenched quite a few times before he said to tell you thanks."

"Thanks for what?" Ian meandered back toward the house.

"For being where he can't be for Taylor. I think he really does see her as a sister."

"That's it?" Ian stopped at the stoop.

"No. He also said that if we were to provide any information to him, on her behalf, he might be persuaded to ensure its safe-keeping or get it into the right hands."

Ian's cheek muscles pulled up his lips. "Not just astute but stellar."

"Exactly."

"You think he came over just for that?"

"No." Tripp's single word came out serious. "He needed to tell me that there was some disturbance at Taylor's house. The ground got pretty messed up overnight. Not that it wasn't already, but apparently, the scientists that showed up this morning mentioned it."

"Hmmm," Ian said.

"Seems a bunch of animals must have traipsed through the site. Deer. Maybe dog or coyote. The thunderstorm did a damn good job of flattening everything out, but left those footprints."

"Well, then." Ian kept his inner worry contained. "We found the photos."

"Yeah? And?"

"Sherrill was just about to tell us more about them when you interrupted."

"Well, why the hell did you answer the phone then?"

"I thought it might be important!" Ian stomped up the steps. "Next time you call, I'm gonna ignore you." Laughter came through until Ian hovered his finger over the off button.

"One more update."

"Oh?" Ian leaned against the frame of the house.

"Your source in Alabama called and said Tanner Meadows died in a bar fight in Tennessee three years ago."

"Son of a bitch. I was hoping he'd have his fingerprints all over this somehow, and we'd be done with it."

"I know." A sigh came through the line. "The mystery continues."

15

Ian followed voices until he found Taylor and Sherrill in her kitchen along with the album they'd searched through before. Unlike his apartment in New York and Lexi's homestyle, modern but cozy place in North Carolina, Sherrill's kitchen screamed commercial. Stainless steel appliances and sleek, silver pots mixed with black granite and marble counters.

"Nice place you got here." Ian took a stool as had Taylor and Sherrill.

"Everything okay?" Taylor sipped from a tall, frosted glass.

Sherrill slid a third in Ian's direction.

"Thanks." Fresh-squeezed lemonade moved across his tongue—not too sugary and not too tart all at once. "Nothing major. Just checking in."

Taylor gave him a small nod.

"So, what'd I miss?"

"Nothing yet," Sherrill said. "We just got the drinks ready."

Ian took another swig of the fresh beverage.

Taylor's fingers circled her drink, but she didn't bring it to her lips. A few blinks. A click of her nails. "Who're those people in that picture, Sherrill? The real ones."

Sherrill failed to hide the smirk behind her own glass, but set it down and opened the album again. "The man was a farmer who worked my great-grandparent's land—Marge's parent's land."

Ian dropped the glass to the counter with a thud. "You're not telling me he was a slave, are you?"

Sherrill held up a hand. “Oh, no. Not at all. My great-grandparents were very progressive-thinking. Back then, they rented out their lands. *To anyone*. They had a whole slew of farmers working them, according to the records I’ve found. They paid rent, helped feed the family, and the farmers reaped the rewards of owning their own businesses. It was a very modern way of working.”

The air Ian held gushed from him. *A farmer working his lands. A farmhouse.* “Why do I sense some sort of . . .”

Sherrill’s grin spread. “Relationship? Tryst, perhaps?”

Ian nodded.

“The story my grandmother told is that her mother and father found the two together once, under one of the biggest oaks at the edge of the lands—right where its roots would meet the small pond at the back of their property. They begged them to keep their secret.” Sherrill sipped some more. “They did, of course. Though my great-grandparents liked to keep an eye on them after that. They said the two shared glances, small waves and hellos, but outside of those, no one knew. Of course, no one in their right mind would have dared attempt a relationship like that back then. So, these two were either crazy, or they must have shared a love that went beyond their time.” She tapped the Taylor-looking person in the photo. “We live in a different world today—one not bound by cultural, racial and ethnic rules.”

“What happened to them?” Taylor scratched at her right ring finger.

Ian’s own itched each time she did it.

“My grandmother never said.”

“Who photographed them?” Taylor asked.

“My great-grandmother. Cameras had just come out back then, for commercial use, that is, and her father had been asked to work with it. She tracked his footsteps as much as possible, I believe.” Sherrill took the album back, thumbed through until she returned it, another page of sketches appearing. “The other thing my great-grandmother was fond of was inks. She loved making them from plants and made a semi-sort of ballpoint pen shaft for herself that she could fill with her inks."

"Very inventive," Taylor said.

"Yes, indeed." The images Sherrill showed off had a deep blue-grey tone to them.

"Why haven't these faded?" Taylor asked.

"I wish I knew. I only attribute it to my great-grandmother's own form of magic. She was a very, *very* unique woman. She used to say, and mind you, this was when she was in her upper nineties, and I was less than eight—so my memory could be off. But she'd say: If people knew who they once were, they'd have had a heck of an easier time dealing with who they are." She turned farther into the album and sighed. "This is my great-grandmother's self portrait."

"Ooh!" Taylor shifted forward, her fingers scratching her ring again. "What's that on her hand?"

Ian peered closer. In the ink of the image, on the woman's right hand, a design had been etched. Like his tattoo. And Taylor's. Only completely different.

"Ah, that's her tattoo. A self made one, supposedly, because no white woman of prosperity would be branded openly like this back then." Sherrill chuckled. "So again, you can see just how unique she was."

Ian raised an eyebrow, noting Taylor continued to twist at the band on her finger. That she didn't stare down at it suggested to him that the action was more habit than anything, but he didn't remember her doing so during any of the last few days. His own itched, but he forced himself to ignore it.

Sherrill turned to the back of the album.

A small, envelope-like folder attached to the inner back. Her fingers slid inside, and when they came out, she had a photo in between her fingers. "I took the liberty of making copies of all the images before we heirloomed them ... you know, just in case I wanted to reframe them." She slid two toward Taylor. "You can have one if you'd like."

Taylor held it. She stared at it. A flip brought the other side over. In the lower corner, words waited to be read in an old handwriting: *My Dearest. Remember me.*

"What's this?" Taylor's voice carried at just above a whisper.

Sherrill's shoulders rose and fell, though with a slight incline toward Taylor. "I don't know. Almost all the photos have writing on them. It was customary early on to help date them."

Taylor's nails made no sound against her skin as she scratched at her finger again.

"You okay, there?" Ian asked. "You been digging at that the whole time."

"Sorry. It's itchy." She pulled off the ring.

"Oh, wow," Sherrill said.

Taylor rubbed at her right ring finger and wiped it on her pants leg. "I must have gotten a bug bite." She looked up to Ian and wiggled her hand. "Sometimes it does this."

"Is . . . that a tattoo?" Sherrill asked.

"No. It's been there all my life."

Sherrill scooped up the ring Taylor had pulled off. "What's this one that you wear?" She turned it around as if studying it.

"It's my grandpa's. He gave it to me before he passed away."

Sherrill's nod coincided with her, 'Ahh'. "You stay connected with your family through heirlooms like this one." Sherrill rose from her stool.

Taylor narrowed her eyes. "I guess." Her head bobbed up and down. "Actually, yes." She stuck the band as far up on her other ring finger. The switch to her right gave her an odd, out-of-balance sensation.

"I want you to see something." Sherrill opened a drawer and withdrew a large magnifying glass. At the counter, she held it over the photo of the Taylor and Ian lookalikes. "It takes a magnifying glass to see it, but it's there. Look at the woman's hand."

Ian snuck next to Taylor, their faces touching at their cheeks.

Taylor took in the face staring back at her, what looked to be light eyes, blondish hair, smooth skin and cheekbones that matched her own. The man beside her held an expression of pain and happiness—a mix Taylor understood well.

"Do you see the pattern inked around this woman's finger?" The humor in Sherrill's voice had Taylor shifting in her seat.

She squinted but could only really make out a faint line around the woman's right ring finger until she put the magnifying glass over it, and it came out in full relief. "Oh. My. God."

Behind her, tension radiated from Ian's body.

"That symbol is there, on her finger, isn't it?" Sherrill asked.

Tingling encompassed Taylor's arm. The same design, barely visible with the glass, but definitely there, showed. Taylor couldn't tell on the man's finger as his dark skin and the photo's depth of field prevented her from seeing it.

"It's no wonder Lexi sent you to me." A small laugh accompanied Sherrill's smile. "My grandmother used to laugh and tell me that her mother believed if you marked yourself in one life, that mark would carry on into the next." She gave a small chuckle.

"Do you believe that?" *Why do I believe her?* Taylor dug at her finger again.

Sherrill took Taylor's hands in hers. "Like I said, my great-grandmother was unique. So yes, I believe it."

"So, this woman and I have the same mark. Does that mean we're related? Is she one of my ancestors? How is this possible?" *Are we the reincarnation of these people in the photo?*

"Now that, I don't know. In all honesty, I don't know who these people are or why my grandparents kept these photos, but they did. For a long time, they hung right where Lexi said—next to the mantel." The chime of five p.m. rang through from a Grandfather clock somewhere in the house, and Sherrill laid her hands back on the countertop. "Would you like to stay for dinner?"

"Actually . . ." Ian leaned forward after his complete and utter lack of participation in the conversation. "We've got another appointment. With Tripp's sister."

Sherrill's smile bloomed. "It's been a few weeks since I talked with Missy last. How is she?"

"Busy," Ian said. "Seems someone gave her name out to a few potential clients, and she has three different houses to design the interiors for."

Sherrill's expression didn't change. "Sometimes, one needs a boost. Other times, they need a downright kick in the butt." A light laugh rang through the kitchen. "She's not so different from her brother but even more headstrong. Please tell Missy I said hello."

"Absolutely." Ian took Taylor's hand as they followed Sherrill to the door and stepped into the evening sun.

"Thank you for everything, Sherrill." Taylor infused her voice with kindness despite the frustration of the hours-long conversation and more questions than answers result.

Sherrill pulled Taylor in for a hug.

Ian moved in for the same. "Nice to finally put a face to a name."

"You, too, Ian. I hope you find what you're looking for."

Once in the confines of the car, Taylor turned to Ian. "Do you think we are those people? Is that even possible?"

"I don't know." His grip on the wheel suggested he might have some of the same problems she did with their little adventure.

She pulled her hand away. "I hate mysteries, Ian. I read the end of books before I hit chapter three. I hate not knowing what's coming or going, who is and who isn't. I hate that my life doesn't have order anymore. Yet, you don't even seem fazed by this."

He leaned back against the seat. "I'm processing. It's what I do best. Get the facts. Lay them all out and figure out what they mean. Then, make up my mind. But right now, I don't feel like I have all the facts. So, I can't be fazed or not fazed. I just … am."

"Doesn't it bother you that we could be the reincarnation of two people from a hundred years ago?"

"Key word, *could.*" Ian bumped his head against the frame of the car a few times. "Lexi has told me hundreds of times that she's never wrong. But, I just don't know." He turned toward Taylor. "We are who we are. You're sitting right here next to the real me. Those people in the picture aren't actually us."

"I know. I know. You're right." She ran her fingers around her tattoo band again. "But this … this symbol … this thing on my finger. Your finger. That has to mean we're the same, right?"

"I have a freckle on my ass, Taylor. So does my dad. Does that mean we're the same person?"

She laughed and fell back against the seat. "Ugh! All this is so frustrating. There are so many balls up in the air."

"Can I just say that that analogy really doesn't work? Especially when talking to a guy." He started the car and navigated them onto the street. "Because, you know, our balls just don't float."

More chuckles came from her. "Strings to pull? Is that better? It's like intertwining stories, one crossing over the other. I'd swear, though, something inside me says they're all connected. And, like we all know, history does like to repeat itself. I'm just waiting for it to explode right in front of my eyes."

A right took them farther away from downtown. "Well … when it all boils over, flames up, sparks, whatever, we'll see what happens. But right now, I'm getting hungry, and Missy's waiting. Well, probably not waiting as she doesn't know how to sit still, but you women know what I mean."

Taylor heaved a sigh.

"Go ahead. Say whatever it is you're holding back." Ian stopped at a traffic light, the blare of another car's radio rumbling theirs.

"The whole last week has been one weird experience after another, and I can't explain any of it. Can't explain why I have a permanent ring on my finger, either, but for some reason, I never really cared before—or not enough to do anything about it. Now, though? It might connect me to a woman from forever ago who doesn't exist anymore. And that really freaks me out."

Ian turned onto a road with a mix of gorgeous homes, some in mid-repair and others in downright need of being torn down. "Well, since you don't like mysteries, go in reverse. Pick this one apart. Deconstruct instead of build." The car stopped at the curb in front of a dilapidated Victorian. "Just don't do it with a sledgehammer. That obviously doesn't come with a happily ever after."

Taylor rose from the car, wishing for a moment she could think beyond the flurry of questions running through her head. *A photo of a person who could be buried in my yard, found by some woman who saw it on a wall. A tattoo I have on my own finger. Two people who look like us. What in high heavens is going on?*

"Ian!" The high pitched voice forced Taylor to turn. A tiny woman with a crop of short, black hair and a smile as wide as her face bounced as she made her way down the weed-strewn path. "You made it." She stopped when she reached Ian, held out her fist and waited.

He stepped to her, bumped it and grabbed her, twirling her around in a fierce hug.

"I'm so excited you guys got to come by!" When he let go, the woman walked closer, her hand outstretched. "I'm Missy, Tripp's sister." The resemblance to her brother showed in her eyes.

Taylor extended her hand to meet Missy's.

"It's so good to finally meet you," Missy said. "Working together by fax and email doesn't give you nearly the same impression, and Ian there wouldn't say boo about you." She wagged a finger in Taylor's direction. "I knew something was up months ago." Missy slid her hand back but stopped. "Is it real? Did it hurt like hell to have one done like this all around your finger?

I've got a tat on my lower back, but there's enough flab there not to hit bone." She turned Taylor's hand sideways and flat again.

Thanks to the itching, Taylor hadn't replaced her ring to cover the design.

Missy dropped her hand. "Oh, sorry. I'm the nosiest of everyone, aren't I?" She stuffed her hands in her pockets. "I want to apologize first that I won't be able to do dinner. The owners of this house—" She thumbed over her shoulder toward the gorgeously decrepit home. "—came to town today, too. So, I only get to hang right now. Then, we're camping inside for the night."

"Camping?"

"Oh, yeah. It's how I learn about a house. Wanna check it out? Missy asked.

Getting to the core of a condemned house like the one before would bring normalcy to her life. If only she had one of her own to renovate, she'd have done it—in a heartbeat, as they said in the south. "Oh, yeah. Show me the bones."

Taylor cringed as she said it. Ian chuckled, and Missy tilted her head as if to ask, "What's the joke?"

16

"Was this condemned?" Taylor asked. The exterior retained only half of its cover, with siding planks hanging as if spider webs held them up.

Missy's eyes sparkled. "Probably should have been."

Ian took a step through the dirt-encrusted yard. "Looks like you have your work cut out for you, Miss."

"You have no idea. The last tenants left half their furniture, plus it sat for a while, and pipes burst from a winter storm. It's like a dream project because the new guys want to incorporate whatever went on when it was first built in 1803. I've done all this research on homes from this area and from that time period. Got my tent all set up."

"Why are you ... camping here?" Taylor had never heard of a designer going to such extremes. In most cases, they gave her plans, color palettes and instructions. Nothing more, nothing less.

"Like I said, I do things a little differently. Come on." She waved them forward.

Ian hung back. Taylor stepped with Missy but glanced over her shoulder. "Coming?"

"Nah. You go ahead. Looks a little—"

"Oh, my God, Ian." Missy stomped her miniature frame back to Ian, grabbed his arm and pulled. Despite her stature, he followed. She inclined her head, nudging Taylor forward through female-only communication methods. "Go up the front steps but stay to the right. The left planks are kinda shot," Missy said, still dragging Ian along.

"Afraid of a little dirt, Ian?" Taylor smiled at him, remembering his horror at her self-imposed shed demolishing activity of the week before.

Once inside, Missy let go, and the three of them stood in a two-story foyer Taylor could envision Scarlett O'Hara walking through.

"I remember getting all your sketches and interiors for Lexi and Tripp's house. They were amazing, Missy. You totally nailed the feel of the place." Taylor walked through dust, dirt, grime and history. Plaster fell. Wallpaper peeled. Boards popped up through the floor, yet the house held an air about it—no one could deny it would have once been beautiful. Her hands itched to dig into the wood, to peel back the layers and help in the renovation process.

"I live and breathe my surroundings," Missy said.

"I'm sorry?" Taylor ran a hand over the newel post, a solid mahogany, pockmarked and scratched.

"When I design a place, I stay in it. Let it speak to me. I wait to hear what the house wants instead of just what the owners want."

"What the house wants?" Taylor tried to keep her voice normal, but suspicion and wariness had run rampant in the past few hours, and around Lexi and Tripp. Though, that would explain how Missy had given Tripp and Lexi's house so much intrinsic character.

Missy giggled. "It's okay if you don't believe in my methods. I'm a little eccentric. I get that from my brother." She nudged Ian with her elbow. "This house though … well, it doesn't want to speak. It's gone quiet, and I think a bit resentful."

A knock and sing-song, "Hello," had them all turning toward the front door. "We're early, Missy. Sorry!" A woman with a bright shock of red hair pulled in a tail at her nape and a man with the darkest black hair as anything Taylor had seen, joined them.

"No problem, Joyce. Randy." Missy nodded to both of them and offered them each a handshake. "This is my cousin Ian—"

Cousin? Taylor withheld the laugh. The fact they shared not a bit of family resemblance should have clued in the two new people.

"—and his girlfriend, Taylor."

Girlfriend? Taylor refrained from commenting and with a nod and shake, noted the Celtic pattern snaking up Randy's arm and the full sleeve of tattoos on the other.

"It's so nice to meet you all." Joyce held her hands up and spun once. "What do you think of our place?"

"It's a junk heap," Ian said.

"It's got so much potential," Taylor said.

Joyce and Randy both burst into laughter, bumping into each other in the process. She advanced toward Taylor, her hand outstretched again.

Taylor's immediate instinct told her to turn and run, but she firmed her feet against the floor. *When did you become a coward?*

Joyce took Taylor's hand, closed her eyes and hummed. Those eyes popped open again no more than a second later. "Has she spoken to you?"

Taylor pulled from her grasp. "Say what?" She stopped the jiggle in her arm by making a tight fist.

"People who are connected in past lives can often communicate with themselves. I was just wondering if she has?"

"How—Wha—" Taylor stared hard at Ian, though how he'd have said anything when they were together the whole time and they'd just met Joyce, she didn't know. Had he shared with Missy before they arrived? Before they flew up? "She who? What are you talking about?" Ian gave only a blank stare. A switch to Missy offered a bright smile. Taylor swallowed hard. "How—"

"You see possibility in a building that is crumbling down upon itself. I see beyond our life today—into the shadows. Call me a psychic if you must, but I prefer Spiritual Naturalist. I am one with the earth." Joyce's smile never left her face.

Taylor's breath backed up in her lungs.

"But, you know nothing about what I'm talking about, do you?" The grin stayed in place.

Missy stepped forward. "I was just giving them the grand tour. You want to come with me? See where I'm set -up for tonight?"

"Of course."

Missy went with Joyce and Randy to the base of the stairs. Three steps up, Joyce stopped, turned and held out her right hand, palm up. "Knowledge is shared in order that we do not repeat our faults but persevere into the future." She swirled with her left index finger overtop her outstretched appendage. "Just something to think about."

Missy offered a slight shrug, and Taylor stared, more dumfounded than before their conversation.

Ian appeared at her shoulder, his lips at her ear—a welcome distraction. "She's a bit of a freak, now isn't she?"

"Given what we have going on, that's not a moniker I'd stick on anyone but ourselves."

Ian shifted against her, his breath tickling her neck. "Point taken." He tucked a strand of hair behind her ear, sending a tingle through her body.

"You two look so sweet together," Missy called from the balcony above.

Taylor lifted her chin. Joyce, Randy and Missy paused together, their arms resting on the wooden banister, a front row, center stage spot to the Ian-and-Taylor show.

Joyce smiled. Missy giggled. Randy grinned.

The barrier gave way.

Their screams filled the space as the railing fell toward Taylor. Her arms flew up and, with them, an unseen wind.

Bodies stopped falling.

They hovered, midair, hands clenching and releasing, flailing and moving as if there might be a bar, a plank, a rail to grab on to—some way to swim toward the floor.

Taylor lowered her arms a little at a time.

The three people floated their way down toward the first level, hands and feet reaching the beaten planks just before a screech of wood against wood somewhere in the rafters jostled in a way it shouldn't, and a low rumble began somewhere beneath where Taylor and Ian stood.

"Get outta here!" Ian's yell coincided with a shake of the whole structure.

Glass burst from an upper story window, cascaded down from the ceiling, and rained upon them as they jolted forward. Ian pushed Taylor toward the front door.

A long yawn sounded around them.

"The roof!" Missy yelled as she bolted through the opening.

Joyce followed.

Randy behind her.

Taylor stopped. As if entranced, she stood and stared at the crumbling wood all around her.

"Go! Go! Go!" Ian's voice reached her, but Taylor envisioned herself covered by it all.

Buried in the rubble.

Not wood. Soil. Filling a grave.

The roof shuddered. A beam landed just in front of her, rocking the floor and throwing her backward. She landed on her butt, braced with her arm behind her and jarring her rib.

Yet, still, she stared.

It's going to bury me.

Alive.

Again.

Her body flung rearward, pressure at her gut dragging her through debris until she landed on her back, staring up at sunlight all around her.

As if torn from a vision, the house came back into view.

Two feet away, the porch bowed inward; slats popped up with

deadly sharpness.

Hands slid under her armpits and pulled. The force yanked at her shoulders, sending stabbing pain through her arm and her chest, taking her farther away, into the grass.

The house's front facade began a slow slide until it fell inward, a cloud of dust shooting up into the air, and the remainder of the four sides collapsed in upon themselves.

Beside her, Ian knelt, his chest heaving. "Son of a bitch." He turned to Taylor, ran his hands down her cheeks. "You're okay. We're all okay. What was—"

"I made it fall." She braced a hand on her knee and managed to get to her feet, wobbling and trembling. "I made it fall! How could I do that?" Bile rose up her throat. *This is all my fault. I made that fall. I broke an entire house!*

Yellow-geared men jogged up to her. "Ma'am, are you okay?"

I made it fall. I made it fall. I made it fall.

If she hadn't used the air to save them, the house wouldn't have crumbled. If she hadn't saved them, she'd have been responsible for their deaths—or at least their injuries.

Both churned her stomach.

Her body swayed. The ground rushed up to her, or she to it, and she hit the grass again.

"Taylor!" Ian broke through the jumble. "Get an EMT over here!"

The voice mixed in her mind but didn't stop the onslaught of emotion or the fazed view of life around her.

"We need to get this woman to a hospital."

Her head lolled to the side, though she knew Ian cradled her.

"You're bleeding." He gripped her arm, sliding it back.

Panic kicked in. *My hands!* Her breath hitched. *Please let me go. I can't breathe.*

"I'm right here. You're okay." As soothing as he might have thought his voice, her constrained arm did her in.

It always did.

"Can't—" Her head shook as consciousness reclaimed her. "Can—"

Ian let go. "Taylor." He said her name right at her ear. "You've been hurt." His fingertip stroked her shoulder.

"It's not you." She turned her face away from Ian's gaze.

"I know, but you've got a gash running from your shoulder to your elbow."

A quick check to her right showed blood pooling through her shirt and down her arm. "No hospitals. I can't—no, I just won't."

"May I?" Joyce knelt at Ian's side.

Remorse and guilt flooded Taylor. She pushed up to sit, the effects of manipulating the air wearing off. "I'm so sorry, Joyce. I—"

"You're sorry for what? Saving our lives?" Confusion coated her question.

"But . . . your . . . *house*." A pulsing throb marched up and down Taylor's arm.

"My life." Joyce took Taylor's hands. "Tell me. Please. Confirm that I didn't fall from a second story balcony and not land flat on my face. Tell me you can manipulate the elements."

Taylor faced Ian, back to Joyce and to Ian again. She dropped her chin but bounced her head up and down.

"Well, I'll be damned," Joyce said as Ian said, "Son of a bitch."

"But your hou—"

Black-soled work boots hit Taylor's line of vision. "Ma'am, I'm Dave—one of the EMTs. I really need to transport you to the hospital—"

"No!"

"Can you do anything here?" Joyce asked.

Dave dropped a bag at Taylor's side. "Let me see it." He ripped her shirt the rest of the way up her arm. "It doesn't look deep, probably won't even need stitches." He pulled out cleaner pads. "But . . . it's our recommendation—"

"No. I'll find a doctor." The first touch of antiseptic shot arrows through Taylor's body. *Should have asked for some Vicadin.* Dave scrubbed so hard on the gash that Taylor cried out.

Joyce gripped Taylor's hands between her own. "Truly, my friend. What happened here was not your fault."

Dave let go, moving back to his pack. "Last tetanus shot?" He sat at Taylor's side, soaking a cotton ball in a clear liquid.

"Three years ago."

"That's good, but what with the age of that building, you should ask a Doc if you need an update. Let me get some heavier gauze to wrap this. And, you're absolutely positive I can't take—"

"I'm *not* going to the hospital."

"I'll be right back." Dave stood and departed.

"So, Taylor—" Joyce took Taylor's hand and with the other motioned behind her.

Shooing Ian away? Taylor checked over her shoulder.

"You'll be … okay?" Ian pointed behind him. "I'll just go check on Missy."

Taylor nodded. "Yeah. Yeah, sure." She adjusted back to Joyce.

"I caught you off guard, I think, yes? But, given what you can do, maybe not?"

Taylor nodded. "A little. I'm not used to people—" She didn't want to say, 'knowing I can control the air,' because, with few exceptions, no one knew.

Joyce's lips curved. "I understand. We, in my profession, maintain confidences as well. And, I've been wrong before, so I try not to push." She crisscrossed her legs underneath her. "Can you manipulate anything else other than air? Create fire? Move the earth? Bend water?"

Taylor shook her head. "Only the air."

"Fascinating."

Not always. "Why?"

Joyce's lips curved in a giant smile. "When I touched your hand, I sensed three lives before this one. The latest is the closest to you. She needs to talk to you … to … communicate as she's in pain. Those before her are silent but echo through your soul along with traces of other gifts."

Taylor glanced down at her hands, the conduit to her gift, and one she used only in emergencies. The previous lives claim, though, that interested her more. "Um … *how* can you … feel those lives?"

"Most of us have no recollection and never even engage with what or who we once were. But … just like an alcoholic is never cured, or a smoker can still have a craving after twenty years of not touching a cigarette, we may be able to feel, breath, taste and touch part of our past whether we interact with it on a daily basis or not."

A zing of pain shot up Taylor's arm. "What am I supposed to do?"

"You have a gift for a reason. You're going to need it. I don't know how. I don't know when. But you will. It's why you have it. Listen to the echoes. Really listen to them and maybe, just maybe, she'll speak to you."

The clomp of rubber-soled feet signaled Dave's return with his satchel.

Joyce rose. "Missy has my number if you have any questions."

Taylor reached out again. "But your hou—"

"The house clearly wanted to be left alone, Taylor." Joyce took Taylor's hand and patted the top. "We aren't here to be masters of our domain, but to let what lives and breathes around us control small bits of that." She knelt at Taylor's side again. "This one said goodbye—in permanence."

"But—" Taylor cringed as Dave rubbed smelly, stingy cleaner on the massive scratch, his deft hands making their way around her arm.

"No buts. We aren't the only ones that live in this world, that breathe and share in what the earth gives us. What we see with our eyes is only one part of what our brains comprehend. I hired Missy because of her reputation for listening to the unsaid sounds, seeing what isn't on the surface. She's told me numerous times that this house wasn't talking. Its soul had already dispersed. I didn't believe her. Now, I do." She left Taylor with the medic.

"That's one big mess, isn't it?" Dave nodded toward the house.

"Yeah."

"Crazy how stuff happens like that."

"You don't know the half of it."

17

"Why in the hell aren't you over there with her?" Missy punched Ian's arm for the third time with the same question, though her hands shook as she returned them across her chest.

Ian recognized the nerves, despite the bravado in her tone. "Because brat-face, I came to check on you." Joyce walked toward them, sidestepped onto the grass and joined Randy with the fire crew. "She doesn't even seem fazed by this."

"You haven't called me that since I was ten . . . you know."

"Called you what?" Ian kept Joyce and Randy in his peripheral vision, watching as she went into his arms and his came around her.

"You're so in love with her you can't think straight."

Ian couldn't hide the flinch. "Say what?"

"Get your ass over there. I don't care if she beats you to a pulp. You owe her. I owe her. I mean, she saved my life, for God's sake!"

Yeah, she did.

What Taylor had done etched into Ian's mind, yet it didn't surprise him. He'd expected it but didn't know why. His best friend and wife both had talents no purebred humans would ever have. Why couldn't some blonde chick from the backwoods of North Carolina have one, too?

How could I not have known?

"Ian?" Missy's voice broke him from his thoughts. "Aren't you going to go to her?"

Ian held up a hand. "Gimme a sec." With a hand in the air,

he wagged a finger, giving up on the coddle-Tripp's-sister idea. "How in fuck's name do I owe her? She saved your life, not mine."

Her lips curved. "Yes, I know. I saw what she did, Ian. I was a party to hovering over the floor for a millisecond. And I will be forever grateful. The fact that these kinds of talents exist—I just—wow." Her eyes grew larger for a moment before returning to normal. "Unlike Joyce, who probably thought it was a normal activity given what she is, *I'm* not going to forget it."

Ian raised an eyebrow.

"Ever. I'm never, ever, ever going to forget falling like that and landing like I had a bunch of pillows waiting for me." Missy held out her hands. Both shook. "See? I'm still freaking out. But I'll be fine." Those hands moved back to her chest. "We Fox girls are tough shit, Ian, but I'm going straight home and taking a hot bath so I can get my mind off what happened today. Her though? You've got her here, away from family, away from people she can talk to—since you seem as surprised as me about this—so I'm guessing, this revelation is not one the world knows."

Missy's shove did little to him given her small stature, but he took notice and marched toward Taylor. Ian's cell buzzed before he'd gotten halfway. Since the medic continued to wrap her arm, he withdrew the phone from his pocket.

Michael's name showed up on screen, and Ian hit connect.

"Tell me you've got something interesting and useful." *And give me something to get this situation out of my mind.*

"No." A serious, wary undertone put Ian on edge.

"What's wrong?"

"Grams fell bowling—"

"They took her bowling? With slick floors? She's ninety-six, for God's sake!"

"No, Ian. She was playing it on a game console." He offered a slight chuckle. "They say she's fine, but . . . I gotta go up there and see her."

"Of course, of course." He nodded to himself. "Can you get

to Stewart in two hours?"

"Yeah."

"I'll meet you there. We'll fly up together."

"Mom and Dad are already on their way. Thanks, bro," Michael said before he clicked off.

Ian finished the distance to Taylor without hesitation, held out a hand and brought her to her feet. At her turn, Taylor's gaze connected straight with Ian's, and his heart lurched.

He'd have to leave her, couldn't risk taking her to New York since she ought to still be in North Carolina.

Her head adjusted to a slight incline. "You look like you saw a ghost." One hand held tight to the bandage on her arm. "Or a woman who can move air. I'll totally understand if you want ru—"

"I need to go to New York. Right now. Might be gone a few days." Ian's chest tightened as he said it—a pull on muscles he'd only ever attributed to playing sports too hard. A rub up his rib-cage did little to ease it. "Why don't I get the plane, have it take me up to New York, and you can head back down to—"

"I'll go with you." She reached but withdrew her hand as her eyes glossed with what he expected to be pain.

"That's not a good idea. Your bail was for in-state residency only. And, I'm not Tripp, so I can't make you disappear fast if we're about to get caught."

Her lips trembled, inciting a wave of emotion through Ian.

"Hey." He pulled her close. *Screw the law.* "Come with me. If I need to stay, I'll send you back."

"I don't want to be alone right now." She nodded against him but disentangled herself and ran her hand along her bandage.

"You might not like meeting my family this early on in a relationship."

Taylor tilted up to Ian. "Are they psychopaths?"

"No."

"Cops?"

Ian snorted a laugh. "No. My mother will smother you. My father will want to take your temperature and monitor your blood pressure—"

"That's right. He's a doctor. I need one." Taylor pointed to her arm. "They're the perfect people."

"You have no idea," Ian said.

Eyes closed, Taylor took in the fragrance of Ian's aftershave and, for the second time in one day, tried not to think about the thousands of feet of empty space between airplane and earth. She leaned back against the chair, thinking through the events of the day.

"Taylor?"

"Yeah?"

He linked his fingers with hers. "What you can do with your . . ."

"Gift? I've always thought of it like that." She tightened her hold on his hand, needing the connection—the touch. "What do you want to know exactly?"

"Can you fly?"

A chuckle escaped. "No."

"Well, that was the obvious question," he said.

"Of course."

"So if this plane heads south, we're still goners?"

Thank you for the mental picture I was trying to avoid. "You don't have a parachute or two on board this tin can contraption?" She kept her eyes closed and her head on Ian's shoulder but bounced with a small laugh.

"Is that a yes or a no?"

She gave him a small shrug. "I can move stuff. I can sorta *hold* incredibly heavy weights. I can levitate things. I can push and pull. I can't fly, though. I can't make me do stuff, just affect stuff around me. And, it always ends like you saw at the house. The more time I use it, the more mental effort it takes—the faster I crash."

"So ... no Superwoman costumes as a kid?

Taylor giggled. "When I was little, I wanted to fly so bad I'd crawl out my window, climb on the roof of the porch and prepare to jump. No sooner than my arms were outstretched, Mama would be standing on the sidewalk, her hands on her hips. She didn't have to say a thing. I'd just crawl back in."

"So, she knew what you could do?"

"No, no. She thought I was spirited. Works to my advantage with my current profession. She still thinks, someday, my fascination with power tools will fade, and I'll become the demure southern woman she is."

"Does she know what you can do now?"

"Oh, no. I've been smart enough to keep that under wraps. Only a few people know ... you and Tripp, for example."

"Tripp?"

Taylor nodded. "One of the guys on the renovation job mispositioned a ladder. It headed backward, and I pushed it up. Tripp happened to be there when I did it."

"And, he told you he saw?"

She shook her head. "I could just tell."

"And Riley?"

Taylor opened her eyes and pushed away from the seat's back, leaning toward Ian. "Yes. You're awfully curious."

"It's my job to ask a lot of questions. It's what I do. Tripp's the one with a ..."

"Gift? Is whatever he can do related to what he's doing for me without telling me exactly what he can do?"

Ian waved a hand through the air as if to agree without agreeing.

"You can't say. I wouldn't have either if—"

"You hadn't kept three people from splatting along the floor and probably busting through the boards and down into the crawlspace."

"Slab. It was built on a slab."

"Well, then," he said. "Ouch."

"That's what I thought, too. You're learning an awful lot about me, but what about you?"

"I'm an open book." Ian's lips curved.

Taylor burst out a laugh. "You're better fortified than Fort Knox."

Ian adjusted until his face came within an inch of Taylor's. "Give me your best shot."

She dipped her gaze toward his lips. "College?"

"Boston."

Taylor's brow rose. "Name of the last woman you dated."

"Dated?" His tone carried a distinct hint of sarcasm.

She gave him her best smirk.

"Let's just say she was a dancer at a club in the Keys. We were on a job. She was there. And, this was all before Tripp met Lexi."

"Favorite color?"

Ian laughed and pushed closer. "Blue." He didn't shift his focus.

"That's not fair." The huskiness in her own voice suggested Ian's answer affected more than her mind. A bump and the flip-flop of her stomach suggested the plane descended.

"One more before we land."

"Do you really think—I mean, do you really believe we could have a past life . . . together?"

He said nothing for a moment. His hand slid behind her neck and he pulled her in for a sweet kiss. "Do you?"

Three hours after the house collapsed, Taylor and Ian landed and taxied to an area reserved for private planes. She hadn't answered him; he figured because she harbored a measure of disbelief herself. He did. Rather than dwell on it, Ian refocused himself on getting to Grams.

Michael joined them in the cabin moments after the plane parked. "Wow. You guys look like shit. Been digging in the dirt?"

Ian would have grabbed Michael into a long, extended head lock if they didn't need to continue on their journey sooner rather than later.

"Don't know if you remember me or not, but I'm Michael." He extended a hand toward Taylor.

She took it, shaking her head. "Taylor Marsh. Have we met?"

Their pilot closed the outer door. Lights illuminated in the cabin, and seconds later, the engine whirled.

"Yeah. At Lexi and Tripp's wedding. Why are you two covered in dust? Been out scavenging more bones? The one Tripp sent wasn't enough?" Michael secured himself in the seat opposite Taylor and Ian.

"A house fell on us," Ian said.

"Dude. You got quite the life."

"Folks . . ." Their pilot came over the small intercom. "We're set to take off. Be in Rochester in about forty-five minutes."

Their bodies pressed into the seats with the momentum of taking off into the sky.

Ian let himself relax and closed his eyes as the plane banked to the left. "You get anything done on the sample?"

"I only had it a few hours before I got the call. But, I got some friends working on it. That lab you guys got us access to is sa*weet.* This is totally going to jack up the research component for my finals. But anyway, they'll call me if anything cool happens. I got a hottie from Horticultural Science to come in and test the soil samples, and a guy getting his PhD in forensics is going to look at the wood from that shed."

"You sent them bones, soil, wood—everything?" Taylor's surprise brought Ian out of his resting place.

"Yes. The goal is to prove you had nothing to do with it, right? So, we sent . . . *everything* . . . Lexi and Tripp got their hands on."

"But . . . how—" Taylor started.

"Remember, they have their ways." Ian tightened his fingers around her knee, massaging in the hopes she wouldn't ask more. She knew too much for his own comfort—without having Tripp explain.

Michael chuckled behind his hand.

"What's up with you?" Ian asked, glaring at Michael.

His brother's eyes darted down and back up. "She's 'the client', isn't she?" He air quoted with his fingers.

"Yes." Ian rubbed at Taylor's thumb. *She's got a scar down the back side, doesn't she?* He traced over that area. *Yup.* A slight chill raced up him. The sense of familiarity grew stronger with each moment he spent with her, yet Ian couldn't explain it, not even from what Sherrill suggested, Joyce had said or anything Taylor shared.

Did he believe they could be reincarnated?

"So, what'd you think about my brother here posting your bond?"

Ian closed his eyes and forced himself not to jerk back. He ventured a glance at Taylor and caught her wide eyes.

"I mean, all that dough and his condo in New York as collateral. You must be out of this world special."

Taylor squeezed Ian's hand. "I-I wasn't sure on that."

"Luckily for you, Taylor, Ian's the most loyal and trustworthy person I know." Michael crossed his index and middle fingers. "He and Tripp've been tight since before I was born. They don't do anything without each other knowing about it. So, if he believes you enough to do that, seriously, you're good in my book." He held out his fist as if Taylor should bump it.

She shifted forward, did exactly that and relaxed against Ian again. "I like knowing you have such good friends and that I can be one of them."

Michael's face lit up with a deviance even Ian would have to wonder about. "Grams is gonna love her."

I know. "Do you know any genealogy people, Michael?" Ian

opted to change the subject in favor of an idea and to get away from the mushiness.

Michael scratched the underside of his chin. "Not off the top of my head, but the school is full of nuts who study what *used* to be instead of what *can* be. Actually—" He wagged a finger. "There's this blonde I see at the library a lot. She's always got those family tree things scattered on tables around her. Why?"

"Let's add them to the search team. I want to—" Ian held out his hand. As if Taylor understood, she rummaged in the bag she'd brought and removed the photo. "I want someone to look these people up."

"Who are they?" Michael squinted at it.

Ian looked to Taylor. Her eyes held only concern.

"Holy shit! That's you! You do one of those old-timey, western photo things?"

"No."

"Then, who? That ain't Grams, but I'd swear, hand on a Bible, that that's you, but if that's not Grams, that can't be Gramps. What gives?"

"We're not sure exactly," Ian said.

"This pic has to be from sometime after eighteen-fifty, probably closer to nineteen-hundred, right? Since that's when cameras had first come out?"

Ian went on to give Michael the details he'd learned from Sherrill. Taylor piped in with her own thoughts every once in a while.

"So, if you swear these people aren't you, why am I looking them up?"

"We just want to know more about them."

"Uh-huh. Sure. There's something fishy goin' on." He pulled out his phone, snapped a shot of the photo and handed it back to Ian. "So, you need me to look someone up who's deader than dirt, for a reason you won't really say, and all I gotta do is ask a hot girl out to do it?"

Taylor's head pressed against Ian's arm, he presumed in an acknowledgement. "Yes," he said.

Michael smiled. "Well, shit, yeah. I can do that."

18

Greater Rochester International Airport welcomed the plane at almost eleven o'clock. Visiting hours at the hospital wouldn't start until nine in the morning the next day, so Ian booked rooms at a hotel.

Ian held out Taylor's key. "You're on the right. I'm on the left."

She took it, flipping it between her fingers. "Ian?"

"Yeah?"

"I don't want to be alone. I'll pay for my room if I can just—"

He stepped toward her, pulled her against him and crushed his lips against her. "God, I was hoping you'd say that."

Taylor rubbed at another spot of grime between her fingers. Her arm ached; her ribs throbbed. She wanted, with a passion, to take a hot bath—assuming she wouldn't die—and to sleep.

The king-sized bed bounced under her as she dropped to it. "You barely know me, Ian, yet you've been helping my . . . me . . . every step of the way, have your brother doing stuff that's probably illegal and don't seem to mind the neurotic nature of my life right now. Why? How is that possible?"

Ian's keys fell with a clang to the only dresser. "If you were worth connecting myself to in a past life, you ought to be worth helping in my current one, right?"

"So, you do believe it." Taylor ran her fingers under her nose, pinched the bridge and pressed at her eyelids. "I mean . . . it's probably all just a coincidence. A … familiarity. Right? That's the logical answer."

Ian took her hands away from her face, kneeling in front of her in the process. "I'm not a man of many words, and hell no on sappy ones. But, I'm a damn good judge of character, and everything that has happened explains a lot about the last half a year. At Tripp's wedding, I swore I'd met you before. The more I spend time with you, the more I—the more I want to."

"Could it be so simple, though? I have a gift for … some reason. Those pictures … let's say they were, somehow … us. These memories that keep popping up and these feelings. Is it supposed to be this way?" Taylor ran a finger down the side of Ian's face. "But … what if this life … this fourth try … what if it's us, and we've failed all the times before. What if we fail again?"

His chuckled warmed Taylor's heart. "Now, that's the spirit. The perfect pessimist." He kissed her knuckle. "Let's pretend for a moment that this is life four, and it's us that's the mission. Maybe the new motto is fourth try's the charm."

She brought her hands back.

He stiffened.

"No, no, sorry. I'm just really dirty," she said. "You could be right. I just wish … I wish I knew more."

"I've done a lot of research in the last week. Ish. I already knew about the design. We have the photos. We have stories. We have an infinite number of possibilities. Maybe instead of pushing it, we just see what happens in this life and roll with it. Be a little spontaneous. Like, for example, would you like to take a bath? This room has a Jacuzzi."

Her eyes widened. "I would, but maybe a shower would be better. You know … to keep myself from drowning again."

"I didn't mean alone." Ian stood.

Taylor followed, her heart lurching at the insinuation in his tone. Spontaneous? Despite her aggressiveness when it came to their kiss at Lexi and Tripp's house, Taylor rarely jumped in with both feet unless she knew what would happen. When it came to men, in fact, she took her time like no other of her friends.

Ian continued walking backward, her hand in his. She made each step with him. Their gazes stayed locked on each other. In what Taylor had expected to be a standard bathroom, she found a whirlpool tub, just as Ian had said.

It would easily fit two.

Seeing really meant believing, and in that instance, all impropriety vanished. "Ian?" Taylor undid the top three buttons of her ruined silk blouse, attempting to mask the pain from moving her arm.

He started the waterfall. "Yeah?" With his glance back, she let the silk fall to the ground. His eyes took on those of a hungry tiger.

She reached behind to undo her bra and failed to hide the wince as tearing pain swept through her right arm. "Dammit."

Ian stood at her toes while the river of water raged on in the circular tub. "Let me." He moved around her, his fingers working against her spine until the cotton loosened and fell along the length of her arms. His hands slid around her side, rubbing against her skin and bringing the hairs there to a stand.

He ran a finger along the underside of her breast until his hands cupped her and pulled her against him.

"I so hope you're not expecting to get in that tub alone." Hot breath hit her ear.

"No. I wasn't."

His hands slid lower until his fingertips graced the edges of her jeans and made their way to the center. Button. Zipper. Undone. He pushed down until fabric no longer covered her hips.

She lifted her foot at the touch on her ankle. Repeated with the other.

He kicked the jeans to the side and stood in front of her again. "This is going to need some TLC." His fingers rested against the gauze, peeling from the top in slow, deliberate actions. "Luckily,

I had my dad as my coach for the healing of all things human, and the EMT handed me strict instructions to wash and rewrap it. I think now is as good a time as any. Don't you?"

Water spurted as the jets kicked in. Ian stopped the flow, leaving bubbles to froth.

Taylor held out her arm. "Just . . . be gentle."

He took hold of the top layer and unwrapped from her shoulder to her elbow. On the second layer, a line of red had etched a path of whatever had run along her arm.

"Eww," Taylor said. "I deal with cuts and stuff all the time, but that is just gross. It looks like a snake."

Ian tugged the layer closest to her skin.

Taylor cringed. "No, keep going." The gauze pulled at her wound, yanking at hairs where the skin and blood had matted to it. "Ow. Shit. Keep going."

Over. Under. Over. Under. Each unwind added to the torment until Ian unraveled the last of it, and her arm no longer throbbed just burned.

Heat ran through her at the press of his lips to the wound. She closed her eyes as he inched his way up, never touching the line that she knew would scar. Up, farther until he reached her shoulder, each kiss brought a mix of fire and cool. Of desire and worry. Pleasure and pain.

Ian continued up to her neck, adding the imprint of his lips. Each nerve ending woke under his caress. His hands found their home at her hips but roamed their way up and down as his tongue teased.

Water grumbled in the tub, and he maneuvered them to the edge, continuing the exploration of her body—of every inch.

Taylor wanted more. She reached low, and he pushed her hands away. "Hey—"

His lips silenced hers, though their smiles merged. "Not your turn right now."

Fingertips danced along her spine, reached down and trailed

back up. Instinct pushed her hips against his, their only separation the fabric still around his body. She closed her eyes, picturing the feel of his skin under hers as if they were one, as if they'd been together forever. Her imagination roamed, taking what her hands couldn't reach and bringing the softness of his skin, the hardness of his muscles, the indentation in his thigh where he'd fallen off his bike and been scarred.

She pulled back with a jerk.

"You feel it, too?" he asked.

"Wha—what . . . exactly?"

"You have a freckle on the side of your hip." His hand reached down, skimming over the side. "I didn't see it. Yet, I know it's there." His lips started anew, descending from her breasts to her belly button. "And here, you have a scar from when you had your appendix out."

She shivered under his touch. *How can he know?*

Ian went lower until his fingertips ran along the inside of her thigh, lighting a fire in her core. "And here, you—" He stopped, rose again until their eyes met. "You had stitches from falling off a horse and landing on a rock." His eyes glazed for a moment before he seemed to refocus.

She'd never fallen off a horse, but she did have a scar in just the place he'd noted.

Taylor didn't understand, but she also didn't care. Whether her current life or a previous one, she wanted him. She wrapped her good arm around Ian's neck and pulled him in so their lips merged. With what little flexibility she had with her other arm, she yanked at the buttons on his shirt, slipped it off his shoulders, and with eyes closed, ran her hands along the smooth skin of chest.

The wind kicked up around them, the trees whispering as skin to skin, her entire body heated. The pond's water lapped at the sides of the grass where they stood, he shirtless and she wishing she could be. If only her mama hadn't tied her corset that morning.

"May I?" he asked.

She arched back as he kissed a line down her neck. "Please, kind sir," she said, bemused by his formality. He'd always been that way, so serene and demure, following her lead.

Their lips played along each other's as he undid the strings he'd learned how to retie to prevent anyone suspecting their trysts. With her breasts exposed to the night sky, he suckled them, massaging and cupping her as she liked so.

"'Tis your turn, my darling," she said.

One leg and another slipped from his pants, and she reached for what she wanted most.

His groan came as approval. His hip thrust added to the torment against her own body. Another tug toward the water and he proceeded. She stepped in. He did the same. She lowered. He, too. One leading. One following. A ballet of desire, drawing each other down and into the water.

The warmth rushed over her. As her arm sank into the liquid, she tensed, the liquid seeping into the wound.

"You continue to suffer."

She forced her arm farther down. "It is nothing that time will not heal."

He reversed their positions, sitting behind her and holding her against his muscular body, his erection pressing into her spine. "You'll take care, this time, to return the leathers?"

"I will. You are not at fault for my transgressions, my love."

He draped her arm along the edge of land where water wouldn't reach and entwined his fingers with hers, keeping it from being immersed.

"You are so kind to me, John."

"And you to me, Claire. So many days I pray for our circumstances to be different."

She rested against him, the natural ebb of water caressing her with feathery touches as his lips did the same, building within her the need for release. "Our lives are given us by God. I will never stop loving you."

"Nor will I." His hands slid down her side, caressing and soothing with each pass as the water did the same.

"Then by night, we shall share, and by day, we are nothing more than daughter of the tailor and beautiful farmer—no! Land owner." She closed her eyes, letting the warmth take over. Rather than wait for him to acquiesce, she lifted up, turned and straddled him. "Shall I entice you further, my love? Will you cease to worry about our futures and simply love me with your whole heart today?" She slipped farther forward, encompassing him with her body but not yet consuming him.

His jaw worked in his silence. "I will never stop. You are my destiny whether anyone can know or not."

A rise brought them in contact with each other and a descent filled her with him, sending pleasure through her body the likes of which a fire master couldn't have created in the sky. She closed her eyes, drawing him in fully and savoring the moment she'd craved for what seemed like lifetimes but had only just been a fortnight since their last.

Opening her eyes, she stared deep into his. His hands found her hips. She breathed in as she rocked against him with a gentleness that sent flutters along the surface of the water. Beneath her, his need for completion built, visible in the set of his jaw and repeated clench of his hands against her hips. She kept their pace languid but jostling the crystal clear liquid with each thrust.

Pleasure rippled through her, a lifetime of pure ecstasy where she could believe in a lack of physical and mental anguish, or torment of the heart, and simply be with the man over whom she loomed. The man she loved. The man who loved her. A man who knew his worth whether or not the world understood.

One hand stayed attached to her thigh while the other roamed her skin, slick and heated with desire. She kept up their pace, pulling and pressing, jostling them and water with an increase in speed. Their rhythm matched, creating a small wave that bounced against her back.

The muscles in his chest jumped as she continued their merging, the blending of two lives into one.

In sync. Together. Forever.

With his intense stare, the fierce grip on her hips and the flutter of his lids, she let herself go, taking her moment of release along with him and savoring in a secret moment.

Taylor woke to darkness.

As her mind cleared, and her eyes adjusted, she flipped from her side to the other and collided with Ian. Her pounding heart calmed as his slow and regular breathing filled her mind with ease.

"You okay?" His groggy voice whispered in her ear. "You yelled out John a second ago."

She switched back to her other side, snuggled in, pressing against him, and murmured, "Just a dream. A dream." She tensed as her throbbing arm reminded her of her night, of what she'd shared with Ian in the tub, and of the vision she'd had that seemed as real as life. "I have no idea who John is."

It had been surreal. Vivid and vibrant. Emotional. It had caused her to crave him again and again.

Why haven't I told him?

"Go back to sleep. Everything's better with the sunlight." Ian's arm snaked out, wrapping around her torso in a comforting hug.

Just a dream.

I want what I had before.

19

Taylor bolted upright for the second time. She spun to the left and found Ian gone. Her heart raced. She ripped the covers off and jumped from the bed, sending a pang through her chest and arm. Her race to the bathroom ended in a collision with him mid-exit.

His hands reached out and grabbed her biceps, sending a wave of torturous fire through her. Her stomach curdled, and she cried out.

He released her as if his clutch had branded his hands.

She fell backward against the wall, rubbing up and down her arm. A ridge raised along the surface.

Ian caught her chin before she could study it more. "Come in here." A deep breath of air escaped him.

Taylor stepped with him into the blinding light. He wore nothing but a towel around his waist. One half of her wanted to grab the edge and make it fall to the ground. The other part of her wanted to scream at whatever had happened to her arm.

"Oh." Ian's single word did not infuse confidence.

"Please tell me I don't have to go to the hospital. Please, Ian."

His head bounced left and right. "Let me call my dad and see if he can help. I doubt he has any privileges in Rochester, but he actually went to school here. Just don't look, and . . . let me call him."

Taylor forced herself not to turn.

The triple knock took both their attentions. "Housekeeping,"

Michael said through the door.

Ian's snarl came out with a laugh. "Get ready, and let me know if you need anything."

She nodded.

He laid a kiss to her forehead, which only made her heart flip-flop worse than it had as she'd laid against him. Ian's voice trailed off as he closed the bathroom door behind him. Despite his suggestion otherwise, Taylor turned her arm toward the mirror.

The gauze had come loose, and what had once been red had turned a deep, purply blue. Her stomach cramped, sending bile up her throat. She dropped to the toilet, prepared to toss her last meal. She'd seen her crew sever fingers and even once watched a femoral artery spray at the beat of a heart. None of them affected her the way her own injuries did. With one hand, she spun the shower knob. As steam filled the room, her stomach calmed. She stripped the gauze and basked in the warmth of the spray, hoping it would wash out whatever infection brewed.

Fifteen minutes later, she walked out, a towel wrapped around her hair, another around her body.

Ian sat on the edge of the bed, flipping channels on the television. He turned toward her as she approached her bag. "Can I help?"

"I'm good." Though she wished she'd packed more than the dinner outfit Ian had made her promise to bring—for a dinner than never happened. "Just . . ." She fiddled with the zipper and failed.

Ian gave it one good yank. "My dad's coming over here to look at you, and we'll all go over to Grams'. Though, if you want something other than your black dress, I can offer you these." Ian pulled out a teal T-shirt with a spiral pattern over the sleeve and a pair of jeans Taylor recognized as her own. "The top comes from the gift shop, and the jeans I had washed this morning before you woke." He handed them to her. "And, since you slept naked with me, I was able to have your extras—" He held up her black, lace panties with a finger. "—carefully cleaned. Michael brought them back."

Taylor snatched them with her free hand, though she smiled and leaned up. The light kiss she'd meant to give him he took with abandon. When he let her go, she swayed, and he caught her.

"You okay?"

"Yeah, just a little … head rush." With a wink, she took her clothes and headed back to the bathroom.

"You're probably going to need help with that, you know."

"I can manage."

After three tries with her bra, in which she failed with greater results each time, Ian appeared within the frame of the door. "Want me to help you now?"

Taylor's shoulders fell. "Yes. Please."

He moved behind her, pulled and clipped. "I can't remember a time where I added one of these back."

"There's a first for everything." Taylor managed the rest of her clothes with little difficulty.

Another knock had Ian backing up.

"It's your dad!" A cheery voice sang out.

He nodded to Taylor and opened the door as she relocated to the interior again. The man who entered was mid-fifties, maybe early sixties, if even. Behind him, his spitting image followed.

"Hi, Michael," Taylor said from her spot on the edge of the bed. "Thanks for playing laundry man."

He waved in return.

"You must be Taylor." Ian's dad came in, traditional black bag in hand.

She held out her right arm but pulled back at the shooting pain. "Yeah. Sorry, I'm—"

"In some trouble, I think." He took the desk chair, pushed it up to her. "I'm Reggie. Ian and Michael's dad." The skin tone matched Ian's lighter coloring and eyes, but he duplicated Michael's face. "So, what happened here?"

"I'm in construction and was looking at a house. Instead of fixing it up, it came down around me."

Reggie stopped his work. "You're in construction? Like, get your hands dirty kind of work?"

"Yes." The stereotypical jock-as-construction attitude and need-to-put-men-down-to-the-right-rung-on-the-ladder gene activated.

"Well, I'll be damned." Reggie turned toward Ian. "This boy wouldn't get his hands dirty if you promised him he'd be doing work in the ocean."

"I'll go in the ocean, Dad. Just not in the dirt." Ian stood with his arms crossed, leaning against the far wall. Michael slouched on the bed.

Facing Taylor, Reggie circled a finger around his ear. "Don't listen to him. Now, Tetanus shot?"

"Three years ago, I believe."

His fingers ran up the edge. "That's probably good then. May need to get you on some antibiotics. Allergic to anything?"

"No."

"Good. Good. I think it's just gotten infected. I wouldn't recommend stitches . . . we don't want to close in any bacteria. And, it's not deep, just long. Probably will be just fine and nothing to worry about. Now, Ian here, he's a whole 'nother barrel of problems."

"Wha—" Ian started.

Reggie waved him off. "He thinks he's going to get away with me checking you out and not giving you any advice about him."

"Da—"

"So, all I gotta say is, I hope you know he's never once brought a girl home to meet us. Not even for prom. Headed there and never came back."

Taylor pinched her lips together to hide the smile, though she expected her actions did no good.

"And—" Reggie withdrew a tube of some antibiotic cream and

rubbed it along the gash. "He's never talked about anyone like he has you. His mom would be up here telling you all these things if she didn't get queasy at the sight of a bug bite." His deft hands added to the soothing sensation along her skin. "She made me promise to embarrass him on her behalf."

A peek at Ian, and his hands covered his face.

"He used to find baby animals and pretend he was their doctor. Never had a problem getting them to go into the box so he could save them. Always had a problem letting them out afterward." Gauze wrapped back around Taylor's arm. "Then, he went off to college and didn't follow in his father's footsteps. Never totally understood that, but hey, what can you do?" His gaze bored right into Taylor.

"Nothing?" she asked.

"Exactly." His lips curved. "Gotta just keep on movin'. Keep on keepin' on. I'll have one more doctor in the family eventually." His head tilted toward Michael. "Until then, Ian's done just fine—he and Tripp."

Taylor couldn't stop the grin. Parents loved to gush about their kids to the complete and utter embarrassment of those kids—no matter their age.

"So, Dr. Sands—"

"Reggie, doll. Call me Reggie. Dr. Sands is for the people who pay for my house, cars, office, etcetera."

Taylor giggled, falling in love with Ian's dad. Her heart lurched as her gaze met Ian's. *Yes, I am falling in love with him. And I'm a hundred percent sure that means again.*

How is that possible?

Ian's mom met them at the entrance to the hospital where Grams had been admitted.

"Hello, gorgeous." Her fingers went straight to his cheeks, pinching like she always did. He kissed both her cheeks, and she pulled him in for a tight hug. "Now, tell me why this beautiful, young woman hasn't been up here before." She let go and moved to Taylor, taking her hand and tugging her in for a hug of equal size before Ian could warn her about Taylor's ribs.

"It's nice to meet you Mrs. Sands," Taylor said. Ian noted her pursed lips just before she said it.

"Oh, call me Georgia." Her hands ran up and down Taylor's good arm. "I'm just so honored that you'd make this trip with Ian and Michael. You're such a sweetheart to do that." His mom hooked her arm through Taylor's and led them through the outer doors.

His dad's hand hit Ian's shoulder. "You leave her with your mother, and you may never find her again. She's been waiting for you to bring someone home for so long I think she just may adopt her."

"I've brought girl—wom—people home before." Ian thought back as he said it.

"Nope. Not a one," Michael said from his other side.

"That's not helping, bro."

"How long you know this one, Ian? A day? Few weeks? A year? How long you been keeping her from us?" his dad asked.

Forever plus three lifetimes, I think. "Week and a half . . . ish."

"That's not true," Michael said as they met up with Taylor and Georgia at the elevator. "You probably saw her, Dad. At the wedding."

Ian grabbed Michael in the headlock he'd wanted to use on the airplane.

Laughter rang out from their parents, yet neither tried to stop the melee. Onto the elevator, they continued with Ian overpowering his smaller, younger and less powerful brother into submission. As the doors opened again, Michael said, "Uncle".

Ian let him free. "You're damn right you lose."

"Boys, now, let's be on our best behavior for your grandmother." His mom clicked her nails against the surface of the nurse's desk before asking for Mae Sands.

"Hey, bro." Michael crooked a finger at Ian.

Ian leaned in close.

"You remember Jessie from way back when?"

"Little nerd girl from next door?" Ian asked.

"Yeah. She works here. If you see her, I'm not here. Got that?"

Ian furrowed his brow. "Why?"

"Long, long, long, long time ago story."

A chuckle came from a room down the hall and had Ian turning his head. "I think I know where Grams is." He didn't even wait but grabbed Taylor's hand and pulled her with him. "Dibs!"

"Why are we hurrying?" she asked.

Ian shot a glance over his shoulder. "Because if I don't get you in there and introduce you to Grams, they will, and it'll go like, 'Ian's brought a woman with him, Grams. Aren't you surprised?' and it'll go on and on and on like that." They reached the door as the shuffle of feet hurried behind them.

After the knock, Gram's voice called out, "Come in already. What are you waiting for?"

Ian passed through the curtain, Taylor in tow.

"Ian!" Grams's wrinkly old-lady face lit up. Her gray hair had been slicked back into a bun just as she liked it. Deep-set, mocha eyes brightened, and she pulled her standard red robe tight around her shoulders before holding out her arms.

He slipped from Taylor's grip, but waved her forward as he dove in for a hug only Grams could give. For a ninety-six year old, her embrace rivaled that of a WWF wrestler.

"Why are you in here, Grams?" Ian asked.

"Boy, I don't know." She patted his cheek. "They just keep saying they want to make sure nothing's broken, yet I already been through so many tests and x-rays ... can't they tell already?" She patted his other side. "Enough about me, though. Who's this doll you've brought with you?"

Ian turned to Taylor, waved her forward and slid his palm

against hers. "This is Taylor Marsh, Grams. She's . . . ah . . . she's my girlfriend." Saying it out loud sent happiness through him.

Grams motioned with a finger for Taylor to come near. "Let me look at you, dear."

Taylor stepped forward but didn't let go of Ian's hand.

"Lean down here."

She did as asked, shooting glances at Ian.

Grams cupped Taylor's chin in her palm, turned her head right and left as if studying her form and figure like a horse. Ian expected her to ask Taylor to show off her teeth at any moment.

"You're a nice fine specimen there, aren't you?"

Taylor chuckled. "Specimen, ma'am?"

"Ooh! We got us a southern girl. Ian, you did this right. You're heading back to the roots." She patted his hand, leaving Taylor to stand upright again.

"Grams, I don't have anyone." Ian turned to Taylor. "She's got me."

The door to the room opened with a cursory 'knock-knock' said by Ian's mom. "Sorry, Mama Sands, but we gave you all three whole minutes to schmooze before we just had to come in."

"Now, Georgia, you know I'm fine. Don't know why I'm in here, and why ya'll came up, though if we can go home, I'd like that a lot." Grams pushed up as if to rise.

Everyone in the room started forward, holding out their hands as if to press her back down.

"Now, Mama," Dad said. "You know the docs here are good. I promised you'd be on your best behavior if we came up to say 'hi'."

She leaned back into the pillow and straightened her gown. "At my age, if it ain't broke, good. If it is, well, make it so I can get around. I'll stay until three in the p.m., and you three can take me home." She nodded to Michael, Ian and their dad in succession.

"Let's just wait and see what the professionals say, Mama," his dad said. "Oh, and on that note, let me step out." He nodded to Taylor. "I'll be back in ten . . . or if I'm gone longer, I've probably been suckered into some treats by a candy striper, and no one should come looking for me." He winked before the door closed behind him.

"Fine. Fine." Grams crossed her hands over her lap. "I want to know more about this beauty Ian has graced me with." One hand patted the bed on the far side, nearest Michael.

Without even saying anything to her, Taylor hitched a hip up and sat on the side of the bed.

"So, darling. Ian a courtin' ya yet?"

Taylor bit at her lips as if to tamp down her smile, though Ian knew his grandmother would love every inch of the expression. "I'm not much into . . . courting."

"Just like his daddy. After the one girl, and she gave in way too soon."

Ian's mom chuckled behind her hand. Michael flopped into the visitor's chair.

Grams turned to him. "You over there."

He sat upright. "Yeah, Grams?"

"You need to take a lesson from this here brother of yours. Don't wait until you're ancient to marry right. I had my Reginald for sixty years, I did." She rubbed at her finger where she still wore her centuries-old ring—one given to Ian's Grandpa by his mother and passed down. Only Ian's dad hadn't used it, saying his mom should keep it until her last breath.

"I'll watch every one of Ian's moves, Gram." Michael sent a wink Ian's way.

Ian offered him an eye roll in return.

"Any advice on these boys, Ms. Sands?"

"Oh, darling, call me Grams. Everyone does. As for advice? Well, they're good boys. Anyone tells you otherwise, you send them to me."

Taylor's soft laugh and touch to his Gram's hand broke any resolve Ian had at keeping Taylor just out of reach of himself.

The door opened behind them, Ian's dad returning with a vial and unopened needle. “Miss Marsh? Care to join me in the room next door?” He gave Taylor a wink and shook the package.

Ian’s mom coughed into her hand. “I-I—”

“Oh, you go on, dear,” Grams said. “We all know. Michael—” She pointed one wrinkled finger his way. “Take your mom out to those vending machines, and buy her a strong drink.”

Michael stood, took his mom’s elbow and escorted her out the door.

“You come on back once you’re done there.” Grams nodded to Taylor as she exited with Ian’s dad. “Now. You. Boy. Sit.” She patted the side of her bed.

Ian did as told.

Gram’s hands came together, her fingers running between the others until she plucked her ring off her finger and held it out. “Gimme your palm now, Ian.”

He held it out as demanded.

She dropped the ring to it, grabbed his hand and curled his fingers around it. “I’m ninety-six years old, Ian. I know things.” She tapped her temple. “I know when a man loves a woman so much he can’t see straight. You might not know it yet, but it’ll be there.”

“Grams—”

“Shush, boy. That one there?” Her head swayed back and forth. “Somethin’s there. Back in my day, we called it magic.”

Ian toyed with the ring. “Grams, I can’t—”

“You can, and you will.” Her finger tapped his knee. “Your daddy didn’t want to take my ring because I was still alive.”

Ian held back his comment about her current state.

“But, your Grandpop, well, he gave me this ring with the instruction to pass it on.”

“When you die, Grams, not now.” Ian held it out. “You’re not going anywhere.”

“How ’em I gonna pass it on then, boy? If I’m dead?” Grams chuckled her sweet old-lady sound. “And, I’m countin’ on bein’ 'round for another, oh . . . four years at least. Got to show up the world and get my presidential birthday card."

"Then, I can't take this—"

She shot him a glare from which a Navy SEAL would have cowered. "You sassin' me, boy?"

Ian's lips twitched. "No, ma'am."

"That's right. Hand me that." She pointed toward a small bag on the table across from the bed. After he'd handed it to her, she unzipped it and rifled through. Ian could only hope she wouldn't have more to force upon him. Her fingers dawdled until she leaned back with a contended sigh, a Mickey Mouse ring in place of the other on her finger. "Now, that's better. He gave me that one, too, for our fiftieth wedding anniversary." With a nod, she closed her eyes and smiled. "We went to Disney together. What a fabulous trip."

The door swished a second later. "Grams!" Michael said. "You're sprung, old lady."

She popped open her lids. "Finally, someone talked some sense into them docs."

Despite Michael's excitement, his face held a hint of worry.

Ian recognized it well.

An orderly came in wheeling a chair in front of him. "All righty, Mrs. Sands. Let's get you home."

Michael tilted his head toward Ian. "Outside."

Michael pushed Ian to the hallway's wall. Staff milled about, laughter rang through the air, but the scent of antiseptic permeated the space.

Ian spun them so he could keep an eye on Gram's door for when they brought her out. "What do you need, Michael?"

"Um . . . this is going to sound really weird, but I got a call from Marcie—on the team testing that bone?"

"Yeah?" As Ian acknowledged his brother, Taylor and his dad

stepped from the other room.

"Well ... they're still running tests, but they did this one quick one, and they look for these markers and—" He blew out a breath. "And, well, they all match." His finger scratched at the side of his head.

"Match what?" Ian's heart stumbled as Taylor smiled.

"Um ... Taylor's DNA matches the DNA from the bone ... for those markers."

"What? How's that possible? Isn't that as unique as fingerprints?"

"Yeah. It is. Unless she's an identical twin. Thus why they think something went wrong." Michael wrung his hands. "We're all still in school, man. Marcie's got the most experience of us all, but maybe you guys need to let the pros do this stuff."

"Do it again."

Taylor joined them as Michael finished up. "Do what again? You two look like you're conspiring."

Without a thought, Ian wrapped his arm around Taylor's waist and pulled her against him. "Nope. Just chitchatting about Grams going home."

"Yes, yes, yes, I am," the woman of the moment said. "And none too soon, I must tell you. These hospitals are full of germs I don't need."

Taylor turned toward Grams, a smile on her face. Before she rounded the halfway point, her face went slack, and her body collapsed to the ground.

20

Her body lays across a pyre but not in effigy. A single flame flies toward the mound, thrown by his own hand. As the fire grows upon the rise, he stands at its edge—a perimeter made for a single witness.

Orange bleeds into blue. Blue to red. The colors sear the wood, smoldering and igniting under her unmoving form. Each lick of flame emboldens him.

Searing heat licks her toes and dances its way toward her ankles, thighs and arms. Her body jolts, though she does not attempt escape—the centerpiece to her own life's finale.

His lips curve upward.

A scream fills the air, sending birds to the sky—the flapping of wings barely audible over the building inferno's roar.

He bristles—a momentary worry she may rise from death's clutches.

The blaze accepts her body as its fuel. Kindling snaps. Sparks fly upward, adding to the smoke-fogged air.

He twirls a single red rose between his fingertips, thorns digging into his pads. His gaze remains fixed on the fire, and the woman who can no longer be defined.

Deer run from one side of the clearing to the other, away from the unceasing heat. Not even nature wishes to be beholden to the man, yet it cannot separate itself from his deed.

A bellow sounds from the center of the pile as it collapses upon itself. Cascading rivers of liquid flow along the sides.

The fire sings, whistling a deep tune and claiming, for itself, everything within its reach.

He remains in place, a grin reaching across his face, growing with each crackle.

Each pop.

"In death, we have parted." The rose twists between his fingers until flakes and dust settle in the center of the destruction, a wide circle where once her body laid as if at rest.

A dying spark sustains itself as if holding out hope for more fuel. He crushes it underfoot, stomping out the final vestiges of life on the scorched patch of earth. "No man, save me, shall ever have your love."

A flicker of blue catches his eye. On bent knee, he runs a fingertip over a soft, velvet square. That it survived the fury surprises him, yet he does not react, for he has already accomplished his mission.

He holds out the rose, its bloom full and bright. It hovers above the center of ash. "Never again will you betray me." Decisive contempt fuels his voice.

He opens his hand.

The flower drops to the ground, sending puffs of white ash into the air.

"The betrayer reaps her own sorrows."

Her demise is his success.

Taylor could no longer differentiate between realities. Words held no meaning. Time meant nothing. Fire consumed her. For all she knew, her body laid across a pile of wood. She tried to move, yelled and screamed at herself to fight, to rise, to depart.

None of it worked.

Tanner's face etched itself in her mind's eye. That followed with Ian's. Round and round they went, mixing and merging within her dream state.

Flames.

Bath.

Falling house.

Fire.

Water.

Earth.

The hotter the air flamed around her, the more she cried out. Whether sound escaped, she didn't know. Encompassed by flames, soaring and shooting into the sky, and crying out within her mind, she managed to turn enough to take in a blaze around her. To see it grab her calves, circle her arms and melt her skin.

A form stood to the side—the silhouette of a man she'd loved for centuries.

She called for John over and over, begging him to stop. To help. To cease. To save her. To kill her.

If her heart could tear in two, it would have. The only emotions she had left sizzled as the fire took everything away.

Her view moved to pure darkness.

Ian slumped against the wall outside Taylor's hospital room door as nurses and doctors rushed in for the fifth time in as many hours.

Codes had been called. Numbers rang out. A controlled panic followed. Taylor's temperature soared. Her body riddled with a fever reaching above one-hundred and seven degrees had nurses and doctors working every bit of magic they possessed to prevent brain damage.

He slid until his butt hit the floor, and his head fell into his hands, balanced against pulled-up knees. Night had passed with a flurry of activity. Grams had gone home, Michael to his hotel, and Ian's parents to theirs. Taylor, though, she'd never regained consciousness. Morning had calmed, but with the five o'clock hour on Monday, chaos reigned again.

"Here." Michael's voice reached Ian. "You need to drink. Eat. Nourish yourself before you fade to gray."

Ian's head lifted, though the strain on his muscles from sleeping in a chair and sitting slumped over for much of the time sent tingles of numbness through him. He took the cup from Michael and breathed in the hot chocolate. "Thanks." A sip seared his lips but gave way to pleasure.

"Let's go to the lounge."

"I want to stay." Ian drank more, letting the cocoa wash away the grit in his throat. The nurses and doctors all thought Ian her fiancé, so they'd given him special concession to remain with her. He didn't want to lose his status or the opportunity. He needed to be there—compelled by unspoken, inner forces.

"I need to talk to you."

"You can talk here." The door slammed open and shut as another cart of something-or-other breezed by.

"No, Ian. We can't. You're distracted and worried . . . and waiting for them to call out numbers that would mean she's dead."

"I am not."

"Are too. Now come on. I have some news." Michael lifted Ian with a heave.

With a feigned reluctance, he rose and went with his brother into the lounge, the space empty, and closed door blocking the hospital sounds. "Okay, what?"

Michael pulled a seat from beneath the table and pointed to the one across from him. "Sit."

"I was sitting. Out there. Where I could listen."

"You really are into this chick, aren't you?"

Ian yanked the chair from under the table and fell into it. "Okay. Now what?"

"I want you to talk to Marcie."

"Who?" Ian dropped his head to the table.

"Marcie. She's a forensic geneticist who's decided to go to med school. She took a creative writing class elective that I was in."

Ian wobbled his head against the surface.

"She's part of the team I assembled for you . . . for that girl you're dying to find out stuff about."

"Oh." Exhaustion took away Ian's ability to be excited about talking to a member of Michael's team. The beep of cell phone numbers being pressed had him popping up his head. "Now?

"Yes."

"Fine, I'll—" Ian stopped at the shuffle and muffled voices on the other end of the line.

"Um, hello?" A sweet, Indian voice joined them.

"Marcie?" Michael asked.

"Yes, this is."

"Hey. This is Michael. I have my brother here."

"Oh, many thank yous for calling."

Ian nodded.

"She can't see you nodding, bro. Go ahead, Marcie, tell him what you told me a few minutes ago."

"My apologies for the interruption, but Michael wanted me to give you results … straight from the horse's ass."

Ian snorted a laugh. "I believe you mean straight from the horse's mouth?"

"Right, yes, sir."

Oh, please don't call me sir.

"I am to tell you, in no uncertain terms, that the DNA markers between a Miss Taylor Marsh and this bone sample are the same. I am so sorry for your loss."

She's watched way too much television drama. "She's not dead," Ian's hands clenched together on the tabletop. "Can you test it again—"

"No," Michael said. "It's conclusive. If Marcie says it, it's the truth. I told you, man, she has the most experience of any of us."

"Mr. Ian?" Marcie's sweetness came through again. "You say she is not dead? Why do we have a rib then?"

"That's a long story. Are you absolutely, positively—"

Michael held up a hand.

"The percent margin of error is point O-O-O-O-O-one."

"It couldn't be a family member or—"

"No," Marcie said.

"Is there anything else you can tell me about the bone?" Ian scratched at the side of his head.

"Ah . . ." Paper shuffling came through the microphone. "The bone comes from a female, approximately nineteen to thirty-one years of age." Marcie stopped for a moment. "We date the bone at one hundred and twenty years." More rattling and dings came through. "That is all."

"Thanks, Marcie," Michael said.

She clicked off.

"How can your girlfriend . . ." Michael pointed out the closed door. ". . . who is very much alive . . . also be dead?" His brows came together in the middle.

Ian slouched further against the table, thoughts of Sherrill's photo from a hundred years ago, the tattoo, the symbolic nature of it and the potential for reincarnation.

"Even identical twins, whose DNA matches ninety-nine point nine, nine, nine percent of markers, have some differences. I'd say the odds are pretty impossible unless Taylor's been cloned."

There can only be one answer.

Ian shipped Michael off in the plane the next day, vowing again to stick to Taylor's side. He'd added a 'please go ask the hot blonde out and get details on the genealogy question', though didn't tell Michael why. His hunches didn't always work out, and he didn't have a particular one about the photo or details Sherrill had given them, but a vibe told him to look into it.

Yet, as he stood outside Taylor's open door, peering in, he wondered how much his presence or any of the tasks he'd undertaken helped or would even matter if she didn't survive.

If her fourth life ended in the hospital's ICU in Rochester, New York.

A rush of staff brought at least half a dozen people into the room, and just as had happened before, for the second day in a row, her body heated up like a small inferno. People moved around each other, running wires and lines from walls to Taylor's bed.

Still Ian stood, watching.

"Mr. Sands?" A lab-coated doctor stood in front of him.

"Yes?" Ian ran a hand over his head.

"I have in my notes that Ms. Marsh was brought in last week, in . . . ah . . . ." He flipped over his paper.

"North Carolina," Ian said.

"Yes . . . for a reported drowning, is this correct?"

Ian nodded.

"And just recently, she was nearly buried by a collapsing house?"

"She just got a gash from that. It didn't cover her or anything."

"Her body's immune system may simply be struggling to maintain itself after the two events" The doctor tapped his pen on the clipboard. "We'll keep working on her. I'm not giving up."

Me neither.

A call out of 'Doctor' left Ian alone again.

Love couldn't be the reason he wanted to stay. He didn't know Taylor long enough to love her. Yet, something inside him compelled him to be at her side, and with each passing hour, that connection grew stronger, even as she failed to heal.

His cell buzzed. Ian reached for it, pressed against his eyelids and said, "Hi, Michael."

"Oh, my God, Ian. You are not going to believe this."

He wanted to say, 'Try me', but fatigue and stress ruined his sense of humor.

"I talked to Janie—that's the girl who's in the library—the one I was telling you about."

"Yeah, yeah," Ian said. "I remember."

"So, get this. She's working on a 'Six degrees of separation' thesis, trying to prove that everyone is related."

Ian waved a hand through the air to speed up his brother, forgetting for a moment they were in different cities. "Got it.

Move on."

"Yeah, so I'm telling her about you and blondie, and she says, 'Well, why don't you just Google it and see what comes up?' So, I sat next to her at the table, you know, feeling her out a little. She's hot in that nerdy, I-know-more-than-you way."

"Michael, please. My head can't take it."

"Oh, yeah. Sorry, bro. So, we're talking, and she flips open her laptop. A few clicks later, she's at a website that traces people's ancestry back for . . . ages. And, since she's working on this project, they've given her free access. So, she types in George and Marge's names. Gets Marge's parents as Loren and Amelia, finds out they lived on Weaton Farm—"

Ian shivered at the name of the farm.

"—which is in North Carolina. Turns out it's about three miles from Lexi and Tripp's. Anyway, they were a big sharecropping farm way back when. It's a massive, five thousand home neighborhood now, but the original structure is still there."

Ian would have stopped Michael since he knew that part of the story, thanks to Sherril, though the relational location to Taylor's home unnerved him.

"So, she takes a few more clicks and finds out Weaton Farm is connected to an unsolved murder from the eighteen hundreds."

Ian dropped into a chair in the lounge, but his body stayed tense.

"I mean, man, she gets all this from a simple Google search. I didn't even know they still keep data on crimes, murders and crazy shit like that from way back when." Michael's breathing increased as if he'd been walking up a flight of stairs.

A tremor ran the length of Ian's form as a screech accompanied a slam of a door through the phone. "Where are you, Michael?"

"Taking a walk back toward the Genetics Lab. Been on my way since I called."

"Did they find something new?"

Another squeal. "I don't know, but I said I'd check in. Hey,

Marcie," Michael said.

Ian kept the phone at his ear but dropped his elbows to the table.

"It gets better, too. The case is about a local girl. She disappeared one night. Poofed into nothingness. Fingers were pointed straight at one of the local farmers. He, on the other hand, had not disappeared and was tried—" Michael snorted. "—Tried, my ass, and hanged for her murder despite never finding the body. Typical of the day, but geez. That bites."

"So, okay, last bit before I let you go. According to good ole search engine number one, the farmer was Jack Howard Mchanga, and the girl was Isabella Claire, last name T-A-I-L-O-R."

Taylor Claire Marsh.

"She was apparently the local tailor's daughter, and he was ... apparently nothing but a farmer."

A farmer.

Shuffling filled the earpiece. "You know ... if a white girl and one of us were shacking up back then ... boy, that would've been ... I can't even say it out loud. I looked 'em up, too. The info I found listed her birthday as June twelfth, eighteen sixty-five, and the day she went missing as May thirty-first, eighteen eighty-five—"

Nineteen years old.

"—and his birthday wasn't noted, but his date of death was November seventeenth, eighteen eighty-five."

My birthday. Shit. Shit. Shit.

"Skin color did dangerous things back then," Michael said.

A bone that matches Taylor's DNA. A photo that looks like us. A murder. Who killed her? Me, because we couldn't be together? Is that why she's seen my face? Aw, shit. This can't be good.

Ian jumped from his seat, whipped open the door and started for Taylor's room, intent on grabbing her wallet for a look at her license. People continued to go in and out. He spun toward the nurse's station, his breath coming in fits, and a mounting worry tickling the base of his skull.

Maryanne, one of those who'd befriended him, tilted up from her computer. "What can I do for you, Ian?"

"Really weird question—"

"Ian?" Michael's voice came through the phone's speaker.

"Let me call you back." With the close of his phone, Ian took a deep breath. The nurses on the unit all thought him the greatest fiancé ever, not knowing he had no formal connection to Taylor. "This is going to sound weird, but ..." He sucked in more air. "Could you tell me Taylor's birthday?"

Maryanne cocked her head. "You don't remember her birthday? Typical male." She waved him away but typed on the keyboard. "Ah ... June 12—"

Shit. He held up the phone. "I gotta—I gotta go make a phone call." He walked away without another look back.

These people are us.

And I killed her.

21

Heart pounding, Ian raced toward the hospital exit, desperate for sunshine and a lack of coincidences. He hit send on the phone as he reached the doors, his palm slapping his forehead on his burst outside. "Well, shit."

Twilight engulfed the front courtyard. The entire day had passed, and he hadn't even noticed.

"Hey, man," Tripp answered on the second ring. "How's—"

"It's official . . . we've been reincarnated. And, something happened to us last time that ended up with me dead and her missing." Having spewed out the words faster than he'd expected to, Ian dropped to the bench. He breathed in the night air. Crickets or cicadas chirped behind him as cars rushed by on a road he couldn't see, thanks to buildings blocking his view.

"What the hell are you talking about?"

Ian leaned his head down to knee level. "Her DNA matches that bone we took."

"I know. You called me yesterday. We said we'd keep looking."

"And, Michael did some genealogy digging. Turns out her disappearance is still floating around the Internet. From a hundred years ago!"

"Okay, but how do you know it's you and her?"

"Current girl is Taylor Claire Marsh. The girl Michael found was Isabella Claire Tailor."

"That's not—"

"Current boy is me. Past boy was Jack Harold Mchanga."

Tripp chuckled. "Your middle name is Harold."

"Exactly. And Jack is another word for John, and that for Ian. And she yells 'John' in her sleep sometimes."

"All coinciden—"

"No." Ian shook his head, sucking in air. "Mchanga is Swahili for 'sands'. Ian Harold Sands. We are those people in the picture, Tripp. He was hanged November seventeenth—"

"Your birthday."

"And her birthday is June twelfth, which is also actually her birthday." Ian stood, paced toward the small fountain and back. "It all fits. I know it. I feel it." *Just like I feel the tie-in with her.* "There is no question. Sherrill said her grandparents saw the two people from the photo together. They couldn't be together. Class and skin color would have prevented it. Then ... she disappeared. Someone pointed a finger at him, the town said it was me ... and he—I—he was hanged. Rightly so if he—me—I killed her."

"Well, if that's the case, be happy you aren't them, then. You're you ... today. Without race and class restrictions. Sounds to me like you're getting a second chance. Or, in your case, a fourth."

Ian nodded to no one. "Exactly what I think. Damn finger tattoo. But this is ridiculous, you know? This doesn't happen to normal people." *I wouldn't kill someone.*

Tripp laughed. "Like what Lexi and I can do? Or Taylor?"

"You never said anything about what she could do."

"Did you think I would?"

Ian shook his head. "Of course not."

"Good. So, maybe it's all connected. You know, me, Lex, Sherrill, Marge, George, you, Taylor."

"I'm not Zeus's pawn, Tripp. This isn't a game. You knew what you had to deal with. That was a game. It can't be when the rules aren't obvious or clear or even defined. Zeus wasn't that mad."

"Think again." Tripp chuckled again. "No one ever said Zeus didn't stick things to people, Ian. So ... what're you going to do?"

Ian ran a hand over his head, digging his fingers into his scalp.

"I have no fucking idea."

"Think through this logically. If what you said is true . . . and you are them from before, and you did—though I'm not saying you did—kill her before, and this is try number four, maybe this time you're supposed to find a way not to do it. Maybe you're not the Romeo and Juliet type this time around, but you're the kick ass and take names."

"This is *not* a game."

"Okay. Okay, man. We'll go with that theory for now. How is Taylor, by the way?"

"Fucked up." Ian went on to fill Tripp in.

Would a god pit two people against each other who also might love each other? What kind of sickness is that?

"You sound tired, Ian."

"I'm exhausted. Have you ever tried to sleep on a guest chair for anything other than a nap?"

Tripp's mirth diffused more of Ian's tension. "No, and I hope I never have to. But try to get some sleep. A few hours, at least."

"Yeah. I need to. Maybe I'll crash on a couch in the lobby." Ian traipsed back into the brightness of the hospital, to the zing of antiseptic and night cleaning routine. A buffer whizzed and spun to the right, so Ian went left.

Lexi's voice calling for ice cream overruled Tripp's. "Gotta go. Get some rest. If there's one thing I've learned about being a pawn to Zeus, it's that I work better when well rested. Or after lots of sex."

Ian snorted a chuckle—the first of the night—and hung up. As he walked the hall, the signs for 'Blood Bank' and 'Donation Center' gave him another idea. He slowed as he approached the double doors.

"Ian?"

He turned at the female voice. The woman walking toward him made him want to give Taylor up or consider a threesome. A moment of recognition hit him, but he couldn't place her face with the Asian-set, green eyes, toned skin, the clipped back, long, black hair or beautiful smile.

As he stared, a flood of memories hit him.

Of the bratty girl-next-door who followed Michael around like a lovesick puppy. The same girl he wanted to not see, though Ian had to guess Michael hadn't gotten a good look at her in a few years. He'd have changed his mind for sure if he had.

"Uh ... Jessie?" Ian hadn't seen her since she'd been twelve, so he could have been wrong, but he didn't think so.

"Yeah." She stepped to him, offered him a short hug and let go. "How are you? What are you doing here? I thought you lived in the big city." Her hands wiggled in the air like he'd seen dancers do on stage.

That and the contrast with the white lab coat sent a wave of confusion through his overtired brain. Jessie'd been Michael's tag-along, the younger sibling he never had and never wanted. She couldn't have been more than twenty-three to Michael's twenty-five. The firmed figure, braces-less teeth and smooth skin would have appealed to anyone. Ian kept all his comments and thoughts to himself, realizing he'd been staring for far too long.

"Uh ... Ian? What *are* you doing here?" She ran a hand along his arm.

Good question. "Here with a friend." *Lover. Multiple lifetime partner? Victim?* He didn't know how to describe Taylor.

Jessie cocked a hand on her hip. Her laugh breached the barrier and had his own grin sneaking out. "Girlfriend, Ian? Fiancée? Wife?"

"Could be a guy friend." He offered her a shrug, though she'd been dead on.

She zipped back and held up her hands. "Right, right. Okay. You look like you haven't slept in days. From what I recall, you and sleep were well acquainted. I can't see you staying awake long nights for a 'guy friend', unless ..."

"Oh, no. It's not like that." He rubbed at his eyes as exhaustion overwhelmed them, and pressure wanted to force his lids closed. "She's . . . yeah . . . fuck." Ian banged his head against the cement wall. "I need—"

"Someone to talk to?"

"No. To do something. Productive."

"It's nearly midnight. Maybe you should get some sleep?"

He waved a hand. "Shit. I was thinking I should go give blood."

Jessie guided him away from the doors. "They aren't going to take you in this state. You'll give them the impression you're a walking germ-pool. You need sleep, Ian. Have you pulled out the chair in the room? It's not great, but better than sitting upright."

The chair pulls out? Holy fucking cow! Why didn't anyone mention that?

They continued walking down the hallway. "Who's your girl?"

"Taylor Marsh." He said it with such a monotone even he didn't recognize his own voice.

Jessie the pig-tailed ten-year-old, at least in Ian's mind, stopped and smiled up at him. "Room five-twelve?"

He nodded.

Her brows creased. "Really?"

"Yes. Why?"

She hesitated. "She's a really popular case around here, and I've just been assigned to the team."

"Ian, it's Dr. Mathias—I mean, Jessie."

Jessie? Pressure on his shoulder stirred him enough to flutter his lids open. An inhale brought an over-clean, sterile scent and a hammering heart. He flipped over and stared into the wide eyes of her face. "Jessie?" A hand down his face didn't wake him as much as her expression. "What's wrong? Why are you—Is everything okay?" He shot a glance toward Taylor and her bed.

Jessie nodded. "She's stable."

Slow beeps filled his mind from the monitors attached to

Taylor. "What time is it?" Ian asked.

Jessie tilted her watch up. "Six."

Ian whirled on her. *I actually slept for three hours on the pullout.* "No wonder I gotta pee like a bitch." He'd spent the two hours after he'd met Jessie doing exactly what Tripp suggested—scouring the Internet for historical data.

Jessie hid her chuckle behind a hand. "I can get you a urinal."

"I don't think so."

"Go relieve yourself and come see me at the desk. I gotta leave, but I have a question for you. And, if you want to freshen up, best to do so before the staff changes at seven."

"I'll be out in a sec." Ian maneuvered himself to the bathroom, emptied out a day's worth of liquid, scrubbed at four-day's worth of scruff and splashed water on his face. Wrinkles had taken over his clothes, and he reeked from the soap he had to wash his hands with every time he even touched Taylor.

"You look like shit," he said to himself. "How the hell did you end up babysitting a girl you barely know, who can't talk to you and who you might have murdered?" He dropped his head, pounded his fist against his heart and stared back into his own eyes. "You better find something that makes all this all go away." At his exit from the room, Jessie's head popped up from behind a screen.

She fisted her hand. "You love her, don't you?"

"Uh . . ."

Jessie chuckled. Her eyes darted to the left and right. Night and morning staff had already begun their change of shift. "Come with me." She led Ian to the conference room again and closed the door once he'd entered.

"You're holding back." A shiver of worry hit him. "What is it?"

"No. I just wanted to ask you something."

"Okay."

"The ring—design—tattoo thing on her finger. It matches yours."

"Yeah, it does." The hairs on the back of his neck stood up. "How did you—"

"I remember a lot of stuff from when I was little, Ian." Her lips curved. "Are you guys … is that a new kind of marriage thing?"

He ran a hand over his head. "No. Not like that."

She bobbled her head. "It bugged the living daylights out of me when I saw that design yesterday during rounds and couldn't remember *where* I'd seen it. Seeing you brought it all back."

"Brought what back?"

"Um … so, I studied in Greece for a summer—two years ago. Wanted to broaden my horizons, as they say …"

Translation: Find a man.

"… and the woman I lived with had a tapestry on the wall. It was of that tattoo you have—which … why put it around your finger? I always wanted to know. It had to hurt, what with the sensitivity of the skin there and—"

Ian held up a hand. "It was just the right place, that's all." He dropped into a chair.

"But on your finger?" She held up both hands and waved them. "Sorry, that's getting too personal. She told me about it—the design, that is. What a history."

"Your hostess did? What did she say about it?" Ian leaned back.

Jessie's cheeks flushed, her eyes dipping down and returning. "You really want to know?"

Ian nodded.

"So … she said to me, 'Jessica … you need man in life. Man need bosom of woman to survive. Man who not play games. Not man with lifes.' I had no idea what she was talking about. Still don't really, but she was so sweet and so kind. I actually thought—" Jessie shook her head and waved, dropping her hand to the back of a chair. In her prim and proper, I'm-a-doctor-and-you're-not posture, she said, "My profession teaches me to listen, learn, take in the facts and find answers. So … naturally … I asked her to tell me more, and I spent three hours enraptured, listening with a big glass of wine in hand."

He remembered Jessie's incessant curiosity. It had been one of the many reasons she followed Michael around as a kid, always asking questions of him or of Ian. He hitched up his chin, dropping it against his palms, waiting for her to go on. When she didn't, he said, "Maybe you could tell me more? What else you learned? I do love a good story."

"You *really* want to hear it? It's just an old ... romantic thing." Jessie sat and clasped her fingers together on the table, cheeks flushing again.

Damn right, I want to hear it. "It would be good for me to think about non-medical issues for a while, don't you think? And, I do have this thing, so the stories are all ... cool to know."

Jessie turned her watch toward herself. She nodded. "Yeah. Okay." Her gaze met Ian's again even as those cheeks burned.

Why the continued blushing?

"She called the design 'love roots'. Now, before you freak out—Adonia was the local storyteller. Big on tale. Small on funds. That's why she took in boarders. And, some people paid her for her stories, believing they would extract wisdom or prophecy. So, the longer the story, the better for her. 'I give you for free,' she said to me." Jessie wagged her hands back and forth.

Ian wanted to say, 'Move on with it', but he held his lips shut, waiting for her to proceed.

"Anyway ... Adonia said the design was a symbol of a game." Jessie sighed just a tiny bit.

Shit. Shit. And triple shit. This is *a game.*

"The game begins with the design appearing—" She pointed to Ian's finger. "—and ends in someone's death. All good Greek stories do, right?" She chuckled behind her hand.

Yeah. Sure. Ian nodded her forward.

"The little root things are like the scoreboard. They show the number of tries the person has to find and win their soul mate's love or be destined to an eternity of searching but never finding.

Think Romeo and Juliet in Greek." She flicked her finger against the table, cheeks flaming again. "'Make sure find love', she said. She was always giving me advice."

So, the thing we didn't get right is finding each other? But, there's a picture of us. If we found each other before, then we succeeded. We won. Right? Ian sat up straighter.

"Wouldn't that suck? To do something over and over without resolution, and when the finale comes, if you've failed, you live for eternity without the one thing you wanted most?" She lifted up toward Ian, with a look of longing in her eyes. "You know, like Sisyphus, the one who had to roll a rock uphill only to have it fall back down every time?"

"Uh, yeah. Very true." *How is it a game if we found each other before? Aren't we meant to be together?*

"Of course, with the Greeks, there's always a catch."

And, here comes more.

"'Tree without earth, weak. Tree with earth, strong.' That's what she said, anyway. I really have no idea what it means. But . . . I gathered, since it's related to roots, that if the two don't have a foundation somehow, they aren't strong enough to stand together, and they fail."

"How do you know who's playing the game?"

Jessie pitched her head to the side. "Uh . . . I don't know. Does it matter? I mean, it is all a crazy story about unrequited love and the tragedy that is everyone's life when they don't care for the one right there in front of them." She turned, eyes toward the floor. "Or don't care back."

Ian forced a laugh. "Right. Would suck to be those two, wouldn't it?" He pushed out another chuckle for show.

She waved a jewel-less hand through the air. "So, anyway, you get the picture."

What does all this mean?

The redness returned to Jessie's face. "Maybe never to give up? Never look at someo—something as nothing more than—" She shrugged and picked at a nail.

Once again, Ian didn't realize he'd spoken out loud. He had to get a handle on his mental ramblings.

Jessie ran a finger in a loop on the table and sighed. Her chin lifted, cheeks brightening again. As quickly as she'd risen, she dropped her head to her arms on the table. "I'm sorry, Ian."

"What for?"

Face muffled by the table, she said, "Seeing you here. You just . . . bring back a lot of memories."

"I hope some of them are good ones."

Jessie oh so slowly dipped her head down and back a few times before lifting up and turning her watch toward herself. "Hey, it's way past my bedtime." She rose and held out a hand, and Ian shook it. "I hope I don't see you again . . . I mean tonight . . . or tomorrow. I'm off. Sorry—" Hand through hair, she took a deep breath and said, "You know what I mean, right? I hope your girl heals quickly. Don't give up on her, Ian. Medicine is part art, part luck and part science. There's no telling what we don't actually know despite the amount of study we've had. Every person is different, and while their physiology is basically the same, what works for one person may not for another."

"That why you already wear a lab coat and Michael doesn't?"

Her face couldn't have gone redder.

Michael. Unrequited love. She have a thing for him still?

Jessie angled her head down before lifting it back to face Ian. "I skipped the second and the seventh grades, Ian. When you're frumpy, really smart and your parents don't want you to get involved with the boy next door, and the boy next door wants nothing to do with you, the next best thing is to dive into school. I finished college at nineteen and got accepted to medical school at twenty." Jessie stopped. She fidgeted. "Hey, you know, if you see him, tell him—well just tell him I said 'hi', okay?"

Still in love with the boy next door. The story only brought up those memories. "Yeah, sure."

"Take care, Ian." With that, she walked away.

Ian stayed in his chair, thinking through Jessie's story. He put what he'd learned about the design, the symbolism with his blips of memories he knew he didn't have, Taylor's call out of 'John', Michael's revelation that Ian, as John, had killed her in their last life, too, her drowning and the bones.

It all swirled in an unintelligible mess with one big question looming.

Why did I kill her if we were together?

Fire.

Dreams.

Sounds.

Pain.

Darkness.

Water.

Cold.

Earth.

Air.

Taylor drew in a breath. Her lungs brought in cool freshness. A thought to herself suggested she let it free. Her lungs obeyed.

I'm alive.

She tried to force her eyes open, but the action revealed nothing but solid black.

Her body shivered, or so it seemed.

Tuning in for sound brought her nothing.

Am I alive?

A squeeze of her hands gave her no sense of touch.

What the hell is happening?

She tried to move her shoulders, but her arms failed to budge. Pressure built at her back.

My hands. Why are my hands tied behind me?

Taylor gasped, her breath catching in her throat, memories and thoughts jumbling together without coherence.

Ian!

At the thought of his name, her heartbeat slowed. Quiet took over until her mind no longer whirred.

He'd loved her.

Calm.

She'd loved him.

Freedom.

She'd said goodbye.

Torment.

He'd killed her.

Hate.

Neither wanted to be separated.

Desperation.

Both vowed to return.

Desire.

One failed to accept.

Insanity.

22

Feet shuffled around Ian as he stood at the counter again. A cup of toffee-flavored mocha from the hospital vending machine rested in his hand. His gaze stuck on the door to the room the doctors wouldn't let him re-enter while they made some adjustments to Taylor's medications.

With so many doctors, nurses and technicians going in and out, he'd stopped watching the who, just looked for any sign he could return, or that something had become worse.

A gasp and a, "Get a doctor in here!" had him tilting his head, and one of the dozen physicians who'd attended to Taylor disappeared into the room, the door not quite swinging closed behind him.

Standing at the counter left Ian with no immediate access and straining for sound.

"What's wrong with her?" A feminine voice said with a bite as strong as whiskey on a first taste.

A pen tapped against metal. "Honestly, Mrs. Marsh, we don't know."

Taylor's mom?

"Diagnostically, she's had a fever we could barely control, but tests show no infection." More taps and shuffling of papers.

"That is not an acceptable diagnosis," the woman said.

"What happened to her arm?" a deeper voice asked.

That's not Riley. Who? Her dad?

The doctor reiterated the story that had been told and retold, by Ian, by his father—to anyone who'd asked.

"Why would she be here in New York?" the woman asked.

"There's a gentleman who can answer that question for you."

The click against the tile floor suggested a tapping in place versus a walk. "What's your prognosis?" The bite of her tone wouldn't be missed by anyone and had Ian leaning his head back against the cement wall near the door.

He caught sight of a couple nurses with eyebrows raised, leaning toward each other with conspiratorial whispers.

"Right now, we don't know what's going on with your daughter. We're running through all her recent records, from her time in the detention center, the hospital in North Carolina. She could have picked up a virus."

"A detention center . . . a hospital . . ." Derision coated the woman's tone. "What on earth are you talking about?"

"Maybe we should take this outside," said the deep voice Ian assumed belonged to Taylor's father.

"I agree." Back to the doc. "We'd like to keep her the least stressed as possible."

Sounds grew louder. Ian searched for a place that wouldn't look obvious toward his eavesdropping if they noticed.

"She was in a jail?" The voice still came from within the room.

Had she not heard the doctor? Ian stood with fists clenched, preparing to give the woman a few choice words.

"Honey, relax," the man said. "Tay's a big girl. If something happened, she doesn't have to tell—"

"Don't you tell me what she should and shouldn't tell me. I'm her mother."

Bingo.

"We've been down this road once before. I won't have someone getting my daughter in trouble and—" The clicks didn't tap but grew louder. The would-be Taylor clone stood in front of Ian. "You."

He stared down into a petite, twenty-years-older face that

matched Taylor's. "Me?"

"What did you do to my daughter?" The set of her jaw and the pursed lips brought on a wicked witch effect.

Ian kept his hands in his pockets, hoping to stem his own irritation and not piss off the woman before him. "I'm sorry, what?"

"They told me you've been here with her this whole time. What did you do that would put her in here?"

"Whoa, there. I didn't *do* anything." His own tone ratcheted up a notch.

"That's exactly what that other bastard said." Her finger poked into Ian's chest.

A man Ian presumed to be Taylor's dad filled the frame of the doorway behind her, his eyes cast down to the ground with a shake of his head.

Ian pulled her finger away, banking down his anger.

"Janet," a voice called from down the hall.

She shifted. The man behind her did the same, a smile growing on his face.

Ian spun to Riley walking toward them. *Son of a bitch.* Ian's heart flip-flopped. Two men. One woman. *Riley.* Could he be the one that took their triangular existence to its end?

"Riley!" Janet ran to him, wrapped her arms around him. "Why is she here? What's going on? Why was she in jail?"

His gaze hit Ian's. "I'll explain everything I know and will tell you over a cup of coffee." His hand slipped to Janet's. "Come with me."

"Oh, no. I'm not leaving her here, helpless and—"

"Take a valium, Janet," Taylor's dad said. He ran his hand through his hair as soon as it escaped his lips. "Shit. I'm sorry. This is just—"

"Come with me," Riley said again. "You, too, Jeff."

"What about—" Janet pointed toward Ian.

"He's . . . a friend." Riley pushed at her shoulder and led Taylor's parents out the double doors of the unit. He returned a second later and held out a series of papers along with Ian's laptop bag. "I was asked to give you these."

Ian unfolded the pages as his mind reeled with possibilities. A scan gave him enough. All charges had been dropped in the arrest of Taylor Marsh. *The forensics guys finally figured out what my brother's team already did?* Ian flipped a page. "Taylor's mom wasn't even a spec in her mother's eye when those bones were buried." He continued to scan.

Riley ran a hand over his head. "Exactly. You can get your bond money back."

"I don't care about that." Ian continued to look through the paperwork, double checking that nothing remained to ruin the moment. "How did you know she was here?"

"I asked." With that, he tipped his head as if he wore an invisible cap, spun and left.

Ian pulled out his cell and pressed '1' to speed dial Tripp.

"Something up?" Tripp asked after the first ring.

"Taylor's parents and Riley just showed up. What did you tell them?"

"Nothing. They must have found out on their own." Behind Tripp, Lexi's voice broke through with unintelligible commentary. "Just pick up the phone. This would be that much easier," Tripp said.

"Hey, Ian," she said.

"Hi. So, please tell me—"

"So ... Emma heard from Janine, who served dinner to Taylor's parents last night ... that the Marsh's found out Taylor was up here. Don't know how. Didn't know they were heading up. I did wheedle out the back story. When Taylor was in jail the first time, her parents ... well ... they hadn't ... they didn't do a very good job because they were pissed she moved to Alabama in the first place. Apparently, they thought she made it all up to get attention, like she'd done when she was little. Done what, though, is the question. But anyway, they promised Taylor that if she ever found herself in the same situation, they'd be the squeaky wheel. So, it took them two weeks to get to Alabama, and by then Taylor'd gotten herself out. She doesn't have the best relationship with her mom because of it, so I'm guessing this is mom and dad's way of making up for last time."

"That's fucked up." Ian rested his arm against the wall. He thought back to his parents, to Grams and Michael. They'd have taken her in without question. Grams already loved her. He let out a deep sigh. "They don't know me from shit, so I guess all they have for their only child is what happened before. Can't blame them for that."

"Good attitude to have," she said. "Stay positive. I'm sure all will be fine. Just be nice to the in-laws."

"Not until they find out I killed her in another life. I probably put those bones there."

At Lexi's gasp, Ian filled her and Tripp in on what he'd concluded.

Back in the bed-chair in Taylor's room, Ian sniffed his pits. The stench permeated his shirt and made him realize just how long it had been since he'd showered. No one had mentioned it, but after day five, he should have gone back to the hotel. He had, after all, kept and paid for the room.

He just couldn't bring himself to leave Taylor, even if the story Michael told suggested he had been responsible for her death the last time they'd been involved. Tripp and Lexi hadn't believed it. 'Come up with a new explanation', they'd said. The mere thought of hurting Taylor tore at his heart. He leaned forward and touched her foot, the closest spot to him.

"I don't know what happened, but I'm going to find out."

When she didn't respond, he opened up his laptop, happy to have a faster tool than his phone for research.

Ian connected to the network and clicked on his email.

Distraction first, then digging. The latest message came from Tripp.

I-

Didn't mention this last night since you seemed to be processing in that brain of yours, but Jefferson Wiley from Alabama State Corrections called. He had some details re: Tanner. Look for them in your email if not already.

-T

Ian scrolled through his inbox, searching for Jefferson's name, but came up with nothing. For all he knew, the guy hadn't yet sent the info. Just in case, he checked his junk mail. Sure enough, a Mr. Jeff Wiley's name showed up in the list, having been sent two days before.

Ian clicked the link.

Mr. Sands—

Our records indicate Tanner Joseph Meadows is deceased as of…

At the knock on the door, Ian skimmed the rest and closed the laptop.

With the second knock, he said, "Come in."

Riley walked in.

Alone.

"What're you doing here, man?"

"Taylor's parents wanted me to apologize on their behalf. They're … a little distraught right now. I left them to talk over their issues before they come back up."

"You came all the way to New York to tell me they're sorry?" Ian tucked his shirt into his pants on the off chance Taylor's parents did return. For some reason, despite the lack of a fresh scent and the massive wrinkles, he wanted to make an impression—hopefully a good one.

"Actually, can we maybe go to another room for a minute?"

With a glance toward sleeping Taylor, her wires and tubes, lines and immobile form, Ian nodded. He and Riley headed toward the conference room. Once inside, Ian took the same spot where he'd sat when speaking with Jessie.

"I came to ask for your help," Riley said, closing the door.

"Me?"

Riley nodded. "It would be unethical to ask Tripp, and I've been told to recuse myself, anyway."

"Weren't supposed to come up here, were you?" Ian leaned back in the chair, motioning Riley to the one across.

"Took a few days off," Riley said, sitting. "Taylor's important to me."

Ian kept his hands clasped at his lap.

"There was a technicality in Taylor's release. No one wants to think the police are inept, or the DA or the judges—and we're not—but somehow . . . *somehow*, the warrant to search her home came with a date before the date Taylor called. By a couple days, actually. They were preparing to execute it that afternoon."

"How's that possible?"

Riley shook his head. "A tip?"

"Who the hell would know?"

"I wish I knew. It gets weirder, because when you secure a warrant, it has to be notarized. The signed dates lined up with the day Taylor found the bones, but the notary's stamp was two days before that. The clerk could have screwed up, not turned her dial, but I don't know, and she's sworn an oath that she wasn't even in the office that day. I'm probably just being paranoid. Faine claims he was given it by his supervisor and he by his." Riley waved a hand through the air. "It doesn't matter. All that does is that the SBI did finally come out with it. Those bones are old. *Really* old. They're now looking into the land there for cemeteries or any former grave markers. But, well . . . I don't know. I was sure this was all because of Tanner—"

"He's dead." Ian shot a figurative air gun through his own temple. "Bar fight not long after he got out of prison for setting up Taylor."

"Damn." Riley ran his hand through his hair. "I was hoping there was an easy answer to the niggle at the back of my mind."

Ian chuckled. "Easy answers don't make the search any fun. Why would you think of him for this, anyway?" The buzz of his cell phone vibrated his leg. He grabbed it, noted the caller ID said 'unknown' and pressed 'off'. "Sorry, that was probably Tripp. Keep going."

"Here's something else weird. The bones' hands were bound, behind the body. Like this." Riley stood and twisted his arms behind himself.

Ian offered a nod but said nothing.

Riley let go of his own arms. "That position is one Taylor goes spastic in. Has since she was a kid. I just figured since Tanner probably knew that, it would be a damn good way to torture her. She'd find the bones, see the hands and wig out, you know? Added to that, they were buried and ... well ..." Riley hung his head. "Whoever produced the warrant, which is a mystery in and of itself as no one in the office is taking blame or credit, documented it as a murder because the orientation of the skull suggested the person was buried alive."

"How would they know that?"

Riley shot a finger toward Ian. "Exactly what I wondered, but the judge signed, Faine showed up, and the ball started rolling. I just can't figure out how anyone would have known."

"Two days before?"

"Yes." Riley ran a hand through his hair. "I kept thinking Tanner could have gotten those bones out of a museum since they've dated them to about eighteen eighty and to a—"

"Female of approximately nineteen to thirty-one?"

Riley's head snapped up. "Yes. How do you—"

"Same way I found out about Tanner before you. It's my job to be in the know." Ian tapped his temple.

Riley angled his head toward Ian. "Is there anything you don't already know?"

What I'm going to do about Taylor? Why I killed her. "Didn't know about the face-up stuff. That would've wigged me out.

And all the reasons for the fevers that the docs don't understand. Don't get that, either. Don't know why she drowned in a bathtub. Not quite sure why the sky is blue, but that one I could probably look up."

"You know she hates water? And fire. Tried a bonfire once in high school on the beach." Riley sat again. "I tell you what, her eyes couldn't have gotten bigger." His eyes widened as though in example. "Her entire body stiffened like she'd been flash-frozen. She couldn't move, yet she stared into the flames so I could see the reflection on her pupils. I had to drag her out of there."

He knows so much about her. Stuff I don't. Riley's comment reminded Ian about Taylor's freeze on the patch of dirt at her house. The phone started up again. Tripp could call back later.

"You ever see her do her air thingamajig?"

Riley chuckled. "Caught her once—rather, I was being nosy when I was about fifteen, and her parents weren't home. Thought I'd catch her naked."

Ian's laugh would not be contained. Fifteen with that sort of temptation would have gotten the best of any teenage boy.

"She was in her parent's yard, and the wind was whipping her hair into the air. Trees were rustling. Everything was moving inside the circle of her arms. God, she was beautiful." The wistfulness in Riley's tone tugged at Ian. "Since then, I've kinda watched her. Seen her push ladders back up against buildings she and her crew are working on. If a storm brews, I'd swear she holds it off as everyone gets to safety. You hear about that parachutist whose pack didn't open, and he dropped to the earth?"

Ian shook his head.

"He fell right toward a pond in a house she was working on. Everyone says there's no reason for him to have survived, but he did. And with only two broken legs."

"You saw her save him?" His phone started up again.

Riley's head moved back and forth. "Don't you think you should get that?"

Ian reached for it, but it stopped. 'Unknown' graced the screen again.

"Taylor had horrible dreams for a week after that and stayed with me a few nights. She'd cry out when I thought she was asleep. 'Why didn't it work?' After the third time, I said, 'What didn't work?' and she responded with, 'My air. I didn't reach him fast enough', and that was it." He shrugged. "She hasn't kept anything from me since."

Because you know her, and I'm only a figment of some imaginary reincarnation.

The phone started again, and Ian snatched it. "What?"

"Ian?" Maryann's—the nicest of all the nurses at the hospital—voice crashed into him.

"What's happened?" He stood and started for the door.

"Nothing bad, Ian. Nothing bad. Your girl's waking up."

23

Blinded by light, Taylor blinked. For a moment, disorientation plagued her as it had every other time she thought she'd woken. A shiver tore through her—one that registered in her limbs to the point her fingers jiggled. She'd watched herself die three times, each in more detail than the last, and she didn't want to do it again.

Please tell me I'm alive.

A turn to the right showed her a wall. A shift to the left, a curtain.

This is definitely not heaven.

A blob of indistinct color moved as she turned left and right.

Ian? Ian. Ian!

Taylor tried to focus but stared through a spider web-like, translucent yet opaque film.

"Ian." Her voice came out garbled, thick with sleep and morning.

The form stirred.

"Ian?"

The form came at her with a speed that had her pushing back in her bed and raising her arms.

"Taylor. Hi, baby."

Not Ian. Who's voice? Riley? No. Who?

"Tay, it's your dad."

"Daddy? Wha—" She pushed up, wanting to sit as her lids blinked to clear away the fog. Knowing her speaker helped define his shape—the strong jawline and angled cheekbones. A few more blinks brought his ashen color and orangey-brown eyes into focus. "What happened?"

"You're in the hospital." His hand took hers.

"Where's Mama?"

"She's getting some food for the boys—for Riley and Ian. Seems Ian wouldn't leave your side for the last few days and hasn't eaten much. Riley followed us up this morning." He chuckled, a sweet sound that filled her ears. "You've got them both pining over you. How'd my tough girl manage that?"

Riley pine for me? Not a chance. Her dad must have been mistaken. She tried to push up again, but a weakness overtook her as if she'd lain in a bed for a month and hadn't risen once. "How long have I been here?" Her fingertips found the bed's button, and it lifted her up.

"Five days. Well, this is the fifth, apparently."

Her eyes wanted to shut, but her mind needed to hear more. "Why's everyone here?" A few more blinks and her vision cleared. The room, a light cream, held four different plants, some pink, some white, others a mix of wilting wildflowers, as well as a few cards on a table. Her father sat on the edge of her bed in T-shirt and jeans, her hand in his.

"Honey, you've been flush with a super-high fever they think is related to that cut on your arm." He picked up the call button. "I could get the nurse for you." His smile couldn't have gotten wider.

The door to the room burst opened as soon as he laid the device down.

"Taylor!" Not a nurse, but her mom, and behind her, Riley and Ian. Her mom ran to her, wrapped her arms around her and sobbed into her shoulder. "I'm so sorry, baby. I can't believe it took so long. We came as soon as we heard. We should have been here sooner."

Taylor eyed her father. He gave her a great big grin, a small head shake and a nod.

She let her mother go on, runny mascara coating Janet Marsh's perfect face. *Ten bucks says she'll fix that in the bathroom mirror in less than thirty seconds.*

"Good afternoon, my friend." The nurse, Maryann by her name tag, laid a stethoscope against Taylor's chest. "Welcome back to the real world. I'm going to call for the doctor and have him come in."

"Okay." Taylor lifted her head. Her eyes darted to Ian. When his gaze met hers, she smiled.

As if he'd read her mind, he stepped past Riley. Her mom rose from the bed and headed straight to the bathroom.

Taylor held out her arms.

Ian joined her.

Anger she'd been consumed with in the midst of her torture-filled confinement vanished with the merging of their lips. What had seemed a lifetime of separation, of living and dying, return and demise culminated in that one moment. She clung to him, pulling her body against his as a need to be tied to him filled her. "It's really been five days?" She kept her voice a whisper to prevent her parents hearing.

Ian nodded. "Five hard ones."

Two doctors entered the room. "Ms. Marsh," said a male/female voice. "Welcome to the land of the living."

Ian scooted off the bed as the two doctors stood at the end.

"If everyone would please excuse us, we've got to run some tests."

Taylor's mother emerged from the bathroom, her mascara perfectly reapplied. Her dad stood and took her mother's arm. "We'll just be outside," he said.

They walked toward the door, grabbed Riley and tugged. "Come on, Ian," Janet said.

Her mother may never have admitted it, especially so soon after meeting a man Taylor had feelings for, but she recognized the tone. Somehow, Ian had won her over already.

Ian waited in the hall, Riley at his side, as Janet broke apart from her embrace with Taylor's father and walked toward them.

She took Ian's hand from the counter. "I want to thank you, Ian. You've been here the whole time—" Her eyes filled. "—I don't know how better to thank you."

"None needed."

"I don't know why you'd give so much of yourself to her when you barely know her. But for that, I thank you." She moved away.

For the next three hours, doctors and nurses flitted in and out of Taylor's room, Taylor's mom returning with them. Since no screaming, no codes, nothing but calm escaped the room, Ian went back to the conference room.

He used his time to do more searching using his laptop. While he had plenty of data stored about the Branches of Life, he needed to search about his and Taylor's former lives, too.

Taylor's ability. The photo. The DNA. Names. Dates. Missing persons. Murder. It all mixed in Ian's mind.

His thoughts returned to his friends.

Tripp and Lexi had been given impossible odds and found the loophole.

In his own case, Ian found nothing except cold hard facts and huge coincidences even a Junior DA could argue against him.

Two more hours passed before Janet ventured to the room Ian occupied, with Riley at her side, and stood in the frame of the door. "She's showering and getting dressed." She glanced up toward the far wall. "I can't believe it's almost ten."

Ian turned to the clock there. Sure enough, the day only had two hours left in it.

"She'd like you to join her, Ian . . . when she's done, of course." Despite the sweet tone, her lips pursed.

Don't like being kicked out? Or don't want me to see your daughter naked?

The three exited, but only Ian returned to Taylor's room, where she sat in the chair he'd slept on. He slipped onto the spinning stool the doctors and techs used each time they came in to treat Taylor.

"Do you believe in second chances, Ian?" Taylor's fingers dug into his arm. "Or thirds? Maybe fourths?"

Ian chuckled.

"Do you, Ian?" Her tone held a firm insistence.

"You like to ask deep, philosophical questions." He traced her cheek with his fingertip. "I believe everyone has a chance to make up for what they've done, but that most people don't know how to get through the problems that got them in trouble in the first place." *Like how I killed you, and why and how I can avoid that now.*

"I think I have another chance."

He nodded. "You just may. The docs say there's absolutely nothing wrong with you."

Her smile grew. "I know. They want me to stay the rest of the night, but I want to get out of here. I want to go with you and to enjoy that hotel room again." She rubbed at the long scratch on her arm that had become a white scar along her skin. "I want that date you and I were supposed to have."

His heart flip-flopped. "How about you stay, just to make sure. It was a rough night … nights, plural." He tucked her hair behind her ear.

"We barely got started, Ian. I want that chance." She ran her thumb over the tattoo-like band around her finger.

Ian's heart tightened in his chest. "There's a lot I've found out in the last couple days."

She stopped him with a finger to his lips. "I'm sure there is, but Ian?"

He stared deep into her eyes.

"Not now. Just take me home or get me out of here. Being … here … can't be good for me."

"Your mom's probably going to think I coerced you into leaving, you know." He stood and took her hand, pulling her to her feet. She wobbled, and he righted her, holding her steady.

"Mama never believes anything unless she sees it, Ian. Bad or good. I get a little of that trait from her."

Despite Taylor's desire to leave the hospital for fun and frolic, her weakened state had her sound asleep by midnight. Ian rose, returned to his laptop and his research on Greek mythology, magical history and anything else he could come up with that might lead him somewhere other than where his heart told him to go. His biggest problem came in what he didn't know. That left him unable to find any solid answers.

As the sun rose, filling the hotel room with warm light, Taylor stirred. "Ian?"

He moved back to the bed, leaving the laptop with its screen up. A kiss to her lips ignited the fire within him, but until she hammered a nail again, he had no intention of tempting any more fates.

"What were you doing?"

"Research." He snuggled with her on the bed.

"All night?"

He knuckled his eyes, tired but desperate for answers. "Yeah."

"Want to tell me about it?" She entwined her fingers with his.

"Not yet. You're barely over it all as it is."

"Dammit, Ian. Don't coddle me."

He jerked back.

"I woke with my heart tearing in two thinking I'd lost you forever ..." Her breath hitched. "Thinking I'd never see you again, that a week wasn't enough, especially with all that went on. And thinking, damn, why didn't I see this right? I remember everything we've been through in this life. The branches. This symbol—" She pointed to her finger and took his hand. "One left. This is our one left."

"I know that."

"Then tell me, Ian." She shifted, facing him straight on. "I want to know what you know. I want to know why I thought I'd never see the light of day again, why I have to reconnect with you this way." Her tone adjusted to one of desperation. "So, tell me. Right now."

A breath whooshed from him. "I thought you might think I was batshit crazy, but given that little tirade, I'm pretty sure you are instead of me."

Taylor crossed her arms over her chest even as a small smile breached her face.

"You know the DNA sample that we sent to Michael?"

"Of course. Emma practically tore off the inside of my cheek rubbing that swab against it."

"It's your DNA."

She didn't even flinch.

"And the two in the photo?"

She angled her head back up.

"There's no doubt one was you—given the DNA. You and me is my guess, given the look, the rings, etcetera." She still hadn't changed her expression, so he continued. "The names are ringers. Her birth date is your birth date. His death date is my birth date. And, you know the bones in your yard?"

"How could I forget them?" She slumped against the headboard. "They started all this mess."

"She—you—she was buried, presumably alive, with her hands tied behind her back."

Her face tilted down.

"You can't stand having your hands tied behind your back. I've seen it. Nothing breaks you except, based on what Riley told me, fire, water and earth, which coincidentally are three of the four elements. Outside of those, you seem to be the toughest chick on the planet. Then, there's the last element. Air. Which you can control."

A small laugh escaped her.

He described the game as Jessie explained it to him, linked it to Zeus and tied it back to himself and Taylor.

"So, it bothers you that you could kill me, but not that I could kill you? Now who's batshit crazy?"

A laugh burst free from Ian. She had a point, but not the right one. "Yes, it bothers me." *More than bothers.* "But, if we keep restarting this process, then it's obvious, I keep killing you. Therefore—" He took on the tone Tripp used to prove a point. "—something's fucked up."

Taylor stared at him.

"You called out John, Taylor. You cried out that name as if you were in pain. That was his name. My name. We're in the game. You. Me."

"You're wrong, Ian."

He clenched and released his fists. The pieces of the puzzle all fit. "How am I wrong? What do you think will happen this time?"

"I said his name in passion. I loved him. He loved me. I could feel it—every bit of it. The longing, the deep desire. When we were in the hotel, in the tub, I—I had a vision, a memory. It was all real." She inched up and ran a hand along Ian's arm. "There's no way in hell he killed her, me, her back then. He didn't. This is our opportunity. Our chance. I know it. We just have to look at it differently. Since we know what happened before, we can—"

Ian shook his head, closing his eyes and heaving a breath. "It's not fourth time the charm. It's third time. And, third time didn't work. Probably for a reason."

"You don't know that a fourth won't." Taylor cupped his cheeks in her palms. "You feel these connections, Ian, but I can see them. When we're most intimately connected, I live it. I know how we felt about each other. I know it."

A small smile took hold of Ian's lips. "You're a funny girl, Miss Marsh. Anyone else would have run from the room screaming that she was a dead woman walking, yet you're here trying to convince me I'm not going to do what is clearly coming." Ian inched toward the edge of the bed.

Taylor grabbed his arm. "Don't leave."

A rumble came from his stomach. "How about you take a shower, I'll get us some breakfast, and—"

She jumped up from the bed but leaned back into it. "Yes. A shower. I really, really, really want one."

"Is fifteen minutes enough time?"

"Give me twenty since I'm slow on my feet. That is, unless you want to join me?" She wiggled her hips but only for a second, reaching for the wall and stabilizing herself again. "I really hate being weak. Messes up my life."

"Go on. Relax and enjoy it."

As Taylor maneuvered to the bathroom, Ian went back to his computer. With the water pouring and his laptop's cursor blinking in the username field, he closed the machine. "I'm not going to put you through a fourth." Ian heaved a sigh. "I'd never put someone I love through that kind of pain."

Taylor's out-of-tune hum came through the door, crushing Ian's heart in on itself. He opened the door, not worrying that she'd hear. She should have been expecting him to leave.

Two doors down, he knocked on Riley's entryway. It took a second knock before a groggy, half-lidded Riley opened the door. "You know it's not even eight, right?"

"It's not like you're on vacation."

Riley squinted, tilting down and returning to Ian's face. "Why do you have your laptop bag?"

"Can I come in?"

With the door open, Ian entered. He turned as Riley stood in the walkway. "Would you believe me if I said Taylor and I are reincarnated people who have had three chances to make a go of it but failed?"

Riley didn't even flinch.

In five minutes, Ian relayed the story about the rings around his and Taylor's fingers, her dreams, and about the game. Riley said nothing, but his eyebrows worked overtime as if processing the information between up and down movements.

After a moment of silence, Riley said, "So, you think by walking away, by giving up, you'll keep her safe?"

"Not give up. Save her. It's a self-sacrifice kind of thing. If we're not together, I can't hurt her. I'm not interested in playing Romeo and Juliet. Alive is far better than dead. Just get her to go on about her life, and make sure she stays safe. I'm sure you can deal with it."

"You're going to piss her off you know."

"Better a pain in the heart than a nonworking one. One will heal. The other . . . well . . . it won't."

Riley nodded. "All right, then."

Once Ian found an ally in Riley, his decision stuck. He stepped forward and held out his hand. "It's been fun. Well, not really, but you understand, right?"

Riley gave him a half-smile.

"Ten minutes. No more. She'll be out of the shower, and you have to be there."

"I will be."

"She's all yours." His voice broke as he walked through the door.

Taylor sang along to the thrum of the shower head's pulse until her fingers pruned and she figured she'd used up enough of the water to warrant the huge hotel bill Ian had to have footed.

With her hair in a towel, she sauntered into the room, but Ian hadn't returned with breakfast. She cocked her head.

Something had changed, she just didn't know what.

The knock had her spinning toward the door, a goon-like smile taking hold of her face. She adjusted the towel around her waist so she could drop it as soon as he entered and tiptoed to the door.

At the second knock, she opened it.

Her gasp came with her attempt to keep the towel secure and the one around her hair from falling to the floor. "Riley! What are you doing here?" She scrambled backward, making sure her butt didn't show under the short towel. A drop to the bed and crossed legs helped cover her a little—at least the parts that counted.

Riley stepped in, closing the door behind him, his face blank.

Taylor's heart sank. "He left, didn't he?"

24

Taylor sat on her own couch, in her own living room, with her own mug of hot cocoa in her hands. Through the unencumbered window, she watched as geese landed in the empty patch of grass that had been covered in sod that morning. She'd worked from sun up to sun down, recreating the peace and tranquillity she'd intended to give to that splotch of land before she'd been jailed, hurt, sick and put on health arrest for a week and a half. It burned her psyche that she hadn't been allowed to exercise, that her mother hovered, and, more so, that Ian hadn't even called.

At the footsteps on the hardwood floor, she turned.

"What should we do today, darling?" Her mom dropped onto the couch with an air of grace and tranquility.

Taylor scanned the room, from her baby blue walls, chair rail and moulding she'd installed years ago, to the marble backsplash around the fireplace and the antiques that graced the mantel. The effect should have made her feel better, not worse.

"Come on, Tay. We can get out for a walk, or I can drive you to the park—"

"Stop it, Mama." Taylor closed her eyes at her biting tone. "I'm sorry. I'm just not in the mood to 'do' stuff right now just for the sake of doing." She snuggled deeper into her chair, an overstuffed, country contemporary in denim, but would have preferred to run outside and chop a log into a zillion pieces just for the rush of energy that would flow through her body.

Her mom put her hands on her knees and stood. "Well, it

has been a week. Maybe I should stop hovering so much." Guilt wracked Taylor.

"I'm sorry, Mama, really. I'm not used to being coddled, and I feel like that's all anyone's doing. Not just you. But Lexi. Emma. Riley. I know ya'll are trying to make up for lost time, but really, I'm okay with how it was. I like my independence, and I don't need someone here every hour of every day. I need to get back to work, to my projects, to making money and—" Taylor set the cup on the table and stood, dropping the blanket in the process as she moved to her mother. She wouldn't say 'forgetting Ian' though she knew she should. Her arms snaked around her mom's waist. "Thank you for being kind during this battle, but I think it's over. There won't ever be another of these instances."

Hands ran up and down Taylor's back. "And, you're sure you want me to leave?"

She chuckled. "You live five miles away. I can send smoke signals if I need you. And yes, I know how."

Her mother's fingers threaded with Taylor's. "I really do wish that Ian would stop by again."

Taylor's heart lurched. "Riley's been by every day. Just like you and Daddy. Ian . . . well, he was . . . just a friend."

"Could've fooled me." With that, she slid away and, grabbing her purse, went to the door. "You'll call me if you need anything, right?"

The doorbell chimed.

An inner excitement ran through Taylor with hope Ian might make a surprise return.

"I'll get it, Taylor."

"Thanks, Mama."

A soft creak came with the opening of the door, and Taylor made a mental note to oil the hinges as she sank back into her seat.

"Oh, hello, Miss Agnes," Taylor's mom said. "What can we do for you?"

"I made some sweet rolls this morning and thought Miss Taylor might like some."

Taylor's lips cracked into a smile. When home, her across-the-street neighbor popped out of her house only long enough to ply Taylor with sugar before she and her husband would be off traveling the world again.

"I'll be happy to give them to her," Taylor's mom said.

"Would you, dear? Thank you for that."

The shuffling at the door didn't bring Taylor out of her spot. Her mom could drop the dish on the counter before leaving.

"Oh . . . I forgot." Agnes's old lady voice cracked.

"Yes?" Taylor's mom said.

"Frank and I will be heading to Maine in two weeks. Then we have a cruise through the Pacific over the summer. If you know of anyone wishing for a nice, furnished rental, have Miss Taylor call me or come by. Someone like that nice young man we had last fall."

Nice young man from last fall? Taylor couldn't recall any visitors from the fall, only the summer—when a family with two kids had planned to relocate and used Agnes's home while they found their own. Taylor had been too busy with the reconstruction of Tripp and Lexi's Victorian to be neighborly. She cringed at the thought her mother would find out she'd failed in her southern hospitality.

"Ah, okay. I'll tell her," her mom said. The same creak sounded until the door clicked closed. "She brought you some cinnamon rolls, honey. They're warm, too. I'll just leave them on the table."

"Take one to Daddy, please." Taylor stared out the window. A crow landed in the center of the yard, scattering the other two birds to the sky.

Cupboards opened and closed. Tupperware burped. "All right, then. The rest are on the stove." Rubber-soled shoes squidged their way toward the door.

Taylor took a deep breath, and two clicks later, silence filled the room.

A crow winged into the air.

Another chime from the doorbell tinkled through the space. *Mama can let herself back in.* Another ring had Taylor clambering up and heading toward the door as the bells sounded a third time. She grabbed the handle and yanked open her barrier to the outside world.

Emma and Lexi stood on the other side. "Hi," they said together.

Taylor faked a smile while inside she cringed. "Come on in." The idea of having guests didn't appeal to her, but ingrained training-by-Janet-Marsh kept that tidbit of information from surfacing.

The two of them exchanged looks before walking in, grabbing Taylor's arms and pulling her from the house.

"Hey! What're you doing?"

In the middle of her driveway sat a stretch limo.

Taylor dug in her heels as her two so-called friends dragged her farther. "I'm not going anywhere until you tell me where you're taking me."

Behind the limo, Tripp's car sat, idling, and her mother stood at her own car, the door wide open.

"Seriously. What are you doing?"

The driver of the stretch stepped out, walked to the back and held open the door.

Taylor yanked herself free. "Stop it right now."

Emma and Lexi both let go, though the smiles upon their faces remained.

"He left *me*, remember? He thinks he's going to repeat a cycle and kill me."

They both stood with their arms crossed over their chests.

"Hello?" Taylor snapped in front of their faces. "Anybody home?"

A giggle came from her mom.

"It's been a week and a half, Taylor." Lexi broke the silly standoff. "We gave you the week to get your wits about you. We gave Ian a week to get over himself. The extra few days have been just plain silly."

"Martyrdom is just not fashionable these days." Emma mirrored Lexi's stance, though the small hump on Lexi's stomach had her standing out more than her sister.

"Ian's not going to kill you," Lexi said.

"And, you would know this how?" Taylor ran a hand through her hair. "You're the one who pointed us to the photo. We have the rings, and we know about the game that ends in my death. Or his."

"Yes, we know." Lexi bobbled her head to each shoulder before righting herself again. "But Ian's not that kind of guy."

"Do you really believe he'd do that?" Emma asked. "Truly?"

Taylor heaved a sigh. "Of course not. And, I told him so."

"I told you before that you're meant to be together, and I'm never wrong, Taylor. I know this is right for you and Ian," Lexi said.

"Oh, well then. Since you said so ..." Sarcasm coated her words. "I doubt he thought he would kill me in previous lives, either. But, when all is said and done, the evidence is kinda conclusive. I do have to agree with him, even if I don't think he'll do it again."

"It's circumstantial, and I can understand his position, but I swear to you ..." Lexi tapped her foot on the ground. "... this is not the eighteen hundreds, not a time where races are separate, not a time where men dictate the rules and lives of women. That was then. This is now. That's a major *game* changer."

"And, you think lives and circumstance change the path we're on?"

Emma and Lexi turned toward each other, Emma facing Taylor again first. "Let me tell you about what you *think* life will be like and what you can do to change the course of it. My sister here ..." She thumbed over her shoulder. "... She and her man are living proof we humans can screw over Zeus. 'Cause he is the instigator behind all these riddles and games. Not for a minute did I let Lexi wallow in the inherent conflict in her life—and let me tell you, it was just as bad as yours but in a completely different way. Now . . . she fought me as much as she did Tripp, but as you can see, they are together, godly Greek conflict or not. So, hell yeah, I think you can change your path."

Taylor hadn't yet learned what exactly happened to Tripp and Lexi, except that it related, somehow, to her and Ian. "But, it's not the same."

Emma stuck her hands on her hips. "Why? Because they knew what they were walking into? And you don't? Dude, so not true. That was even harder for them because Lex couldn't wrap her head around the solution even when it punched her in the face." Emma took a deep breath. "So . . . when I say 'you can change your path, young grasshopper', I mean it. I believe it. You just don't let the past screw with you. Take it by the balls and yank it."

Taylor spurted a laugh, hiding it behind her hand. "But—"

"She doesn't believe us," Lexi said.

Emma shook her head. "Time to bring out the big guns."

"Do you know who Metis is?" Lexi smiled as she asked.

"No."

"She was Zeus's wife," Emma started. "The most important woman in his life, in fact. She meddled just like Zeus did, but not in the same way. He screwed with humans. She screwed, ha ha, literally, with him." When Emma stopped chuckling, she said, "Her name alone means wisdom and cunning. For example, she was the one who gave Zeus a nice, little liquid concoction so he'd make Kronos throw up Zeus's own brothers and sisters. Gross, but that's what we women do. We look out for each other. For our futures. For our children. For love." Emma let out a long, sarcastic sigh. "Every mythological loophole comes from her. That includes her ability to give gifts."

Lexi added, "Like fire, water, earth and air. Or mental gifts like

Tripp and I have. Or whatever."

That had been the first real time Lexi had defined her gift. Had Ian told her about Taylor's? She pinched the bridge of her nose. "Wouldn't I know if I had a way to fix this?"

Emma held her palms up to the sky and waved. Lexi blew a breath.

"You know," Taylor said.

They both shrugged.

"You think the fact I can manipulate air is somehow related?"

They both nodded at the same time, in exactly the same way.

"He loves you, Taylor," Lexi said. "But, he's just as stubborn as you. If he says he's going to keep away? He will. He doesn't break his own rules."

"If you want to give this thing you got goin' on a chance?" Emma waved a finger in the air. "Then, you gotta take the boy by the balls and tie 'em in a knot about your finger and just hope to hell what Metis gave you will fix it all. *If* anything happens."

"But how is air going to help me not die? I mean, besides the obvious?"

Lexi and Emma squished up their noses at the same time.

"Ya'll do that a lot, don't you?" Taylor pointed at one and the other and back.

"So we're told," Lexi said. "Just remember, I know you're meant to be together. I have no idea how it's going to happen, I just know it. And, I'm never wrong."

Taylor put her hand on the limo's frame but didn't enter. "What if it all turns out to be true? What if he does kill me, and I have to live all the rest of my lives ... to infinity ... miserable? How am I supposed to deal with that?"

"You can either believe Lexi or my magic eight ball. It came up with 'All signs point to no'," Emma said as Taylor rolled her eyes. "What if this is part of the roller coaster ride, and this time you've figured it out before it can all blow up in your face? Are you really going to give up a chance to try? Isn't that what life is all about?

You're born. You die. In between, you do ... stuff. Where there's a will there's a way. Don't let a Greek god screw with you more than he has. Lexi and Tripp are a testament to that."

"You're being very cliché today, Em." Lexi nudged her sister's hip. "In your heart, Taylor—deep in there—do you really think Ian is going to hurt you?"

Taylor didn't believe it. She never had. That mental picture had never come to her like the rest of her past-life memories. She shook her head as she whispered, "No. But—"

"No buts!" Emma and Lexi said together. Lexi pushed Taylor inside the car. "Sometimes, you're the lemon and sometimes, you make lemonade. Now get in the limo, and go squeeze the fruit."

Taylor chuckled, having absolutely no idea as to the relevance of Emma's comment.

"The limo will take you to the airport," Lexi said. "The plane is waiting. There's a service that will meet you at the FBO for a ride to Ian's place. And, here's a key just in case you need it."

"Why—"

Emma's glare stopped Taylor.

She glanced at her sweats, T-shirt and flip-flops.

"His brother Michael is helping us." A grin shot across Emma's face. "So, don't even worry about Ian not being there or anything."

"What if the lemon is too sour?" Taylor hoped she'd used the analogy in context.

Lexi laid her hand on Taylor's shoulder. "Then you add some sugar."

Taylor burst out a laugh as she dropped to the seat, and the limo driver closed the door.

Michael grabbed the door and slammed it shut. "Sit down already."

"Damn you." Ian stared at the flat panel in the apartment he'd once thought he'd have to give up. Michael had been bossing him around for an hour, and despite his half-witted comeback, Ian didn't have anything better to do than pick a fight.

Michael plopped back on the couch. "I said sit."

"No." For all that happened the week before, a year could have passed, and Ian not have known it. He paced to the window, where the late afternoon sunshine sifted through.

"Your pacing has got to stop." Sound ceased from the television.

Ian spun to his brother. "What do you want me to do, Michael?"

"Anything but this. This—" He waved his arms up and down Ian's form. "—isn't you." Michael stood and marched toward the kitchen, rifled and returned. "Look at this." He held up a blue, button-down dress shirt.

"What about it?"

"It was on the counter. The *counter*, Ian. You don't leave stuff like that out. You're meticulous. You're anal retentive." Michael shrugged. "You value your stuff, respect it, take care of it. You're who I aspire to be, but man, today? You've been thoroughly distracted. And wrinkled. And . . . and just not you. Why?"

I've been thoroughly distracted for almost two weeks; you just weren't here to see it. "I need to get away." Long strides took him to the door.

Michael jumped into Ian's path.

"Move," Ian said.

"No." Michael crossed his arms over his chest.

Ian tried to step around his brother.

Michael moved into his way again, his chin lifted. "It's Saturday. It's sunny. You can even smell the disgusting hot dog vendor on the street as he clogs up all the arteries I'm gonna have to fix one day."

"I said move." Ian forced firmness into his tone. The head shake from Michael broke Ian's resolve. He stepped to Michael, wrapped his arm around his neck and tugged him into a headlock.

"Shit, man." Michael's hands grasped at Ian's forearms.

"You gonna let me leave? That was your recommendation last time I was trying to get some blonde chick off my mind."

Michael chuckled. "And look how that turned out."

Ian tightened his hold.

Michael's foot slipped between Ian's legs. A second later, the two crashed to the ground.

Ian let go, scrambled to Michael's upper body again until he ended up within Michael's clutches. "Son of a bitch! When did you get so strong?" Ian pulled at his brother's hands but didn't succeed in moving either of them.

Michael's body flailed until he managed to flip them over. "I wrestled in high school. Don't you remember, or have you gotten too old?"

At Ian's snort, Michael relaxed his hold just enough for Ian to grab his leg and tug at it. If anyone saw them, they'd have to wonder at the contorted mess of limbs the two of them created.

Michael's squeeze pulled at Ian's hamstrings. "Too much for you, old man?"

One knock and both turned their heads to the door.

A grin crossed Michael's features. "Cry uncle, and I'll let you go."

"No." Ian stretched his arm, capturing the hem of Michael's jeans.

Michael zipped his foot away, bending into a position Ian couldn't even describe. Another knock forced them both to look up, though Ian's position made it difficult to do so.

"Gonna answer that?" Michael asked.

"No," Ian said.

"Well, we need a tie breaker, so whoever is on the other side gets dibs." The doorbell chimed through the apartment, and Michael drew in a breath. "Come in!"

"The door is locked." Ian lightened his hold, intent on rising.

Michael grabbed and tugged him into a crouch. "Oh, no. You're not getting away that easy. Come in!" he said again.

"Why—"

The door creaked an inch. A foot. It opened wide.

Taylor stood in the empty space, her hands over her lips. "Well, well, well." She jangled a key, pursing her lips as if to hold back a grin. Neither Ian nor Michael let go, though Ian's heart did a flip-flop. "This isn't quite the welcoming committee I was expecting."

"Oh no, don't you stop." Michael's grip tightened around Ian's arms.

Chuckling, Taylor closed the door behind her and dropped to the arm of the couch. "Need a ref?"

"Yeah," Michael said as Ian said, "No."

More laughter came from her. "You two have reputations to uphold, and I didn't think wrestling on the floor was going to fit it, but now I see it suits you both." She angled a finger at each of them in turn.

Even in her half-mussed clothes and with the tendrils of hair falling around her face, Ian wanted her.

"So, how might one win this game?" A slender finger tapped her chin. "I believe it requires one opponent to pin the other, right?"

"Yes," they both said at the same time.

"And, this could go on and on and on and on at this rate, right?"

"He's going to get tired faster than I am since he's so old and decrepit and celibate." Michael's snark had Ian snaking his hand around Michael's wrist.

In one tug, Ian yanked his brother around to the flat of his back, tugged up his knees, twisted and had Michael's face against the floor.

"Ooh," Taylor said. "Sorry, Michael, but I'm pretty sure Ian wins."

Ian let go, and his brother fell flat to the floor. He stood, wiped at his pants, rubbed his hands together and stared at Taylor. "Your turn."

"What?" Her shriek came fast as Ian moved toward her.

He reached her before she could even rise from the couch, laying his palms against her cheeks and his lips against hers. Her arms snaked around his neck, squeezing his body closer. Softness reached the edges of her lips, trailed across to the opposite side and returned. She opened, letting her tongue dance with his.

"Ahem."

She pulled him nearer, wanting more, desperate for the touch of his skin against hers, for the roughness of his chin's shadow against every inch of her body.

"Ahem."

Their kiss—an experience that tied together centuries of a past with the singular presence of that moment—never faltered.

"A-*hem*!"

Her smile broke Ian's touch. "I think Michael's trying to tell us we're in a public space."

"It's my apartment," Ian said. "He can leave."

"You wouldn't do that to me, would ya? I came all the way up—"

Taylor snuck a glance at Michael.

He jiggled keys in his hands without adding any sound, his head angling toward the door.

She closed her eyes.

Ian stayed silent, rubbing his forehead against hers as the door opened and closed again.

"Your brother's a good man."

Another touch to her lips. "I know. He wouldn't let me leave today, even though I told him I didn't really want him around. Or want to be here. He knew you were coming, didn't he?"

She nodded with her head still against his. "Yeah. Lexi and

Emma … and Tripp put him up to it."

"Damn them." He pulled away.

"Don't you go now, Ian Sands." Taylor tugged him back.

He relaxed against her again, melding her to his body, his arms wrapping behind her. His lips caressed her neck. "God, I missed you."

"It's only been a couple weeks," she said. "Ish."

"It felt like years. Decades. Centuries. Like I had you in my hand and someone took you away, and then I got you again only to have to leave you."

She trailed her fingers up and down his neck. "Well, if our powers of deduction are right, that's exactly what happened."

He stiffened within her hold. "It's going to end badly."

"Maybe. But, what if it doesn't? What if there's a pawn to our rook?"

"If the psycho lady—"

"Psychic, Ian. Actually, she said all she could do was communicate with the dead. I'm not sure what that makes her if she can't see futures. Lexi, on the other hand, seems determined to prove we're meant to be without telling me how she knows."

He chuckled against the skin of her shoulder. "And, she's supposedly always right."

Taylor pushed at his chest so she could stare into his eyes. "Different time. Different place. And, what if you kill me … say … when I'm ninety? I'd have lived a long and happy life by then. We have no conclusive data on me in the previous instances, right?"

Ian spun away to the mantle. "How can you look at this so calmly?" One hand rested against the wall.

Taylor shuffled over to him. "I don't *feel* it, Ian. I don't feel like you're going to hurt me. I had three really long dreams while I was … incapacitated. I only told you part of what I experienced. Each was amazing and full of life, a love so strong I could barely breathe when I was around you—"

"And, they ended, didn't they? Just like last time. Both of us dead. That wasn't an unsolved murder with a lynch mob. I killed you, and I buried your body. The proof is in the pudding as you southern girls say, and those bones were right there. End of story, except, here we are again."

Taylor rested her head against his back, his heart beating under her ear. "You don't feel it?"

"I feel connected to you. I did the moment I met you. Actually, even before that just on the phone about that damn house in North Carolina. I don't dream about it, Taylor. I can't see it. There's no way to explain."

She reached up and pressed her lips to his. "I know. Trust me, I know. I might have some memories, but I feel it, too."

"My life will never be the same if I do something to hurt you."

"You once said I was the tough chick who uses power tools. I'm not weak. I'm not one to sit around and wait to see what bad experience will fall down upon me. I don't feel it . . . in here." She tapped her chest above her heart. "If I did, I'd be running away so fast you'd see nothing but a blur. But, I don't feel that. I just feel . . . desire. Need. Want." She sucked in a breath. "Love."

25

Tendrils of Taylor's hair flew up before she could control it.

She grabbed at strands and patted them flat, taking the whole tail and resecuring it.

"Um . . ." Ian circled a pointed finger. "That's kinda freaky."

"Sorry. Yeah. Does that sometimes when I'm a little emotional."

"What else can you do with the air?" Ian tugged at Taylor's hand, nudging her toward the couch. "If you can prevent three people from belly flopping against a wood floor . . . what else?"

Taylor offered him a small shrug. "That's kinda it. Like I told you before, I can move stuff. I don't use it much . . . not since my college years." *Not since Tanner.* Taylor stared into Ian's eyes. She read a question in the deep green—one to which she'd kept the answer to herself.

He didn't move, didn't shift—didn't blink.

"Tanner knew about my gift." She said it on a whoosh of air.

Ian jerked back. "What?"

She wanted to reach out and grab his hands to get him back close to her. "Something happened on campus one day. Two men fell from the top of a bell tower they were in the process of renovating. I didn't see what was going on until . . . well . . . until they hit the ground." The memories sent a jolt of pain through her heart. "The third lost his footing right afterward, and I couldn't see him dying when I was standing right there, so I pushed the wind toward the tower." She took a deep breath. "That current nudged a branch from one of the big oaks into the scaffolding and then him against the facade of the building, so it looked like he slid down to a safe level."

"And Tanner saw you?"

She shook her head. "Not exactly. He was the third guy." Her throat dried up on her. "Can I get some water?"

Ian scrambled up and dashed into the kitchen. "Evian or Voss?"

"Straight from the tap. I'm not a fancy girl."

Clatter emanated from the kitchen. He came back with a glass and a bottle with big lettering on it.

"Very cultured, Ian."

"It's New York. Who knows what's in the pipes?" He took the same spot again, tucking his leg up under himself and twisting off the cap.

"How much did you pay for this?" Taylor smirked at him.

"Does that really matter?" He took a swig.

"Humor me."

Ian raised an eyebrow. "Probably about five bucks."

Her eyes popped open. "Per bottle or a case?"

"Does it *matter*?"

"I'm trying to get a handle on you. Mid-thirties, single, uptown New York apartment that I know you put up as collateral for me."

He stopped in mid-sip. "Is this confessions day with Ian and Taylor?" A small chuckle accompanied his sip. "Should we be lying on a couch as if talking to the best shrink?"

"Confessions, yes. Shrinks, no." She held out her glass.

Ian clinked it. "So, yeah, I put up my apartment."

"Even before you got to know me?"

"Isn't that obvious?"

"Why?"

"Finish your story about Tanner, and maybe I'll tell you."

"Fine." She set the bottle on the glass coffee table. "So, he'd been up there, watched his buddies fall—they didn't die, by the way. For some reason, they'd surrounded the base of the pedestal with tarps and both of them fell into them. Broke a couple legs and a few ribs, but that was the extent. Talk about lucky." Taylor waved the thought away. "So, Tanner's up there, and down below is me, and he said when he felt the air push him back up, he turned, and I was standing there. My hair was blowing in a breeze that didn't affect anyone else, and my hand was held out in such a way that he knew I'd had something to do with it. He asked me out as soon as he got down. And, on our first date, that's all we talked about."

"Kinda selfish, don't you think?"

Taylor busted out a laugh. "Ian, you're too funny."

"I try. Though, I'm not sure what I did to make you laugh like that. I'll do it again if I get a repeat performance."

She bit back the bubbling giggle. "Nothing. Nothing. Just being you. So … on Tanner, it's selfish of him to talk about things that can't happen in this world? Wouldn't that peak your curiosity enough to have endless conversations?" Her hand landed on Ian's leg. "He was curious. Unfortunately, that turned into an obsession I didn't even see coming. He wanted me to try stuff, to practice, to test the limits of what I could do."

"And. did you?"

"Yeah. That's also how I learned to really control it, and why I don't use it unless I need to."

"Tanner's dead, you know."

Taylor nodded. "Riley told me. I don't believe it."

Ian flinched.

She waved her hands back and forth. "Not that you're lying. But he faked it before. For all we know, he needed to get out of town because he'd set up another woman of his dreams."

"He really is. They confirmed with DNA and dental records."

"Which can all be faked."

"You really are cynical." He leaned in, his lips a breath from hers. "I kinda like that in a woman."

Taylor chuckled and gave him a quick kiss. "You haven't answered my original question. I think I ponied up enough. It's your turn now, mister." She poked a finger into his chest. The touch made her want him more. "So, tell me, Ian . . ." Taylor teased his lips with her tongue. ". . . why did you agree to potentially lose this place?"

"What else would I do for a friend in need—especially a hot one." His smile crept in.

She sucked in air but kept her lips glued to his. "You didn't even know me at the time." Her words came out barely a whisper.

"You might have had dreams. You might have spent days dying under the watch of a dozen doctors. Remember what I said about the phone calls? That and the wedding made me insane for months—kept my life out of balance. I felt it. Knew it."

"Love at first sight?"

"Or first lives." His lips formed into a smile a second before they crushed Taylor's again.

The buzz of a fire alarm tore them apart.

"Son of a bitch!" Ian said as Taylor covered her ears.

Ian braced his hands against his own and nodded toward the door. The emergency lights flickered. The scream of the siren grew and retreated. Ended and restarted.

"This isn't a test." Ian's head shook. "We gotta go."

Taylor couldn't move. Thirty-gazillion stories up. Fire below or above, she didn't know. Didn't care. Just as with a pool or a house falling down around her, she froze.

Ian tugged at her arm.

Her body failed to move even as her mind called out to her to snap out of it, to go, to take the stairs and get out.

Ian's face appeared in front of her. His hands clamped around her arms. A small shake had her looking down at him, seeing but not seeing him. The mere thought of a fire that could consume the whole of her sent her body into a panic.

Another blast of sound hit her ears, but Taylor couldn't make herself budge.

Ian disappeared from view. A jingle of keys followed. A second later, he winged her into his arms and ran out the door.

A one week course in fire safety in college did not prepare Ian for three dozen flights of stairs with a one-hundred-and-thirty-pound weight in his arms. On the landing of his floor, all four doors remained closed. He headed toward the stair exit, bumped it with his hip and headed in. The blink of the emergency lights flashed through the well, adding a red haze with each new appearance and blare.

With each of Ian's steps, Taylor's stiffness relaxed until her weight evened out in his arm. He kept her tucked in, refusing to get them both stuck in a high rise fire. *No way this is how I kill her.*

After one flight down, the scent of burning plastic made his nose twitch.

At the second level below, they met with the couple who'd moved in across the hall from him. The man clung to his wife, who Ian had to guess would pop her watermelon-sized belly at any moment.

Their slowness pushed him to a stop as the alarm made them all jump.

"Go around us," Jacob said.

Ian started to do just that, but Taylor wiggled out of his hold. He pulled her back in.

"I'm okay. Don't know how, but I'm okay, now." She stirred until her feet hit the tread below them.

Jacob and his wife continued down, one step at a time, she heaving great breaths as he held her hand and mumbled at her ear.

Way too many flights to go.

Jacob and his wife came down two more steps, and she cried out.

"Carry her!" Staring at Ian, Taylor pointed at the struggling couple.

Another three people broke through from the fire door, their voices a jumble of sounds that Ian couldn't pick out. He spun to Jacob. "You know how to hold in a chair position?" The look Jacob gave Ian said 'no'. Another glance to Taylor got a 'do it'.

The newest folks in their group pushed past without pausing as Ian walked up three steps and showed Jacob how to hold his hands. "I'm Ian," he said as Taylor nudged the woman into their arms.

"Ellen," she said between pants. With a turn to Jacob, she added, "And, I want to move to the 'burbs."

He chuckled as she settled into their hold.

"Keep your pace with mine," Ian said. "Slow around the corners."

"I heard someone say there was a kitchen fire and to stop on twenty for the elevators there," Jacob said.

Ten flights to go then.

Ian's arms burned as he kept Ellen's weight on his side and maneuvered down the steps. His body may have been tuned to the woman in his arms, but his mind stayed fixed on Taylor, one step ahead of them and calling out obstacles.

Two more flights down and they met up with another group chitchatting and meandering their way. "I heard this was just a test." "Someone said a toaster blew up." "Damn high rises. Can't keep their fire contained." Each of the voices gave Ian a picture of the face, yet he refused to look, keeping his gaze trained on Taylor.

Another thirty stairs and his legs cramped, but he pressed on, gritting his teeth and willing his ear drums to deal with the continued siren.

Twenty stairs later, the foursome stopped, along with at least two dozen others as four firemen waved their arms in the air. "From here you can take the elevators. Everything is contained on thirty-two. Nothing to worry about. Just a small kitchen fire. You'll be back home soon, but we do want to complete the evacuation."

Ian helped Ellen to her feet as they stood in front of the bank of four elevators.

Taylor tugged on Ian's shirt. "Can we keep going? I don't like being up here knowing there might be flames above us."

He switched toward where Jacob and Ellen stood, still clinging to each other as she continued her pants and breaths. With a ding, the elevator opened, and the crowd rushed forward.

"Please, Ian. I'm a little claustrophobic and a lot fearful of fire."

"All right, then. Let's go."

Unencumbered, the trip down took just over five minutes. As soon as they exited the lobby, along with a rush of people from the elevators, Taylor turned to Ian. Behind them, four fire trucks waited, their lights flashing. A few police cars sat caddy-corner to the building, blocking traffic or redirecting it. People stood, crammed together on the sidewalk and in the street, some moving away, others staying in place as if to snub the would-be fire.

"Ian," she said as he said, "Taylor."

She ran a hand through her hair as Ian wiped one across his scalp.

Never before had he been so in tune with a woman.

"Let's go back to North Carolina," he said as she said, "I really can't stand New York."

Her mouth opened wide. "You want to go . . . back?"

Ian slid his palm against her cheeks and touched his lips to hers. "My brother once said that my place is wherever Tripp is, but I think he was wrong. My place is wherever you are." Someone jostled him from behind, and Ian repositioned himself and Taylor farther into the mixing crowd.

"Do you mean that?" she asked.

"I just carried a woman down almost ten flights of stairs not knowing if the building was really on fire or not. If that had been Lexi and Tripp and I had to do that, my heart would have been pounding in my chest. I'd have had one of your panic attacks not knowing if we'd get her out. And, she's just a sister to me. God, Taylor, what if that was you?"

"But, isn't New York your home? Isn't this where you're meant to be? I've been in your life a couple weeks and some of that I've been in a coma-like state, and others I've been in ja—" She stopped at Ian's glare.

"What really made you come up here?" People bustled about in Ian's peripheral vision, jockeying for space, moving in and out and probably pick-pocketing a few of those standing around idle.

Taylor didn't respond.

"Something else?" Ian asked.

Her lips firmed.

"The real reason. Tell me the real one. Not about the daring duo of womanhood who love to meddle, especially in my life."

Taylor's smile brought Ian's out. "I never wanted you to leave. Even with the story and conclusions you made, and when Riley explained why you left—all the coincidences. Lexi and Emma reminded me what those are." Her eyes closed.

He sighed, dropping his forehead to her. "I really did think leaving was best, that if I weren't in your life at all, there'd be no chance I could hurt you. But, Taylor, I've been going out of my mind again just like before."

She opened her eyes.

"I'd planned to get the plane and fly down today. Was just pacing my apartment waiting for the phone call that would tell me it was ready. I didn't tell anyone what my plans were, except Tripp."

Taylor snorted a laugh. "And now, I see where his wife gets it. Master manipulators, wouldn't you say?"

"Given they can cheat . . . uh . . . it makes their roles even easier for them."

She reached up and kissed the corner of Ian's mouth. "I want you to be with me, no matter what happens to us. I'm not willing to let a 'what if' from a history that doesn't belong to us screw with me."

"You know, that sounds as bad as someone saying they want to marry a prisoner, right? You're signing your own life sentence at the hands of a man who pretty much wants to have sex with you every minute of every day."

A laugh burst from Taylor. "Bluntness is your forte, Ian."

"I know." His grin spread. "Now, North Carolina, and we see where this goes, or we go back up and see how many more toasters self-combust while we're there?"

"You need to know more about me first . . . I . . . panic sometimes. It's happened more since I've met you. Might get worse."

"I'm not going to pick up a handsaw, fix a faucet or toilet. Either you can do it, or I'll hire someone."

"I spend twelve hours a day outside with a ton of guys. Some go shirtless. Some are pretty ripped."

"I'm not opposed to a threesome."

The burgeoning crowd pressed closer to them as if listening in on their back and forth conversation. Laughter flowed around them.

"I don't like pools. I don't like bonfires, even though I'm an outdoorsy, girl."

"What're you guys listing?" A bystander jumped up to them. "Sorry. I'm bored waiting for this ridiculous fire alarm."

"Whether to stay in New York with me," Ian said. "Or to go to North Carolina, where she lives. Probably forever."

"Go with her!" a woman said, sidling up to the man who'd interrupted. "That's so romantic."

The guy rolled his eyes.

"They've been listening." Taylor tried to turn, but stuck in Ian's hands, she came right back to him, her body bouncing with her laughter. "This is so embarrassing."

"I'm going to want to take a lot of trips because of my work. I'll want you to go with me."

Taylor smirked. "I don't like boats."

"I don't like slow."

Groans rang out through the growing crowd. "Go with her!" More female voices shouted out.

"I like steak," Taylor said.

"Me, too. I think that seals the deal." Ian crushed her lips with his, wrapping his arms around her as the crowd cheered. "Guess it's time to get my redneck on."

26

The plane banked left, Ian sitting at Taylor's side. She snuck a peek out the window. The city, on the edge of the Atlantic Ocean, stood tall and proud as if waving her away and wishing Ian well as he left New York behind.

"We have a couple hours to kill. Ish." Ian leaned forward, elbows resting on his knees.

Taylor shifted to him. "I could think of a few things to do."

His muscles flexed under his shirt. "Could you now?"

"Yes." The sound came out low and sultry.

His hands clenched together. "Anything interesting? Or just plain normal?" He added a soft kiss to the edge of her lips.

She tilted as he did, their movement a dance that shifted only as the plane increased its altitude in a smooth glide toward the heavens.

"You know . . . I don't think I've done so much first base stuff since I was ten," Ian said.

Taylor's laugh hit the roof. As her mirth subsided, she faced him again. "Ten, Ian? Really?"

"I'm just that good." A small shrug accompanied his smirk.

"I might have to test that theory. Again." She grabbed his shirt, tugged him forward and covered his lips with hers. Rather than let him lead, she did, slipping her tongue between his lips and pushing their kiss further. Taylor nipped the side of his jaw up to his lobe. She stretched out her hands, reaching for his. "Mile high club?"

The belt of his seat unclipped faster than she could blink. A second later, Taylor found herself whisked into his arms and perched on his lap. Ian's hands gripped her as if he needed to hold tight to keep her in place.

She kissed the underside of his chin, moving down his neck to where his shirt separated at the first button.

A low growl rumbled in his chest. "I've wanted my hands on you since I first heard your voice. I've wanted to touch you at every opportunity. Being apart again was a total waste of time and energy."

She nipped at his skin. "Then, let's make up for that."

His hands gripped her hair, and he pulled her forward until her breasts pressed against him through the sheath of her T-shirt.

"I've wanted you since the first moment I saw you." She nipped at his ear. "Whatever happens from this point forward, I want to know I satisfied one of my many little fantasies." Her tongue teased back to his lips.

"Anything. At this point, if you told me you'd planned *my* murder, I'd still be willing." He slid from the seat, following as he lowered her to the small space between the two rows.

"There's not a lot of room down here." She wriggled until her shoulders fit between the two chair legs.

"I can deal if you can."

Looking up at him from the floor, she reached for his buttons, undoing each one with slow, measured precision. "I can."

The sight of his chest, uncovered, with a fine layer of dark, soft hair, forced a tremble through her body.

John.

She slid the sleeves of his work shirt over his shoulders until he drew out of each, one by one. She yanked on his belt, and he undid the tie, sliding it from the loops.

Never before had a farmer's breeches been so desirable.

John braced himself above her. "I know the space ain't big, but—"

"With you, any place will do." She ran a hand down his face, the day's growth of beard roughening her palm. With a wide grin, she worked to press down the fabric at his waist, her hand slipping between wool and skin, short nails brushing against the side of his thigh.

He closed his eyes, and a long moan left his lips.

"Anticipation is much of the enjoyment, wouldn't you say?" She slid her hand down and around until she reached her goal.

He lowered until his lips touched hers. From left to right, he nibbled while she caressed.

A bump of turbulence brought Taylor back to their moment, to Ian, and to the realization she'd just experienced another of her out of body memories, yet her hand remained firmly around his reality.

"What's wrong?" His eyes held nothing but concern.

Taylor smiled. "Nothing." With eyes closed again, she willed the memory to come back. "Nothing at all."

He repositioned to the side, lying with her in the straw in the upper loft of the barn, just under the easement, in the crook where no one would ever search. His finger stroked a line along her face.

"Where are your thoughts?" she asked.

His lips curved. "Would you, if the circumstance differed, consider marrying the likes of me?"

She couldn't contain her smile. "Without a doubt. I would marry you today if Father would but allow."

His smile remained as hers grew.

She took the opportunity to reverse their positions until she lay above him. His hands moved with speed but matched the sensual dance and play they'd found themselves in before. Fingertips unraveled her rear corset's ties, and she rose up so he could smooth the cotton over her shoulders, down her arms and expose her torso. His hands cupped her breasts, sending tingles through her. She lowered again, hair falling from her ribbon and onto his face.

He separated the strands, sliding his hands between them and cupping her cheeks. A tug brought her down to his lips, his hips driving up as she nibbled his ear.

With her touch to his thigh, he let go and pushed at his trousers, removing them with a few quick movements.

She repositioned herself against him, the way a tree roots with the earth, each extension fitting as if made to be together. Skin to skin, dotted with perspiration more from eagerness than exertion, and with their gazes locked on each other, she took him inside her.

His eyes shuttered as her own did the same. Lost in the beauty of her own thoughts, John became the only man Claire could picture—the only man she ever wanted. The only man with whom she would ever share of herself.

A bump jostled her, and Taylor opened her eyes again to find a grin across Ian's face.

"Where did you go?" Ian asked.

"With you. Always you," She lifted her hips just a bit.

Ian drove into her with a slow, painful back and forth like a violin's bow across a low note, gauging just how long it could hold out before it had to reverse course.

The tease drove pleasure through her.

She closed her eyes again, savoring.

Each touch of his hands on her body, his lips against her skin, and their simple connection made her want to cry out for more. He'd move slow and tease, build to a crescendo, and she'd hold off on her release, desperate to remain connected with John.

Her lip throbbed from her bite, their whispered words the loudest of their sounds as horses whinnied and the hiss of a feline followed the bark of her daddy's sheepdog.

John levered up onto his elbows, wrapped one arm around her and spun them so he lay across her again. "Would you deny my wish to pleasure you?"

She reached her arms above her head, giving the entirety of herself over to him, his fingers grasping and intertwining with hers. "As you wish, my love."

Warmth spread to the farthest reaches of her body, branding her with the scent, touch and taste of the man above her. A kiss to her cheek, and her legs tightened around him. A touch to her neck, and his speed increased. A lick at her lips, and her entire world rocketed toward the sun in a blinding fury of passion.

Their chests heaved against one another, neither prepared to move, as if she had fused with him in a mating dance made to last centuries—as right as if they'd repeated an event that tied them across time.

"Taylor." Her name came out a loud whisper into her ear and snapped her back to the plane.

She wanted to respond, but her heart lurched as it had so often since she'd met him.

Throughout the centuries.

Ian added a soft kiss to the side of her neck.

She sucked in air to keep her voice steady and said, "You really know how to please a woman." She stroked his back, running her fingers along the ridges of muscle. "I believe I've always known that."

"Only you." He started to shift, but Taylor held him in place. "Aren't I heavy?"

"Nah." She drew lazy circles along the side of his rib cage. "I'm . . . happy right now."

The plane bucked.

"We're descending already, you know." He didn't move from his spot, but instead entangled their fingers again. "We've been on our way down for a while, actually."

"Doesn't your pilot have to remind us to buckle up?"

Ian chuckled. "I think he did. I remember something coming through the speaker, but I was a bit preoccupied."

The bump of wheels against ground had them both laughing, and the thruster of the single-engine plane reversed, sending their bodies forward by an inch.

"Guess we missed a lot of the flight." Her fingernail ran low on his side.

Ian jumped with what she assumed to be an unexpected tickle. "S'okay by me. Though I'd swear you were in another world a couple times. You said John again."

"My lives are mixing. When we . . . you know, do this?"

His chest bumped against hers. "This . . . meaning when you make love with me?"

Her cheeks heated. "Yeah, that."

"You're embarrassed, yet you've started each of our experiences."

"Which is very unlike me. Anyway . . ." She patted his cheek. "I . . . experienced another time. It happens each time. Sometimes with a kiss. Sometimes all the way. It's . . . amazing, Ian. I'm here, yet I'm there and in both . . . I—"

As their speed decreased, Taylor realized they needed to dress. Fast.

She pushed up, but Ian held her down.

"You . . . what?"

"We're about to surprise our pilot."

"Enh." His shoulder bumped into her armpit. "That's not what you were going to say. What was it?"

"You want him to see your dangly bits?"

The grin coupled with a laugh brought her own chuckle. "Trust me. It's not dangling."

"I can't believe you let him open that door. Why? Why? Why? Why? Why?" Taylor slid out of the car and stepped onto the sidewalk toward the path up to her house.

"Enh." Ian shrugged for the umpteenth time.

"You said that on the plane, Ian. And, I have asked repeatedly. Are you a sexual show-off? Do I need to worry what might end up on the Internet?"

"Enh." He held open the front door but grabbed her arm as she tried to pass. With one quick pull against him, he laid his lips along hers.

Taylor's body melded against him. "What was that for?" she asked when he released her.

"Enh."

"Great. Now he's a caveman." The sarcasm in her voice mixed with giddiness as she strolled into her house to the smells of the raspberry potpourri she kept stashed in each room, to familiarity, to normalcy. A flick of the interior switch illuminated the room. "Home, sweet, home." She dropped her keys in their bowl, breathing a sigh as a smile took hold of her lips. "Would you like something to eat?"

"What, the peanuts and half a can of Coke on the plane weren't enough?" The front door closed. Ian's footsteps echoed through with a cadence and weight she'd come to recognize. "This is ... uh ... country." He chuckled as he took a seat on a bar stool.

She assumed he referred to the denim-patterned walls with white accents, the hanging pots and her collection of ceramic teapots, rather than the stainless steel, marble countertops or the empty fridge. "We didn't have peanuts—"

The look Ian sent her said 'duh' without words. "Tell me what you were going to say on the plane."

A shiver started in her spine but she banked it, forcing herself still. "Um ... so, I don't do a lot of cooking." Taylor spun to her cabinets, withdrew a box of cereal and set it on the counter. "Cheerios?"

"So, you're going to just ignore me?" Ian took the box. "You do know this has a best when used by date, right?"

"Of course." She laid her hands on the countertop, but grabbed the pile of mail she'd set on the edge and rifled through. She'd managed to ignore it all through the week, not realizing how much she'd acquired.

"And, this expired about three months ago." He chuckled.

"Well, shoot." Taylor shifted toward her clock. "And, it's eleven already. I don't think anything but one or two fast food joints might be open. Or the grocery store."

Ian stood and walked around the counter where Taylor separated bills from junk and coupons from personal stuff. He ran his hands down her arms. "You said your lives are mixing."

Taylor eyed the mail again. "Hey, check this out." She waved an envelope at Ian.

He lifted her chin. "What were you going to say?"

With a sigh, she said, "I was going to say I was in love with you. In that life. I was. And, I feel ... I feel ..."

"You feel it now." He ran his hand behind her head and drew her closer. "Just like all those little things I can't know about you but do. Like how you love the smell of lavender, but not sage. How you cut your finger on the fence while pretending to bark orders so you could watch me at work."

She jerked back.

He held her in place. "I don't know how I know these things. I just do. But, if you loved me ... if I loved you ... why would I kill you? Why wouldn't I want to savor every inch of you?"

"I don't know. Oh!" Her lids went wide.

"What?"

"What if ..." She slipped out of his hold and paced across the kitchen floor and back. "What if you did it because I asked you? What if it was a Romeo and Juliet thing, and seriously, we were waiting until the times were right?" She wagged a finger in the air. "What if it was our own plan to get to number four?" Taylor reached Ian and laid her palms against his cheeks. "What if *we* did it, on purpose, and now we're here, and we know, and the world isn't going to separate us?"

"Like hell it will."

She smiled up at him. "This is awesome, Ian! This has to be it. There's no way I would hurt you, and no way you would hurt me, so this had to be our plan." Taylor wrapped her arms around him as his hands slid to her lower back. "This has to be it!" She giggled as if the answer had always been there. "I love you!"

Ian stiffened.

Taylor forced herself to calm and angled her head until their gazes met. "I love you, Ian. I've never met a man like you, and I've never had feelings like these. From everywhere. From all over. I'm—we're—"

"Connected." He dipped down and pressed his lips against hers. "I've never told anyone I love them, Taylor, but I don't want to screw this up."

"You don't think my theory is right."

He shook his head. "Not in my gut. Not like those feelings I get about you. Yes, I—"

She patted his cheek. "It's okay. We southern girls like to love. I think it'll hit ya soon enough." With that, she grabbed the mail that had fallen to the counter. "Oh! Look. It's from Sherrill."

Ian leaned forward, and Taylor shook the envelope in front of him. 'Photos—Do not bend.' had been stamped on both sides.

"Think she sent us copies?" Ian asked.

Taylor pulled out a knife to slide through the tape. An inner envelope slid from within the cardboard packaging. A quick rip opened the first, and a sticky note and two photos slid to the marble surface.

Ian picked up one while Taylor took the other. "This is the one she showed us," he said.

"This isn't." Taylor waved the second one with a sticky note attached to it, too. "Dear Taylor, I found this one as I was scouring another box. Sorry that I didn't have it at the time you were here. Thought you might like it. All copies of course, no harm done if you destroy them. Sherrill." Taylor pulled the note off and dropped it in the trash. "Oh. My. God." Her hand flew to her chest as the photo fell to the counter.

Ian snatched up the image.

She shook her head. *This isn't possible.*

The photo tilted left and right in Ian's hand, like he studied it. "What do you see that I don't see?" he asked.

"What *do* you see?" Her hand shook.

He angled it to the left. "I see another of the supposed you and supposed me. I see a barn. I see cows. You're talking to someone." He pulled the photo in closer. "I'm not getting your reaction."

She took it back and stared at it. *Barn—the one we made love in our last time. Ian. Me. Cows. Check.* The same old, faded, black and white reflected back at her—the same as the original Sherrill had provided. "That face. Here." She pointed to the one her 'supposed self', as Ian called them, seemed to be talking to.

"What about it?"

"That looks like . . . Tanner."

Ian ripped it from her hands again. "No, it doesn't."

"You've seen him?"

"Of course. We had them send us his mug shot from Alabama when he was finally booked, and the photo from the identification at the morgue. They matched."

Taylor's shoulders relaxed. "Okay." *Not really.* "I'm probably just tired. Seeing things. Or really confused." She didn't believe herself.

"That's to be expected with all the travel. Don't worry about it. I will, though, send it up to Michael and get his team to look into it."

She leaned into him. "Thank you. What would I do without you?" *Again.*

Ian chuckled. "I know *some* things you wouldn't have done." He gave her a wink along with a kiss.

Taylor bumped her hip against his as her stomach grumbled. "How about food?"

"I know who we can bug." Ian tucked the photo back into the envelope.

Taylor waved both arms in front of her. "Oh, no. I'm not about to go to Tripp and Lexi's at this hour—"

"No, not them. Tripp would fry me over coals he lights and flames himself. So, not him. Emma owes me a few, and she's a really good cook."

"What is between you two?" Taylor asked as she grabbed her keys, preparing to go.

"Nothing romantic, if that's what you're worried about." He raised an eyebrow.

Taylor wanted to ask more but she valued privacy. She'd just have to trust him. "What about the grocery store? It's open twenty-four—" At Ian's glare, Taylor stopped. "Okay. Emma's. Least you can do is let me put on some clean clothes. I've been in these all day."

Ian nodded, and Taylor forced herself not to race to her bedroom—the one space in her home where she'd added girly touches.

The baby blue walls accented with taupe trim and her white four-poster bed called to her. She ignored them and went to her dresser, pulled out clean jeans, a T-shirt and fresh underwear. "Commando?" She weighed the panties and bra in one hand before she stuffed them back in their drawer. She might have been somewhat demure in her previous life, but with Ian, she'd never experienced more pleasure and wanted to prove to him that love would conquer all.

The mirror in the bathroom showed bags under her eyes, mussed hair—the dregs of fatigue and a body ravaged by what the doctors had termed "an unidentifiable virus." Taylor called it living-through-multiple-lives-and-dying-three-times. Just the thought brought her mind back to the photo in her kitchen.

She stared at herself. "That was Tanner. Wasn't it?" Her shoulders dropped. "No. Stupid-head. You're just tired."

27

Ian stalked toward the front of Emma's white, clapboard, single-story house on the edge of town, despite the lack of light, no car in the driveway and no sign of life.

"Shouldn't we call her or . . . maybe just forget it? She's obviously not here," Taylor said. "Or, she's in bed. Sleeping. Like normal people."

"Which is all the more reason to break in and pilfer through her fridge."

Taylor grabbed his arm. "They told me you were the good guy. That you didn't do all the bad stuff. I'm all about the southern hospitality, Ian, but this is a bit much."

He squished up his lips and jiggled the keys. "I promise, I have permission. You'll just have to trust me."

Taylor stopped him again. "What if she's sleeping, and her car's in the shop? Aren't you going to surprise her?"

The curve of his lips moved into his every essence. "All the better. I owe her still, despite my saying she owes me."

"But—"

"Taylor, seriously. Calm down. You don't know Emma the way I do. I spent almost two weeks with her babysitting Lexi eons ago. We learned a lot about each other, such as, one—" He held up his finger. "—she's a night owl and loves to party. Two, she loves a practical joke. Three—" Ian held up another finger but didn't go on. "I don't know if there is a third. But this is not a B and E job. I have a key and the alarm code—which she never uses."

"Fine, fine."

With Taylor at Ian's side, they entered to a silent and dark house.

Ian flipped on the light as he called, "Emma, you home?" but received no response. "Like I said, she's a night owl. C'mon." He took Taylor's hand and dragged her toward the kitchen, flipping switches as he passed through.

"Wow," Taylor said.

"What?"

"This kitchen is made for a chef. And, you said she's in real estate?"

"Yup." Ian pulled open the cool side of the side-by-side refrigerator. "Have a seat at the bar, milady, and I shall serve you."

Taylor froze. "You used to call me that."

"Call you what?" Container after container, he brought them out—each one labeled with a date and contents—followed by a bottle of wine and placed them all on the blue, granite countertop.

Taylor took the closest seat to the door. "Milady ... you used to call me Milady."

Ian eyed her as he opened containers, extracted servings and popped them into the microwave. "Maybe that's because you were—are—were—" He forced himself calm. "Dammit, that was a trap wasn't it?"

Taylor laughed, filling the space around them. "No, not a trap at all. Mama doesn't think I'm much of a lady, either."

Ian stayed mute as he opened containers, exposing lasagne, barbeque and mixed greens, and popped some into the microwave to warm up. He poured Merlot into two of Emma's champagne flutes and took a seat on the red leather barstool next to Taylor, downing the serving of wine he'd given himself.

"What does wine do to you? Relax you or make you want to table dance?" he asked.

Taylor chuckled into her glass. "It's relaxing. Like my work.

It might seem like the wrong career, but I love it. You know this place is just as homey as mine. Do you know who did all the work?"

He shook his head. "No idea. It functions, and someone else made it happen. That's what makes me happy." The microwave beeped, and Ian went to it as the front door slammed.

"Oh, my freaking hell." Emma stormed into the kitchen, threw her black bag on the counter and faced Ian and Taylor respectively.

Taylor set her glass down as Ian put her plate of food in front of her. "We'll just—"

"Sit," Ian said. "What's wrong, Em?" He continued on with the dishing out of food and the follow-through warm-up.

Emma yanked at the red bow keeping her blond hair tucked behind her head. "You will *not* believe this guy I went out with. Three weeks and nothing. No sex. No kiss. Just wanted to get information for some article about Rune. Dammit. Am I losing my touch?" Her hand patted her chest over the red, sleeveless v-neck that glittered under the simple kitchen lights. "Have I gotten old? Is almost thirty and a half too much for people? It's not like I was looking for a permanent thing." She turned to the fridge as Ian took his seat again and winked at Taylor.

She opened her mouth as if to speak, but he shook his head.

Emma turned back from the fridge, one hand still on the handle. "Am I ugly, Ian?"

Minefield! Minefield! Abort! Abort! You already screwed up once tonight. Do not answer. Walk away! Run! Ian filled his mouth to avoid having to add any commentary.

Emma dropped her elbows on the counter. A second later, she lifted up and grabbed a glass, poured it full of wine and leaned her hip into the edge. "Maybe it's the jeans. They are my fat pants."

Ian nearly spit out his food, his lips fluttering and pursing to hold it in.

Taylor chuckled. "I have a pair of those, too. Best things I ever purchased." She held up her glass, and Emma clinked it. "So, where'd you meet this guy? Any place I should stay away from?" Taylor's fork hit her plate as Ian turned to her.

He pointed to himself with his pasta-wrapped utensil.

Taylor's shoulder nudge set his nerves tingling, though he wondered for a second at her comment about seeking out others. Before she could speak, he forced his dinner down, leaned over and took her lips with his. Taylor's brief shriek faded before he let go.

"What was that for?" she asked.

"To remind you why you don't want to go to the bars and joints Emma finds herself in where stupid men hang out who don't take care of her." Ian offered Emma a wink.

She rolled her eyes at him and pulled a bucket of ice cream from the freezer.

"I was trying to be supportive. See if I offer to empty out your fridge again in the future." He waved his fork at her again.

Her chuckle sent the tension flying from the room.

"So, this guy?" Taylor interrupted their banter.

"Met him at the grocery store. He was buying melons, you know, and holding them up like boobs."

Ian sat straight. "And, that turned you on to him?"

Emma waved. "He wasn't actually doing that, Ian. Just weighing them, and I told him he should be careful with the produce otherwise someone might mistake him for a transvestite."

"You did not," Taylor said, her fork clattering to her plate.

"Why not? It worked." Emma shrugged as she dug into the ice cream. "I should have seen it coming, though. He'd ask me questions about me, but mostly, he was scoping out the city." She sucked on a big spoonful of some chocolatey-looking frozen concoction, probably one she'd made herself. "Then, tonight—" She stopped, squished up her lips and pointed to them.

"Got peanut butter stuck to the roof of your mouth?" Taylor asked.

Emma nodded. A few more shakes of her head occurred before

she opened her mouth again. "Phew. Okay, so, tonight he says, 'Well, Emma, my work in town is almost done. I'll be taking my leave of you soon."

"He sounds polite," Taylor said.

"He sounds like a pansy." Ian earned a glare from both women. He backed off and focused on his food.

"So, I asked him when he was leaving. And, he said 'soon, soon', but I might not see him again, so he wished me well." Her fist slammed on the counter. The plates and glasses all jumped. "Can you believe that? I totally got blown off."

Ian kept his eyes cast down.

"All you men suck," Emma said, though Ian heard the love.

He popped back up. "Okay, who's this dastardly dickhead? I shall take my leave of you two beautiful women and go pummel him. If nothing else, for making you so mad you messed up my foraging."

Emma belted out a laugh. "Oh, God, Ian. You can be funny when you aren't trying to be mean." She stood straight again and stared at him. "You'd do that for me?" Her hands crossed over her chest.

"Enh. It's nothing." He added a small shrug.

Taylor's laugh mixed with Emma's.

"Jason Porter hasn't seen anything if you're coming after him."

Taylor jerked so hard her entire seat wobbled.

Ian caught her before she toppled. "You okay?"

She coughed into her hand. "Did you say Jason Porter?"

"Yeah." Emma waved another spoon full of ice cream.

Ian's worry ratcheted up a notch. "What's wrong, Taylor?"

"That's the name of one of Tanner's friends—the ones who fell off the bell tower in Alabama."

Taylor pushed the stool back from the counter and stood. "What does this guy look like, Emma?" Taylor's hands shook, and she clenched and released them in a bid to relieve the tension.

"Jason Porter isn't a particularly unique name." Ian scooped up another bite of his food.

"I know. I just—I need to know."

"Okay," Emma said. "He was … um … about six feet, maybe a little more. Dark hair, pretty super-white, like no tan and had brown eyes. Actually his hair was brown, too."

Taylor dropped her face into her palms. "Not him. Thank God." She tugged at her hair, stepping away from Emma and Ian. "I just can't help but think Tanner's involved again. With me. The bones. Something. Whether it's a legit concern or not."

Ian wrapped his arms around her. "Hey." His voice soothed even as torment reigned in her mind. "Remember. One … he's dead. Two … how in the hell would he have known those bones were there? He couldn't have. So, he's not involved in that. Three … well, I'm not sure there's a three."

"Coincidences are just that," Emma said. "Odd combinations of stuff that people make more of in their heads."

The firmness of Ian's chest warmed Taylor as her frustration mounted, ebbed, grew again and slowed. "I'm so tired. That's got to be what it is."

"We'll just be going now," Ian said as if he could read Taylor's thoughts.

"Take some leftovers?" Emma asked.

"Later. Taylor owes me breakfast. From scratch."

Emma pointed her spoon at Taylor. "I saw your fridge last week. All you have are sweet rolls and old, dry cereal. You'll be back by nine. With empty stomachs." She nodded, licking her spoon in the process.

Taylor reached her arms above her head, smiling when she hit her own headboard. The realization that no dreams had plagued her sleep arrived as she rolled beneath her blankets and found

Ian's eyes open, his gaze fixed on her.

"Good morning." Her purr would have told anyone how she'd slept.

"Hi," he said back. "Sleep well, I take it?"

She closed her eyes. "Yeah. Very. How long you been awake?"

"Five minutes. Or less. You moved. I woke."

Taylor leaned forward and snatched a kiss from Ian's lips. "You know what I'm craving?"

"What?"

"One of those sweet rolls Emma reminded me of last night. My neighbor brought them over yesterday. I didn't even get to eat one before I was whisked away to New York for the day."

Ian pushed up from his spot. "Where are they?"

Taylor's brows furrowed. "They were on the counter, but Mama probably put them in the breadbox or the microwave since I never even locked up."

Ian leaned forward and kissed her. "Then, I'll find one and bring it to you."

"Really?" Her eyes opened wide. "I didn't take you for a cook."

"Yes, really. And that's not cooking. Plus … I can find food when I need to." He slipped from the bed without grabbing any covering.

Taylor's little-girl giggle took hold. "Are you about to go into my kitchen stark naked?"

"Yeah. Got a problem with it?"

Her fit of laughter continued even as she grabbed pillows and stuffed them behind her back to prop herself up.

"What're you doing?" He stopped at the edge of her bed.

"I'm watching the show. Don't want to miss the second act or the encore performance."

Ian strutted the rest of the way through the door until he disappeared from sight. Taylor tracked his footsteps through her house, down the hallway, into the wide expanse of her living room and to the kitchen. Cabinets opened and closed. The sucking sound as the fridge doors opened and the swishing as they closed reached her.

"Taylor?"

"Yeah?" She pitched her voice so he'd hear, and she wouldn't have to get up.

"I'm not seeing any rolls."

"Check the breadbox."

"I did." Silence ensued. "Actually, I'm not seeing a few things. Didn't we leave the mail from Sherrill on your counter? So I could send that picture to Michael?"

Taylor threw the covers off, grabbing her robe on the way out of her room. Panic set in, tightening her chest. "What do you mean?" She went straight to the spot where she'd left the photos. A run through of the envelopes left her with bills and junk, but nothing from Sherrill. She strode to her microwave, to the pantry, even checked her fridge. No sweet rolls.

"Maybe Mama came over. Let me just call her." A turn brought her to the wall phone, and with a few presses of buttons, the connection rang out.

"Hi, Baby. Back already?" her mom asked.

"Yeah. Late last night. Um …"

"Need me to bring breakfast?" A small chuckle came from the background. "You didn't eat all those sweet rolls already, did you? That'll add a few pounds."

Taylor rolled her eyes, happy not to be seen. "You took one to Daddy, right?"

"Yes. He ate it right up last night. Said it was the best one since … well … forever."

"Okay. Good."

Mumbles from within her parent's home came through the line, but Taylor couldn't understand them. "Your daddy suggests you heat up the extras in the oven for a pinch over ten minutes instead of wasting them in that microwave. They taste much better that way."

A shiver raced down Taylor's body. She faced Ian and closed her eyes. "Thanks, Mama. I gotta go, just wanted to let you know I was back. Oh, and Ian's with me."

"Aw, darling, that's great. Does he need a place to stay while he's here?"

Taylor nearly snorted her laugh but managed to hold it back. "No. He can stay at Tripp and Lexi's." She gave Ian a wink. A point to the phone should have told him the real reason for her answer.

"Well, how about your father and I treat you two to dinner one night?"

"That'd be great."

"Okay, let me see what night we're free, and I'll call ya'll back. How long is Ian staying?"

"Uh . . ." Taylor wanted to say 'forever'. "Not sure. Just call me and let me know."

"Okay. Take care then."

"Thanks, Mama." Taylor replaced the phone in its cradle.

Ian snuck up to her, his hands against her hips. "You're shivering." He pulled her tighter against him.

Taylor laid her head against his chest. "Someone's been in my house."

28

An immediate need to race through the rooms with a weapon in hand filled Ian. "What do you mean, someone's been in your house? I've been here. Your mom has." He misinterpreted on purpose.

Taylor's head moved side to side against his chest. "No, I mean, someone . . . *else*."

Yeah, I know. "Do you have a cleaning service?"

"No."

Damn. "Anyone else got keys?"

"Just Mama and Daddy. And Riley—"

Riley.

"—but he only has them for emergencies."

Emergencies. Right. Ian held Taylor out so he could look into her eyes. "You need to call him."

"And do what? Ask him if he's been in my house and stolen my sweet rolls—"

"And the photo."

Taylor spun away from Ian. "He wouldn't do that, and it was midnight. He'd have been asleep." She paced the length of the kitchen, to the bay window, around the table and back. "He wouldn't."

Ian held up his hands. "He could have borrow—"

"Riley wouldn't do that without telling me. He's a police officer. He has high standards." She stared up at Ian, her feet braced as if for attack.

Ian went to her and took her in his arms. "Through all my years, there's one thing Tripp and I have always vowed."

"What's that?" Her arms went around his neck.

"To listen to our gut. If it's talking, and it's not gas, it's important."

Chuckles bumped her against him. "And what is your gut saying?"

"That Riley needs to know about this."

Taylor rolled her eyes as well as any teenager. "If I tell Riley about this, he's going to flip out, and will try to hide me under a bush or lock me up 'for my own safety'." The latter part came out as pure sarcasm.

"Sometimes," Ian said, "we do what we have to do."

Three phone calls and one drive-thru run later, Ian and Taylor's car crunched gravel in Lexi and Tripp's driveway. Riley's black pickup waited, with him standing at the front. Emma rocked in a chair on the wide expanse of porch, and, Ian assumed, Lexi and Tripp waited inside. He parked, grabbed the bags of biscuits and goodies from the back seat, and slipped from the car.

Riley pushed off from his truck, tucked what looked like a cell phone in his jeans pockets and didn't even look toward Ian.

As soon as Taylor got within his reach, he put his hands on her biceps, holding her still and in front of him. "Tell me why you asked me if I'd been to your house."

"I will, but I'd rather do it once—"

"You think someone has, then. Who?"

Taylor shook her head. "I don't know."

"This needs to be reported—"

"I'm just a little leery of having any more police around my house, Riley."

Ian held up the bags, nudged Taylor with his shoulder and walked away. From within his peripheral vision, Riley let go, and both he and Taylor followed.

On the porch, Emma stood, opened the door and waved them in. "Sherrill's scanning the photos for you," she said as they passed. "She'll text me when she's done and send them to us."

Ian gave her a small nod. "Thanks."

"Good morning." In the kitchen, Lexi sipped from a cup, a pile of saltine crackers at her side, while Tripp stood leaning back against the sink.

When Ian dropped the breakfast on the table, Lexi jumped up and ran from the room.

A door somewhere in the back slammed shut, and Emma went after her.

"She upset about something?" Ian asked as the scent of bacon, eggs, biscuits and gravy wafted from the bag.

"Or is that morning sickness?" Taylor asked.

"The second," Tripp said. "And God help me, I'm gonna die if I have to eat crackers for breakfast again." He grabbed an orange and white wrapper from the table, unfurled it and bit in. His eyes closed as if heaven itself descended upon his taste buds.

"My sister spent the first trimester doing the same thing," Riley said.

Ian took a seat, motioned to Riley and Taylor to do the same. Tripp dropped onto the end stool as Emma came back in.

"She says to eat, hurry it up and throw all remnants away." Emma grabbed a biscuit and dove into it as fast as Tripp had.

"She been like this long?" Ian asked as he savored his own hand-held goodness.

"Almost two weeks," Tripp mumbled behind a bite. "Was fine for a while, and then it hit her. Every morning, she comes in here, sips her tea ready to eat some crackers, and it either all comes back up, or she pounds another portion or two down. I don't get it."

"All day?" Taylor asked.

Tripp shook his head. "Usually by noon, she's good *if* she's been sick. If she's having a good day, she'll eat like a horse from the moment she wakes up."

"It'll end," Riley said. "Katie swears she'll never have another during those first twelve weeks."

"She's on her third of the brood, isn't she?" Taylor bounced with a small laugh.

Riley nodded, his hands tucked in his lap. "Don't you want a whole bunch, Tay? Something like a half dozen to fill up your Mama's house to mess it up on purpose."

Taylor shot Riley her middle finger.

"You can eat, you know," Emma said to Riley. "It's gonna go to waste if you don't, thanks to Lexi's overactive sense of smell." Emma slid a wrapped package to him. "You want kids, Riley?"

He took one of the breakfast sandwiches. "I don't think about it much since I'm not married." His emphasis on the last part came with a direct glance toward Taylor.

Sitting between them, Ian swiveled back and forth to catch the looks.

"How long have you two known each other?" Tripp asked.

"All our lives," Riley said. "She was the girl next door through high school. I've seen the pigtails, first bikinis, braces, acne, all grown up—all the stages."

"And, you never made a move?" Tripp asked.

Ian shot his best friend a glare.

Tripp grinned.

Riley chuckled. "Would you have wanted to date Emma?"

Emma batted Tripp with her hand. "That's just mean."

"What? I didn't say anything!" Tripp shirked away from another slap. "That would be like dating Missy. *That's* gross."

"Exactly," Riley said.

The five of them munched in amicable silence for a few minutes until Lexi stood in the doorway again. Tripp jumped up, and Emma stuffed wrappers in the bag, Riley helping. "It's okay," Lexi said. "Heard the ding of email and checked it. Got this from Sherrill." She waved a paper in the air before handing it to Tripp.

"I'm actually kinda hungry." Another step brought her closer to the table. "Maybe I could—" She turned and ran again.

Tripp hung his head. "This bites. She's probably going to be like this for the rest of the morning, so we can get started anytime."

Emma threw away or stored the remainder of the food and came back to the table. "Whoa." She sat and picked up the photocopy of the pictures. "That *is* totally you two." She brought it closer, pulled it away and brought it in again. "And that's totally Jason Porter."

"What?" Taylor and Ian said.

Emma turned the photo around, holding it in front of herself, and pointed to one man. "This looks like Ian." Her finger ticked to the right. "This one looks like Taylor." She went farther in the same direction. "And, this one looks like Jason. Right? Do I win a prize?"

"Who the heck is Jason Porter?" Riley snatched the photo from Emma.

"Oh, my lord," Riley said, photo still in hand. "That's Tanner."

"Son of a bitch," Ian said.

For the second time that day, Taylor's body shook with an uncontrollable movement. If anyone else had recognized Tanner, it would have been Riley. They'd met once, when Riley'd tried to get her to return to North Carolina and had stayed for the better part of a week trying to convince her.

A month later, Tanner pulled his prank-of-a-lifetime.

"Tell me why all three of you look like you're in the eighteen hundreds," Riley said, his steepled hands resting on the table.

Taylor recognized the gesture. Calm fury—one Riley had perfected over his years on the force. She squelched her internal groan. "Was this what your gut was telling you, Ian?" Taylor asked. "Was this why you didn't think we'd beaten it?"

"Not exactly, but what if he was there, and he's here now—" Ian ran a hand over his head, pursing his lips.

"Then how?" Tripp asked.

"The mind can really play tricks. Maybe—" Ian turned to Tripp. "You got your computer?"

"I'll get it." Tripp disappeared with a scrape of chair legs against the floor.

"Tay?" Riley's simple call of her name held the undertones of one ready to burst.

"I'm just gonna go check on Lexi." Emma scooted back and followed Tripp, leaving Ian, Taylor and Riley together.

"Taylor Claire Marsh. Speak. Now." Riley poked one finger onto the table. "If Tanner Meadows is somehow alive and around here, I need to know. And, I want to know how he's involved in this … thing—" He turned to Ian. "—that you got her caught up with."

A bubble of Taylor's own anger built inside. She opened her mouth to speak as Ian's chair scooted forward with a screech against the floor.

Hands clasped on the table, in much the same way Riley's had been, Ian said, "I didn't bring her into this. It's a game. A fucking messed up one. And now, with these three faces, I'm thinking there's some sort of connection." Ian pointed to the photo.

Taylor held up a finger. "But the game is only us two."

"Jessie recounted a story she was told." Ian adjusted until he faced Taylor. "You know how that is? One person tells a story, another retells it, and the little details change. Who knows if this is related, but I have a feeling … and I told you I listen to my gut."

Taylor sat back, rubbing her hands up her arms.

Ian switched back to Riley. "I think Tanner faked his own death. Again. And took Jason's name. I think he set up Taylor … somehow. I think those two people in that picture are actually Taylor and I, but in another life. It's obvious Tanner was there, too … somehow. But, what his role is, I don't know."

Riley let out a deep sigh. "And, you really believe all this? What you told me in New York wasn't just some … scheme?"

Ian leaned farther across the table. "Do you believe she can move the air?"

"I've seen it with my own eyes," Riley said as Emma, Tripp and Lexi walked back in.

"Seen what?" Emma plopped down in the seat closest to Riley while Tripp opened the laptop.

Taylor dropped her head into her hands. A squeak brought her head back up.

Tripp turned a laptop around until it faced her. "Is this Tanner or Jason, Taylor?"

Her heart lurched as the face stared back at her. The one on the left, clean shaven and unsmiling, matched the one on the right—closed-eyed and with the pallor of death. "Not Tanner. But not Jason, either."

Tripp turned it to Emma. "You recognize him?"

Emma nodded. "Jason."

Taylor shook her head again. "No." She closed her eyes. "It's the third guy. From the tower incident."

"What?" Riley beat his fists into his temples. "Why didn't you tell me?"

"I didn't know!" Anger surged through Taylor's words as the news boiled in her gut.

"Would you give me that data, there, Tripp?" Riley nodded his head toward the laptop.

Tripp and Ian turned to each other and back to Riley. "Sure."

"Great. I'm going to take this to my lieutenant and do some digging. We've got ourselves an identity thief—"

"Who was here recently," Emma said.

Riley nodded. "I want to do a little canvassing, too. And, Emma, I'd like to talk with you about your interactions with him." He turned to the others. "I suggest you all try to relax and let me handle this."

Taylor wanted to say 'thank you, yes, take it!', while at the same time, she knew Tanner's involvement meant misfortune would be right around the corner.

"No," she said as Ian said, "I think putting this back in the hands of the police is a good idea."

Taylor swung around to him, her hair hitting her in the face. "Wait . . . what?" She didn't want anyone hurt on her account, including Riley.

Ian stared straight back into her eyes. He took her hand so their ring fingers connected and smiled. "We're going to let them do their job." His head shifted until he faced Riley. "If Tanner messes with Taylor again—"

Riley held up both hands. "Don't say it out loud." A second later, he covered his ears and sidestepped toward the door. "Emma . . . would you mind joining me out here for a second?"

She jumped from her seat and glided after him, the door slamming shut behind them.

Taylor whirled to Ian. "What's going on?"

Ian twisted to Lexi as soon as Riley left. "You'll do this, right, Lex? You'll look for him so I can go have a little chat with him? All I need—"

Lexi sipped at more of her tea and closed her eyes, leaning into Tripp's shoulder. "Sometimes, I hate this gift."

Taylor wanted to ask 'what gift?' but ingrained manners kept her silent while inside curiosity ate at her.

"Please, Lexi?" Ian asked. "I've never asked, and I just need you to tell me where he is."

Tripp held up a hand. "She doesn't do people, Ian. You know that."

"That's bullshit, and *you* know it." Ian slammed his hands against the wall. He spun toward Lexi. "This is more important than—"

Tripp rose, stormed toward Ian, and shoved at his chest with both hands. "Than what, Ian? The delicate nature of my wife?"

Taylor scrambled up, standing between the two men and moving to block Tripp when he slid to the side.

He picked her up by her biceps and spun so she'd be behind him. "You, stay out of this."

Ian responded by scrambling forward and sending Tripp back a few feet. "Do not try me, man. And do not mess with her."

"I can take care of myself." Taylor's rage burst from her.

Ian pounded the counter by the sink, his focus still toward his friend. "Now is not the time to deny me, Tripp. I've spent all my life following you and doing the digging, the research—fuck, everything—"

"Except going in and getting the job done."

"Don't fuck with me, man. We're equals in our partnership."

"Don't ask for what crosses the line."

Already, Tanner's involvement stretched a brother-like bond thin—a result that tugged at Taylor. "Stop—"

"I . . . didn't . . . cross." Ian's fists clenched. He drew one up and shook it at Tripp; for a moment, Taylor considered he might take a swing. "You went looking." He whirled to Lexi. "You did. On your own terms, you went looking for us." He pointed at Taylor. "And now, when I need you to do it for me, for other reasons, you won't?"

"I—" Lexi started.

Tripp's palm met Ian's shoulder and pushed him back. "Get out."

Taylor would have gotten in the middle, but despite her strength, both would bowl her over and ultimately do whatever they wanted without her.

"Tripp, no!" Lexi pushed back from the table and stood, her hands falling to the surface as she did. "Whoa. Head rush." She swayed. Tripp caught her before she fell.

Ian went to her. "I'm sorry, Lexi." A mix of kindness and irritation came through Ian's tone.

"Get the fuck out of my house, Ian." Tripp set her back in

her seat.

"No." Lexi shook her head. "He's right, Tripp."

"I won't have him asking stuff of you when you're not in a position to—"

Lexi crossed her arms over her chest. "Really? You asked me to look for Jill's husband. You asked me to look for the owner of the bone. And, I did both." She gave Tripp a curt nod. "Just because I said 'no people' doesn't mean I'm not going to use every gift I have to make sure our family is safe, Tripp. You ... of all people ... should know that."

Ian snickered as Tripp shuffled backward.

Taylor leaned into the frame of the door separating the kitchen from the living room.

"You think that just because I get a little sick and have to eat crackers and tea, and faint occasionally ... that I'm weak now?"

"No."

"Yes, you do." She flicked the top of Tripp's head. A small snort escaped Ian. "And you." Her finger headed in his direction. "You know I don't look for people. But, this is an exception. You also know I can't do it ... without Tripp. And, he's obviously not going to agree until I do and until you aren't fighting. So, that means you two have to make this right." She waved her hand toward the men. "Kiss and make up."

"Fuck, no," Tripp said to Ian's, "Are you insane?"

Lexi and Taylor laughed. Tripp and Ian turned toward each other. Tripp showed no emotion but held out his fist. Ian's smile broke some of the tension as he connected with it.

"Now ... apologize," Lexi said.

"Gee, Mom," Ian said. "Do we have to?"

She tapped her fingernail on the table.

"I'm sorry," Ian said as Tripp said it, too.

29

Two Fridays later, neither Riley nor Lexi had found Tanner—or rather, neither had provided any news that they had. Ian had his fill of watching Taylor rise with the roosters and chickens, dress in the dark and yell at him to get a move on because she didn't have all day to waste.

Thanks to her incarceration and hospital visit, her renovations had all fallen behind. She'd needed to get back to work, and Ian refused to let her out of his sight, though she'd relegated him to the car with a stern warning not to step foot on her project again unless he'd be willing to help. She had almost three weeks of work to make up since she acted as general foreman for her crews, and in her absence, they'd all slacked off.

Within the confines of the passenger seat of the car, Ian sat with his laptop and continued his research efforts while monitoring the scene before him. Taylor directed, pointed, yelled, and only once did Ian see any sign of excess wind in the area. He'd chuckled as a roofer slid but stopped short of falling off the edge. On the ground, Taylor had stood, her clipboard in one hand, the other outstretched toward the man, her lips moving as if to chastise his failed safety efforts. She'd only pressed at her temples afterward as if the pain of using her gift hadn't been too bad.

If nothing else, Ian learned she ran a proverbial tight ship and understood why Tripp had wanted the infamous 'Taylor Marsh' for his own house's reconstruction.

A knock on the window brought Ian from his laptop screen.

Taylor stood just outside. With a click of the key, the glass slid down.

"Want to make a run for some lunch?" she asked.

"Can't I just order it and have it delivered?"

The roll of her eyes said 'no'. "It might do you some good to leave for five minutes, Ian."

"Not until we know where Tanner is."

"The man's not in town anymore. Riley's been by fifteen times this week. He's shown those photos around and around, and only those downtown even saw Tanner or Jason or whoever he is. If nothing else . . . if he shows up here, I got twelve crew inside, four outside and a cell phone."

"But not me."

Her fingers tapped on the roof of the car. "Seriously, Ian. What's he going to do? Go into town. Get some lunch for you and me. Bring it back. By five, I'll be done for this week." She straightened, her head disappearing from view. A second later, she reappeared. "Oh!"

His heart lurched until her smile reappeared. "What?"

"I forgot to tell you that I made up a whole week thanks to your little push with the plumbers." She reached in with her head and added a kiss to his lips. "Wanted to thank you for that. You're quite the negotiator."

His grin snuck out. "I'm good at the business side of . . . stuff, and—" Taylor's single raised eyebrow eyes stopped him. "What?" he asked.

"Before . . ." Her voice came out a throaty whisper. "Before . . . you were a farmer. You were . . . building a business." Her eyes took on a faraway focus. "You were—you were just getting started. And, you asked my father—to help—that's how we met. I saw you. I mean. I remember." She tilted down to him. "Watching you through the farmhouse windows. Seeing you with my father, learning how to properly budget." She blinked a few times, and her gaze returned to Ian.

He reached out for her hand. “Maybe I learned back then.” He turned her hand over and kissed her palm. “I have a feeling I learned a lot around the time I met you.” He let go and laid her hand on the car’s window frame. “And on that note, we need to go out to that farmhouse still.”

“We?” She leaned her arms on the edge of the door. “Have you decided to start working with me?”

Ian chuckled.

“You’re really not going to let me out of your sight, are you?” Taylor asked.

He shook his head.

“I could make up even more time if you’d get a little dirty.” Her brows flashed up and down. “And, spend time … just with you.” She ran a finger down his cheek.

“I’ll get dirty but not with power tools.”

The call of Taylor’s name took her away from the window again. Her second in command, one Ian had run a few background checks on, shook his head with his cap in his hand. The two conversed for a minute before Taylor came back.

“Please, please, please go get lunch?” She batted her lashes at him like some demure southern belle.

Ian’s lips curved despite his desire to stay resolved. “Fine. I’ll be back in fifteen minutes, but if anything happens, you call.”

She leaned in for another kiss. “Will do. I want a chicken sandwich, please.”

“Yeah, yeah. I’ll play errand boy but only ‘cause I kinda like you.”

“I’ll play helpless girl, and you can be a fire fighter tonight, how about that?”

Ian’s laugh jumped out. “Am I gonna have to play the girl?”

Taylor’s hand shot out and punched him.

He rubbed at the spot on his bicep where she hit. “You didn’t pull that one.”

“You deserved it.” She sauntered off, gave him a salute and

followed her crew back into the house.

A switch to the driver's seat and Ian headed out.

Taylor trudged her way back into the house, following around until she reached the interior bathroom. Two men added tile to the walls but had called her due to colors not matching. A check of the outside of the box revealed the source of the problem. Box number one listed the correct tile and box two a single number off.

"Just do what you can, and I'll get more for Monday," she said.

"We can come in this weekend if that helps, boss," one of the guys said.

Taylor noted the information she needed on her clipboard. "I'll see if they're in the store, and if so, I'll take you up on that." She stepped away, pulling her phone out at the same time as it buzzed. The number on screen didn't show but came through as unknown. She let it go to voicemail as she walked out into the sunshine.

With her back to the house, she navigated her way to her address book and dialed the kitchen and bath store. Her phone buzzed again while it rang, but the same 'unknown' came through, so she ignored it.

". . . Kitchen and Bath, how may I help you?"

Taylor almost missed the response with the phone away from her ear. "Hi, this is . . ." She went on to describe what she needed.

An incoming call buzzed her phone again.

Riley's number popped up. Taylor itched to answer it but needed to finish out her conversation.

"So, you need to replace just the one box?" The woman on the other end of the line talked as slow as Taylor's neighbor.

"Yes, ma'am. I do. Just the one."

"All righty, then. I can have that back . . ." The phone buzzed again with Riley's number. ". . . well, yeah, actually, we do have them in stock."

"Great." Taylor interrupted. "I'll pick them up tomorrow morning."

"Okay—"

"Thanks." She hung up as her phone buzzed again with the 'unknown' number. Rather than ignore it, she answered, "Taylor Marsh."

"Ms. Marsh?"

She tensed at the clipped tone. "Yes."

"This is Kenya with Smart Alarm—"

Taylor's body shivered.

"—We've received notification that your alarm has been triggered. Do we need to send fire and emergency services—"

"I'm not there, so . . ." Taylor ran toward one of her company trucks parked at the edge of the lot. ". . . yes, please send them." She hung up and climbed into the cab, grabbed the keys in the ignition and started it up as her crew ran from the house. "Back later, guys!"

Wheels kicked up gravel as she spun out onto the road.

"Two miles away," she said to herself as she fiddled with her cell to dig up Ian's number.

The sounds of sirens rang through the open window under a clear blue sky. "Shit!" Pressing the accelerator, she pushed the truck through the back roads toward her home.

30

Ian dawdled on his return, enjoying the air-conditioning in Tripp's Jaguar, when his phone rang. "Ian Sands."

"Ian, it's Riley."

"Hi—"

"Are you with Taylor?" Worry coated the question.

Ian's heart thumped hard in his chest. "No, why?"

"They just put out a call for police and fire to her house, and I can't get through to her."

"I'm two seconds from the driveway to her job site."

"Have her get over there . . . and Ian?"

"Yeah?"

"Stay with her."

Ian cocked his head at nobody, the question playing through his mind. "Any reason I should ask why?"

"Yes, actually. I'll meet you at her house." Riley hung up as Ian pulled into the driveway.

He noted a few missing cars but no one outside. A skip through an open door didn't reveal anyone, either. "Hello?" Ian's chest heaved with the rush of adrenaline at Taylor's absence.

Someone popped their head out from one of the rooms. "You lookin' for the foreman?"

"Yeah. She here?"

"Went into town to get some tiles for the bathroom, I think."

"Thanks." Ian slapped a hand against a door frame as he took off toward his car. With his cell in hand, he dialed Taylor's number but received no answer. The door to his car slammed as he got back into his seat, revved the engine and took off down the drive, turning toward town and hoping she'd stay there long enough for him to find her. As he drove, he tried her cell, once, twice and five more times.

She didn't answer any of the calls.

Riley stepped from his car as Taylor drove up. "They got in touch with you?"

She ran toward her house, but he grabbed her arm and pulled her back. "Let go." Taylor yanked herself free. "This is my house." Her bungalow gave no hint of a problem except for the somewhat audible screech of the alarm coming from inside.

Riley caught up to Taylor as a fire truck pulled into the driveway. "I've called Ian. He's on his way."

She walked the length of her front porch, noting the curtains were open with no sign of being disturbed. Taylor moved around to the side and peered in. "It's a false alarm, Riley."

He stood to her side. "You don't know that."

"Why would I have any reason to believe otherwise?" Taylor narrowed her eyes.

"Just let me—"

"No." Key into lock, the door opened. Taylor marched over to the alarm panel, entered her numbers and silenced the inner squealing.

"I can look with you."

"Riley Dale, I *am* a big girl. How many times have I got to tell you that?" She dropped her keys on the counter and began her inspection. The table stood as it had that morning, with chairs tucked tight up underneath. Taylor went back to the living room.

Nothing.

She searched the length of the hallway, popping her head into the bathroom, the second bedroom and her office.

Nothing.

Turning back, she slipped into her room. "Everything's fine, Rile—" She froze.

On her bed lay a red rose, its stem wrapped in a velvet ribbon.

Taylor dropped to her knees, gasping for air, a burn racing through her as a memory took hold.

The blaze accepts her body as its fuel. Kindling snaps. Sparks fly upward, adding to the smoke-filled air.

A touch to her shoulder made her scream. She jumped and scrambled away until her back hit the edge of something.

Her location six feet beneath the surface of the earth, with her hands bound behind, prevents escape. He'd planned well, taking away her ability to save herself.

"John! No!"

Something touched her arms.

He twists her hair around his wrist and pushes lower, forcing himself to move backward toward the outer edge of what should be paradise. "Not this time," he says. "You will not betray my love again."

The intensity of her fear grew until Taylor couldn't hold up her own head. She curled in on herself.

He twirls a single red rose between his fingertips.

On a final breath, the world went black.

Ian stood over Taylor, his face set in a scowl. "Taylor." His voice cracked.

"I don't know what happened." Riley knelt with him.

Ian hadn't smelled anything odd, hadn't seen anything out of the ordinary. Nothing. "Let's get her out of here." He lifted her into his arms and followed Riley out of the room.

"Ian?" Taylor's soft voice stopped him.

He tightened his hold and moved again toward the living room couch.

"I need to breathe."

He relaxed but only a little, dropping to the sofa with her still in his arms. "Are you okay?" An eerie worry came through his tone.

She nodded against him. "What happened?"

"You tell me." His own breath hitched. "You were screaming as if someone was torturing you."

"And you kept yelling 'John'," Riley said.

Ian drew in deep. *John again?* "Calling for me or—"

"In absolute terror," Riley said.

Taylor rested her head against Ian's chest. "The-the … flower."

"The rose?" Riley faced Ian. "You didn't give that to her?"

Ian shook his head. Uncertainty reigned as to whether he wanted to press or not.

Taylor snuggled up against him, her head fitting just above his heart. "And the ribbon. Why did he leave those for me again?"

Ian's heart lurched. *Again?* A knock on the door had Ian tilting up and cut his question of 'He, who?' short.

He glanced at Riley and gestured with his head for him to check it, and Riley stood and headed toward the door.

"Oh, hello, dear." Agnes's voice reached Ian. "Is everything okay? I saw the fire trucks. I hope there are no problems, no gas leaks or anything."

"No problems, Miss Agnes," Riley said from around the corner. "Just a little alarm system on the fritz."

"Oh, well. Those alarm systems … that newfangled technology. A good dead bolt is so much simpler."

"She's a little batty," Taylor whispered.

"I'll be sure to pass on that advice to Taylor, Miss Agnes," Riley said.

"Speaking of which … is Miss Taylor available?"

"Uh …" Riley started.

Taylor extricated herself from Ian and went toward the door. She wiped her hands across her face and through her hair before straightening her shoulders. "Miss Agnes, so good to see you."

To anyone else, Taylor probably sounded sincere, but the slight warble suggested to Ian whatever had happened still bothered her.

"Oh, Miss Taylor! Did I catch you while working?"

"Not you, but that alarm."

Agnes giggled an old lady sound. "Silly technology. Anyway, we're about to leave for our trip. I was hoping you could water my plants? I was going to ask Andy, but he won't be staying after all."

"Andy?" Taylor asked.

Goosebumps formed on Ian's arm. He rose and walked, without making any noise, toward where Taylor and Riley stood.

"Oh, yes. Stayed with us last fall? You remember, dear? He stopped by today," Agnes said. "Asked about you, too."

Ian rounded the frame of the wall and waved at Agnes.

A small pat to Taylor's forearm accompanied Agnes's slight lean forward. "That Andy was such a kind boy, but I like this one you've got here much better." Her giddy, granny laugh normally would have made Ian smile.

"I'm glad to know I've won you over," Ian said. "Who was I competing against again?"

"Why Andy George, of course. Didn't I introduce you?" She patted her blue-rinse hair as if to tap her memory into overdrive.

Taylor swayed, but Ian held her up. "I-I don't think so, Miss Agnes," Taylor said. "I'm sorry I didn't get to meet him."

"Oh, but I was sure I had. Nice fella, about Riley's height, with those European features, the blond hair."

Taylor shook her head.

"Oh, well. We were hoping he'd stay again and house sit." Agnes shrugged. "But, what can you do? You young whippersnappers always galavanting off."

Speak of the devil galavanting off. Agnes had stopped by at least once a day while Ian had stayed with Taylor. She'd regaled him with stories from her trips with her husband.

"He only swung through town just this afternoon and told me he had other plans."

Shaking took hold of Taylor's body.

"What's going on Taylor?" Ian whispered at her ear.

"What … did he ask … about me?" Taylor asked.

Agnes's smile creased every inch of her face. "Oh, you know how men are. He asked how you were getting along, if any suitors had come by. He remembered you being somewhat solitary during his stay last year. I told him you had your Ian here." She laid her hand on Ian's forearm and squeezed. "You are smitten with Miss Taylor, aren't you young man?"

Even as Ian thought, '*Who is Andy George, and why does he have this affect on Taylor?*' he smiled. "I believe I am." His hold on Taylor didn't decrease, but he took Agnes's hand in his. A blush filled her cheeks, pinking them up like a little school girl's.

"Well, I best be going."

"I'll walk you home, Miss Agnes." Riley nodded toward Ian and pushed forward with Agnes.

"Have a good trip," Taylor said as the door closed behind them.

With every step, Taylor wobbled, and Ian had to steady her. "Tell me what's going on. Who is Andy George?"

"One of the three." She fell to the couch and leaned forward, heaving air. "From the tower accident in Alabama." Taylor shook her head from one side to the other in a way Ian understood to be deliberate. "He's doing something. Planning. He took this Tanner guy's name, faked his identity and set me up before. Why?" Before Ian could speak, Taylor continued, "Then, he comes here and takes Jason's name and a shining to Emma, gets information and tells her he's leaving. But … Andy. Is he being all three of them? What did he do to the others?" Taylor popped up. "What the hell is he doing, Ian?"

Ian wished he had an answer. "First, we don't know that Andy is Tanner. It could be complete coin—"

The glare Taylor sent him stopped him.

"Okay, so coincidences aside ... I don't know, but I'm not going—"

"You think you can stick to my side every minute of every day for the rest of my life? I've got Tanner-Jason-Andy following close on my heels. I know he was in my house today."

"How?"

"The rose. In the middle of that mess in Alabama was a rose, tied in a velvet ribbon. Just like today." Her tone hardened. "And, it was there today. And, it was there ... before. Before now. In our life before. He dropped it on my grave as he buried me."

"He? Did you see his face in a vision or—"

"No." Taylor yanked at her hair. "I just—I don't know."

Ian took her hands and rubbed with his thumb. *He was in the photo. If he was there before, could he have killed Taylor? Why?*

"He's been this shadow looming over my life for over ten years, Ian!" She broke Ian's thoughts. "Maybe ten lives! Or at least four!"

Ian motioned for her to inhale. "Come on. Breathe a little."

Her rigid shoulders relaxed. "What's he doing to me, Ian? Why? Why now?"

"Well—"

"What if that photo was him, and what if he's involved in this, and what if that means the game isn't over, and what if we fail, and I never hear you tell me you love me, and ..."

"That's your worry?"

"All of it is! I don't know what's going on, and I hate it!"

Ian crushed his lips to hers. When he slowed and parted, he rested his forehead against hers. "I love you, Taylor. I have for three lifetimes, and I do now. I love your work ethic, how you support people, that you're building a business and that crazy-assed, southern accent of yours. So, there's one less thing to worry about, okay? I love you."

She touched his lips. "Thank you."

"Now, before we keep going. I had a thought. For sake of argument, if there were three players ... well, Tripp and Lexi both have the same symbol on them—"

"Are you ever going to tell me what they can do?"

Ian chuckled. "Ask them one day. They'll tell you, I'm sure."

"Okay.

"So, as I was saying, they have a matching symbol. We have a matching symbol. If he's involved in this thing with us, he'd probably have the same, right? That's logical, at least. Do you remember if he had this?"

Her eyes went wide. "No." A head shake followed. "Oh—how could I not—"

"What?" Ian asked.

"When I first met him, he'd been working and had gloves on. Then, he said he was into leather making—like belts and ropes and stuff. And his hands were either super-stained or covered in band-aids. What if he was hiding the tattoo from me? What if—"

Ian took her hands, which had moved around wildly, and held them still. "Surely he wasn't like that all the time."

Taylor hung her head. "No. You're right. I'm projecting what I want to remember."

"Lexi and Tripp's are in slightly different places. I'm assuming you *saw* all parts of Tanner's body? Did you … oh God, I can't believe I'm asking this … but did you … have sex with him? Or at least check out … *that.*"

Her hands fisted within his grip "He was my first, Ian." She said it with such softness Ian's heart flip-flopped. "God, I wish I hadn't. Now, of all times, I wish I'd listened to Mama."

He ran a hand down her cheek, the pain in her eyes tearing at his heart. "We all make mistakes." He pulled her in toward him, laid her head on his chest and breathed deep. "I hate to make you think about it. But … did you? Notice?"

"Yeah, I remember and no. Nothing … *there.*"

Ian brought her in for another hug. "It's okay. We'll figure all this out."

❧

Taylor lifted her head and stared right into Ian's eyes. "So, if it's not game related, then why? What?

Ian laid his lips against hers again, making her heart swell with emotion. "If we find Tanner and can sit down with him, maybe a conversation or two will net us some answers. Let's go see if Tripp and Lexi have had any luck."

Taylor had been thinking the same, wanting to ask, or beg or plead for them to search for Tanner again—however they went about it. "You sure?"

"Yes, so let's go."

31

Ian pulled up outside the real estate office Lexi shared with Emma, and he and Taylor exited the car. Emma walked out of their single-story building, followed by Lexi and Tripp.

"Not right now." Emma directed her words to Ian and Taylor while waving Lexi and Tripp toward their Mini Cooper. "Get a move on already."

"Where are you going?" Ian asked.

"Ultrasound day," Tripp said.

"You gonna find out what it is?" Ian slung an arm over Tripp's shoulder. "Hoping for a boy?"

"It's a little early for that," Emma said. "Now shoo, you two."

"They're just going to date the pregnancy officially ..." Lexi leaned against Tripp's chest. "Though, I could tell them to the day when it happened."

Ian and Emma said 'eww' at the same time as Taylor laughed.

"We'll be back by dinner time." Lexi extracted herself and moved to Taylor. "I can see what you want to ask. I haven't had any luck. But, I'll try again when we get back."

"Thank you." Taylor wrapped her arms around Lexi and squeezed. "It means ... a lot ... to have friends like you two."

"We'll be back," Tripp said. "Lock up for us, Em."

"Already done. I'm coming with." She scooted around them both toward her own car. "But unlike you two, I'm coming back to get some work done."

Ian gave Tripp a salute. If Taylor hadn't been in the middle of emotional torture, she'd have been happier for them.

"I need to get back to the site and finish off the day's work. I'm still behind, and the last day of the month is . . . coming up way too fast. Payday is upon me." She ran a hand through her hair. "If I don't run numbers tonight, I'll have nothing ready for next week."

"I can help with that," Ian said.

"You'd like to help? Or you just would for me?"

Ian raised an eyebrow. "Both."

"I'm going to have to see about how to pay you . . . unless you'll work for free."

"No one said anything about not getting paid." He offered her a quick kiss. "I will take an IOU, and my preference is sexual favors."

She slapped his chest as a grin popped onto her face. "You can be in the most stressful environment ever and still think about sex, can't you?"

His hand went over his heart. "Whatever do you mean, Milady?" Ian shifted against her, his center pressing to Taylor's—the rock hardness telling her just *how* he felt. "Hey, remember when my parents said I'd never brought anyone home?" Ian asked.

Taylor nodded.

"They weren't kidding. Most of that's because I knew every girl wasn't the right one. And, somewhere in there, I felt the need to 'sow my oats' as Grams said. But, like I said earlier, I'm in love with you, Taylor . . . in a way I've never felt before. In a way I've never wanted to be before. So hell, yeah, I think about sex all the time. With you. No matter what happens in the next eighty or so years—no, wait, that would make me a hundred and fifteen . . . sixty years then—I want you to know that."

Taylor poured herself into the kiss. She pressed, pled, begged and responded with every ounce of love she had. Ian's hands went to her waist. Hers tangled together around his neck. She wanted nothing more than everything he'd offer.

When she surfaced for air, she smiled and stared into his eyes. "I love you, too, Ian. I feel like I have for three centuries." Another kiss ignited tingles through her body. "What if our eighty years ends badly?"

"Well, then we should make the most of it now. Remember I asked about a date? One we never got to go on?"

Taylor's eyebrow winged up, a smile taking over her lips. "Yeah."

"No time like the present. Tonight. You and I. Dinner. A little fun. Let's take our minds off evil and past lives and just enjoy the one in front of us."

"What about Tanner?"

"We'll deal with that. Afterward. Tomorrow. Maybe Monday. He sounds like a good Monday job. The perfect epitome to ruin a good week. And, Riley's already on it, I'm sure. When Tripp and Lexi get back, I'll ask them to look again. For tonight . . ." He took her hands in his. "Let's let this be the start of our future. Just us."

Sweat beaded on Taylor's brow as she and the carpenters secured the last cabinet into place. The two hours of work, with her as an added hand, helped bridge the two-day schedule delay she still carried on the project.

Taylor wanted to get another hour or two in, but the crew had been at it for almost twelve; to ask more would kill her reputation for decent work schedules and make her late for her date with Ian.

Marty walked up to her, his face the picture of exhaustion.

"We callin' it a day, boss?"

"Yeah. Think we should."

"It's six, anyway. Want us back tomorrow?"

Saturday. She closed her eyes for a second. "Only if you can."

"I think I right can. Mark, too. Maybe Jose and Jock, even."

"Thanks." She laid her hand on his shoulder. "I appreciate it."

He nodded. "We do, too. You're too good not to work for." He tipped his hat and trotted off with the rest of the crew in his wake.

Of course I am when I pay double overtime.

Taylor dropped her gloves onto an overturned bucket but changed her mind and picked them up only to plop herself on it.

"You're lookin' a little grungy." At Ian's voice, she lifted her head.

"I'm feeling it, too." A quick check found no other places to sit. Taylor rose. "I could do for a hot bath and some dinner."

Ian moved in a step closer and pushed her hair up under the cap she wore. A hunger filled his eyes as his hand slid down the side of her cheek, sending shivers through her. Her eyes closed on their own, leaving her defenseless and filled with desire, awakening every nerve.

She opened her eyes. Her hands reached for his shirt and pulled him against her. Ian didn't even push away. Their lips merged as dirt and grime met with refined New York elegance. Taylor chuckled, pulling herself out of the moment. "You do realize we look a sight, right?"

"I'm sure we would if anyone were looking."

"Someone's always looking in a small town, Ian." He bristled under her touch. "What's going on?"

"Nothing." His hand slipped to hers. "Let's go have our date."

"I need to clean up first."

"Um . . . okay."

The simple answer had Taylor narrowing her eyes. "Where to?"

"Home."

Good. She followed Ian back out through the house, locked up and stared at her truck in the driveway. "Why—"

"Because I knew you'd be grimy and not want to get the soft leather of Tripp's Jag dirty."

"But you're wear—"

Ian touched her lips with a finger. "Tonight, you are not to ask questions about how I make stuff happen. I have a phone and a laptop. And money. Tonight, is about you."

With a giant smile, she slid into the passenger seat of her truck. A sniff of the air had her turning her head as he joined her. "What's been in here?"

"What do you mean?" He started the engine, his lips tight.

Taylor breathed in deep, inhaling the scents of grilled meats and vegetables. "Food, Ian. It smells like food."

"Maybe I ate. Or, maybe you should stop asking questions."

She pursed her lips together and clamped them with her finger, watching as the scenery between the house she'd been renovating and her own house passed. Trees, shrubs, small and large neighborhoods filled with houses, families and kids running around in the late evening springtime. A longing tugged at her heart. *I want that, and I feel like I've wanted it forever.*

Ian pulled into the driveway with a bump over the gravel covered ditch.

Taylor gasped. She drew her hands to her lips, turned to Ian and spun back. As the truck came to a stop, she jumped out and ran to the middle of her yard.

A small, white awning ruffled in the breeze, covering a single table with two chairs. A fire burned in the pit she'd made just for that purpose, and tiki torches lit the space, prepared to ward off the evening's more irritating creatures.

Ian appeared at her side. "It's all I could do on short notice."

Taylor turned into him, drew her hands up to his face and pulled him down for a kiss. "Can I change before we sit?"

"Yeah. I'll be waiting."

"Ten minutes. Ish." She added a small smack to his lips and darted off to her house, stripping her clothes in the process, knowing with Agnes gone, no one, anywhere, would see her.

Under the hot water, the grit and dirt of the day as well as the tension drained away. Water sluiced over her, down her body, sending licks of heat to every nerve ending. Ian had created a picnic over the very spot that had messed up her life and brought back the security and love she had with her house. She couldn't have asked for a better start to their future, as he'd put it, and to get Tanner out of her mind.

Taylor stepped from her home, after spending only five extra minutes, to find Ian stoking the fire, his back to her. He turned as she walked down the three steps onto her grass, his soft, green-collared shirt opened at the top but tucked into khaki slacks. Blades tickled the underside of her bare feet as her white, summer dress waved in wind she created just with her own movement.

The sun dipped below the tops of the trees at the back of her property and set the entire area aglow in a warm, orange light.

Something took hold of Ian's expression, keeping him a solid, stone wall Taylor couldn't read. She flattened her hands along her sides, wiping the perspiration that accumulated under his stare.

He held out his hand, and Taylor noted he, too, had gone barefoot. "You're beautiful," he said as she said, "Slumming it, Ian?"

Their smiles matched as they kept their gazes fixed on each other. The sounds of nature filled the space, mixing with the small laughter of children from somewhere Taylor couldn't see.

Ian shifted toward the table where a silver platter sat in the center. A lift of the lid revealed two plates of steak, sizzling as if they'd just been taken off the grill. Taylor whipped around and found the grill on her back deck pulled out. "You cooked?"

Ian lifted a bottle of Merlot from an ice bucket and filled their glasses. "I warmed . . . with explicit instructions."

Taylor couldn't help the laugh or the overwhelming love that flowed through her.

Ian motioned with his fork for her to begin.

A hint of chocolate came through as she sliced a piece of steak. "You got this from Dulces, didn't you?"

A half-smile graced his face. "Where else would someone go on a first date?"

"But, you made it a picnic." Juices from the meat coated her tongue.

"I thought coming here, being a part of what started it all and hoping it would be positive would be a good thing. You know . . . overshadow the bad."

Taylor waved her fork, a red potato stuck to the tines. "It is. This couldn't be more amazing."

In the distance, a coyote made its first call of the night, and the crickets around them buzzed their evening tune. Ian scooped up a forkful of rice as Taylor dove into grilled vegetables. She savored each bite, each morsel, wanting more, as much as she wanted Ian in her life.

Their gazes only strayed as they piled their forks. Few words passed between them. His presence seemed enough.

The last of their natural illumination disappeared as they finished, and Ian leaned toward the ground. A second later, twinkly bulbs lit the interior of their tented roof.

He held out his hand and stood as soft music carried on the breeze. "May I have this dance?"

A check of her plate showed it empty, the flavors continuing to tease her tongue. Her palm slid against Ian's as naturally as if they'd made the same move for centuries. His body hugged hers, swaying to the slow rhythm of a symphonic orchestra.

Taylor laid her head onto his shoulder, basking in the atmosphere, in the moment, and in the truth. She'd known Ian, in a way no one could describe, from the moment their hands shook at Tripp and Lexi's wedding. That their lives entwined in some game no longer mattered. He held her in his arms, and she wanted him.

Ian's lips found her lobe. Taylor's sigh contradicted the goosebumps up her arm. She stretched, giving him access. He trailed soft kisses to her shoulder, brushing the single strap down. Their bodies moved in unison, she letting him lead.

Dusk darkened the surrounding light, bringing with it the chill of evening, though heat seared between their bodies. Each of Ian's touches scorched Taylor. Each kiss branded her as his.

Taylor's strap slid lower until she pulled her arm from it. His hands slid around her back as their lips played against each other. His press forward leaned her back. Trust kept her in his arms until she lay against the soft grass.

Ian ranged over her until he fit along her body, his weight lightened by the propping of his elbows on either side of her. Taylor worked at the buttons of his shirt, one by one, undoing them.

Muscles jumped as she caressed. A finger under the collar and a push had his shirt falling off his shoulders. Ian slipped his arms out, leaving his torso exposed.

His arms shook.

"Tired?" Her own tone came out a lazy drawl.

"Aroused."

The mere mention spurred her forward. A twist and a zip freed him from his pants. "You sure you want to do this out here?" More sultry sexuality made her smile at herself. Only with Ian had she ever been the one to make the move.

"Here seems to be the right place." Ian nipped at her chin, moving up to her lips.

Taylor wrapped her arms around him and pulled him down upon her. His hand slid down her side, a finger-walk over fabric brought it up until his palm met the flesh of her inner thigh. She moaned her desire, spurring him to torment closer to her center.

Her lips explored every inch of his face, delighting in the fact that she recognized him under her own touch. Fingertips traced his cheekbones, his ear and down his shoulder to his chest, teasing until he shivered.

His hands slid up to her breast, down to her inner thigh and back, eliciting lines of heat from the core of her body to her head.

A suckle arched her back.

A nip elicited a groan of pleasure.

A kiss relaxed.

Their touches continued, tormenting each other until Taylor's need for him overwhelmed. She drew herself up, transposing their positions.

A tug of his pants lowered them.

A lift of her skirt raised it.

A descent merged their bodies into one.

Ian's thrusts speared her with sensations, bringing to mind years of time spent together that could only be imaginary—the lake, dust-covered ground, the hayloft of her parent's barn. Each a moment they should not have come together, tempting fate, testing even time itself.

Taylor rocked against Ian's hips, drawing him in as deep as possible, wanting their connection to remain.

Never to sever.

Memories played out in Taylor's mind with each draw from or rise to Ian. Against a rock wall. In a grove of trees. Amidst the sunshine in a field of daisies.

The harder his thrusts, the more those snippets, those momentary windows into their prior lives surfaced and faded. She leaned forward, laying her lips against his as he continued to provide the pleasure she'd always dreamed she'd be able to accept—from the right man.

Tension surfaced in his legs, driving Taylor toward her own peak.

No words need have been spoken.

No thoughts need have been shared.

No memories broke what remained between them.

Together.

Forever.

Pleasure consumed Taylor, sending a dizzying array of sound, movement, light, darkness, joy and happiness through her—a cacophony of life as in that moment two became one.

32

Taylor trailed lazy fingers along Ian's side as their breaths slowed. A light breeze moved through, causing a shiver.

"Cold?" Ian's rough, sated voice didn't mask the happiness.

"A little." She laid a small kiss at the side of his lips. "But, I would like to stay out here. Want me to get a blanket?"

His hands slid low. "I'm good."

Taylor chuckled as she pushed herself up. "You stay here."

Ian yanked her back down. "But, I'm going to be cold."

She nuzzled her nose against his. "Ian?"

"Yeah?" His fingertips traced along her back.

"I think all our lives merged tonight. I didn't have that out of body experience I've had before. I just . . . it was just you and me."

He turned until their gazes met. "Really?"

She nodded against him. "Every other time has kinda taken me with it, but this was . . . different. This was . . . today—real, if that makes sense."

"I think I get it, yeah."

"So . . ." She walked her fingers up his chest again. "I have a feeling. A gut feeling, since you like to listen to yours. That we won this time. Like maybe it's over. Really. I feel it inside."

Ian tilted up her chin and touched his lips with hers, but he didn't comment.

A deeper breeze blew over them. He may not have believed, but she did. On a sigh, she said, "Let me get us a blanket. I'll be back in two minutes." Taylor lifted her body from Ian's, bringing herself to a stand and holding her dress to her chest. On a second thought, she let it fall to the ground. "More for you to think about until I get back."

He tucked his hands behind his head, leaving himself fully exposed. "A little cocky are you now?"

"Look who's talking." She swirled a finger in the air, circling his midsection.

"You know what they say." He shrugged, a smile playing along his lips.

A laugh burst from Taylor. "Okay. Be right back." Her walk from their tent to her house met with a growing smile and the cool of spring dew under her feet. She picked up speed, hopping up onto her deck as naked as a newborn but sated like a well-fed cat. A look back toward Ian put him in complete shadow, but the lights under the canopy glowed. Her sigh came with pure happiness.

She stepped into her kitchen, skipped the light switch and slipped along the hardwood floors toward her hall closet. A breath in stung her sinuses. "What's that smell?"

"Hello, Claire." The unmistakeable voice and the use of her middle name had Taylor spinning around, covering her breasts with her arms and sliding behind a chair—not that it would hide much.

"Surprised to see me?"

She squinted into the darkness. The moonlight silhouetted his form, leaning against the counter at her sink. "Tanner?" *Oh, God, he can probably see all of me.* The stream of illumination also reached one of Ian's shirts—a long-sleeved button-down Taylor had hooked to the back of a chair that morning. She grabbed it and slid her arms inside, shaking fingers pulling the edges tight and closed.

"Are you afraid of me, Claire? After all this time?" His chuckle rang through the room, the lack of any other noise making it echo back at her.

"I thought you were dead." She forced her voice firm and low, hating that he always used her middle name.

The dark shape grew. Footsteps came toward her. "Not dead, no. Planning. It took a while to figure out how best to get your attention again."

"Again?"

He shrugged. "Once. Twice. Four or five times."

"Five?" Taylor scooted backward more. As he came closer, she caught the glint of metal at waist level.

A gun?

"It's such a small town, Claire. I had to be very, very careful to whom I spoke. Everyone … *knows*. They always have. They always do." Another step back.

She hit the chair at her back. "Knows … *what*?"

"Oh, come on now, Claire. There's nothing to fear. You love me, remember?" The outside light bathed his face as he emerged within the single stream emanating from outside. "You gave yourself to me. You promised to be mine."

He hadn't changed. Handsome but rugged, dark hair, brooding blue eyes. She'd fallen for him once because of looks and attention, but the conversation she'd had with Hough in the jail popped into Taylor's mind. *It's all in the eyes.* His eyes said it all—pure evil.

"Why did you set me up in Alabama?" Taylor's fingers held tight to her shirt. If he came close enough, she'd let go, grab the chair and swing it and knock him over—or so she hoped.

"I thought it was the right time to start the game over."

Oh, my God, there are *three players.* "Game?" Taylor asked, forcing the wobble from her voice.

"Of course. One." He pointed to Taylor. "Two." His finger angled toward himself. "Three." He angled it toward the window.

Taylor. Tanner. Ian. She inched the chair out from the table, keeping it tight against her butt.

"Last time, though … he didn't come. He didn't save you. He

didn't love you enough."

"Who're you talking about?" Muscles trembled in Taylor's arm.

"He wasn't the right one."

"*Who are you* talking about?" She said each word with distinct emphasis.

"The one you love but had not given yourself to."

She wanted to scream. To curse at him. To force him to explain. "*Who?*"

"The cop. Such a pity. It would have been fun to see him suffer a little at your loss."

Riley. He'd been in Alabama to convince Taylor to return home. As much as she wanted to bash in Tanner's face, she also wanted answers. "Why did you think he was the one?"

Tanner raised an eyebrow. "Because he touched you that way."

Friendship. A deep, longing friendship made them intimate on a different level than what she and Ian shared. "Why—"

Tanner jumped toward her. Taylor's legs buckled at his quick movement, her shirt falling open. She straightened and spun with the chair.

He grabbed the back before she could get it off the ground. "Now that, we'll not be having." He inclined his head as he reached for Taylor's cheek, rubbing his knuckles along her flesh. "So beautiful. You were so beautiful before, too. You gave yourself to me, Claire. To me." He spit the words at Taylor. "As you were meant to."

"I don't know what you're talking about."

"A virgin gives only to the man to whom she is destined to be with." His hand gripped her chin. "But, you pushed me away." A crazed, manic hold shone in his eyes.

"I don't—"

He jerked her head. "You lie. I waited for you. You called him. I begged you to stay. You called him. I thought he was the one. To prove it, to show you how much you'd miss me, to bring you back to me, I had to fake my own death."

And still I didn't go to him.

"And, you didn't come. That's when I knew I'd played wrong because you also didn't go to him. This time, I've been watching. For years, I've been waiting. Considering. Planning. At the wedding, I saw. I knew. I worked on your crew. I shook his hand. I verified first."

Ian.

"I was patient. I needed to know if you'd remember. If you'd fall for him." Tanner traced a thumb along her lips.

"You set me up, didn't you?"

"I had to know. He left and came back. For you. I watched. I waited."

You stalked me.

"He knew, too. I could feel it. And with that, I knew our paths had finally crossed, and it was time. All you had to do was give him up, and the game would end. But that ... you did not do."

"Okay, I will—"

He squeezed her lips shut. "It's not appropriate to tell tales, Claire."

She tried to turn, but he held her in place.

"You've even given him your body. You should have remained true to us." Before she could comment, he crushed his lips to hers.

Taylor slid her hands between them and pressed with every ounce of effort inside her. His fingers wrapped around her wrist holding her still before she could force the air to bash something into his head.

His nails dug into her skin. "Ah, ah, ah. Remember, I know what you can do. I've known through all three lives. Fire. Water. Earth. Air." His grip tightened around her. "It's easy to use against you since you refused, each time, to use them to your benefit. My belts did a great job holding your hands back last time, and your efforts only served to bury you faster. Thank you for sparing me the torture." Tanner licked the side of her lips.

A deep desire to wipe off his saliva drove her anger up another notch. She jerked to the side, turning her head as far as possible, expecting another unwanted kiss.

"Those bones. They were beautiful, weren't they? Yours. So lovely. When you bought this house, I knew then this would be the place we'd reunite." Tanner's breath, a sickly nausea-inducing smell, wafted over her nose. "Fate is fickle, isn't she? You could have met him ages ago. Or, found your bones well before now. But, all of us coming together as it did—it could not have been more perfect."

Taylor stayed mute, letting him talk and taking in the details.

"You don't know, do you? About your heritage. Your destiny to be mine."

"Destiny? But, you don't have the symbol."

"Neither would he, if the farmer's wife hadn't etched his skin with it first. And, just days before I dragged you to your grave." With her gasp, he said, "All you had to do was choose me. Four times now you've promised yourself to me only to give yourself to another. Why would you deny me?"

Taylor didn't remember evil or menace in Tanner's voice during their quasi-relationship. "Maybe—maybe I *have* chosen you."

"But, you haven't. I can smell him upon you. Like before. Every time." His voice pitched up.

Snake-like chills slithered up her body. *Get him out of the house, and maybe you can get him into a mental institution.* "How do you … know … all this?" It took determined force to say the words without a sarcastic tone.

A gleam brightened his eyes. "You've been in my dreams since … forever. But, I knew they weren't just dreams. Nothing so vivid could have been conjured by a boy, repeated incessantly as a young man and understood by me. I see you with me. With him. I watch you die on a pyre I built. I hold you under the water. I let the earth reclaim you."

The memories of seeing herself die played out. Had he seen the same from the other perspective? Why had they only come to her after she'd met Ian? No matter the answer, Taylor knew she had to act. "Maybe you're wrong—"

He let go of her wrist, but the release lasted only a second, and a backhanded slap spun her from the chair to the floor. "Your body is a temple. My temple."

Taylor scrambled toward the door. *Get to Ian. Get out. Get Riley.* The repetition ran through her mind.

Her head whipped back as Tanner yanked her hair, stopping her crawl. "Up. Now. It's time to start the game again."

Again? But this is it. This is my last! She lifted to her knees, pain searing through her scalp. With her hands free, she sent air in every direction, knocking pictures and figurines off their shelves. The sparseness of the room left her little to toss at him, and their proximity to the chairs and table wouldn't allow her to levitate them to throw.

"Let me go, Tanner." Grit and fire coated her tone as she stood, his hand still on her hair.

He chuckled. "I don't think so. If I do … you'll go back to him. I can't have—I won't see—" A tug pulled her backward toward him. "I watched him die last time. Stood there with the townspeople around me as his neck snapped."

Rage burned inside her, enough to evaporate any forming tears. *Convince him they were just dreams.*

"Stupid, ignorant farmer thinking he could best me. All it took was one anonymous tip to the town magistrate."

"You're not old enough to have been around when there were hangings—"

His hand covered her mouth, and fear drained her of all warmth. His other hand slid around her bare middle, pressing her to him. "No one would ever have suspected the boy next door."

The photo. He was there because he was … there.

She kicked behind her, but her leg only reached air. A movement with her wrist slid the microwave to the side, but she couldn't focus to get it further.

"I want you to remember me this time, too." Tanner's hand crept from her face and down her arms, bone-chilling cold taking hold of her body. "I want to give you a mark like he did, so next time, we'll be branded together."

"Tanner, really, we can talk—"

He yanked her arms behind her.

Her lungs ceased to function.

The glint of a knife shone in her peripheral vision. *No! Oh my God!* The tip drew nearer as a desperate desire to breathe overcame her. She gulped, no different than when Riley had cuffed her a month before.

"You have a symbol. I give you one, too."

Please, stop! The words her mind formed failed to be spoken as her mind blanked out, growing darker with each passing moment. *I'm so sorry, Ian. This is all my fault.*

The tip pierced the side of her cheek.

An involuntary gasp brought in air to her burning lungs and consciousness to her mind. She threw back her head, ramming him in the nose.

The knife clattered to the ground. Tanner hobbled backward as Taylor sucked in more air. "You bitch!" He covered his nose, dripping red through his fingers.

She spit to the side, wiping her hand over her mouth in a bid to rid herself of even the taste of him.

In that second, he jumped, knocking her over and pinning her to the ground—arms out wide—his legs between hers.

"Do you really think you can fight me? Have you ever been able to? This is our destiny. You die. We start over. Next time, you'll know. Next time, you will be mine. Next time, you will understand what it means to give oneself to a man."

Taylor whipped her head to the side as Tanner lowered his hips upon hers. "Get off me!" The rawness of her throat muted the snarl she'd attempted. She pulled at her legs and arms with all her strength. Until she had better use of her hands, her magical talent would remain a useless artifact of her life.

Like it had been every other time.

A faded memory hit her. She'd had gifts and hadn't used them. Or couldn't. He'd known how to keep her from using them because he'd known of them—just like in Alabama.

He kicked her legs apart. "Once more? For old times' sake?"

"Go to hell."

Tanner's grin took on an even uglier smirk. Hot breath hit her lips. "Never test fate, Claire." One hand reached for his belt. "We were meant to be together."

"Taylor?" Ian's voice breached the door.

Tanner cocked his head. "He calls you by your surname?"

Rage built up in Taylor, still strapped to her floor by the nearly two-hundred-pound man atop her. "My grandpa gave me that name, you fucking pig." She yanked one hand free, flicked her wrist at the chair and sent it crashing into Tanner's head. "Ian! Help!"

With Tanner's body off to the side, she scrambled again. Taylor raced for the gun that had slid near the knife.

Tanner went for the same.

Ian pounded on the window.

Shoulder's bumped as he reached the gun first.

Dammit, no!

Not ammunition.

Flares.

A Joker-like grin took hold of his face as he raised the barrel.

She grappled for the weapon as the sight in her peripheral vision took hold. Her gas oven stood wide open, the knobs all spun to high but unlit.

He's going to create fire.

Tanner pointed straight to it.

Oh. My. God. He's going to kill me again.

The explosion shook the earth, shattered glass and threw Ian from the back deck to a bush behind the house. His body crumpled along the ground, twenty feet from where he'd stood, while flames consumed the kitchen and leeched their way outside, up and over the roof of Taylor's house.

"*No!*"

A rocket of wood tore off from the house and landed on the ground next to Ian. He scrambled upright, his heart pumping, chest heaving. Heat from the house made him blink and back up a few steps.

"No, you son of a bitch! This can't be happening!"

Ian pushed off from his side spot, racing around to the front.

Smoke billowed from every crevice.

Flames raced from every opening.

Fire engulfed the porch, halting Ian's approach.

"Taylor!" he screamed.

33

Taylor held her hands wide as flames took hold of every combustible surface in her kitchen. Her island had become a smoldering mound. Beyond that, only a river of red swirled. Within her own circle, air kept the flames at bay.

Tanner pushed to his knees, coughing and sputtering as black smoke and heat whirled outside of Taylor's barrier.

She pushed her circle farther, encompassing Tanner and preventing the flames from reaching him.

His gaze locked on hers, a madness consuming his features.

At his jolt forward, she backed up.

The air retreated with her, but creaks from the roof reminded her of Joyce's home. Flames grabbed hold of the interior walls. A step into what once had been her living room showed it fully engulfed.

Not an inch of her space existed.

Tears pricked her eyes.

Tanner'd been the literal death of her multiple times, and he would still win unless she kept the air going.

If windows existed, she couldn't see them.

If a door opened, she wouldn't have known.

Staring into Tanner's eyes, she knew the only way to stop him would be to kill him. Yet, she couldn't push him into the flames without breaking her own personal ethos.

Tanner jumped for her, his hands outstretched, a clear intention to grab her neck.

Taylor let one arm fall and pushed him to the ground. Flames grabbed her hair and Ian's shirt, following the air as if seeking fuel and food to grow. She screamed and pushed her arm out again.

The flames upon her died.

Tanner leapt for her again, and she repeated her actions, kicking him forward but bringing fire upon her other side.

Another cry out accompanied the lift of her arm. The crash of roofing and interior support beams came from behind them. The roar of the fire filled her ears as her house began its inward fall.

In front of her, he stood. She stepped backward. He did the same.

She knew he planned for her to die.

She intended to live.

"We need to go, Tanner." Taylor yelled it while stepping back.

A crack above had them both ducking. If the roof fell, she knew she wouldn't be able to save either of them.

"Now."

Fire touched Tanner's feet. He held his spot as if tempting her to let it burn him.

She trod backward. "Please, Tanner. This isn't the way. We can be together—"

He crossed his arms. "Only in the next life."

"Please, Tanner. Please!" Beams fell to the ground in the hallway. Another minute and they'd take them both. *I'm so sorry, Ian. I'm just so sorry.*

No more than five feet separated Taylor from Tanner. Her inner conscience refused to let her budge, as if she'd have to die for him rather than save herself and risk his life.

She closed her eyes.

The snap from above came before she could even move. A beam crashed as Taylor ducked, her hands still outspread.

Tanner's scream barely reached her through the roaring of the fire. She jumped backward, her circle staying with her as more of the roof caved.

Go!

Her body failed to respond to her mind's command.

Go, Taylor. Go! Ian needs you.

Jolted from her stupor, Taylor spun, barreling forward in the hope of an escape. Like when under water, she barely registered which way faced up or out. She kept her hands splayed before her, calling to the little bit of still-surrounding air, and jumped.

Taylor's screams broke as she fell to the grass on the front lawn. She refused to look back, expecting to see a fireball in human form racing after her. Instead, two fire trucks raced into her driveway. They stopped at the edge of the lawn, crews jumping out as the wheels finished rolling.

Ian! Taylor wanted to call out, but rawness took hold of her throat as exhaustion plagued her body. She'd never used so much power of the wind for her own benefit. Never. Not even when Tanner had tested her.

Taylor stared through dry eyes as the fire raged. She pushed up from the ground as water sprayed into the air and something grabbed hold of her arm. She pulled, tried to roll, but it held tight.

"Taylor!"

She gasped and struggled to get away, unable to see, think or hear anything beyond what her memories filled her with and of seeing Tanner swallowed by flames.

He'd known all along. He'd only had to wait for her to fall in love. For her to give herself to John. To Ian.

John hadn't killed her. He'd loved her.

"Taylor, it's Ian." His voice registered somewhere in the deep recesses of her mind.

I should have listened to you, Ian. Trusted your gut.

He'd died. John. Ian. Over and over because there were three. Three.

"Taylor, baby. Come on."

The entire story weighed on Taylor's shoulders like the destruction of Joyce's house.

She could have saved them all.

She should have.

Her head wobbled against a soft surface. Hands grasped her arms, and with a touch to her lips, she blinked her eyes open.

Ian.

Ian.

Ian.

She burst into a fit of tears. He pulled her into his lap as she let every bit of emotion through. Hiccups of sound continued until she no longer listened to herself.

Ian rubbed up and down her back, holding her tight and leaving her to the expulsion of her sorrows—to a lifetime, or three, of death at the hands of a man who claimed to love her.

"Tanner … bones … Ian." She gasped for air between each word.

Water sprayed overtop, hitting her house from above like a beautiful rain shower and sending a stream of crystal through the inky sky. The roof had collapsed. Windows no longer existed. If there had ever been a front door, no one would have known. The orangey-red glow grew and abated.

Had it been only weeks before that her life had been normal, routine and unencumbered?

Ian lifted her from the ground. She snuggled into his shoulder, bracing herself against another onslaught of waterworks and the smell of flesh burning in the biggest bonfire she'd ever seen.

"You're okay," Ian said. "We're both okay." Her body jostled as he walked.

"This way!" An unrecognizable voice snuck its way in. "Let's get some oxygen here!"

More bumping. More movement. She stayed in Ian's arms as they reached an ambulance, and a mask fit over her nose and mouth while a heavy blanket lay across her body.

"Were you in that fire, ma'am?" The EMT snapped on blue gloves as he grabbed stuff from behind him. "And you, sir?" His hand reached out toward Ian. "You've got a nice bump there."

Taylor tilted up, catching sight of the knot and trickle of blood from Ian's temple. She reached, but he pulled her in tighter.

"Wasn't . . . inside." Relaxed back in Ian's arms, she stared out at her home, her eyes attempting closure with each passing second.

A police officer approached the back of the ambulance. "Ma'am."

"Can this wait?" Ian asked.

"No, sorry. We just need to know . . . was there anyone else in the house?" The slight hesitation suggested he already knew the answer.

Ian's hold tightened.

"A . . . friend. T—Andy . . . George. He . . ." Fresh tears sprung to her eyes. ". . . kill himself. I tried . . ." She sucked in air. ". . . stop him." Even the small lie tore at her soul.

The police officer took off, flagging down a fireman. They surrounded the house, but their heads hung low. Taylor understood. No way would Tanner have survived.

His shot into the oven had exploded the fumes. The flames would have stolen her oxygen—her air. As realization dawned, she closed her eyes. He'd have won again if she hadn't tried to save Tanner. The game would have ended as well but never restarted.

For the first time in four lives, she'd won.

Ian kept his arm around Taylor as the EMTs released her to his care. He'd declined any support, explaining that he'd fallen when the house exploded, but had asked that Taylor's neck be bandaged where a small scratch had bled. Fire crews continued to work the flames, with peaks of red reaching into the sky and retreating several times, while the group stood and watched.

"You want to go home?" Ian cringed as soon as he asked. "I

mean, to—"

She nodded. "I know what you mean."

"Should we tell your folks?"

"Mama likes her beauty sleep."

He carried Taylor to the truck, lifted her into the cab and ran a hand along her arm, noting the singed hairs. Watching the woman he loved stand in the middle of a raging inferno couldn't have been scarier. His heart hadn't stopped racing until the moment she'd run out, and he'd splayed his hands along her functioning and very alive body.

Around to the driver's seat, he began the trek to take her away from her nightmare.

She leaned into him, his arm wrapped around her. "I tried to save—I could have—I just—I failed."

He took her slowed speech to be a reflection of using the wind so heavily. "Are you kidding me?" He drove onto Tripp and Lexi's road. "This isn't on you. This is on a fucking maniac of a Greek god. Running us off track with varying stories, no consistency and no way to prepare. The whole situation has Zeus written all over it."

A jerk of her shoulders came as she said, "He didn't know everything, either, Ian. How is this fair to him?"

Ian drove them into Lexi and Tripp's driveway and stopped the engine. He turned to her and stared into her eyes. "Why do you care about him?"

She closed her lids but reopened them. "Because it's not right, and I think it's all my fault. I'm the only one with the tattoo. I did give myself to him. And, as Mama is my witness, that ties me to him. I should have—"

Ian palmed his forehead. "I can't believe this. The guy tries to kill you, and you think it's your fault. I'm going to need therapy."

A small laugh-cry escaped Taylor.

Ian's lips curved. "What?"

"I'm the one with issues, and you need therapy?"

"Yes. It's going to take years for me to learn how to make you not believe this is your fault." Ian held out a finger. "He did this, not you. Not me. Not you to me. Not you to him. *He* killed you three times. And ... do you realize what happened to him tonight is everything that happened to you at once? He died in a fire, crushed under wood, and if you add in the water from the fire trucks ... he kinda drowned, too."

"I tried to get him to come out with me." Her lids fell again. "I tried to make him understand." Taylor blinked glassy eyes at Ian.

He leaned his forehead to hers, took her hands in his and scratched at his ring finger. "I know, babe, but there's nothing you could have done to convince him."

"Why would Zeus torture people like this?"

"Have you ever read about the stuff he did? Or any of the Greek gods for that matter? Lexi and Tripp got off easy." Ian laid his lips against the top of Taylor's head and heaved a sigh. "All the good Greek stories are tragedies."

"And ours? Are we a tragedy?"

"You asked me before if I thought the game was over, and I didn't, but now I do. It makes sense to have three people—a triangle." He tapped his own temple. "That's a game. One that crosses the ages, too. And in them, two people usually win. But no matter what, one always loses."

"But, he didn't have to die!" Tears fell in great sobs.

Ian wrapped his arms around her. "I know, but in all good Greek tragedies, someone dies. It's like fulfillment for the players and ... the creators."

"What do you mean?"

Ian heaved a sigh. "In all the research I did about Tripp's gift, I learned a lot about Greek tragedies. This, now that we know there are three, is like the perfect match to history. The timing is consistent with the performance dates. The plays were actually competitions between three playwrights, which at one point all had linked stories. And ..." Ian chuckled at the memory of what he'd found so long ago. "They were always performed in the open air. Like tonight. What a coincidence, right?"

Taylor scratched at her finger. "I guess. I just hate that he—"

"I know, but, Taylor? We won. We *won*."

She pressed the button on the overhead map light and held her finger up into it.

"What's wrong—oh—wow!" Ian brought his into the same stream of illumination.

"Double wow," Taylor said.

The blue of their tattoo-like rings darkened, the last connector etching itself into their skin.

Both of theirs.

"You know what?" Ian asked. "I'm just going to go with this and pretend it's as normal as a sunrise on a cloudless day. Are you with me?"

Taylor's gaze never faltered as she said, "Always."

34

In the bright, early morning sunshine, the yellow caution tape surrounding the exterior of Taylor's house gleamed. Ian stood at the edge of the makeshift barricade, staring at what used to be the floor. The outer siding had melted and curled onto itself, falling to the ground and shriveling up.

He'd been ogling the nearly flat structure for at least ten minutes while the Chief of Rune Fire walked Taylor and Riley around, confirming, with finger pointing, where the blaze started, how it spread and squashing eruptions they'd thought snuffed but relit like a set of joke birthday candles.

"Well, I think that's it." Greg held out his hand. "Except for this."

Ian peered over Taylor's shoulder. A simple square of velvet lay in his palm.

"It was in the middle of the kitchen." He pressed fingers to his eyes. "I know you said your friend was in here, Taylor, but we find no evidence of him at all. Not even a bone fragment. There's nothing, yet this little piece of fabric survived."

"Isn't that kinda odd?" Ian's mind whirled with possibilities.

"May I keep it?" Taylor asked.

Greg dropped it onto her palm. "That's the thing about fires. They take what they want. They don't always take what you expect."

Ian couldn't have said it better.

"I assume you have arrangements to stay elsewhere?"

"I do, yes. Thanks," Taylor said.

Emma said 'everyone in town knows everything'. As soon as Taylor's house burned, people from multiple neighborhoods came out, offering their help and consolation. Food arrived on platters, yet with nowhere to store it and Lexi's weak stomach, it went to the downtown food kitchen as a donation.

"All righty then." Greg tipped his hat. "Once the heat is gone, we'll do a more thorough inspection, but I'm pretty sure we all already know what happened." He laid his hand on Taylor's shoulder. "Sorry you had to witness that, Taylor. Some people, though … you know, they just aren't right in the mind, and their pain leeches into others in ways we think unspeakable." He patted her again. "You'll rebuild, right? We don't want you to leave."

The smallest of smiles breached Taylor's serious expression. "Probably." She shrugged, but her hand clenched.

Greg walked away.

Taylor and Ian stood, staring at the plot of land before them. Taylor heaved a sigh before she turned to Ian; her arms enveloped him and squeezed. "You were right."

"Of course I was."

She chuckled against him. "I couldn't sleep last night."

"I know. I was right next to you. Dreams again?"

She shook her head. "This time was because … well … I don't want to rebuild here. I—I was actually thinking this ground should be sacred. It's tied to too much out of this weird stuff, but how would I justify that to Mama and Daddy when they helped me with the down payment and—"

Ian's lips stopped her flow. When their kiss slowed, he said, "You want a new house? I know just the person to ask."

Taylor stared out the window as Ian drove them back to Lexi and Tripp's. With their super-late arrival and super-early departure again, they hadn't seen each other.

Lexi ran out, her arms encircling Taylor as she and Ian walked from the truck. "Oh, holy shit, Zeus needs to be smacked on his ass and put in a time out."

"You're not going to talk to your kid like that, are you?" Ian asked, a slight chuckle in his voice.

Lexi continued to hug Taylor as Tripp joined them on the porch. "Don't ask her anything. She'll either bite your head off or hug and kiss you." His hands went to his crotch, covering it as if he'd learned his lesson the wrong way.

"That's what pregnancy will do, right?" Ian asked.

"That's what twins will do." Emma plopped into one of the rocking chairs.

"Twins?" Taylor and Ian said at the same time.

Lexi jumped and hugged Taylor again as Ian slapped Tripp's back with his palm. "Well, damn. You must be good."

Tripp's shoulders lifted and fell. "Must be." A giant grin took hold of his face. "Makes even more sense now why her mood swings are so rampant."

Lexi let go and turned back to Tripp, one hand on the slight bulge in her midsection.

"So, do you know what you're having?" Taylor snuggled into the crook of Ian's arm.

"Nope. Not going to find out, either," Lexi said.

"Much to her sister and very best friend's heartache." Emma rocked back and forth. "How am I going to shop for a sexless baby? Worse, how am I going to shop for two of them?"

The crunch of gravel took all their attentions as Riley's car joined Taylor's truck in the driveway. Taylor caught the slight adjustment in Emma's posture, the quick finger under the nose and over her hair.

"Mornin', ya'll," he said as he came forward.

Taylor moved to him, put her hands on his cheeks and kissed him smack on the lips. "He's dead, Riley."

"I know." Riley wiped the kiss off as if he were ten and not thirty-three. "Dammit, Tay. I do not need your cooties." The group behind her laughed as Ian took her hand and brought her back into the fold of his arms. "Actually, I came to see how you were doing."

"I'll survive," she said.

He toed the ground with his work boot, though the jeans and red Coke T-shirt said 'off-duty'. "Good, good. I'm glad you … made it. The both of ya."

Tripp and Ian both held their fists out. Riley bumped them both.

"You have something to say, don't you, Riley?" Taylor asked.

Riley gave them a small nod. "Um … I found out how the search warrant came through two days before you found the bones."

The entire group turned to him.

Riley scratched at the side of his nose. "I hate to say it, but it seems Jeremy Faine's been … well … taking some bribes. He's been under investigation for some stuff I can't say about … and I did some of my own investigation. Seems someone else had put two and two together before me. Saw the report this morning."

"That must have been why he came after me so hard," Taylor said. "So, what's up with him?"

"Ah …" Riley ran a hand through his hair. "I can't say. I'm sure the news will get wind, though. Maybe just wait for that. He won't be any trouble from now on, though." Riley bundled Taylor in another hug. "I'm just so glad this is over. Forever."

A sense of peace washed over Taylor. *It is over. All of it.*

"Call me if you need me, Tay." Riley saluted as he went back to his car.

"Riley, wait." Ian drew himself away from Taylor, stepped to Riley and took him away from the porch, their heads bent close to each other.

Riley stopped. He made no move forward or back. A second later, he pulled Ian into a great big bear hug, turned toward Taylor and smiled.

"Looks like the cat and the mouse are eating together," Lexi said.

"No doubt," Emma said.

Ian sauntered back toward the group as Riley continued on to his car.

"What gives, Yankee boy?" Emma asked, a smirk in her tone.

Ian stuffed his hand in his pocket. "Just a word of thanks."

Lexi tugged at Taylor's sleeve. "So, I'm sure you're tired and—"

Taylor shook her head. "Actually, I want to work. I need to. I owe my crew pay checks and tiles and—"

Ian draped his arm across her shoulders. "My kind of girl."

Finally.

"Well . . . ," Lexi started, "even though it's been a few weeks, the buyer for the Weaton Estate still wants to meet A.S.A.P. I think they're ready to move on the project. When . . . do you think we could . . . you know?"

"Lex, she's been through—" Tripp started.

"Now." Taylor grabbed Ian's wrist and turned his watch toward her. The hands clicked to the twelve. "No. I need to take care of a few things. How about three?"

Ian coughed into his hands. "Girl, you move . . . fast."

Emma's eyes grew wide. "Efficiency in motion. That's you, Taylor."

"Work keeps me grounded. It'll get my mind off . . . off what happened."

"I'm with her," Lexi said. "Better to be busy."

Ian took Taylor's hands, kissed her knuckles and stared into her eyes. "Word of warning . . . but all your files went up in flames. I'll go find out who you owe what people-wise, and you do your thing, and we'll reconvene. Sound good?"

"You're not worried about being away from me?" Taylor asked.

Ian drew her toward him and laid his lips on hers. "Not anymore."

"Three o'clock at the main house, then," Lexi said. "See you there."

Taylor followed Lexi and Emma up the steps of the Weaton Estate main house. The falling-apart homestead boasted two full floors of classic, southern American architecture. Her favorite part had always been the wraparound porch that really did go all the way around the building. Had she the financial means to acquire it, and not the bungalow on the other side of what used to be hundreds of acres of farmland, she would have. The home was none other than a piece of American history.

The door creaked on its hinges as Emma pushed it open.

"Watch that board," Lexi said.

"Should you be in here?" Taylor stepped around the rotting wood. "This place could come down right around you." Memories of that happening to her hit her, making her limbs tremble. *It's all over. No more games.*

"That's why the new owner needs you to check it out," Emma said.

The entry foyer had a similar double staircase with a two-level foyer reminiscent of an old plantation house. Taylor imagined herself walking down them, her hand trailing along the banister. "God, this place is amazing."

Ian and Tripp walked in from the back, stopped in the middle of the entry and faced the three women.

"You made it." Taylor admired the molding and potentially salvageable woodwork over each doorframe. "How was your afternoon?"

Ian said, "Boring." as Tripp said, "Good."

Riley showed up with the two of them a second later.

"What are you doing here?" Taylor moved to the opposite side, half-listening and half-imagining what she could do with the place.

"Helping the new owner," Riley said.

Blues and creams came to mind as an idea sprung. "Wait, what?" Taylor stopped and stared at Riley. "Did you buy this place?"

"Nope."

She moseyed to a space she would peg as a traditional living room. "Tripp, do you think your sister would want to work on this with me? To put a bid together?"

"I'm sure she would." His smile bloomed as Lexi went to him.

A fireplace with no mantle or surround stood before her. She imagined a large mirror over the top. Slipping back through to the entry and heading for the kitchen, she turned toward Lexi. "So, who's the owner?"

Ian advanced.

Taylor did the same and laid a small kiss on his cheek. "Wouldn't it be awesome to live in an old house like this?"

A small chuckle came from him.

"Oh, right. You're Mr. New York."

"Well, I don't know about that. Would *you* like to live in it?"

She slapped his chest. "Damn right I would. Who are we waiting for?"

"No one," Riley said again in his simple, southern, country charm.

Taylor stopped and tilted her head. She passed from Riley to Tripp, to Lexi with her great big smile and to Emma until she got back to Ian. "Tell me you didn't buy this house."

"I didn't buy this house."

"Well then, who did?"

"Me," Ian said.

"But you just said—"

Laughter filled the room.

"No, you told me to tell you that. So I did."

Taylor's eyes enlarged.

Lexi chuckled. She lifted up to Tripp. "Told you they were

meant for each other."

Ian and Taylor both spun to Lexi. "What?" they asked at the same time.

Emma and Riley leaned forward, too, as if curiosity had captured their attention as well.

Lexi waved a hand through the air. "So, I already told you I found the photo."

"Oh. My. God. Lexi Shepherd Fox, you looked!" Emma stood in front of Lexi, wagging her finger at her sister. "You looked up the house! That photo was an aside."

The blush in Lexi's cheeks couldn't have conveyed guilt better, but still, Taylor didn't quite understand how Lexi could 'look up' anything or how that related to a house.

"Are you mad?" Lexi's question went toward Ian.

He raised an eyebrow. "So you, who doesn't 'do' people, looked up who the owners of this house should be, and you found Taylor and me?"

Lexi nodded. "That's my gift. Putting two lost things back together. Why else would I tell you to buy it months ago as an investment?"

Ian slapped a palm to his forehead.

Taylor faced him. "You really bought it? You're staying?"

He pulled out a small box from his pocket.

Taylor's hands covered her mouth. "Wha-What's that?" she asked without uncovering.

A cough from behind had them both curving back. Tripp pointed to the floor as Lexi giggled.

Ian rolled his eyes and dropped to one knee, his face sloped toward Taylor.

She pinched her lips together, the smile taking hold of the corners.

"Taylor Claire Marsh, I believe I've wanted to do this three other times but didn't get the opportunity. I'm not one to look a gift horse in the mouth more than … oh … say three times.

To the woman I've loved all my lives but didn't know it … will you share the rest of this life and anything in the future-forever category with me?" He opened the box.

Inside, his Gram's ring stared back at her.

An 'Aww' burst from Emma and Lexi.

Taylor's gaze met Riley's. He gave her a small nod—that little bit of assurance she'd always wondered if she'd get.

"I'm down here in the dirt, you know. In a house that's falling apart. One I was *told* to invest in, and today, *told* you were the perfect woman for." He eyed Tripp and Lexi but returned to Taylor. "I'll learn to deal with this place as long as I can get a sixty-inch in that living room area over there." Ian's smile came through with the point of a finger off to the left. When he returned to Taylor, he asked, "Will you marry me?"

Her nod came out fast as tears pricked her eyes. "Yes, Ian. I'll marry you." Her hands held court over her heart.

"This is where you are, so this is where I want to be. Forever." He'd answered her unasked question.

Taylor jumped against him, cocooning him in her hold. "I can't believe you bought this house. It's going to be more fun than Lexi and Tripp's to renovate. You do realize it's *the* house, right? *The* house. The one Marge's grandparents owned from … the last time. Probably where she tattooed you."

Ian nodded. "Is that too weird?"

"No, it's beyond perfect. It's like a homecoming. My house was one of the old farmhand bungalows. I loved it, but this is just … *this.*"

Ian bent her backward and kissed her long and hard as the group around them started clapping and whistling. When he lifted her up, he said, "I love you, and this time, I'm not letting you go. Ever."

"Is that a threat?" Her smile refused to stay hidden.

"You bet your ass it is."

No lingering echoes flitted through her mind. *Gone. All of them.* She focused on Ian again. *Now, I can start my real future.* "Then, I accept."

"Yes!" Tripp pumped a hand through the air.

"You're excited that I'm finally settling down?" Ian asked, his arm around Taylor, holding her tight against him.

Tripp shook his head. "Nope. Well, yeah, but it's before May thirty-first, so I win."

Ian belted out a laugh.

"What?" Taylor asked.

Ian snorted a laugh. "Weeks ago, the man here bet me I would ask you to marry me by the thirty-first of May, or he'd pay me five million dollars."

Taylor's eyes opened wide as Lexi slapped Tripp's bicep. "You bet that much money that he'd ask me to marry him?" Taylor asked as Lexi asked, "What would have happened had he not?"

"This was a one-way bet," Tripp said. "Sometimes, you gotta play the game to win." He cringed, drew Lexi in for a giant hug to which she responded the same way.

Ian added another soft kiss to Taylor's lips. "Never a better answer given. Wouldn't you agree?"

She laid her palms against his cheeks. "Never better. And I'm so glad we won't ever have to do it again."

ACKNOWLEDGEMENTS

It's amazing how many people touch the story, the words, the construction of sentences, right down to what you hold in your hand—to the final product of a book. Thanking them all would take pages and pages of acknowledgements.

Now, though, I have a few very key people to virtually hug, and a group to give some massive thanks to. Let's start with the key people.

Emma Madden. Have I told you how awesome you are? How your feedback helps me go from story to epic tale? I know I'm not the only one who loves everything you do with a story.

J.A. Belfield. The toughest critic I have but also the one who knows how to set me straight. This story wouldn't be what it is without you.

Wendy Seagondollar. Doesn't even know she's in here, but I'm pretty sure she's my number one fan, and two read-throughs of this book proves that.

The other group of awesome people I need to thank are those who were a part of Hide & Seek's book tour. These bloggers are the heart and soul of book marketing and they deserve so much credit for helping put a book out there. So, in order only of their assistance one year ago: Synchronized Reading, Reviewing Shelf, Rainy of the Dark, Kindle and Me, Babs Book Bistro, JC Martin, Burning Impossibly Bright Blog, Claire Gillian, Long and Short Reviews, Roro is Reading, Bex Book Nook, Known To Read, MoonLight Gleam, Julie Reece, Coffee Time Romance, and Nightly Reading. To all of you, I say ... thank you!

Brian Mullins Photography

Aimee Laine

Aimee is a romantic at heart and a southern transplant with a bit of the accent (but not a whole bunch). She's married to her high school sweetheart, and with him, she's produced three native North Carolinians, two of whom share the same DNA.

With an MBA and a degree in Applied Mathematics, there's absolutely no reason she should be writing romance novels. Then again, she shouldn't need a calculator to add two numbers, either . . . but she does.

AVAILABLE NOW

HIDE & SEEK
A GAMES OF ZEUS NOVEL
LIE, CHEAT OR STEAL,
NO ONE CAN CATCH HIM
EXCEPT ONE WOMAN
aimee laine

www.ingramcontent.com/pod-product-compliance
Lightning Source LLC
LaVergne TN
LVHW050930080826
845145LV00001B/282
9781937744212